His eyes were bewildered, lost and weary, glazed with drink.

"All lying cheats," he mumbled. "Every one of you." Edmond sighed once and collapsed against her breast. In a moment he was snoring softly.

Celeste eased herself from under him, fighting her tears. She crept up the stairs, clinging to the banister to keep herself from trembling in grief and horror. In the passageway, she turned toward her rooms. She extinguished her candles and crawled into bed.

It was hours before she fell asleep. Again and again, she reviewed Edmond's story in her mind. And each time her despair grew. To learn of his dark *hatred* . . . of his deep and bitter mistrust of all women . . .

She moaned and curled herself into a tight ball of pain. How could she win his trust, when almost everything he knew about her was a lie?

Dear Reader,

Harlequin Historicals would like to introduce you to a new concept. Big books! Beginning with October, we will be publishing one longer title a month with books that will include everything from popular reprints to originals from your favorite authors.

Our first longer title, *The Bargain,* by Veronica Sattler is a sexy historical set during the Regency period. It's the story of Lord Brett Westmont and Ashleigh Sinclair, two people who are thrown together in a series of compromising positions, only to fall madly in love.

In *Tapestry,* by author Sally Cheney, heroine Dandre Collin discovers that the rough mill worker who rescues her from a runaway carriage is really her uncle's aristocratic neighbor.

An ex-masterspy grows bored with his forced retirement and winds up creating more mischief than he can handle by taking a wife in *The Gilded Lion,* a sensual tale from Kit Gardner.

Finally, author Louisa Rawlings returns to France as the setting for *Scarlet Woman,* an intriguing story of murder and revenge.

We hope you enjoy all four of this month's titles.

And next month, be on the lookout for the long awaited reissue of *Pieces of Sky* by Marianne Willman, the unforgettable story of a spinster who marries the cruel Abner Slade but finds true love in the arms of Roger Le Beau, her husband's sworn enemy.

Sincerely,

Tracy Farrell
Senior Editor

Scarlet Woman

LOUISA RAWLINGS

Harlequin Books

TORONTO • NEW YORK • LONDON
AMSTERDAM • PARIS • SYDNEY • HAMBURG
STOCKHOLM • ATHENS • TOKYO • MILAN
MADRID • WARSAW • BUDAPEST • AUCKLAND

Harlequin Historicals first edition October 1993

ISBN 0-373-28794-1

SCARLET WOMAN

Books by Louisa Rawlings

Harlequin Historicals

Stranger in My Arms #60
Autumn Rose #86
Wicked Stranger #157
Scarlet Woman #194

LOUISA RAWLINGS

has written eleven historical romances, several under the pseudonym of Ena Halliday. Interested in France since her high school days, she has set most of her books in that country. She has received awards for her books from the Romance Writers of America and *Romantic Times*. When her four children were younger, she enjoyed a suburban, domestic life: PTA, gardening, gourmet cooking and sewing her own clothes. With the children grown and gone, she and her husband find more time for traveling and attending the opera. They now live happily in a Manhattan apartment.

Printed in the U.S.A.

great deal more to gossip about tomorrow.

Chapter One

As usual, the Paris Opera House was abuzz with gossip.

"Monsieur Liszt quarreled with his mistress on Thursday, they say. And reconciled on Friday."

"Who is that handsome man in the brocaded waistcoat? I *must* meet him!"

"Did you hear that the carriage of *madame la duchesse*, your neighbor who claims never to go out, was seen in the Champs Élysées today?"

My dear, her husband has left the city on business. While the cat's away…"

"Do you see that painted creature there? The one in green gauze? I hear her diamonds have a very curious history."

"You don't say!"

From her private box in the first balcony, Céleste Valvert surveyed the people in the rapidly filling parterre below and the circular tiers of boxes above. Her own appearance a moment ago had produced a fresh outburst of prattle, and busy mutterings of speculation. Buzz, buzz, buzz, she thought. Chattering women in rich gowns, and men in splendid evening attire pretending indifference to the gossip. Céleste smiled, her full pink lips curving upward in a subtle expression that owed less to amusement than to cynicism. The hypocrites! Well, they would certainly have a great deal more to gossip about tomorrow.

She nodded to the couple who had just entered the box next to hers, acknowledging the gentleman's murmured "Good evening, *madame*." He had a pleasant face and a gracious manner.

His wife, a well-endowed matron in billows of pink tulle, was not as generous of spirit. She glared at her husband, her round face a mask of disapproval. She snapped open her fan and held it before her fleshy mouth and chin like a screen, as though the diaphanous lace would keep her words from traveling to Céleste's box. "Don't you dare say another word to that Valvert woman!" Her whispered command was a sharp hiss of jealousy, and her eyes were narrow as she surveyed Céleste over the top of her fan.

Look your fill, thought Céleste with annoyance. If she was to be condemned, she would at least take pleasure in it. She turned slowly and deliberately, aware that her violet taffeta gown bared white shoulders and a swanlike neck, and that her full, bell-shaped skirt sprang from a waist so lissome and slender that it scarcely needed the aid of a corset. Her dark brown hair had been parted in the middle and smoothed into two long braids that were coiled about her ears. To accent the amber clarity of her light brown eyes and the broad sweep of her brow, she had put on a fine gold chain that encircled the top of her head, its small topaz pendant resting in the middle of her forehead in the current style. With her lush features—in particular her almond-shaped eyes—she looked like an exotic odalisque in a pasha's harem. She had planned her toilette with care this evening—artful simplicity, innocent but seductive. And all to enchant Paul. She hoped she looked as beautiful as she felt.

The sharp intake of breath from the next box as she completed her turn revealed the success of her planning. The matron was almost sputtering with envy. "Not another word to that creature!" she warned her husband again.

"But, my dear," he said mildly, "we've seen her every night this week. How long are we to ignore her? And, after all, the old baron de Lansac vouched for her when he brought her to Madame de Marsan's soirée before Christmas."

"Bah! The baron is senile! Where was the woman before then? The New Year is already past, and who knows a thing about her? Yet you greet her with warmth. God in heaven! Next you'll expect me to receive her in my salon. A woman of no consequence. The Widow Valvert." The name was uttered with exquisite contempt. "I wonder if there ever *was* a husband. Not that Paul de Beaufort seems to care. He—"

"Hold your tongue," her husband muttered, pulling his wife away from the railing of the box. "She'll hear you."

As I was meant to, thought Céleste, drawing the gold velvet curtain halfway across the front of her own box to shield herself from further malice. The gossips of Paris were the cruelest she had encountered in all her twenty-three years. She sighed. Ah, well . . . By tomorrow at this time the matron's pinched comments would seem like effusive praise beside the fresh gossip. She turned to her servant, who still waited at the door. "All is in readiness, Joseph?"

"Yes, *madame*. Your carriage will be standing at the side entrance below."

"And the inn?"

"Pierre has not yet returned, *madame*. But he knows well enough to come here to the opera house to confirm the arrangements with me."

Frowning, Céleste paced the small space, then sank into one of the little plush chairs. A hundred thoughts swirled in her brain. Arrangements. Details. Doubts. "The menu!" she exclaimed suddenly. "Did Pierre remember to take the menu I wrote down? Monsieur de Beaufort . . ."

"Put your mind at ease, Madame Valvert. The supper will be waiting, just as you ordered. All the gentleman's favorite dishes."

"Nothing must go wrong, you understand."

"Peace, *madame*."

Céleste searched Joseph's face. He was competent and loyal. Of course, as was the case with most of the servants she'd found in her brief sojourn in Paris, his loyalty was bought at a price. He was well along in years, however, and there was in his eyes a look of wisdom and understanding. She allowed herself to relax and laughed softly. "How many assignations have you arranged in your time, Joseph?"

He smiled. "My lips are forever silent, *madame.*" He gave a little bow. "Will there be anything more?"

"The champagne."

"It's been ordered. A waiter will bring it just before the entr'acte, as you requested. Enjoy the opera, *madame,* and leave the rest to me." He bowed again and left her alone with her thoughts.

The musicians had begun to file into the pit. Indifferent to the confusion of sound, they tuned their various instruments; the squeak of the violins was an incongruous counterpoint to the short, sharp blares from the horns, the nasal plaint of the oboes. A single clarinetist rehearsed a difficult arpeggio while the harpist pulled liquid scales from his instrument. The jumbled noises rose in a crescendo, filling the vast hall, and its spectators, with a heightened air of expectation that only added to Céleste's uneasy impatience. She looked beyond the glittering chandelier to an empty box on the opposite side of the balcony.

Oh, Paul, she thought, feeling a presentiment of disaster, where are you? He was usually in his box by this time, leaning forward, his fingers against his lips in an inviting gesture that had come to be a secret romantic signal between them. She would nod in agreement. During the intermission, as she moved through the crowds in the foyer, he would catch her eye and bow in formal greeting. She would turn away nonchalantly. It was a delicious game. Wherever they met, they pretended to be passing acquaintances, no more; they exchanged pleasantries and shared trivial bits of conversation among groups of friends.

But after the opera, or the theater, or wherever was the fashionable gathering of the night, she would go to her carriage and he would be there. Waiting inside. They would take supper in the private rooms of a restaurant, and kiss and laugh and whisper tender words to each other. They were discreet. The many letters they exchanged were carried by private messengers, hired boys who forgot an address as soon as the note was delivered.

But in the month since their meeting at Madame de Marsan's soirée, the gossip—much to Céleste's astonishment—had stirred, risen and grown to epic proportions. She wondered if there was a single soul in Parisian society who didn't know that the handsome and rich Paul de Beaufort, of a fine old family, was passionately in love with Céleste Valvert, the unknown widow who excited so much curiosity.

But where was he tonight? Despite the cool façade she presented to the world, the serene and inscrutable expression that was a part of her natural reserve, Céleste was concerned. She caught herself tapping her closed fan impatiently against her palm as she stared at Paul's empty box.

Perhaps he was angry with her. They had parted three nights ago on the edge of a quarrel—their first. He had blurted out his love for her, and wrested from her the confession that she loved him in return. Then he'd begged her to surrender to him. It was no longer enough for him, he'd said, to kiss and fondle and embrace in her carriage. He wanted more. And upon the instant. When she'd hesitated, taken aback by the suddenness of his impassioned plea, he'd escorted her home in sullen silence.

Now she unclasped her reticule and drew from it a folded sheet of perfumed vellum. She opened it and read—for the hundredth time, and with the same doubts as always—the words she'd penned this morning:

My dearest love, I can no longer deny the passion that stirs my soul. Let the world think what it will. I care not. My heart is too filled with love for you. Come to my box at the entr'acte. There you may learn of the fever that burns in my heart, the strength of my desire. I promise you all before the night is through. Céleste.

She had decided not to raise the matter of an elopement in her letter. When she was in his arms, when the champagne had fired his blood, she would tell him of the snug inn that waited, the intimate room, the supper, the wine. How could he resist? How could he refuse? They would leave the theater before the final curtain fell.

The great gaslit chandelier of the opera house rose slowly; the hushed audience waited in anticipation. Since its debut in their city seven years before, in 1829, the opera *Guillaume Tell,* by the Italian Rossini, had never failed to enthrall Parisians. The first notes of the overture sounded—the deep, mournful tones of a solo cello trembled in the stillness. Céleste scarcely listened as the gentle opening gave way to nervous violins that ushered in a raging storm of blaring horns and loud, crashing cymbals. Her mind was in more turmoil than the music.

Why did she keep thinking of Alex, when her thoughts tonight should be on Paul, on her future? Her marriage to Alexis de LaGrange had always seemed like a misty dream—their meeting, their brief time together, the look of anger and surprise in his eyes the night he'd died. His last, reproachful words. All a gray mist. But tonight, every moment of her time with Alex played out in her thoughts with crystal clarity, like a clouded mirror suddenly made sharp and bright. She sighed. Perhaps, after tonight, she could begin to forget the past and start a new life.

The overture was ending, the wild *galop* coming to a close in a triumphant blast of massed trumpets. And still Paul did not appear. Céleste tried to concentrate on the opera—the story of the great Swiss patriot—but it was no use. The voices, the costumes, the flash and pageantry, faded like empty shadows before the reality of Paul's possible abandonment. Had she lost him? Had her reluctance to give in to his desires that night ruined her chances? Oh, God, she thought, what shall I do if I've lost him forever? She could never forgive herself.

The long first act was nearly over. Céleste had sat like an automaton, applauding mechanically when others did, listening but not hearing, watching yet scarcely seeing. Scattered rustlings in the crowd roused her suddenly from her malaise. What had stirred the gossips now? She looked quickly about her. Her heart thumped in relief. Thank God.

Tall and aristocratic in his evening clothes, Paul de Beaufort had just entered his box, and the drama of it seemed to enthrall the people around him more than the drama taking place on stage. Women whispered, and men turned to gape at him, and then to look at Céleste. In a moment, she saw the reason why.

Paul wasn't alone. As Céleste watched, he and another man escorted an elderly woman to a chair in the front of the box. Paul straightened, staring across the space at Céleste. His handsome face registered frustration, regret and apology. His light brown hair, normally combed to perfection, was in disarray, as though the events of the evening had quite overwhelmed him. He gave an imperceptible shrug as his eyes held Céleste's, then turned toward the back of his box.

The matron next to Céleste gasped as Paul led forward a young woman. "My God, it's Mademoiselle de Malecot!"

It was all Céleste could do to keep her composure. So this was Élise de Malecot. Paul's fiancée.

Céleste studied her rival. Élise de Malecot was heartbreakingly young, pale and fragile, with soft blond hair massed in prim curls at her temples. As Paul ushered her to her seat, she looked up at him with an expression of such innocence and trust that it nearly broke Céleste's heart. Why? she thought with a pang of guilt. Why tonight, of all nights, did he have to bring that woman? Her plans were made; she wouldn't cancel them now. She couldn't. But oh, how difficult for her, and how painful for the Malecot woman, for Céleste to snatch Paul away tonight, under her very nose. It was one thing to imagine the girl learning of their elopement in the privacy of her boudoir, hiding her shame from the prying eyes of the gossips. But to be abandoned publicly, for all the world to see and know...

Céleste groaned softly, filled with self-loathing. Dear God, she thought in anguish, the things we are prepared to do in the name of love!

Paul and his party had settled into their chairs, but the murmurs in the audience continued unabated. It seemed that no one was paying heed to the opera. Heads turned, eyes scanned first Paul and Élise, then Céleste, looking for a flicker, an acknowledgment, any hint of emotion.

Her face frozen in a stiff half smile, Céleste felt as though she were playing out a charade for the benefit of every man and woman in the audience—prying interlopers and voyeurs at the spectacle of love. This lack of privacy was unavoidable, she supposed. But it shamed her nonetheless.

"Madame?"

The soft voice made Céleste jump. She turned in her chair. "Oh. Joseph. You startled me."

"Forgive me, *madame,* but Pierre has returned. Everything at the inn has been arranged to your pleasure. And the waiter is here with your champagne. I'll have him open it, then leave. Is there anything more, before Pierre and I return to the *hôtel?*"

"Does the coachman know the way to the inn?"

"Of course, *madame.* Anything more?"

She hesitated. God forgive her. She took the note from her reticule and held it out to Joseph. "Take this note to Monsieur Paul's box. No, wait! You might be recognized as coming from my household. Find an usher instead. See that he gives the note to Monsieur de Beaufort just before the entr'acte. *Discreetly,* you understand. Now leave me." She needed time to compose herself. She had her own drama to play out. And she *would* play it out, even if it killed her.

She leaned forward in her chair, smiled at Paul and put her fingers to her lips in their secret signal. He looked startled. He glanced uneasily at the young woman beside him, a frown creasing his brow. But when he raised his eyes to Céleste again, the frown had vanished. And when he put his own fingers to his lips in an answering sign, she breathed a sigh of relief. She had won. Élise de Malecot might be a momentary sting to Paul's conscience, but the girl's powers were scarcely enough to cancel his ardor, his burning passion for Céleste.

She watched the waiter open the champagne and put out the glasses in readiness, then dismissed him with a nod of her head. The long first act had concluded. The singers took their bows amid wild applause and left the stage. The great chandelier was lowered once again, filling the theater with light. Céleste drew the curtains across the front of her box until only a foot or two remained open. The enclosed space was dim and intimate, lit only by the low-burning gas lamp on the inner wall. She heard the sound of the door opening.

She composed her face into its most seductive smile and turned. "Beloved . . ." she whispered.

Chapter Two

"A charming greeting, but a waste of time." The man who stood in the doorway, scowling at her, was certainly not Paul. Nor any woman's beloved, from the look of arrogant contempt he cast upon Céleste, as though any woman would be beneath his notice. He was not quite as tall as Paul, but he was solidly built, with an imposing breadth of shoulder and a way of standing, leaning slightly forward, that was distinctly menacing. His short hair was black and curly and wild, and with his swarthy complexion he looked like some savage corsair upon the high seas. His firm jaw was angular, his mouth was set in a hard line, and his pale blue eyes, vivid against his dark skin, were the coldest eyes Céleste had ever seen. He seemed to be in his mid-thirties. He stepped into the box and closed the door behind him.

Céleste frowned in annoyance. At any moment, Paul might walk in. "You seem to have made a mistake, *monsieur*," she said coldly. "This is not the box you were seeking."

"On the contrary, *madame*. I was invited." His mouth curved in a mocking smile that was even more unpleasant than his frown.

For the first time, Céleste noticed the piece of paper in his hand. Dear God, her note to Paul! Her impassioned vows of love. She burned with embarrassment. She whipped open her fan and briskly fanned herself to cover her discomfiture. "My letter was meant for Monsieur de Beaufort. It was given to you in error."

He laughed sharply. It was an ugly sound. "It was not given me. I waylaid it. Besides, I *am* Monsieur de Beaufort. Edmond, comte de Beaufort, to be precise."

Of course. He had been the other man in Paul's box. A relative, no doubt. She had paid him no heed—all her attention, all her hopes had focused on Paul. "This is an unforgivable effrontery, *monsieur le comte,*" she snapped. "You had no right to take the letter. Paul—"

"Was the Beaufort you wished to seduce?" His eyes bored into her, seeming to study the effect of his cruel, bold words.

She would give him nothing to use against her. Her expression remained inscrutable. "Whatever is between Paul and me is our affair. No one else need be concerned."

"Tell that to Mademoiselle de Malecot. Tell that to Paul's mother, who called me away from the country to see if I could talk some sense into my imbecile of a cousin. I arranged this little opera party tonight simply to see the creature who had turned Paul's head. But, my God—" he sneered, brandishing Céleste's letter "—you are more brazen than I would have thought possible."

Her amber eyes narrowed. "I think you had better go."

"So that you can write another letter to Paul? I think not, *madame.*" He reached out and turned up the gaslight. "Let me see you clearly." The insolence of his gaze as his eyes raked her body made Céleste's blood boil. "Yes, I can see what Paul saw in you. As can you, every time you look in your mirror, I'll wager. I never knew a beautiful woman who wasn't aware of her power. What are you? Twenty-two? Twenty-three...four? Not innocent, that's apparent. Your mouth is too ripe—it's been kissed many a time, I think. Your eyes are filled with knowing, cool and assured. Eve, after the fall. And your body..." A cynical laugh. "Well, I suspect you know exactly what your body is capable of. Tell me, are you soft and melting in a man's embrace? Or hot and passionate? Do those white arms drape themselves about a lover's neck in gentle surrender, or do they cling with desire?"

Céleste's hands curled into fists at her sides. Her teeth ached from clenching them. "You will please leave," she said.

"Not quite yet. I want you to understand precisely what is at stake here. The Malecot marriage has been arranged because it is of benefit to both our families. Mademoiselle de Malecot comes with a fine old name, a good dowry and a spotless reputation. You, *madame,* on the other hand, are an adventuress, to put it kindly."

Céleste wrapped herself in frosty pride. She had been discreet and secretive. "Because the gossips can find nothing to say about me," she said coldly, "do you now choose to malign me without cause?"

"On the contrary, the gossips have much to say about you, Madame Valvert."

It distressed her that tales were being spread. "And of course you believe all you hear," she said with contained anger. "Scarcely the sign of a gentleman, *monsieur.* For all your title. Well, despite the gossips, Paul and I love each other truly. *Love.* Do you understand what I am saying? Do you think your family can win against the power of Paul's love for me?"

"I'm sure he *thinks* he loves you, the poor fool. At his age, every stirring of the flesh seems like love."

"He's not a child. He knows what he wants."

"At twenty-five, he thinks that a woman of experience will open the door to paradise. At thirty-six—" Edmond de Beaufort gave a little bow "—he will know that only a woman of virtue can bring a man lasting happiness."

She lifted her chin in defiance, ignoring the insult. "That's for him to decide, and there's nothing you can do about it."

"There's a great deal I can do." He strode past her to the edge of the box, opened the curtains a bit more and glanced out at the theater. "Good," he said, nodding in satisfaction, and moved toward Céleste. Before she realized what was happening, he had reached out and pulled her to him, one strong hand going about her waist in a fierce embrace, the other sliding up from her breast to clutch her throat in a deadly grip. He bent his head and pressed his lips against hers.

It was scarcely a kiss. It was more a smothering pressure against her mouth and nose that kept her from exhaling what little air could pass the choking fingers at her neck. She uttered little squeaking sounds and struggled in his arms, aware of his awesome strength, of a terrifying savagery that could snuff her life in a moment. At last, she managed to wrench her mouth free. She stared into his eyes. They were colder and more frightening up close than she could have imagined. "For the love of God," she gasped, her body trembling, "I can't breathe!"

He eased his hold on her neck, but his long fingers remained curled around her throat. "Then kiss me again, of your own free will. With a little passion, if you please. Unless you want me to snap your neck here and now."

She hesitated for only a moment. He seemed perfectly capable of killing her to keep her away from Paul. And she wasn't so foolish as to risk her life with this cold-blooded monster. She frowned in distaste, put her arms around his neck and lifted her face to his. In response, he drew her closer to his hard body. The heat of the hand at her silk-covered waist burned her almost as much as the hand that still rested on her bare neck.

She stared in surprise. Edmond de Beaufort's blue eyes had suddenly become soft, hazy with desire, and his hot breath brushed her cheek. Dear God, she thought, is that what this is about? Did he hope to make her his own? She laughed, softly, mockingly. "Are you so jealous of your cousin, that you wish to taste of his pleasures?"

She had been mistaken. There was no warmth in those eyes. "I find nothing pleasurable in this, *madame*," he growled, crushing her mouth with his. This time there was less cruelty in the kiss. His lips were firm, yet strangely caressing as they moved over hers. Still, she felt violated, helpless and impotent against his strength and power. She was bewildered by this man who demanded her kiss yet seemed repelled by her.

Then—still holding her close—he began to move, forcing her backward, step by halting step. And when she felt the railing of the balcony against her back, and heard the gasps of surprise from the spectators behind her, she understood all. No, no! This charade was for *Paul*. Paul, who must still be in his own box. Paul, who would see her kissing his cousin. She tried to break free of Edmond de Beaufort's arms, groaning in angry frustration beneath the pressure of his kiss. Instantly his fingers tightened on her neck in warning. Knowing herself defeated, she relaxed in his embrace and felt an answering release of the deadly pressure on her windpipe.

The kiss was interminable, but at length her torment ceased. With a smile of satisfaction, Edmond de Beaufort dropped his arms and stepped back. "Beloved . . ." he murmured, his voice a scornful echo of a lover's tone.

"You monster," she said. She could still feel the pain of his fingers on her neck. She put an involuntary hand to her throat and looked anxiously toward Paul's box. The expression on his face made her heart sink. Disgust, horror, betrayal. She shook her head in denial, desperate to send him a message, to negate what he had seen. But how could she refute the evidence before him—evidence that had set the gossiping tongues of the onlookers to wagging again? A seemingly rapturous kiss, a man who smiled in contentment, and a woman who put a trembling hand to her throat as though she hadn't yet recovered from her passionate transports. Curse Beaufort. Curse him for ever and ever.

With a final scowl for Céleste, Paul turned his attention to Élise de Malecot. He offered her his arm and escorted her and his mother from the box. No doubt he planned to parade Élise before his friends during the intermission, making a great show of her status as his fiancée, her acceptance into his family circle.

I must reach him before he reaches the foyer, thought Céleste in panic. A hurried signal, a whispered word—anything to convey to him that her love for him was undimmed. That her heart remained constant, no matter what he'd seen. She made a desperate lunge for the door of her box. But Edmond de Beaufort had guessed her intentions, and moved quickly to bar the way.

"Alas, no *madame*. Now that I've found you—" his voice was sharp with mockery "—I cannot think to share you with the world this evening. We'll spend the entr'acte here. Alone, just the two of us. I see you've thoughtfully provided champagne. Good. Shall I pour you a glass?"

"Let me pass," she said.

"Don't be absurd."

"What do you intend?"

He shrugged. "It's very simple. We'll stay here, enjoy your champagne and leave when the opera is done. I'll escort you out of the theater under the watchful eyes of the gossips, take you to your carriage and see you home. By which time Paul and Élise will have gone on to supper together. I regret that you yourself will have to do without supper tonight, Madame Valvert. But I doubt that either of us could endure the other's company for that length of time."

"And if I refuse to leave with you?"

His eyes narrowed. "Though I dislike striking a woman, I'm quite prepared to render you unconscious. Then I'll carry you to your vehicle, allowing the onlookers—and Paul, of course—to assume you've swooned with passion. A nice touch, that. Don't you agree?" He smiled cruelly. "I could almost wish you'd resist me."

The man was intolerable! Perhaps if she called for help... She turned and started for the edge of the balcony.

Beaufort was quicker than she. He grabbed her wrist, spun her around to face him and took hold of her shoulders. His fingers dug into her tender flesh. His eyes blazed in fury, but his voice was cold and controlled. "Don't cross me," he said softly. "You'll find I'm far more dangerous than my cousin. Now, you'll either sit down and behave yourself, or I'll drag you to the front of the box and repeat our performance. Is that what you want?"

She rubbed her hand against her mouth in disgust. "I can't think of anything more abhorrent." She glared at him in frustration. "It seems you have won, for the present. Now kindly allow me to sit."

"A wise decision." He let her go and held out a chair. She sat with as much dignity as she could manage under the circumstances. He opened the door and signaled to an usher. "Go to Monsieur de Beaufort's box and bring back my top hat and cape. They're marked with my crest, just so." He pulled a calling card from his pocket, embossed with his name and coat of arms. He handed it to the usher, along with several large coins. "Then go and see to it that Madame Valvert's coachman has her carriage at the ready."

"Begging your pardon, Your Excellency, but I believe *madame's* carriage is already waiting at the side entrance."

"Indeed?" Edmond de Beaufort swung back to Céleste, his eyes glinting with malicious humor. "Don't you enjoy Rossini, *madame?*"

Deliberately she stared beyond him, to the door that had just closed after the servant. "May you be cursed," she muttered.

He laughed—a dark laugh, bitter and chilling. "Adam was cursed when the first woman came into this world, *madame*. Why should I escape his fate?" He paused, brooding, then seemed to shake off the darkness. "Now. Let me pour you some champagne before the music begins again. *Guillaume Tell* is one of my favorite operas." He handed her a glass of champagne, poured one for himself, and sat down next to her, his free hand draped across her shoulder. It seemed a casual gesture, but the tension of his body, leaning close, made it clear that she was as much his prisoner as if he had tied her to the chair. She dared not try to rise or cry out, lest his fingers find her throat again. The curtains of her box were partially open; in the dimness, Paul and the others would see only the intimacy of her tête-à-tête with Edmond de Beaufort, little realizing her danger.

She had never felt more helpless in her life. "It's a wonder you have time for opera," she said scornfully, "with all your interfering in your cousin's affairs."

"In point of fact, I was here in '29, when the composer first presented this opera. Were you so fortunate as to hear it on that occasion, *madame?*"

Good God, she thought, now we're to make small talk? Well, she was as good at games as he. She sipped her champagne, smiled nonchalantly and shrugged her shoulders. "Alas, I wasn't in Paris at the time."

"A pity. You were in—?" There was a motive to his small talk, after all. He smiled blandly, waiting for her to finish the sentence.

Oh, no, she thought. It's not as simple as that, my fine count. "I was in..." She hesitated.

"Yes?"

"A place other than Paris."

He laughed softly, saluting her neat evasion with an upraised glass. "The mysterious Widow Valvert. You're far too clever for poor Paul. Why can't you be sensible and leave him to Élise?"

"I told you, Paul and I love—"

He cut her off with an impatient shake of the head. "Enough! If that's all you can say, you're not even worth engaging in conversation. I suggest you hold your tongue and keep your own counsel. I'll do likewise." Scowling, he downed his glass of champagne, poured another and slouched in his chair to concentrate on the opera in angry silence.

His dark mood persisted for the remainder of the opera. Céleste had begun to think he was oblivious of the music, until the soprano, reaching for a high note, struck it wrong and screeched. Beaufort flinched, as though the sound had physically pained him. How curious, thought Céleste, that such a brute should have a sensitive side. She examined him more closely, turning her head only a slight degree so that he wouldn't be aware of her scrutiny.

He really was extraordinarily handsome, in a dark and overbearing way. His profile was finely chiseled, with a straight nose and a magisterial chin. His brows were slashes of black across his forehead, and his penetrating blue eyes were veiled by the longest lashes she had ever seen. Paul de Beaufort was handsome, with the unseasoned good looks of a youth; his cousin Edmond had the face of a man.

That thought reminded her of Paul. She had scarcely looked at him since the opera began again. It was too painful to watch him, bending to Élise, whispering in her ear, laughing and kissing her hand. He clearly intended to make Céleste burn with jealousy.

What *shall* I do about Paul? she thought. Tonight was already a disaster, a loss she couldn't remedy. But tomorrow—? There was no way she could be certain that a note would get past the vigilance of his meddling cousin. However, Paul hadn't ridden in the Bois de Boulogne for several days. Perhaps, if the weather was fine tomorrow, she'd seek him there. If not, he might be at Madame de Cloquet's musicale on Thursday.

She sighed. Her brain was spinning, her thoughts heavy with uncertainty. But, until she spoke with Paul, there was no way to know how much damage his cousin's interference tonight had done.

Edmond de Beaufort stirred in his chair and prodded Céleste with the hand that still rested lightly on her shoulder. "Come. It's nearly over. I don't wish to be caught in the press of people. I might lose you, my dear. And that would break my heart."

Curse him, he was enjoying himself! "But it's your favorite opera," she countered, her voice tinged with sarcasm. "Don't you want to stay for the final chorus?"

He stood up and pulled her to her feet. "Your charming presence will more than compensate me for missing it." He helped her into her velvet pelisse, swirled his opera cape about his shoulders and picked up his top hat. "Besides, the conductor is abominable tonight. Dragging every tempo. The final chorus will be a trial, best left unheard. Come. By now there should be patrons enough in the foyer to report back to Paul on the intimacy of our departure." He put one arm possessively about her waist and escorted her from the box. Past watchful eyes and down the wide stairs to a side entrance, he played his part to perfection—the attentive lover, clinging to his new mistress. And how was she to escape, when he held her so closely?

Her coachman leapt from his seat as they hurried into the frosty January night. He touched his whip to his tall silk hat in salute. "Are your instructions still the same, *madame?*"

Edmond de Beaufort cut in before Céleste could reply. "What is our destination, my good man?"

"The Three Feathers, at Saint-Leu-Taverny."

"A country inn?" Beaufort smiled down at Céleste, his mouth twitching. "How romantic of you, my darling." He fished in his waistcoat pocket, pulled out a gold piece and pressed it into the coachman's hand. "However, the plans have changed. *Madame* and I will merely ride around the city. I leave the route to you. In about a half hour, you may proceed toward *madame's hôtel....* I've forgotten the address."

Céleste started to cry out, to silence her coachman, but it was too late.

"Twenty-six rue de Provence, *monsieur,*" he answered.

Céleste's heart sank. Now Beaufort knew where she lived.

Lit by the flickering gas of the street lamps, Edmond de Beaufort's eyes glittered in triumph. "Yes, of course. The rue de Provence. I'll rap on the coach when I want you to stop.'' He hooked his arm firmly under Céleste's elbow and guided her into the carriage, then followed, taking the seat opposite her. The street lamps shone intermittently on his face as they rode, highlighting the sharp planes of his cheekbones and making him appear all the more evil and satanic. He laughed softly, cruelly. ''The inn of the Three Feathers. How charming. It would seem I saved my cousin just in time. I assume from your note that you have not yet granted Paul the last favors.''

''You may assume whatever you wish. You haven't won yet.'' Her voice was as cold as the night air.

He watched her in silence, his long fingers drumming on the crown of his hat, which he had set beside him. ''I wonder . . . Even with Mademoiselle de Malecot there, you were prepared to run away with Paul. And . . . how did you put it? Bestow all before the night is through? Very bold. Very headstrong. Yet you don't seem that sort of woman. I can't help but wonder if your surrender to Paul did not have a deeper design.''

''What do you mean?'' Céleste asked tightly.

''A beautiful woman like yourself must have known dozens of men. I find myself wondering if you're not . . . 'in trouble,' as the English say. By some ne'er-do-well who seduced you and vanished. And now you hope to provide for your 'mistake' by trapping an innocent like Paul.''

It was too much for her to contain herself a moment longer. With a cry of outrage, she leaned forward and slashed at his face with her closed fan. The ivory stick left a bright red streak across his cheek.

''Vixen!'' He leapt at her and threw her down on the seat, pinning her shoulders against the cushion with savage hands. He bent low so that his face was above hers, near enough that she could feel the angry puff of his breath. ''Don't challenge me,'' he said through clenched teeth. ''I'll win every time.''

She was frightened. There was no denying it. He was strong and threatening, filled with dark hatred. And all she had for weapons was her words. But perhaps she could shame him into releasing her. "Do you plan to choke me again? To prove how brave you are? This has nothing to do with Paul. Only your pride."

"My family's pride. And I'll do whatever I must to see that you don't disgrace Paul, or the Beaufort name."

She stifled a sharp retort. The man was too menacing to battle openly. Besides, it wasn't in her nature. "Let me go," she said, her voice low and controlled.

He ignored her words. He continued to hold her down, his iron hands pressing on her shoulders. His eyes narrowed ominously. After a long, dangerous silence, his voice emerged from his throat as a hoarse growl. "By God, you're seductive. You make a man's blood burn. I have half a mind to take Paul's place. It seems a pity to waste that country inn."

Céleste gasped in horror. If she had learned nothing else about Edmond de Beaufort tonight, she had learned that he was capable of anything. "You wouldn't dare!"

"Of course," he went on, "I wouldn't be nearly as solicitous a lover as Cousin Paul. But he probably looks at you and sees a Madonna. I see you for what you are."

"Curse you! Paul and I love—"

Her words were cut short by Edmond's mouth slashing down on hers. His lips were hard and demanding, forcing her to submit to the urgency of his kiss. This was not like the cold, cruel kisses he'd taken in the opera; now his mouth burned on hers, hot with desire. He seemed to inhale her lips with his own, and when she moaned softly, feeling a thrill race up her spine, he thrust his tongue savagely against her closed lips. She moaned again and sagged beneath his attack, hating him, hating her body's weak-willed response.

Taking one hand from her shoulder, he caressed the downy softness of her cheek, the throbbing warmth of her temple. She shuddered at his touch, his sensual fingers, and parted her lips in docile surrender to his passionate kiss.

Dear God, she thought, as his tongue sought and found the moist grotto of her mouth. What am I doing? Where was her usual self-control? She felt perilously close to tears, and prayed he'd let her go before she shamed herself completely by yielding all to him.

He released her as abruptly as he'd captured her, and moved back to his own seat. For a moment, seeing the misty look in his eyes, Céleste thought he'd been stirred by the kiss as much as she had. Then his expression hardened, and he laughed softly. "Poor Paul," he said. "It's just as well he wasn't here to see *that*."

She sat up with difficulty, quivering in every nerve of her body. "You monster," she whispered.

He shrugged and rapped on the roof of the coach. At once it stopped, and the coachman opened the door. "Let me out here," said Beaufort, clapping his top hat on his head. "Then take *madame* home with all haste." He stepped from the coach, turned, and reached for Céleste's hand. With a devil's smile, he brought her fingers to his lips. "Beloved," he said. He saluted her, turned on his heel, and vanished into the night.

She was glad the ride to her town house took as long as it did. She needed the time to compose herself, to remind herself that Paul was the man she hoped to have for her own, to forget a kiss that had, no doubt, been meant as an insult.

Her heart sank as the coach pulled into the courtyard of her *hôtel* and she saw the hired carriage there. Not tonight, she thought. It was too much. She could deal with them in the morning. She could think clearly in the morning. Tonight she was tired, hungry, confused. Why did they have to torment her tonight?

Her maid, Thérèse, met her at the door. "Good evening, *madame*," she said, taking Céleste's pelisse, reticule and gloves. "We didn't expect your return tonight."

Céleste sighed. Were even her servants to reproach her now? "The sitting room?" she asked, already knowing the answer.

"Yes, *madame*. They came in about a half hour ago. I'll wait for you in your boudoir. There's a warm fire when you're ready to go to bed."

"Thank you, Thérèse. Oh, and you might bring me a little supper. I didn't eat tonight. Bring it to my rooms." She remembered that she'd have to send Pierre to the Three Feathers in the morning to pay the proprietor for the uneaten meal and the unused room.

"Very good, *madame*." Thérèse nodded and moved out of the vestibule, toward the kitchen.

Céleste sighed again. There was no use delaying the inevitable. With a sinking heart, she trudged up the staircase. The sitting room door was ajar, and lamplight was spilling into the passageway like a golden tide. Céleste hesitated outside the door.

She could guess where they would be sitting. Alex's mother, her face pinched into that expression of combined disapproval and self-pity that was her normal aspect, would be perched on the edge of the desk chair, while her nervous hands compulsively straightened and restraightened the blotter and inkstand and pens, the books and oddments before her. Alex's father, Vicomte Philippe de LaGrange, would be taking his ease on a settee or a comfortable sofa, his head back, his eyes closed. He would seem to be asleep, except for the fact that every once in a while he would frown, flex the fingers of his left hand and rub at the empty, pinned-up sleeve where once had been his right arm. Céleste pushed open the door and went in.

Madame de LaGrange immediately rose from her chair to challenge Céleste. Her evening gown was crushed from hours of sitting. Her fashionable coiffure, an elaborate arrangement of high poufs and curls, embellished with feathers, flowers and strings of beads, had begun to droop. She folded her arms across her ample breast, her eyes dark with accusation. "It was a pity you didn't stay until the end of the opera," she said. "The hall was in an uproar the minute it was learned that you'd left with the count. My God, the scandal! That shameless embrace! What in the name of heaven possessed you to entertain that man? Tonight of all nights, when *monsieur* and I—" she nodded toward her husband, who still sat on the sofa with his eyes closed "—when we were imagining you well away at Saint-Leu with Paul de Beaufort."

Céleste couldn't bear to look into her mother-in-law's eyes. She lowered her gaze and moved away from the woman's overbearing presence. "I'm sorry," she murmured, then raised her chin—a small, proud gesture in her own defense. "But surely you understand that the appearance of Paul's party was unexpected. There was nothing I could do."

The older woman's mouth was tight with bitterness. "And so you lost your courage."

"No! I sent the billet-doux. But Edmond de Beaufort intercepted it."

"Bah!" Madame de LaGrange swirled away from her in a cloud of yellow satin and lace. "Careless. Stupid."

"The man *forced* himself upon me. Surely you don't think I welcomed him. Or invited him. Or that I enjoyed his kiss." She stopped abruptly, aware that her body had flooded with warmth at the memory of Edmond de Beaufort's mouth on hers. It only added to her sense of failure.

The viscount opened his eyes. Céleste was dismayed to see them filled with tears. It was too painful to endure. He looked so like Alexis, with his dark blond hair—now graying—and his blue-green eyes. Céleste held out her hands in supplication. "Please understand."

LaGrange rose slowly, moving with great dignity across the carpet to place himself before Céleste. He blinked, and the tears spilled down his patrician and still-handsome face. He lifted his hand and blotted them. Then, with a swift and savage movement, he swung his upraised arm in a circle and struck Céleste's face with the backs of his fingers.

The force of the blow sent her tottering backward, gasping. She cradled her stinging cheek and looked up at him, seeking a spark of pity. *"Monsieur..."*

He was implacable. "Did I once call you 'daughter'?" he asked mournfully. "Your husband curses you from the grave."

She had reached the end of her self-control. She sank onto the sofa and buried her face in her hands, fighting against the tears. "I know," she whispered. "I know."

Chapter Three

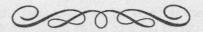

"Well?" Madame de LaGrange's mouth was a pinch of displeasure as she stared up at Céleste from the open window of her large, finely appointed carriage. "Have you found him?"

Reluctantly Céleste bent low in her saddle to meet the older woman's sour gaze, then shook her head. "I've spent hours in the Bois. Paul didn't come riding. I'm sure of it."

The vicomte de LaGrange leaned his head out of the window next to his wife. He squinted against the thin winter sun and surveyed the narrow road that meandered among the bare trees in the Bois de Boulogne. "Were you followed?" At Céleste's negative response, he motioned with his fingers. "Come, then." His breath was a frosty puff on the air.

Céleste sighed as she slid from her saddle and tied her horse to a tree. Despite their disappointment and anger last night, Alex's parents had left her *hôtel* with scarcely a word—only a terse command, ordering this meeting. But they had had all the intervening hours to catalog their complaints against her; today's recriminations, she knew, would be long and bitter. She settled into the carriage and sat opposite them, feeling like a prisoner in the dock, facing a bank of judges. The carriage moved off slowly.

Madame de LaGrange shivered, pulled up the window and then began to stroke the small gray dog nestled in the velvet cushions beside her. "Now, Pépin, isn't this cozy?" She looked up at Céleste and made a face. "Pépin and I hate it when we have to hire a coach to visit you at your *hôtel*. A horrid little coupé. Not nearly as comfortable as this one. Isn't that so, Pépin?"

Monsieur de LaGrange grunted and rubbed at the stump of his arm. "Oh, indeed, yes. We should take *this* carriage to visit her in the rue de Provence. Perhaps our crest on the outside isn't enough. We could hang a banner, as well, announcing to all of Paris that the LaGranges are plotting with their son's widow—the mysterious Valvert—against the Malecots! Would that please you, wife?"

Madame de LaGrange dismissed him with a flutter of hands. "Oh, don't be droll. You know what I mean." She frowned at Céleste. "You look peaked. Didn't you sleep well?"

"No." She had dreamed of Alex again.

LaGrange sighed—a martyr's sigh. "You might at least have had the sense to take a sleeping draft to get a good night's rest. Your allure is the only weapon we have." He indicated his empty sleeve and sighed again. "God knows I'm useless to avenge the family." He stared at Céleste with his mournful eyes—eyes that were so like Alex's. "Or perhaps you *want* to fail."

"No! Of course not. Haven't I pledged myself to you?"

How strange life can be, she thought, examining the elderly couple across from her. The LaGranges had never liked her very much; in fact, they had never approved of Alex's marrying her. Yet she'd spent the past year in mourning at their château in Normandy, under Madame de LaGrange's critical glare and Monsieur de LaGrange's heavy sighs of regret and recrimination. Her filial duty was the least she owed them. Her obedience to Alex's final wishes. The LaGranges were the only relations she had in this world.

And now she was helping them to destroy their lifelong enemies, the Malecots. In humble atonement for her sins.

Or perhaps it was one last homage to Alex's memory, though it seemed a shabby final tribute.

Madame de LaGrange's voice was sharp and demanding. "How soon do you think you can arrange another assignation at the Three Feathers?"

"I don't know. It took almost a month to stir Paul's desire. At least to the point where I was sure he'd be willing to elope and betray Elise de Malecot. And now, after last night...that accursed Edmond de Beaufort..." She rubbed her gloved hand across her mouth. "I won't know until I meet Paul again."

"And Edmond de Beaufort? Do you intend to meet *him* again?" It was more a scornful accusation than a question.

"Of course not! I told you, he forced himself upon me last night, to drive Paul away." She sighed. "But I fear I haven't heard the last of him."

"Where's the bottle of wine now?" asked the viscount, frowning in sudden thought.

"It's still in the coachman's box, where I left it yesterday. I didn't want to send it ahead. Not until Paul and I reached the inn."

Monsieur de LaGrange swore under his breath. "Get it back and put it in safekeeping. These hired servants... Who knows? The wretch could steal it or replace it."

"*Sample* it, even!" cried Madame de LaGrange. "My God, have you no sense?"

Céleste nodded in agreement. How stupid of her. "Yes, yes. Of course. I'll get it back directly." She eyed them with a look that held an edge of resentment. "But I still don't know why *I* have to drink it, as well as Paul."

Monsieur de LaGrange's tight face expressed the strained tolerance of an adult for a rebellious child. "How could you refuse to drink? The man would be suspicious. You propose a toast in honor of your 'love,' you open a rare and special bottle of wine...and then you *refuse?* No, your objection would be absurd."

"And then, you don't have to drink very much!" added Madame de LaGrange in her sharp voice. "Half a glass or so should be enough. Just be sure Paul drinks several glasses. The dose should make him sleep like a child until you're discovered in the morning, but you will merely be a bit drowsy."

Monsieur de LaGrange leaned back in his seat and closed his eyes. "A rare bottle of wine. Very old. Very rare. Very special." He laughed softly, a dry laugh, devoid of humor. "From the cellars of the Baron Julien de Malecot."

"It seems so needlessly cruel," said Céleste, reviewing the plan once again in her mind. She was to persuade Paul to write a letter of rejection to Élise de Malecot, then arrange for the letter to be delivered instead to the girl's maternal grandmother—a powerful duchess, and the woman who held the family purse strings. The old woman's shame and disgust, caused by her horror of any scandal that touched upon her kin, would lead her to drastic measures. If the Malecots were so foolish and unwise as to choose a bridegroom for Élise who allowed himself to be found at an inn with a woman of questionable virtue, then they didn't deserve her continued support. She would immediately cut off the Malecots without a sou. Or so the LaGranges hoped.

"But to use a doctored bottle of the Malecots' very own wine to set the scandal in motion..." continued Céleste. "Salt in the wound. Malice that Paul doesn't deserve. Why must you choose *that* bottle?"

"Oh!" Madame de LaGrange threw up her hands. "You can keep the bottle from his scrutiny, can't you? A man in the transports of love wouldn't ask to see the label!"

The viscount sighed and opened his eyes. "I chose that bottle for a final irony. Have you forgotten? *That* was the gift from Baron Julien de Malecot, with his regrets for..." His voice thickened, and he fell silent.

Céleste twisted her hands in her lap. Of course she remembered. It had been thoughtless of her to question, even for a moment, the depths of Monsieur de LaGrange's grief.

She hurried on, to finish the interview. The burden of remorse was beginning to suffocate her. "And in the morning? After we're discovered?"

"Once the scandal has ruined the Malecots for good, the 'Widow Valvert' can vanish, never to be heard from again. As we arranged. The Widow *de LaGrange* will return to the family estate in Normandy. We will follow in a few weeks."

Céleste frowned and stared at the frost on the window glass. In some ways, that was the part of the plan that gave her the most unease. To spend the rest of her days with them in that gloomy Norman château, where the sun never seemed to shine...

"It *is* what you want, isn't it?" demanded Madame de LaGrange. "The quiet life in the country? You've told us often enough."

"Yes, of course, but..."

Monsieur de LaGrange fixed her with the mournful look that always made her feel guilty. "I suppose it seems a burden to you, to care for us as the years go on. That's a child's duty. A *grandchild's* duty. But, with Alex gone, where are your ties to us now?"

She squirmed in her seat. He knew just which notes to sound. "You haven't lost my loyalty," she murmured at last.

He smiled sadly. "I feel sure that Alexis, watching from heaven, will approve of your conduct."

"But...Paul," she said, voicing a thought that had come to trouble her more and more. "We'll be revenged upon the Malecots. And Paul, being a man, will survive the scandal easily enough. But what did he ever do to you to deserve a broken heart?"

Madame de LaGrange lifted her dog and put it into her lap. "If you feel that way," she said, her voice sliding into a whine, "marry Paul de Beaufort. *Monsieur* and I can do very well without you. Marry the man, if his feelings are of such concern to you."

Céleste shook her head. "I couldn't. Not after I'd disgraced him."

"Well, it doesn't matter to us!" snapped the older woman. "Just so you see to it that Élise would be too shamed to take him back. Ever! I think it would be a good idea if you could arrange to get into bed with him—un-clothed—before you drank the wine."

Céleste felt the heat in her cheeks. "I'm prepared to scandalize Paris. Ruin the man's reputation. And my own. But I'm not prepared to allow him the final liberties. I told you that from the first!"

"Such impertinence!" Madame de LaGrange clapped her hands together in annoyance. Pépin lifted its head from her lap and whimpered. "Do you forget what you owe us, miss?"

Céleste clenched her fists and swallowed her anger. They were right, of course, and she was wrong. "If you have nothing more to tell me today," she said tightly, "perhaps you should return me to my horse. I want to write another letter to Paul, in case my first one was intercepted."

The viscount leaned forward and patted her hand. "Now, now. *Madame* and I do not wish to be harsh. We rely on your judgment. The *appearance* of scandal is what we want. The extent of your undress is entirely up to you." He rapped on the roof of the carriage with his cane. At once it wheeled about to return to the spot where Céleste had left her horse.

They rode in uneasy silence for some minutes. Monsieur de LaGrange sat with his eyes closed. His wife—far less comfortable with the quiet—petted her dog, fidgeted in her seat, and cleared her throat loudly. When no one responded, she burst out in a torrent of words. "It would have been so perfect, had you managed to elope with Paul last night. The gossip in the opera house was not to be believed! Both of Paul de Beaufort's women in the same place... My God! It was *delicious!* If only you had seized the opportunity..."

"I'm glad I didn't," admitted Céleste. "Not with Élise de Malecot there. I'd never seen her until last night. I didn't know... She's so fragile...."

Monsieur de LaGrange's eyes shot open. "She's a Malecot! Isn't that enough?"

"But she's young and blameless. And if the old duchess withdraws her support, how will Élise ever find a husband without a dowry? It seems so cowardly and underhanded to hurt innocent people. What do Élise and Paul have to do with a feud that's been going on for more than fifty years?"

LaGrange's eyes burned with rage and pain. "If they must be hurt, so be it! If Élise never marries, the Malecot line will die out. As the LaGrange line is dead. I am sixty-one years of age! How much longer do I have? I want to know that the Malecots are totally destroyed before they lay me in my tomb!"

"And I must be a part of your fanatical hatred?" Céleste was beginning to regret the whole ugly scheme. Edmond de Beaufort had looked at her with such scorn in his icy blue eyes. She had felt soiled and degraded just imagining what he thought of her.

LaGrange was now trembling violently, torn between fury and a deep grief that seemed about to pour out in a flood of tears. "Our hatred should by your hatred! Have you forgotten who killed your husband last year?"

"Ungrateful wretch!" Madame de LaGrange chimed in. "Has it been so long since you put away your black crape that you can no longer remember the reason you wore it? Élise's father, Julien de Malecot!" At her grating tone, Pépin looked up and barked at Céleste.

"I haven't forgotten," whispered Céleste. Alex's death had broken her heart, leaving her alone and bereft. A stupid duel. And Alex had further weakened his strength by insisting on being carried home to Normandy, instead of staying in Paris. To see his dear Céleste, he'd told his parents. Though it cost him his life.

Still, though she'd grieved, she'd found it impossible to hate Julien de Malecot. Alex had always been hotheaded. There had been so many duels in his young life. So many dead and wounded opponents. Could she hate Julien de

Malecot simply because he'd won in a fair fight? "But Malecot has repented of his ways," she said. "Didn't he send you that humble letter of apology? And the wine from his own vineyards as a peace offering?"

LaGrange snorted. "Repented? Only because his mother-in-law, the old duchess, warned him. Threatened him for all of Paris to hear. No more scandals. He was to return to his faith and devote himself to his wife—that sickly daughter of hers. Or there would be no more money."

Madame de LaGrange smiled—an ugly grimace. "The fear of being destitute has made a sanctimonious psalm-singer of him. Otherwise, *monsieur* and I would have encouraged you to seduce *him*."

"He'll be begging for alms in the streets, or worse, before I'm finished with him," muttered the viscount. He rubbed at the frosty glass and peered out the window. "We're here. Your horse looks frozen. Send us word the moment you've spoken with Paul de Beaufort again." The eyes he turned to Céleste were dark with condemnation. "I am impatient to conclude this business. If you have any thought in your heart for poor Alex, do not fail in your duty."

The sun disappeared behind gray clouds as Céleste passed the opera house, in the rue Lepeletier. She shivered, but it was less because of the deepening chill in the air than because of the sight of the building—a reminder of last night, and Edmond de Beaufort's cold eyes. Her instincts told her he was a real danger—not just to the LaGranges' plans, but to her, as well. A frightening and powerful adversary. Last night, she suspected, had only been the beginning of the battle.

Not that she could blame him, she supposed. He was defending the honor of his family, just as the LaGranges were stubbornly set on their own path. And she was in the middle, trapped between passions and objectives that left her strangely unmoved. How could she appreciate Beaufort's fierce family loyalties, his defense of dynastic pride, when her own life had been one of wandering, relative solitude, disconnectedness to home, to community, even to country? How could she feel the years of hatred behind the La-Grange-Malecot feud? The pain and suffering on both sides? She, whose life had been serene and free of dark passions?

She knew the history, of course. It had been recited in mournful detail by Monsieur de LaGrange over many a late-night glass of cognac.

The LaGranges had been nobility of the ancient régime, before the Revolution. They were a large and prosperous family, with many sons. The Malecots had been their land stewards for generations.

The feud had begun when Alex's grandfather raped a Malecot woman, who then killed herself. Helpless against their powerful masters, the Malecots bided their time; when the Revolution came, they denounced every single La-Grange, sending most of them to the guillotine. A very few escaped into exile. With the establishment of the Empire, the Malecots found fortune and favor under Napoleon. They acquired a noble title and—in an act of supreme revenge—bought the old, confiscated LaGrange estates.

At the restoration of the monarchy, Vicomte Philippe de LaGrange, now the only surviving male besides his young son, Alexis, returned from exile in England and set about restoring his family's fortunes. He bought another estate in an adjoining parish, but the loss of his ancestral home had rankled.

Within a year of LaGrange's return from England, a mysterious fire consumed the Malecots' château, killing Julien's mother, sister and older brother. Philippe de La-Grange was suspected of the crime by the Malecots. He always denied it, even in his telling of the story to Céleste, but sometimes she wondered. His bitter hatred of the Male-cots—the source of the destruction of his entire family—had always seemed to be the main thread of his life.

A year after the fire, Julien de Malecot's father forced a quarrel with Philippe de LaGrange. The bloody duel that followed left old Malecot dead, and LaGrange with a severed arm and a wound to his vitals that rendered him impotent.

That had been nearly twenty years ago. In the intervening years, there had been such a spate of lawsuits between the families—false claims, trumped-up accusations, charges of libel and slander—that both the Malecots and the La-Granges had seen their fortunes dwindle to almost nothing.

Yes, thought Céleste. The history of their enmity was straightforward enough. But how could she ever feel the passion behind the hatred?

She guided her horse into the rue de Provence. She was chilled to the bone; she'd have Thérèse prepare her a hot bath. She was invited to a rout this evening. She hadn't planned to go when she received the invitation. They were invariably noisy parties, impersonal and showy, reflecting the crass aristocracy of wealth that Paris had come to represent. Besides, Paul wasn't expected. He was dining out of the city with old friends from the university tonight.

But perhaps she'd change her mind. She might glean a few crumbs of gossip at the rout and possibly discover whether Paul would be at Madame de Cloquet's musicale tomorrow night. And she was curious to hear the gossip about herself after that scene at the opera. Edmond de Beaufort had indicated that there was a great deal more gossip about her than she would have wished. If she decided to go to the rout tonight, she intended to listen very carefully.

Chapter Four

She was home at last, and not a minute too soon. The day had turned frigid. She stopped at her gate and rang the bell. At once, her servant Pierre appeared and opened it for her before guiding her horse into the courtyard of her *hôtel.*

"Cold day for a ride, *madame,*" said Pierre, leading the horse to the block so that Céleste could dismount. He was about to retrace his steps and close the gate when a man on horseback rode into the courtyard, climbed down from his saddle and strode purposefully toward Céleste.

It was Count Edmond de Beaufort.

He bowed in salute and began to speak before Céleste had a chance to order him away. "Forgive my presumption, Madame Valvert. I feared your servant would not admit me if I left my card."

She nodded stiffly. "That is true enough." Unlike the rest of her servants, who had been hired in Paris, Thérèse had come with Céleste from Normandy. She was a family intimate, and aware of the LeGranges' plot—no doubt they had discussed the whole scene at the opera with her. She would certainly have barred the door to the count.

"This seemed the only way to approach you," he said. "I had heard you enjoy riding—an *Amazone* who does not fear the harsh elements. I tipped a concierge down the street, who told me you'd gone out earlier today. And so..." He shrugged.

His effrontery was not to be endured. "And so you lay in wait for me, like a spider poised for its prey." Her voice was as cold as the day.

His mouth twitched in a smile. "A spider? I hope not, *madame*. I don't wish to see you harmed. I came merely to speak with you. As one reasonable adult to another." He gestured toward the door of her *hôtel*. "Can we go inside?"

"It would be a waste of time. We have nothing to say to each other." She swirled away from him in a flurry of skirts, then cried out in dismay. Too late, she saw the patch of ice on the cobbles of the courtyard. The heel of her boot slipped, and she felt herself falling. Beaufort's strong arms caught her a second before she would have crashed to the ground. She clung to him, gasping for breath, her heart pounding with the shock of her near fall. After a moment, she recovered herself. "Thank you, *monsieur*," she murmured, and tried to move out of his arms.

He held her fast. And when she looked up and saw the expression in his eyes, she trembled. He seemed to peer into her very soul, with eyes as clear and blue and warm as a summer sky. "How can any woman be so beautiful? So tempting?" His voice was husky with desire.

For one insane moment, she found herself wishing that he'd kiss her; then she came to her senses. She had a duty to the LaGranges. To Alex. She stiffened in his embrace. "Release me, if you please."

He, too, seemed to recover his senses. He lowered his searching gaze and dropped his arms. "Forgive me, *madame*. I spoke out of turn. I only beg you, in all sincerity, to grant me but five minutes of your time."

She was numb with cold. If she must quarrel with him, let it be within the warmth of her house. She nodded. "Very well." She led him into her drawing room and rang for Thérèse. "His excellency and I will have tea," she said, handing the maid her short fur-lined cape, her gloves and her riding hat.

"Very good, *madame*." Thérèse cast a quizzical eye toward Edmond de Beaufort, stared meaningfully at Céleste, then left the room.

The count stripped off his greatcoat and gloves, placed his hat on the glossy mahogany piano, and then took a turn around the large room. He paced like a dark panther, his steps catlike and alert, his eyes darting about as though he were taking the measure of his prey. He paused to warm his hands at the fire. Next, he ran his thumb along the keys of the piano and riffled through the music scores that cluttered its top. Beyond an open door was a room that Céleste had furnished as a studio where a half-finished canvas sat on an easel. Beaufort stepped to the doorway to look about the smaller room, then returned to Céleste, who had seated herself at the tea table awaiting the return of her maid. "A handsomely appointed house, *madame*," he said. "Scarcely what I would have expected to see."

"Did you expect a vulgar, gaudy boudoir, as befits the type of woman you seem to suppose I am?" she said, with more self-control than she felt.

He had the grace to look abashed, color rising to the roots of his dark curls. "From all the stories I have heard..."

"I suppose it would do no good to tell you they are probably lies."

He threw himself onto a velvet divan. "Let's put aside the matter of your reputation for a moment, and speak reasonably. My cousin Paul—he is young. He is innocent. He is easily wounded. He is also lacking in your sophistication and worldliness. He can easily be led by someone as clever and charming as yourself. That can only cause him humiliation in the future, when he begins to realize it. Élise de Malecot, on the other hand, is a child. They will come to love together, mature together, raise a proper family and live in virtue and propriety. Where—in that happy domestic scene—is there a place for you?"

She paused for a moment before replying, choosing her words with care. For all his mild tone, Edmond de Beaufort was the enemy of her plans. She must remember that. "You speak of being reasonable, *monsieur le comte*," she said at last. "But your tone reveals more than you think. Every word is underlaid with scorn. For me. My life. The woman I am, though you know nothing about me. Why do you find it so difficult to believe that Paul and I love each other?"

"I'm willing to accept that Paul is captivated by you. Infatuated to the point of madness. And, though it seems improbable, I could almost be persuaded that you love him in return, and have only the purest designs on his heart." He smiled benignly, as though inviting her to trust in his good will. She was about to relax; then he delivered his final, quiet thrust. "But one point troubles me." His eyes glinted with sudden cunning.

Was this how Alex had felt every time he engaged in a duel? Challenged, ever on the alert for the opponent's blows? She tingled with nervous energy. "One point, *monsieur?* And that is?"

His voice was like silk. "The matter of the inn. I don't think that was Paul's idea. I doubt he knew of it. But if you truly loved him, and wished merely to be his mistress, what would keep you from entertaining him here, at your *hôtel?* It's done every day, with discretion, by women far less clever than you are." He laughed sharply, bitterly. "Even a married woman, with a husband to deceive, can manage an affair without risking the openness, the danger to one's reputation, of a rendezvous at a public house."

"It seemed romantic at the time," she said, hoping her lie sounded convincing.

His lip curled in scorn. "I scarcely believe that. Tell me, is it marriage that you want? Paul is a man of honor. It would be very simple to compromise him into marriage. I think you know that. But only a woman with a corrupt nature would find such a stratagem necessary. And, of course, it quite nullifies your sincere avowals of love."

She had to remind herself that she was supposed to be a woman in love. She suppressed her anger and tried to look hurt. "I find your cynicism distressing, *monsieur*," she said in an aggrieved tone. "I see little point in continuing this conversation."

He crossed his arms against his chest. When he spoke again, his voice was clipped and businesslike. "I'm prepared to offer you thirty thousand francs to leave Paul in peace."

She pressed her hands together, struggling to maintain her composure. She should have expected such an insult. "That's very generous of you," she said quietly. "I'm told that a whore picked up in the jardins des Tuileries costs only twenty francs, and she is expected to perform some service to her benefactor. You called me tempting. Surely you want payment in return for your thirty thousand."

He looked distinctly uncomfortable. "That will scarcely be necessary," he growled.

For the first time, she felt a measure of control over the situation. She pressed her advantage. "And yet I think you want me," she purred. "I'd take an oath on it."

He stood up and began to pace. "You flatter yourself, *madame.*"

She smiled, enjoying his discomfiture. How dare he offer her money, the black-hearted villain! "Perhaps, if you haven't a wife yet, Monsieur de Beaufort, I'll compromise *you* into marriage someday."

He fixed her with an icy glare. "If I were ever to marry, I can assure you I would choose a woman of spotless reputation."

Her stomach lurched in disgust. "What hypocrites you men are! Every one of you wants a virtuous wife, but you don't mind corrupting some other man's wife. Or any woman, for that matter. How many mistresses have you had, Monsieur de Beaufort? Yet you come here to judge me, to buy me, to look at me with contempt. A scarlet woman, not worthy of your cousin's love, your family's name." She rose proudly from her chair as Thérèse came in with the tea. "Take it away," she ordered, snatching up Edmond de Beaufort's hat and thrusting it into his hands. "*Monsieur le comte* is leaving!" Without another word, she turned on her heel and stormed from the room.

"The count de Beaufort! Wait until I tell Monsieur de LaGrange!" Thérèse glided the soapy sponge across Céleste's shoulders and grinned.

"There's no need to inform him," said Céleste, already regretting that she'd told Thérèse the name of her caller. She frowned and sank deeper into the warm tub. "I don't want you to say anything to anyone." Edmond de Beaufort had been in her opera box last night, and she'd invited him into her house today. The LaGranges might misread the situation. She didn't need their criticism on *that* score, as well. "And you're not to tell the other maids in the shops where you run my errands in the rue Saint-Denis."

"Oh, *madame*, a little harmless gossip..."

"From what I understand, there are already too many stories about me." She clicked her tongue. "And in the absence of facts, people invent all sorts of nonsense."

"But isn't that part of the plan, *madame?* The more wicked they think you, the more shameful it will be for the Malecots." Thérèse giggled in delight. "They'll be the laughingstocks of Paris. And now, with the visit of *monsieur le comte*..."

"No gossip, I said. I'll deal with Beaufort in my own way." If she could succeed with Paul, she could ignore his cousin. A far more comfortable solution than an open war, given Edmond de Beaufort's menacing presence. She brushed away Thérèse's sponge. "Enough. Bring me my towel." She climbed out of the tub and allowed the maid to dry her gently.

Thérèse toweled her full breasts and her smooth, flat belly. She made a sour face of disapproval. "Your stretch marks have almost vanished, madame. There's barely a trace." There was accusation in her voice, as though Céleste were accountable to *her* as well, for the loss of Alex's child.

She allowed Thérèse to help her into a fresh chemise and a paisley dressing gown, then moved out of her bathroom and into her bedchamber. "I'll put on my corset and petticoats later," she said. "Leave me now." The reminder of the baby had been a sudden, sharp and unexpected knife to her heart. She sighed and threw herself across the bed, staring up into the silken hangings.

Alex. She groaned and covered her eyes with her hand. She was responsible for his death, and for his last, unhappy days. He had come home to recuperate in her arms, knowing it was unsafe for her to travel to Paris so close to her time. She had been carrying his child—the last hope of the LaGrange line. A sacred burden and responsibility.

And she had betrayed her charge through stupidity and vanity. She had seen his parents making a fuss at his bedside and had felt a pang of jealousy. In her desire to show that *her* love was greater than theirs, she had spent long nights beside his bed, exhausting herself with his care. And then—her final folly—she had strained her body in trying, unassisted, to lift him back into bed after he'd fallen in a convulsion of pain.

After the stillbirth, Alex had borne her presence in angry silence, his eyes filled with condemnation. And when it was clear that he was going to die, no matter what the doctors did, he had clutched her wrist in a savage grip. "Don't forget me," he had said, his voice a painful croak. "Avenge my death. Swear it to me now. Give my parents the honor and devotion owed to them. Pray they forgive your thoughtless destruction of the line." He had sighed and closed his eyes. "I never can."

"Alex," she whispered, and curled herself into a tight knot on the bed. Had ever remorse been sharper, more cruel? And each time she looked at Monsieur de La-Grange's features, she saw Alex's face, his blue-green eyes filled with blame.

But she would atone. She would give them the one thing they wanted besides an heir: the destruction of the Malecots. And then, perhaps, after the momentary shame and scandal, she could escape to the serenity of the country, to the healing balm of a quiet, contemplative life.

But, oh! To be done with it! She jumped from the bed, went into her boudoir and sat down at her writing table. She pulled out pen and notepaper, and tapped at her chin in thought. She had sent a letter to Paul this morning, a letter filled with her love and devotion. She had begged him to arrange a meeting as soon as possible. She had said nothing about the scene in her box—it would be easier to explain away Edmond when she was in Paul's arms.

Pierre had delivered the note to Paul's door, but there was no way to know if Paul himself had received it. It was possible he had, and was still angry because of Edmond and the kiss at the opera. She'd take a different tone in this second letter. She dipped her pen and began to write.

My dearest Paul, I cannot endure the rift that exists between us. It was not of my choosing. I am desperate to explain to you that your opinion of me at this time is a cruel misjudgment. My love for you has never failed, no matter what you may think or suspect. You are as dear to me as ever.

I must see you at once. Come to my *hôtel* directly you receive this letter. I know it is imprudent for you to call on me, but I desire peace and harmony between us. If you are of the same mind, do not fail to come.

She stopped writing. The clock on the mantel had chimed the hour. The shadows were already lengthening outside her windows. Paul would be on his way to dinner by now. It was foolish to send the letter. She put down her pen, sanded the words and laid the note to one side. There would be time to finish and send it if he didn't come to the musicale tomorrow night.

Paul. She thought of him with a pang of regret. He was so sweet and charming. So loving and devoted. So young in so many ways. And so susceptible to her wiles. It didn't seem right to play with his heart this way. The fact that he was so easy to deceive only added to her guilt.

It would be different if Edmond de Beaufort were her prey. She suspected the man didn't have a heart to break. Only desires. And he *did* desire her. She'd mocked him with it, but, upon reflection, she realized it was so. She had read it in his eyes. She had felt it in his kiss.

His kiss . . . She stroked her full lower lip, her body filled with a sudden warmth at the memory. If only she were free to pursue her own life, to follow her own heart and desires . . .

She opened a small drawer and pulled out a miniature of Alex, examining his every feature to remind herself of what she'd lost. His blond good looks, the proud tilt of his chin. His soft eyes. They stared back at her with a look she had seen many a time. A look that seemed to say, "You can never love me as much as I love you. You can never atone."

"Oh, Alex!" she cried in anguish. "Forgive me! Release me!"

Chapter Five

"I tell you, Edmond, I won't go!" Paul de Beaufort stood impatiently while his valet finished tying his cravat, then motioned the man from the room. He shrugged into his evening coat and turned to glare at his cousin, who was seated comfortably behind him in the large dressing room.

Count Edmond de Beaufort hooked one long leg over the arm of his velvet chair and smiled. He could afford to be patient with Paul. As the ranking male in the family, he held all the cards. "And I tell you it's all arranged," he said calmly. "Élise expects you at eight, and Madame de Granville has graciously found places for you at her dining table. I think she plans a few tables of écarté afterward. You know how much you enjoy the game. And it will give you the opportunity to see if Élise is as skillful a card player as she is sweet and agreeable. I must tell you, in the few times I've met her, I've found her delightful. A worthy addition to the Beaufort family."

A half-dozen invitations were tucked into the mirror above the mantel. With a muttered oath, Paul pulled one down and slapped it on the table beside Edmond. "*This* is where I'm going. The baroness de Cloquet's musical soirée."

Edmond raised a quizzical eyebrow. "And the Widow Valvert?"

"I trust she'll be there. She's fond of music. A charming voice." Paul tried to sound nonchalant, but a slight twitch of his mouth betrayed him.

Edmond shook his head. "A charming voice isn't reason enough to disappoint your fiancée. Nor Madame de Granville, who altered her social arrangements on your behalf."

"Damn it, Céleste will be waiting for me. She loves me!" Paul ran his fingers through his light brown hair. "I should have written. Two days... She must be frantic with worry...."

Edmond sighed. It was necessary to keep Paul from ruining his life, but he wished it didn't have to be this way. Why couldn't the boy open his eyes and see the sort of woman the Valvert creature was? Why did he have to be the one to disillusion his cousin? For the first time in ten years—since the death of Paul's father—he resented the burden that had been put upon his shoulders. Making order of Aunt Charlotte's life, seeing to Paul's education, supervising the family's investments so that they would never want for comforts. He had taken it all upon himself, and had never regretted it. And when Aunt Charlotte had written to tell him of the engagement to Élise de Malecot, he'd been almost as delighted as if Paul were his own son—though there was only an eleven-year difference in their ages.

But now, with the sudden intrusion of the Widow Valvert... He sighed again. Well, better to cause the young fool a little grief now than to see him destroy his life with a loose woman. "How can you believe Valvert loves you, when you saw how passionately she responded to me at the opera? I was sorry I had to prove it to you in such a cruel way. How fickle are women of that sort." Paul's expression that night had shown him how convincing his performance was.

"I don't want to speak of it," Paul growled. There was an undercurrent of pain in his voice. "Your behavior was beneath contempt."

"I couldn't think of any other way to bring you to your senses. *Nom de Dieu,* you're about to be married! In less than two months. And to a sweet, innocent child. Have you no thought to what she would think if the gossip reached her ears?"

"We've been discreet," he said sullenly.

"Not discreet enough, if even your mother heard of it and sent for me. And Élise's grandmother, the duchesse de Tallon, has a horror of scandal, I understand. Everyone knows it. Are you prepared to have the old woman disavow the marital negotiations because of your passion for Valvert?"

"Then I'll marry Céleste! I'm not sure I wasn't prepared to jilt Élise, in any event!"

Edmond jumped to his feet in exasperation. "By all the devils, I see that common sense was lacking in your education! Do you know what would happen with a wife like that? Half of Parisian society would close its doors to you. You and your wife would sit at home, vainly awaiting callers who never came. My God, you'd do better to marry Élise and keep Valvert discreetly as a mistress if you're so besotted!" He gripped Paul by the shoulders and gave him a firm but affectionate shake. "For the love of heaven, Paul, choose the sensible course. Marry a woman you can honor and respect. Love will follow. The difference between conjugal affection and unbridled desire is the difference between wisdom and madness. Think of your future."

Paul shook him off. "I want Céleste. And—if she'll have me—I want her as my wife."

Edmond stiffened. So it was to be war. "As head of the family," he said coldly, "I forbid it."

Paul thrust out his chin like a rebellious child. "I defy you."

The impetuous fool! thought Edmond. He hated to have to play his trump card. "Part of your father's fortune is still under my control. Must I withhold your income to keep you from folly?"

Paul frowned, and then sagged his shoulders in resignation. "You're a cold man, cousin. Marriage is simply a social convenience to you, is it not so? A question of advantage. A way of increasing the family prestige and resources. You've forgotten what love is. But I remember a funeral five years ago. I remember a man who wasn't afraid to weep at the graves of his wife and young son. A man who loved his wife. Who married because of love, not practicality."

Caught off guard by the sudden recollection, Edmond turned away from his cousin. To his surprise, he found that his hands had begun to shake. He crossed to a small bureau and took a cigar from a silver box. He struck a match and puffed in silence for a few minutes, allowing his chaotic emotions to quiet. "I've lived more than you, Paul," he said at last. "I've seen more. The cold man before you is a man whose heart was broken. I pass my days in travel, or at my country estates. What difference? I am like a dead man. Each hour is more empty than the last. There's no joy. There's no laughter. And when I come to Paris, it is worse. To see the frantic gaiety and feel like an outsider. To feel that nothing again will ever touch me to the soul. Life can do that to you. As can a false woman. And I tell you, Valvert will break your heart and leave you as desolate as you find me now."

"No!" It was a cry of pain. "She loves me."

"And her explanation for allowing me to kiss her in the opera house?"

Paul looked abashed. "I...I haven't heard from her since that night."

"So much for her 'love,'" Edmond said with a snort. Damn it, he shouldn't be forced to play this game! To tell lies for Paul's own good. Not with the jade's letter burning a hole in his breast pocket at this very moment. It was a good thing he'd bribed Paul's servants to direct all correspondence to him while he was staying in Paris.

And the letter, delivered yesterday morning... By God, the minx was skilled, he had to give her that. Pouring out the most extravagant sentiments, a veritable catalogue of her love. Begging Paul to summon her for a rendezvous. To soothe the fires of her desire. Not a word about the kiss. Not a whisper of remorse or apology. As brazen a hussy as he'd ever encountered.

"When I hold her in my arms," said Paul, "all misunderstandings will vanish."

"And what do you know of her?"

"All that I need to know. She's beautiful, gifted, refined, enchanting. She moves with grace, dignified and serene. Her conversation is witty and clever, her silences profound. I'm distracted to madness thinking of her. Ever since the ball on Saturday, when she confessed her love for me, I sit like an idiot and pluck the petals of the daisies. Will she love me tomorrow? The next day? Is it only a dream?" His eyes burned with fervor. "In short, she is divine."

"Bah!" Somehow, Paul's lavish praise rankled him almost as much as the woman's letter—that sickening, cloying encomium of love. "But what do you really know of her?" he said impatiently.

Paul stared at him, his face blank with perplexity.

"I'll tell you what I've learned," continued Edmond. "Her name is Céleste Valvert. Yes, I know," he said, holding up his hand to silence his cousin. "That is precisely what she claims. But she also claims to be a widow. Yet she has been called Céleste Valvert for some time. Since long before a proper age for marriage. And there seems to be no trace of a Monsieur Valvert."

"How do you know this?"

"I spent the morning with old baron de Lansac, who introduced her to Paris society in December. He's somewhat senile now, but I managed to glean some information. He met her six years ago. She was seventeen. She called herself *Mademoiselle* Valvert then. She was traveling with an old man named Achille Desrosiers. In the days of the Empire,

Desrosiers was a diplomat. And the toast of Paris—its demimonde, as well as its drawing rooms. But when Napoleon fell, Desrosiers retired. For a while he seemed to have vanished, and then stories began to drift back to Paris. He was seen in Frankfurt, Madrid, Florence. Every capital of Europe. And always accompanied by an exquisite young woman."

Paul frowned. "Céleste?"

"Lansac encountered them in Rome, as I say. Desrosiers was teaching music to supplement his modest income. He introduced Mademoiselle Valvert as his granddaughter."

"Why, then, there you are! Could any explanation be simpler? More benign?" Paul smiled his relief.

"My God, don't be naive! Desrosiers always fancied young women. He was never without a companion in Paris, usually twenty or thirty years his junior. I remember your father telling me of his wild escapades, his devotion to the amatory pursuits. He never married."

"How can anyone be sure? A country wedding, a secret marriage, a granddaughter..."

"That's absurd, and you know it," said Edmond gently. "And there's something more. Lansac said that Mademoiselle Valvert was besieged by suitors in Rome. The cream of the Italian nobility. But she never allowed a single familiarity. Indeed, she claimed that she would never marry, but live in contented devotion to the old man. There wasn't a doubt in Lansac's mind that it was a sordid liaison. And when Desrosiers died in Rome three years ago—virtually penniless—Valvert disappeared. And now she appears in Paris with a fine furnished *hôtel* and carriage and servants, rented for an entire year... Yes, I made inquiry. Someone had to play the skeptic. And who is paying for all this? The mysterious 'Valvert,' who left her a widow? Or another patron, who took Desrosiers's place?"

"I feel sure there's an explanation...." There was more hope than conviction in Paul's voice.

"And the stories that are making the rounds in Paris? Stories that hint at liaisons with a deputy of the Chamber? With one of the writers in Balzac's circle?"

"Rumors! Gossip!"

"There must be *some* truth to it. Paul, for the love of God, think of the shame to yourself, to your mother, to all the Beauforts, if your name should be linked to a woman like that."

"I tell you, we've been discreet. And will continue to be so."

"Discreet?" His cousin's blindness was maddening! "The woman was planning a rendezvous at the Three Feathers. Did you know that? The place is notorious for lovers' meetings. The landlord's tongue is as loose as a fishwife's. He's even been known to sell information to the newspapers. *Le Charivari* would have a field day! Don't you see? The woman means to ruin you."

Paul buried his face in his hands. "Even if she's everything that you say, I can't give her up."

Edmond clapped him on the shoulder in a gesture of sympathy. "It's a fleeting passion. We've all known such madness. But a woman like that can't inspire true love. It's the allure of the forbidden, nothing more. What we desire is more tempting than all we possess." He picked up Paul's top hat and gloves from a table and held them out to his cousin. "Be reasonable. Go and dine at Madame de Granville's with Élise. Enjoy yourself. Appreciate the fine qualities of your fiancée, and see how the Valvert woman pales beside a woman of virtue."

Paul nodded reluctantly, took his hat and gloves and wrapped his evening cape around his shoulders. "You speak of Céleste with such scorn. Yet you've tasted her sweet kisses." He looked at his cousin with an expression in his eyes that was very close to hatred. "Can you say that you felt nothing? No stirring in your breast?"

Edmond had a sudden vision of her face, the glinting topaz of her eyes, the fullness of her seductive lips, as pink as a dewy rose in summer. Then he caught himself. What was in his mind that he should allow himself to dwell on the overripe charms of a practised courtesan? The honey of her mouth? He smiled and shrugged, propelling Paul toward the door. "No, of course not," he said coolly. "I felt nothing. Now go and enjoy yourself."

When Paul had gone, he turned and threw the remains of his cigar into the fireplace. Madame de Cloquet's invitation caught his eye. He picked it up and flicked it lightly with his finger.

"I wonder..." he said aloud. Would the brazen creature exhibit herself at the musicale, after what had happened at the opera? He smiled, his mouth curving in a wicked smirk. It would please him to tell her that she'd failed with Paul tonight, and then watch her cheeks turn pale, her mouth tremble.

He thought quickly. It would take him half an hour or so to get across Paris to his own *hôtel,* change into evening clothes, and...

Madame Valvert, he thought, before I'm through, I'll send you back to wherever you came from!

Chapter Six

"Did you enjoy *Guillaume Tell* the other night, Madame Valvert?" The plump matron smirked at Céleste, then turned to smile slyly at her companion, a woman of equal girth in a heavy, patterned-silk gown that made her look like an upholstered chair.

Céleste smiled in return, controlling her face against the merest hint of annoyance. The gossips were determined to disconcert her tonight, if they could. After all, it was her first social appearance since that unfortunate scene with Edmond de Beaufort. And everyone, no doubt, was wondering to which Beaufort she was now devoted. She had been subjected to whisperings, furtive smiles and mocking glances from the first moment she'd swept into the baroness de Cloquet's drawing room.

She was glad she'd worn her pale blue moiré gown, with the wide lace collar that accented the graceful slope of her white shoulders, the low neckline that revealed the tantalizing curves of her breasts. She had wanted to be particularly seductive to Paul tonight. But it pleased her, as well, to show everyone in the room that, despite what they might have seen in her box at the opera, she didn't intend to hide for shame, nor dim her luster like a timid mouse. "I didn't enjoy it nearly as much as *La Juive*, last week," she said in response to the woman's question, as though this were normal chitchat. "Falcon was superb. A splendid voice."

The woman seemed disappointed not to have struck a nerve. "Alas, I wasn't there."

The upholstered chair frowned at the other woman. "But surely, my dear... I saw your husband."

The first woman laughed and fanned herself briskly. "Oh, my dear, that was on Wednesday. He always goes with friends on Wednesday, to meet the pretty young dancers in the *foyer de la danse*. Saturday is my day."

The other woman shrugged. "Men will have their little amusements. Don't you agree, Madame Valvert?"

Céleste nodded curtly and moved away from the two women. The hypocrisy between the sexes never ceased to surprise and vex her—especially here in Paris. Every respectable man—if he considered himself a true man—was expected to go at least twice a week to the opera. Once with his wife, and once with his mistress. He thereby earned the admiration of his fellows. Whereas a woman, were she as wanton as Delilah, as free with her favors as the worst *fille de joie* of the streets, was expected to conceal her affairs with all the feminine skills at her command. She had no doubt the two sanctimonious matrons had had lovers in their time.

She sighed. She wished the baron de Lansac were coming tonight. It would have been pleasant to have someone to keep her company until Paul arrived. To guard her from the gossips with their vicious tongues. And Lansac was so blunt-witted with age, yet still so protective of her because of the old days, that there would have been no rude questions or remarks from others.

She had already decided she would be shamelessly open in her attentions to Paul tonight. And the devil take discretion. If the LaGranges' plan was to succeed, it was important to lay to rest whatever doubts had been raised by Edmond de Beaufort—either in his cousin's eyes, or in the prurient opinion of society.

"Madame Valvert!" The baroness de Cloquet hurried toward Céleste, an awkward, morose-looking man in tow.

"Eugène here has been pining away since you arrived—too shy to approach you, and too stubborn to go home and take poison, as all our Romantic poets suggest for lovelorn young men." Laughing, she introduced Eugène, a Russian count newly arrived in Paris. While she beamed like a doting mother, he stammered out a few clumsy sentences of admiration for Céleste, reddening and staring down at his varnished leather evening shoes with every other word.

Céleste responded coolly. His French was atrocious, but she wasn't about to make it easier for him by lapsing into Russian. Not when Madame de Cloquet's expression—and those of the several guests crowding forward to eavesdrop—made her wonder if she and the Russian count weren't being maneuvered into some malicious joke to amuse the company. Part of the evening's entertainment— like Christians and lions before the Roman horde?

Eugène cleared his throat and tugged at his cravat. "May I call upon you tomorrow, *madame?*" he said to his shoes.

"I receive very few callers, *monsieur*. I am a widow. I live a quiet life."

His head snapped up in surprise. "But that is not so!" he blurted, looking with panic toward the assembled guests. "I have heard . . ."

Merciful heaven! she thought. What slander had they told him? That the Valvert woman received with no discernment? Entertained any man who called? Well, they would not have a joke at *her* expense. "What have you heard?" Her voice was icy, clear and sharp.

Madame de Cloquet had the grace to blush, as though she had suddenly remembered her responsibilities as a hostess. "Oh, Madame Valvert," she said quickly, jumping in to change the subject before there was an unfortunate scene in her salon, "have you heard the sad news? Monsieur Chopin has sent his regrets. We were looking forward to his playing tonight. But, alas, he hasn't been well."

Céleste looked at the baroness, whose eyes held a silent plea. Well, if the woman was willing to back down from an open confrontation, she could do the same. "What a pity, *madame,*" she said graciously.

Madame de Cloquet sighed in relief. "It's too late to find another virtuoso to take his place," she went on. "We shall have an evening of amateur musicians, instead. Though none the less brilliant and talented," she added, as several of the other guests stepped nearer. "My daughter has promised to play the piano. And Madame de Coudray will essay the harp. I have prevailed upon my daughter's piano teacher to accompany her. He's very skilled. He's promised us a Beethoven sonata to begin the program. And might we hope that you will favor us with a song or two, Madame Valvert?"

"Indeed, yes, *madame,*" said a guest. "You sing with captivating warmth. I had the pleasure to hear you at a musicale just before Christmas."

"How kind of you," said Céleste. She didn't think she would sing. There was no point to it—not if Paul wasn't here. And she didn't feel generous enough toward Madame de Cloquet, at the moment, to add to the success of her evening. She turned to her hostess. "It's kind of you to ask, *madame la baronne,* but I fear I must decline."

"I should be desolated not to hear you sing, *madame.*" The voice was low and thrilling and familiar. Céleste whirled to see Count Edmond de Beaufort smiling down at her. "Will you sing for me?" His voice was warm and intimate, but the blue eyes were chilling in their scorn.

The coldhearted devil, she thought. She matched his scorn with her own. "For *you?*" she said. "Do you flatter yourself, Your Excellency?"

Behind her she could hear excited whispering, snatches of phrases: "lovers' quarrel..." "...at the opera on Tuesday..."

He gave a formal bow. "I was in error. I meant to say, of course, for *us.* For myself, you understand, it's a matter of complete indifference." Several women gasped at the remark, which had clearly been intended as an insult.

Indifference? thought Céleste. She felt a wild urge to crack that icy exterior, to bring him down to the level of that foolish, lovelorn Russian count. She turned to Madame de Cloquet with a smile. "I should be delighted to sing."

The baroness clapped her hands in pleasure. "Hurry off, then, before the program begins, and arrange your selections with the accompanist."

Céleste did as she was asked, and was pleased to find that the pianist was familiar with the songs she had in mind. Then, seeming to ignore Edmond de Beaufort, she arranged herself gracefully on a sofa in full view of him. She'd make him regret he'd ever used the word *indifference*.

The pianist seated himself and began the Beethoven sonata. He was passably good, but not so extraordinary that Céleste had to focus her energies on listening. She concerned herself instead with all the charming little movements of seduction that her years among men had taught her. She tilted her head to one side, she moistened her lips, she closed her eyes and leaned back, pressing her handkerchief to her throat when a particularly lovely passage in the music stirred her. Without looking at Edmond de Beaufort directly, she knew he was watching her; she knew he couldn't help but watch her.

She glanced at him only once. Madame de Cloquet's daughter had played—badly, and at great length—and the harpist followed. Her playing was even worse. But she played with such extravagant flourishes of her hands, with such a sense of her own importance, that Céleste found she could scarcely suppress a laugh. She looked up. Beaufort, equally amused, had put his hand in front of his mouth, and was making a valiant effort to hide his smile. Strange, thought Céleste, remembering his astute criticisms at the opera, that such a cold, unfeeling man should have such sensitivity toward music.

At last it was Céleste's turn. She began with a lilting ballad designed to warm up her voice and show it to advantage. Beaufort seemed pleasantly surprised with the quality of her singing; his applause, though initially reluctant, was sustained. She felt a surge of confidence. She'd already drawn him in, without his being aware of it. Her next selection was Schubert's ravishing "Serenade," a song of haunting beauty that described a poet singing at his lover's window. She caressed the notes with all the skill she'd been taught. She moved away from the piano so that Edmond de Beaufort would have an unobstructed view of her, and sang every word to him, her gaze locked on his blue eyes—an intimacy that seemed to deny the presence of any other person in the room.

He frowned. He stirred in his chair. He pressed his lips together, his chest rising and falling with ever-deepening breaths. He was ensnared. Bewitched by her charms, beguiled by her song. When she reached the line "Beloved, come to me," she held out her soft arms in supplication to him; he clenched the sides of his chair as if to keep himself from rushing to her side. And when she closed on a soft F sharp, her voice throbbing with passion, he turned his head away.

There was a moment of silence, and then the listeners burst into applause that almost, but not quite, drowned out the whispers. Everyone had seen. Everyone knew that Madame Valvert had recaptured a lover who, earlier in the evening, had treated her with a lack of kindness.

Strangely, Céleste felt no joy at her triumph, as Beaufort sat like a stone, his blue eyes riveted on her face. If only this were not a game, she thought. If only those burning eyes, that mouth... She dropped her head, waiting for the applause to cease.

Madame de Cloquet stepped forward and held up her hands for silence. "I know we should all like an encore from Madame Valvert. But after that sublimity, how can we ask for more?" She gestured toward the door. "Come, my friends. A little supper."

The guests began to file out toward Madame de Cloquet's dining room. Céleste declined several gentlemen's offers to escort her, and turned back to thank the pianist for his help. They chatted for a few minutes, discussing the merits of Schubert as against Liszt. "Aren't you coming in to supper?" she asked at length, when he made no move to offer his arm.

"In a little while. I want to put away my music. Go in without me, *madame.*"

Bother! she thought. The drawing room was now quite empty; she'd have to go in alone. But as she reached the doorway, Edmond de Beaufort stepped back into the room and wrapped his strong fingers around her wrist. His voice was low and savage. "You may play your little games, Madame Valvert, but Paul isn't coming tonight. He's dining with Mademoiselle de Malecot. I saw to it." He smiled cruelly at her involuntary gasp of dismay, then held out his arm. "May I escort you in, *madame?* Someone with a sense of humor has put us at the same table. And I took the liberty of moving your place card next to mine."

Smiling through her fury, she took his arm. She could play the game as well as he. They passed through a little arched gallery whose wide glass windows looked out upon an inner courtyard that gleamed bright under a full moon, and entered the dining room. Edmond led her to her place, and made a great show of seating her, holding out her chair like a thoughtful servant.

Or a dutiful lover, thought Céleste sourly. He had clearly recovered from his setback in the drawing room. Now it was he who held the field, tending to her every need while the matrons nodded their approval at the lovers' reconciliation. Céleste could not ignore him or avoid him, but had to be content with speaking to him as little as possible. The meal was interminable, with so many courses that she was exhausted from eating long before the servants had cleared away the last platters.

They moved back into the drawing room for coffee. Céleste had hoped to escape Beaufort's saccharine attentions, but he stayed close to her side, even murmuring "Beloved" when he handed her a cup of coffee.

Madame de Cloquet sighed and leaned back in her chair, clearly pleased with the way the evening was going. And well she might be, thought Céleste in disgust, seeing the older woman's smug smile. Tolerable music, a lavish meal, and two adversaries whose alternating seductions and salvos were surely more amusing than a couple of trained monkeys or a court jester!

The Russian count had found a pretty little supper partner who had managed to coax him out of his shell. Now he glowed with self-confidence, leaping into the conversation at every opportunity. "I hear it is the play *Antony* will be— How do you say? Revived? By your Alexandre Dumas."

"Yes," said another guest, fanning herself. "I saw it in '31, with Marie Dorval. A moving performance. She wept real tears."

"What woman wouldn't be moved by a question of honor, such as the play represents?" said Madame de Cloquet.

This was too much for Céleste. She had planned to spend the rest of the evening in silence, waiting for the moment of escape. But she couldn't resist the impulse to enter the conversation. Though she hadn't seen *Antony,* she'd read it, and its depiction of an adulterous love affair and its resolution had angered her. In order to save his mistress's honor, Antony, the hero, had stabbed her just as her husband was about to discover them in a compromising situation. Antony had then nobly claimed that he'd killed her because the virtuous woman had resisted his base advances.

"Honor?" said Céleste, her mouth curving in a twist of disapproval. "Why should the burden of dishonor fall upon Adèle when Antony was equally guilty? It seems eminently unfair to me that, had the woman lived, she alone would have endured the scorn of society. And so he kills her. To *save* her. It's ridiculous."

Edmond de Beaufort raised a mocking eyebrow. "One assumes the man, in killing her, does not come away unscathed. I should think the guillotine is a rather heavy price to pay."

"That sensualist?" she said, fixing him with a pointed stare. "That man with no heart, who has little control over his desires? The guillotine is a fitting reward for his lust!"

He reddened at the openness of her attack, clearly remembering his weakness in the drawing room. "And the woman?" he growled. "That double-dealing creature who finds it impossible to choose between two men? What word would you use to describe her? A word, at least, that can be used in polite company!"

She held her tongue with the greatest effort of will, aware that half the guests had stopped to listen to the exchange. Her head was spinning from the warmth of the room, the closeness of the air, the wine she'd had at supper. Her state of exhaustion from keeping a tight rein on her emotions in the face of the monster's provocations. She turned to the baroness. "Do you suppose I might take a turn in your garden, *madame?* I feel quite flushed."

The baroness exchanged a meaningful look with a friend. "But it's so cold outside," she said to Céleste. "Let me send for your wrap."

"No, please," she said, rising. "I'll just take a breath or two." She swept out of the room with as much dignity as she could manage and reached the garden through the door of the gallery. The air was crisp and cold—as cold as the full moon that stared down at her. She was tempted to go home at once, slip out a side door and never have to see him again. The night air revived her, but she hated to return to the drawing room so soon.

She looked around the garden court. On the other side of the drawing room was what seemed to be a conservatory, dark except for the light from a few small, smoldering braziers to warm the more fragile plants. She crossed the court and went into the conservatory. It was dim and soothing, filled with the odors of vegetation, the heady perfume of tropical plants, the humid closeness of a summer night. She relaxed in the gloom and moved farther into the room, stepping away from the patches of silver moonlight. She would stay here for a little while. Perhaps Beaufort would tire of waiting for her return and go home. She closed her eyes and leaned against a large *jardinière*.

She heard a noise. A soft footfall. She opened her eyes. Edmond de Beaufort stood before her.

His hands reached out to pull her into his arms. "You Jezebel," he growled. "You siren, with your songs. Was there a moment tonight when you weren't performing for me? Tempting me with your every word and movement? Well, damn you, is this what you want?"

He took her mouth in a passionate kiss, his lips molding themselves around hers, his arms fitting her into the angles and curves of his own hard body. She had no will to struggle; it was too unexpected, too thrilling. She succumbed to his domination, trembling wildly, stirred to an intensity of feeling that she had never known. His scent, the perfume of the flowers, the mysterious darkness, the glow of moonlight. Magical ingredients to beguile her senses, to fill her with the longing to stay locked in his embrace forever. She moaned and wrapped her arms around his neck.

"Céleste..." he whispered, gliding his lips across her cheek to linger at the shell of her ear. She felt the sensual stroke of his tongue on the edge of her ear and suppressed a cry of pleasure. At any moment they might be discovered, and yet she never wanted him to stop kissing her.

"I know a little café," he murmured, holding her away to stare into her eyes. "Champagne and oysters. And then, afterward..."

She looked at his handsome face in the dimness and ached with desires long buried. She was filled with a need she had scarcely acknowledged since Alex had died, a fire that was now raging within her, hot and vital as a blazing torch.

"Well?" he said.

She hesitated. It was madness.

He pulled her close to him again. This time his hungry kiss demanded total surrender. His tongue plunged into her mouth in a surging rhythm that brought her to the edge of ecstasy. And when he released her, she sagged against his chest, drawing in great, gasping breaths of the scented air in a vain attempt to slow her racing heart.

"Come," he said. "Why do you resist? Your desire matches mine. You knew it from the first, and so did I. Come."

She was torn, unwilling to say the words that would bind them together tonight. And in the morning? What of her plans? Her promise to Alex? She needed time to think it through, and how could she think with her body pulsing with the thrill of his hot kisses?

His self-assured decisiveness settled the matter for her. "I'll leave now," he said. "Wait a quarter of an hour, then send for your carriage and say your adieux. I'll wait for you at the corner of the boulevard. We'll take my carriage and send yours back to your *hôtel*."

She nodded in agreement. What did she care for tomorrow?

He took her face in his hands. "You ravishing creature," he whispered. "So beautiful. So desirable. A dangerous weakness." He kissed her softly, then slid his hands down her throat and neck to caress the fullness of her breasts. "I'll love you as a man loves. Not a boy."

She stiffened at his words. The fire in her veins turned to ice. A boy. Paul. That was what he meant. She had thought to seduce Edmond when she sang, to shame him with his weakness. But he had seduced her instead. Kissed her, murmured her name, held her close. Made her forget herself. And it had meant nothing to him. Nothing! It was only one more ploy to distract her from Paul.

She willed away the pain that tore at her heart; this was not the time for it. She racked her brain, thinking how she could salvage her pride, turn this humiliation to her advantage. She allowed him a few more kisses, and then she began to laugh. The sound was light, carefree. As silvery as the moonbeams. "Oh, I wish Monsieur Dumas were here to help me with my drama."

He stepped back and frowned. "What?"

"I've been writing a play tonight. Didn't you know?"

"What the deuce are you talking about?" he growled.

She laughed again. "Act 1: The Musicale. She seduces him with her song." She danced around the *jardinière* and sniffed at a fragrant blossom. "Act 2: The Supper Table. He plays the gallant in lighthearted fashion, but secretly he burns with desire." Beaufort made a strangled sound in his throat, but she ignored him and went on. "Act 3: The Kiss in the Conservatory. Not entirely a successful scene, I fear. Dumas would have put a gossip or two into the scene. A few prying matrons hiding among the potted jasmine, eager to report back to the guests."

Even in the dimness, she could see the rage in his eyes. "And the dénouement?" The words came from him in a menacing rumble.

She shrugged. "I haven't worked it out yet. Sweet heaven, don't glower, or I'll think you want the ending that Dumas used in *Antony.*"

"No," he said coldly, regaining his frosty composure. "Antony killed to preserve a woman's reputation. I scarcely think that's applicable here."

Strangely, his opinion of her had lost its power to hurt. From that first moment at the opera, he'd seen her as a shameless woman; nothing she could ever do would change that. Why should she allow it to give her pain?

"I wonder," she said, appraising him coolly. "If we played *Antony,* which role would you take? Antony, who— though misguided and selfish—shows noble sentiments? Or the husband? Narrow, bound by convention, morally uncompromising, sanctimonious. Does it come from his sense of propriety, do you think? Or is he merely outraged that his passions—refusing to be controlled—have made a fool of him?''

He drew a sharp breath through his teeth—a long, hissing sound—and then bowed to her. ''Tonight I leave the stage to you, *madame*. Your performance, as usual, was superb.''

Chapter Seven

"Your tea, *madame*." Thérèse's voice grated like an iron wheel on cobblestones.

Céleste stirred in annoyance, sat up in bed and stretched. "What time is it?"

"Nearly one." Thérèse put the tea tray on a table near the canopied bed and crossed to the windows. She tied back the heavy silk draperies. The winter sun brightened the room, filtering through lace curtains to cast patterned shadows across the carpet.

Céleste stretched again, lifting her heavy brown braid from the back of her neck. "One! Dear God, I shall be glad to return to the country, where a body can keep reasonable hours." She put another pillow behind her back and patted her lap. "I'll have my tea now."

"Very good, *madame*." Thérèse bent her head to pick up the tray. Her eyes were dark, shadowed by the ruffles of her cap.

"What is it?" said Céleste. "Something's troubling you."

"You told me not to say anything to the LaGranges, and I won't," said the maid with a pout. "But when all the girls are talking about it in the shops..."

"Talking about what?"

"That's three times you've seen Monsieur Paul's cousin. I'm sure Monsieur de LaGrange would be very interested. And you won't let me tell him."

She frowned. "What are they saying in the shops?"

"That you and *monsieur le comte* . . . in the conservatory of Madame de Cloquet's *hôtel* last night . . ."

"Oh!" She groaned and closed her eyes, leaning back against the pillows. "Merciful heaven, do they never stop talking in this city?" She opened her eyes and looked with curiosity at Thérèse. "But I thought you were the one who approved of so much talk about me."

"Oh, *madame*, it's one thing to spread gossip about a deputy of the Chamber. It's quite another to make Monsieur Paul so jealous of his cousin that he won't want to go away with you!"

"What do you mean, 'spread gossip about a deputy'? Have you been doing that?"

"Oh, *madame*, I . . ."

"Answer me!" she demanded.

Thérèse faced her defiantly. "It was what Monsieur de LaGrange wanted. To make it all the more shameful for Monsieur Paul when you're found."

"Dear God! And were there other stories as well? Of other men?"

"A journalist, a friend of Monsieur de Balzac," she said sullenly. "And a baron from Dijon. Monsieur de La-Grange ordered me to do it."

It was intolerable, to have such stories spread about! And the thought of the LaGranges conspiring with her servant behind her back made it all the worse. "I thought you served *me*. How dare you blacken my name in this city without so much as a word to me?"

The maid sniffed. "I've been with the family for years. Long before you came to Normandy. I even played with Monsieur Alexis when we were children."

"And so you attend me, but all the while you serve *them*." She waved an impatient hand at the girl. "Give me my tea, then leave my sight. Before I'm tempted to sack you." It wasn't the maid's fault, she realized after a moment. A lifetime of loyalty to the LaGranges—why shouldn't she take their part? Still, she intended to reproach them for it. To spread vile stories and never even tell her! This explained why Edmond de Beaufort looked at her with such contempt.

She sipped her tea, scowling as the maid shuffled toward the door. "Wait," she said. "Since gossip is your mother's milk, what do you know of the count de Beaufort? He's not married, I'm given to understand."

Thérèse turned. "He was. Had a boy, too, I think. They were killed years ago in a carriage accident."

"Oh, how sad." No man, not even one as heartless as Beaufort, deserved such grief. "Does he—" She hesitated. "Does he have a mistress?"

Thérèse shrugged. "He doesn't come to Paris very much. He stays in the country or travels. That's all I know."

She dismissed the girl and finished her tea, allowing her thoughts to drift back to last night. Why had she sung that song to him? Why had she made a scene that common sense should have told her would become fodder for the gossips? Had she wanted to humiliate him? Revenge herself for his high-handedness at the opera?

Or had she, unaware of her own hidden desires, played the oldest game in the world? A nightingale, strutting in her plumage, trilling out her song in the eternal mating ritual? Advancing, retreating, a part of her wanting him and hoping he would want her in return?

She moaned softly, acknowledging the pain she'd ignored last night. All he seemed to want, all he thought about, was keeping her away from Paul, protecting his family name. And even if he truly did desire her, what did it matter? Because of her vow to Alex, her scheming with his parents, her whole world was awry. She had spun a twisted thread of deceit and vengeance that would end when she disgraced Paul and vanished from Paris. And she would never know if Edmond de Beaufort truly grew weak in her arms, as she did in his.

She closed her eyes, trembling at the memory of his lips. Not since those mad days in Rome had she felt such a thrill. Alex had been so hot-blooded, so brash and passionate, sweeping her off her feet with the fever of his desire.

Alex. The chevalier de LaGrange. Careless and blond and beautiful, drinking in Rome as though it were a cup of golden nectar poured for his enjoyment. So hungry for her that he wept in frustration when they parted after an evening of frenzied kisses and caresses that she stopped just short of shameful dishonor.

And she—lonely, lost, warming herself at the fire of his devotion, surrendering to a force she could scarcely resist. She had been caught in the whirlwind, a spinning storm of passion that had swept away her grief and despair. And when, in a wild, impulsive moment—desperate to possess her—he had proposed marriage, she had leapt at the chance. He represented family, solidity, belonging. In the days before the wedding—a hasty affair in front of a village notary—she had allowed herself to dream, imagining what it would be like to be made love to, to be a wife, a mother, the mistress of a real home.

Somehow, the reality had never been quite as wonderful as the dream. Alex's lovemaking had been as wild and reckless as the life he led. She had felt overwhelmed, inadequate to meet his urgent passion with her own. He would rise from their bed and go off alone into the soft Roman night, complaining that she made him feel like a brute.

And when he'd taken her home to Normandy, to his family's modest country estate, it had been worse. The LaGranges, hoping for a good marriage for their son, had been disappointed with a woman who had no title, no money, no illustrious forebears. They had behaved as though she were a poor relation, ordering her around, ignoring her when they chose, arranging for her always to be away from the château when important friends came to call. And Alex, bored with her, bored with a secret marriage he'd come to regret, had gone off to Paris for months at a time to resume the madcap life he'd known before.

A secret marriage. Sometimes she had sat in the loneliness of her room in Normandy, rereading the marriage contract to remind herself it wasn't simply a dream.

She had been delighted when she became pregnant. It was a tangible sign of her love for Alex; didn't everyone know that only a woman who experienced pleasure in the marriage bed could conceive? She would win back the love she so desperately yearned for. She would redeem herself in Alex's eyes, make up to him for his disappointments in bed. When she was the mother of his son, the heir to the LaGrange line, they would acknowledge her openly. Alex had promised it, just before his last, fatal journey to Paris.

She laughed softly, sadly. They had acknowledged her, at last, at Alex's grave.

"*Madame.*" Thérèse stood in the doorway, holding out an envelope. "A boy just delivered this message."

"Give it here." Céleste tore it open, glanced at the signature on the bottom of the page, and breathed a sigh of relief. Paul. He had written at last. He had forgiven her the scene at the opera. Well, perhaps *forgive* was too strong a word, she thought, scanning his terse message.

He would call upon her at four. He trusted she was entertaining no one else today. He would hire a fiacre and come incognito, to escape his cousin's vigilance. If, however, she no longer wished to see him, she should have her servant wave him off, and he would pass her gate without stopping. He would understand.

She smiled as she read the words. In spite of the disasters with Edmond de Beaufort, there was still hope. She would capture Paul's heart once more. Perhaps today she could arrange a new rendezvous at the Three Feathers. For next Monday or Tuesday, if Paul was willing. The sooner this was over, the sooner she would be at peace.

She had already decided she wouldn't go back to Normandy. Duty or not, she couldn't bear the thought of spending the rest of her life with those unpleasant people. She remembered a charming villa on one of the hills outside Rome. With her modest inheritance from Alex's will, she could live there quite comfortably. There was nothing to keep her in France. The LaGrange estates were bequeathed to a distant relative; Monsieur de LaGrange had changed his will after the losses of Alex and the baby.

She looked at Thérèse, awaiting her instructions. "It's from Paul de Beaufort," she said. "He's coming here at four. What shall I wear that makes me look penitent?"

She chose an afternoon dress of dark green cashmere, its simple lines relieved by a small lace collar, which she fastened with a cameo that Alex had bought her in Rome. She looked prim and humble, without disguising the shapeliness of her figure.

She decided to receive Paul in her cozily furnished studio, rather than in the large drawing room or her plain upstairs sitting room; she wanted intimacy for this scene of the drama. The studio was a warm and personal room, not as dangerous as her boudoir with its feminine atmosphere, and its door that opened onto her bedchamber. Besides, she needed something to do with her hands while she gauged Paul's mood.

She was seated before her easel, sketching a bowl of fruit, when he burst into the room. "Paul," she said, looking up with a smile. She searched his face. Did he want a kiss? A formal greeting on both cheeks? A handshake, in the English style? She assessed the angry scowl on his soft young features. No. He wanted nothing. Except, perhaps, to vent his spleen.

He ran his fingers through his light brown curls and glared at her. "I'm surprised you didn't greet me in your bedchamber," he growled. "After the liberties you granted my cousin, it's the least I'd expect for myself!"

She continued to sketch, unperturbed. "I granted nothing to your cousin," she said calmly. "He overpowered me in the opera house. Simply to make you jealous." She smiled

again, like an indulgent parent. "And it seems he suc-
ceeded. Shall I ring for tea?"

"Damn it, I'm not talking about the opera house! Edmond himself told me that it was a ruse. That he had no interest in you. But I neglected to ask him if *you* were
interested in *him*."

"Don't be foolish, my dear." With a graceful turn of her
wrist, she executed the curve of the porcelain bowl in front
of her, then suggested its contours with small, feathery
strokes.

Paul swore softly. He strode to her, snatched the charcoal pencil from her fingers and flung it across the room.
"What happened in Madame de Cloquet's conservatory last
night? Everyone saw you leave the salon to go into the garden. Then Edmond vanished. The baroness and her guests
swear they heard noises from the conservatory. Damn it,
what happened?"

She took another charcoal from the worktable beside her
and sighed. "Your cousin and I quarreled in the conservatory. Over you."

"That's all?" The beginnings of doubt crossed his face.
"And his attentions to you at dinner?"

She put aside her work and rose to her feet. She looked at
him tenderly, her eyes soft with love and sincerity. "Paul,
dearest," she murmured, "how can you doubt me? Don't
you know your cousin wants to make mischief between us?
To keep us apart?"

He kicked angrily at the leg of a chair. "Yes, the devil
take him, I know."

"Well, then . . ."

The doubts persisted. "But you sang to him. A love
song."

She smoothed back the wild curls from his forehead. How
skilled she had become at this vile game. "I sang to everyone. I was thinking only of you, my love."

His eyes shone with devotion. "Do you mean that?" He
swept her into his arms and clasped her to his breast. "How

cruel I was to doubt you, even for a moment. My dearest one." He kissed her passionately, his lips moving over hers.

She responded as she always did, wrapping her arms around his neck and pressing against him with a breathless hunger. But she felt sick. It had never troubled her before—to pretend a passion she didn't feel. She was doing this for Alex, wasn't she? For the man she had loved and called husband.

But now, with the feel of Edmond de Beaufort's kisses still on her lips, burned in like a brand that claimed her, she felt nothing but shame and horror at the intimacy of Paul's mouth on hers. She was no better than a cheap trollop. Dear God, she thought, let it be done with!

She freed herself from Paul's arms, resisting the impulse to flee. She must see this through to the end. "Beloved," she said with a sigh, putting her hand to her heart, "you quite overwhelm me. Go away before I forget myself."

He reached out to pull her back. "I want you to," he said hoarsely. "I want your surrender."

She held him off. "Not here. Not now." God forgive me for this, she thought. "I want our love to be perfect. Not in this commonplace house, with prying servants. A rendezvous. A secret, magical retreat. I'll make the preparations. I'll send a carriage to bring you to me. Tonight, my love, if you are as impatient as I."

His face fell. "I can't. Tonight Edmond has arranged a dinner with the Malecots. And tomorrow..." He clenched his fists in impotent fury. "Tomorrow I'm being sent away. Like a child who has thrown mud on the family crest."

"Sent away?"

"Edmond insists that I go to take the waters at Aix-les-Bains."

She frowned. Edmond de Beaufort was becoming the bane of her life, thwarting her plans at every turn. "To go away?" she said. "For how long?"

He laughed bitterly. "I'll be permitted to return to Paris a week before the wedding. The end of February."

"Merciful God," she breathed, resting her forehead on her fingertips. Six more weeks of this city, of enduring the ugly gossip, of wondering what new schemes the count de Beaufort would devise to confound her. Six more weeks of the LaGranges. She raised her head and stared at Paul with genuine dismay. "But why?"

"Oh, my love... Your heartbreak only binds you to me the more. Edmond thinks if I drink enough glasses from that sulfurous spring I'll be cured of loving you."

"Oh, Paul..."

"It will be unbearable," he said. "Cold. Miserable. To take the baths and then go out into the snow... to drink the waters... God! But what else is there to do? No one goes at this time of year, except true invalids." He threw up his hands. "They don't even gamble!"

"Can't you refuse to go?"

"How can I? Edmond has been like a father to me. I feel a duty to obey. And my mother is near to distraction because of the rumors about you and me."

"I hate the gossip. I wish you could stay. At least for a few days." She clutched his arm in a gesture of urgency. Perhaps the scheme could still work. "Stay for a few days. Tomorrow night. Give me tomorrow night, beloved."

"I promised I'd go," he said with an unhappy sigh. But when she looked desolate, he added quickly, "I didn't say I'd stay for the entire six weeks."

Her thoughts were spinning. It didn't really matter, after all, when the scandal broke. Just so it happened before his marriage to Élise. She put a brave expression on her face. "Go off and take the waters, then. Let your cousin try his best to destroy our love. We know he'll fail. And when you come back to me," she added in a seductive whisper, "I'll plan a night of love to make you think you're in paradise." *That* should bring him racing back from Aix-les-Bains in a twinkling!

"No," he said. "Follow me there. I'm renting a house. Just the two of us..."

She thought quickly. For the scheme to work, the scandal had to take place here in Paris. And if she joined him at Aix, he'd expect her to go to bed with him. "No. I couldn't. To live together openly... I couldn't. I'll wait for your return."

"*Live* together? My God, Céleste, I'm asking you to marry me!"

The suddenness of it overwhelmed her. She fell back a step, her hand to her breast. "Paul. No!"

"The banns can be waived," he said eagerly. "We can marry almost as soon as you arrive."

"But...we scarcely know each other..." she stammered. "To talk of marriage..."

His eyes were dark with reproach. "Did you think it was only a fleeting passion? A flame that would burn itself out? Did you think me as shallow as that? Look." He pulled a snowy handkerchief from his pocket and held it out to her. One corner was embroidered with a delicate pattern of twining leaves and trailing blossoms, superbly executed in fine silken thread of the richest brown color. "Do you remember the day I begged you for a curl?" he went on.

She gasped. "Dear God! You had your linen marked with my hair?" It was a fashionable gesture of love, but one of such intimacy that women blushed to present such gifts to their lovers. She cursed her blindness. How had she failed to realize he was falling so deeply in love? That the diabolical plan would succeed far beyond what she hoped or wished for? Her guilt was like a sharp knife. "Paul, you shouldn't love me so much," she said in anguish. "I'm not worthy of you."

He gathered her into his arms. "Not worthy? You're an angel. A pure, unspoiled darling. Come away. Marry me." He tried to kiss her, but she pulled away.

She clasped her hands together in what was almost a gesture of supplication. "You move too fast. It's all too sudden. My head is spinning. If you love me, go away. Give me a chance to look into my heart. I promise to be here when you return." She wasn't sure she meant it, but it seemed the only way to persuade him to leave.

He grabbed her hands and kissed them passionately. "Come to Aix, I beg you!"

She was too much a coward to refuse him outright. To say the words and watch his heart break. "I don't know. Perhaps Edmond is right. We need this time apart. But if I decide to come, I'll write to you first. That's the most I can promise." She was very close to tears, seeing the grief on his face. "Go now," she said. "I can't bear it."

He nodded, kissed her softly and quickly on the mouth, and ran from the room.

She sank into a chair. This wasn't meant to happen. It should have been a lighthearted affair—a brief, intense passion that would lead to the fateful rendezvous. Nothing more. Dear God, nothing more!

But Paul was young, impulsive. Perhaps that would work in her favor. If he'd fallen in love so quickly, perhaps this enforced separation would help him fall out of love. If nothing else, it would give her time to plan a renunciation that would hurt him as little as possible.

She laughed ruefully. Whoever could have believed that she and Edmond de Beaufort would want the same thing?

"I won't go. It's wrong, what we're doing to Paul de Beaufort. I won't!" Céleste crossed her arms tightly against the bosom of her dressing gown to keep her hands from shaking in anger.

Madame de LaGrange fanned herself in a frenzy of nervous activity. "It isn't enough that we learn of Paul's escape from the city between the acts at the Théâtre-Italien. Oh, no! Now we must endure rebellion from you?"

Céleste sighed and sank into an armchair. She sometimes suspected the LaGranges enjoyed these nocturnal visits, the opportunity to wake her at two or three in the morning with some trivial news or command that could have waited until daylight.

Monsieur de LaGrange, sitting quietly in the desk chair, opened his eyes. "Did you know Beaufort was going to Aix-les-Bains?"

Why did he always force her to defend herself? "Yes," she said with reluctance. "He told me himself, yesterday afternoon."

"And you let him go?"

"Merciful heaven, how was I to stop him?"

"But if he wanted you to follow him, as you said, why are you still here? Why aren't you packing?" The mournful tone was even more accusatory.

"You know what he would expect if I went. Marriage, or..." She jumped up from her chair and went to stand at the window and gaze out at the bright moon on the cobbles below. "I told you, I won't become Paul's mistress. Besides..." She hesitated, then turned back to face them. "I think I've begun to change my mind about the whole scheme."

"What?" squeaked Madame de LaGrange.

"Here is your tea, *madame*." Thérèse stood in the doorway, holding a tray. Her hair was in curlpapers and her mouth was turned down in a sour expression, as though she found her mistress's sudden change of heart worthy of nothing but contempt.

"Do you lose your nerve with one setback?" said Monsieur de LaGrange. He turned to his wife. "You see, my dear. It's borne out once again. There's a subtle distinction between an acquired and a natural breeding." His tone was soft, but tinged with malice. He smiled at Céleste and continued as though the air didn't hang heavy with the implied insult, the reminder that he had been born an aristocrat, while she...

"You needn't take Paul to bed," he went on. "I think you're clever enough to keep him at bay. Merely go to Aix, cement the bonds between you, and bring him back to Paris and the inn. That, I trust, is not beyond your capabilities."

She refused to be drawn in. He had insulted her merely to put her on the defensive. It was more important to make clear how she felt. "No. I told you. I won't involve Paul any longer. When this is done, what would he have? Neither Élise nor me. Only a broken heart. I can't punish him like that."

LaGrange grimaced in pain and clutched his stump. "You cannot punish the man who killed your husband?" His voice rose, sharp and accusing. "You cannot avenge Alex?"

"Ingrate!" added Madame de LaGrange.

Céleste clenched her hands together in frustration. "*Malecot* is our enemy, not Paul! By heaven, I'd rather take a knife and plunge it into Julien de Malecot's heart than cause Paul any more grief!" She waved away Thérèse and the cup of tea. "I want to leave Paris," she said defiantly. "I want to be quit of this whole ugly business. I've decided to go back to Rome. I long to see it again. Perhaps I can even teach singing. In any event, I have enough to live on."

Madame de LaGrange's voice was almost a shriek. "You want happiness, when your poor dead husband has not been revenged yet? Is this how you show your love?"

Céleste was reaching the end of her endurance. "What more do you want of me? I honored him while he lived. I honored you afterward. I kept my mourning in his house, as you wished. What more do you want?"

"What did you ever bring him?" said Madame de La-Grange bitterly. "A dowry? A family name? An heir? He might have made a brilliant match in society. Instead, you seduced him, appealed to his baser nature, so he foolishly married you."

"He loved me! And I loved him!"

"And couldn't hold him. Why do you think he had to go to Paris?"

She held her hands before her like a shield, wishing she could stave off the woman's hateful words. "When he was hurt, he came home to me," she said in her own defense.

"To *you?* My God! He came home to the child you were carrying. He was so proud to have an heir. He wanted to be at home when you were delivered of his son." Madame de LaGrange's eyes were dark with venom. "And you *killed* his child!"

It was the familiar refrain, fashioned to play upon her guilt. But tonight it had a strange effect upon her. She stared at Madame de LaGrange's face, which was contorted with hatred, at the viscount's twisted smile, which was no less malevolent, and shuddered. They were consumed with thoughts of revenge against the Malecots—not just for Alex, but for all the LaGranges who had come before. They didn't care about her. They didn't care *for* her. They would use her, play upon her guilt, spread gossip. Anything. And if she continued to do their bidding, she would become as warped and poisoned as they, seeing the world through a dark cloud of hatred. Hadn't she already gone against her instincts these past two months, behaving in ways that would have sickened the old Céleste? She must escape them while she could.

"I can never atone for the loss of the baby," she said quietly. "I shall grieve every day of my life. But I won't hurt a Beaufort because a Malecot killed my husband. I intend to go to Rome." Her words rang with finality. She turned to LaGrange, defying him to challenge her with his martyr's voice, his mournful appeals to her conscience.

Instead, he smiled apologetically. "How unkind we've been to you. Thinking only of ourselves, forgetting that you have suffered, also. The loss of Alex. The loss of your child. And the strain of these past few weeks. *Madame* and I have not been sufficiently appreciative of your efforts. By all means, go to Rome. Revisit your old haunts. Refresh yourself. Remind yourself of the happiness you and Alex shared. Go."

She stared at him, taken aback by his unexpected gentleness. "Now?"

"This week. Why not? We are not heartless fiends, despite what you may have begun to think. Perhaps reaching the Malecots through Paul is the wrong approach. You were quite right to see it as needless cruelty. I fear *madame* and I have allowed our grief at Alex's death to distort our judgment. Go to Rome for a few weeks. We'll rack our brains to think of a new scheme. When you return, we can talk of it." He stood up and crossed to Céleste. He bent his head and kissed her on the forehead. His eyes were kind and loving, and his smile was warm. She had a sudden, poignant memory of Alex. "Think of it as a little holiday," LaGrange said. "Will that please you?"

She nodded. She felt weary to her very soul. "I'm tired," she said. "All these weeks of pretense..." She looked at him and frowned. "And ugly gossip."

He made no attempt at denial. "Yes," he said in a low voice. "Thérèse told me you asked her about the gossip. That, too, was unkind. And for that I humbly beg your apology."

She accepted him with a nod, then looked around the room, her thoughts already on the days ahead. "The *hôtel* and its furnishings are rented for the year. I suppose I could just close it up until I return. And dismiss all the servants. There will be time enough to sublet it when I get back."

"Why not let Thérèse stay here as the concierge until your return? You might feel differently after your holiday."

"Yes. I suppose that makes sense. Though I must tell you, in all fairness, that—" It was difficult to say the words.

He patted her cheek. "That you might decide not to help us when you come back? Despite your vow to Alex on his deathbed? Yes, I understand. I can read it in your face."

She wavered. He was being so kind. And the reminder of her pledge to Alex... "If I can help you, without going against my conscience, you know I will. If not..."

"If not," he said, his voice suddenly sharp, "I should want your word that you will not interfere with our plans, whatever they may be."

"No, of course not."

"Nor speak of this to anyone. Ever."

"I promise."

"Do you intend to break off with Paul de Beaufort?"

"It's the only decent course."

"Wait until he returns from Aix-les-Bains, then. It would be a kindness to let your image fade in his memory for a few weeks." He held up a warning finger. "But you mustn't tell him why you pursued him, or why you now spurn him. Let him think you've grown tired of him, nothing more. I don't want our names to be mentioned at all, in connection with this or *anything* else. All we ask is your complete silence."

It was the least she owed them. "Of course."

"Do you swear it?"

"By Alex's memory."

"No," said Madame de LaGrange, her eyes glowing with renewed fury. "Swear instead by the bloody wounds that felled him. By the mortal blows from Julien de Malecot's blade. Julien de Malecot, who will have a *grandson* someday!"

Céleste bowed her head, feeling drawn back into the whirlpool of their fanatical hatred. They would always win. For as long as she had regrets and remorse to torment her, they would win.

"I swear," she whispered.

Chapter Eight

"I'll help you with your corset, *madame*. It will be faster."

"No, no." Céleste brushed off the innkeeper's wife and hastily finished hooking the snug garment. She was glad she'd thought to travel with one of the newer corsets that opened in the front—the sort that allowed a woman to dress herself unaided. Country inns didn't always have girls who were capable of serving as ladies' maids. "Just see that my nightcase is packed and put aboard the coach with my trunks and hatboxes." She took a hurried swallow of her morning tea and reached for her petticoats. "In point of fact," she said, her voice tinged with annoyance, "I don't know why you couldn't have wakened me at the hour I requested." Impatiently she threw her petticoats over her head, one by one, ending with a warm, quilted silk. The day was chilly. "I quite clearly asked to be wakened early, so I wouldn't be forced to rush like this."

The innkeeper's wife ducked her head as she made for the door with Céleste's nightcase. "I...I suppose I just forgot," she mumbled. She seemed embarrassed, and eager to be gone.

"But you're sure the *diligence* won't leave without me?"

"No, *madame*. My husband is holding the coach. You have my word you won't walk." The woman hurried from the room and closed the door.

Céleste sighed and put on a redingote of gray merino trimmed with chinchilla bands at the hem and cuffs. She fastened it closed down the front, then pinned on her cameo brooch. She didn't know why she'd taken to wearing that piece of jewelry so often lately. Perhaps now, escaping from her obligation to Alex's memory, she was punishing herself by keeping his gift constantly in her sight.

She gulped down the last of her tea and reached for her gray velvet bonnet. Except for the chaos of this morning, the trip had gone very well so far. Two days in the public coach, with only a few quiet and reserved passengers, pleasant overnight stops at comfortable inns. She tied her bonnet under her chin, quickly arranged the ribbon loops, and reached for her reticule and gloves. But if only they'd given her warning today! She felt sure that her hastily eaten breakfast of tea and toast and jam would sit like a rock in her stomach for hours.

There was a rapid series of knocks on the door, and the innkeeper burst into the room. "Quick, now, *madame,* before the *diligence* leaves!" He hooked his large hand around her elbow and steered her out of the room, propelling her with such haste that she feared she'd slip and fall on the staircase.

"My good man . . ." she protested.

"No time, *madame.* Quick, now!" He hustled her out of the inn and into the courtyard; the carriage was waiting, its door wide open. She had only a moment to see that her several trunks and boxes were piled on the top before she was thrust into the dim interior.

She sat down in a flurry of petticoats and then frowned. *Velvet* cushions? And where were the other passengers? "Wait a moment." she cried. "This isn't my coach!"

A caped figure loomed in the open doorway. "Indeed it is, Madame Valvert." Edmond de Beaufort swung himself into the carriage and slammed the door shut behind him. "Drive on!" he shouted, sitting down across from her.

"No!" In a panic of alarm and consternation, Céleste lunged for the door.

He muttered a curse, caught at her waist and pulled her down onto his lap, his arms wrapping firmly around her. "You're coming with me."

"Curse you!" She struggled vainly to escape his iron hold, to reach and open a window. "If I scream, you'll have to let me go."

"Not at all," he drawled, as the coach started up. "The carriage is mine. My people don't really care who I... entertain. As for the innkeeper and his good woman—they think you're a runaway wife. And I, the wronged husband who has come to fetch you back." He laughed shortly. "The innkeeper was even helpful enough to suggest I take a switch to you."

The enormity of his villainy overwhelmed her. "Oh, you scoundrel!" she breathed, looking over her shoulder to glare at him. "You arranged it all! The lateness of the hour, this mad haste, so I shouldn't notice your deception!"

"I don't think it's seemly for you to lecture me about deception," he said. "Not after the games you've played." His voice was a mocking growl in her ear. "Now, unless you choose to spend the rest of the journey like this, I advise you to behave yourself and take a seat. Otherwise..." He pulled her more closely against his hard body. His hands moved suggestively at her waist.

She wrenched free of him and flounced onto the seat opposite. She smoothed her skirts, putting a rein on her anger. "The last round was mine, as I recall," she said coldly. "You're entitled to this one."

He inclined his head in salute. "A wise decision."

She examined him minutely, as a pugilist would measure his opponent. It was astonishing how a man so handsome, so imbued with dark good looks, should have a nature as ugly and unpleasant as his face was beautiful. That those clear blue eyes should conceal a black heart. "Would you care to tell me what this is about?" She had an uneasy and frightening suspicion of what he intended, but she wanted to hear him say it.

He shrugged. "I've just kidnapped you."

"That's clear enough," she said with a snort. "To what purpose? Have you decided that, since I wouldn't yield to you the other night, you will take what you want? Am I to be your plaything?"

He tapped his fingers together and smiled. "An interesting thought. It hadn't occurred to me. But I'm in the habit of paying for an offer like that."

She had to remind herself that he'd probably heard all of Thérèse's lying gossip. That awareness was all that kept her from clawing his eyes out. "What do you have in mind?" she said crisply. "I assume there's a purpose behind this farce. Something that goes beyond your selfish pleasures."

"Indeed." He nodded. "I thought I'd finally brought Paul to his senses. He agreed to go away. He went. And then my people told me that the fascinating Madame Valvert was closing her house and arranging a journey." He spread his hands in mock innocence. "Where *could* she be going? I asked myself. And the answer came to me in a dream: Aix-les-Bains."

She stared in astonishment. "Merciful heaven! You think I'm going to join Paul?"

"It would appear so."

"Appearances can deceive. I'm going to Rome, on a holiday. I have friends there."

He applauded softly, his lip curling in derision. "Oh, very good. A ready answer. But how convenient that Aix happens to be on your route."

"I tell you, I don't intend to see Paul."

"And I think you do. I think you plan to see him, seduce him and defame him."

He came too close to the truth. "Why should I want such a thing?" She tried to sound indifferent.

"If Élise de Malecot's grandmother, the duchesse de Tallon, learns of it, there'll be no marriage."

"What nonsense! Why should I want to hurt Paul that way?"

"I don't know." He eyed her thoughtfully, his eyes scanning her with a thoroughness that was disconcerting. "If I could learn more about you, I'd have the answers. Perhaps something in my uncle's past . . . But you would have been a child then. How old are you?"

"Twenty-three," she answered in a frosty tone, wondering why she even bothered to reply.

"Paul's father died ten years ago." He smirked wickedly. "But I suppose you could have been precocious."

"Once and for all," she said, ignoring that bit of malice, "I'm going to Rome." She opened her reticule. "Would you care to see my passport?"

"It won't be necessary. I believe you have one. Did you take that precaution so that you and Paul could elope to Rome, far from my control?"

"My God, don't you understand? I have no intention of seeing Paul. In point of fact, I've begun to think that you were right. He's dreadfully young. I plan to put an end to our affair—such as it is—when both of us are back in Paris. So you see, this absurd business has only wasted your time."

"No, I doubt that. I've been inconvenienced, my pleasant life disrupted, my solitude shattered. But a waste of time? No. Not if it preserves Paul's future happiness."

"Oh! Must you be so obtuse? I wish him the same happiness. Let him marry Élise de Malecot and be done with it. Only let me go to Rome. *I don't want Paul.*" She enunciated each word clearly in the hope that perhaps he would understand.

"I've already admired your skill as an actress. You deceived me once before. You'll forgive me if I don't believe you now. I thought you welcomed my attentions in Madame de Cloquet's conservatory. I was wrong. I don't intend to be fooled again by your feminine tricks."

She remembered the fable of the boy who cried wolf. Her kisses had been genuine. Her repudiation of Paul was genuine. But she could scarcely make Edmond de Beaufort understand now. She sighed, temporarily defeated. "What do you plan to do with me?"

"I'm taking you to my château."

"I'm to be your prisoner?"

"My *guest,* Madame Valvert," he said with an exaggerated smirk. "You'll find it agreeable enough. I have a music room and a good library. Billiards, too, if you are so inclined. And the country landscape is pleasing, even in winter. You'll stay until Paul and Élise are safely married and on their wedding travels. And then you'll be free to return to your life in Paris."

"But that's ridiculous. All those weeks? I'll be missed."

"By whom? You've closed up your *hôtel* and left the city. Who expects you to return at any time soon? I assure you, however, that if there is anyone to whom you wish to write, I shall be happy to see the letter delivered. To put his mind at rest," he added pointedly.

The scoundrel! she thought. She was trapped. If she wrote to Paul, rejecting him, it would break his heart without convincing Edmond she meant to give him up. And she scarcely could send a note to the LaGranges! "I suppose you think you're clever," she said. "But I remember once you accused me of trying to compromise Paul into marriage. Aren't you afraid that my presence in your home—unchaperoned—might put you in the same impossible position?"

He smiled mockingly. "If you become difficult in the next few weeks, I could always use marriage as a threat."

She returned his smile with a wry laugh, acknowledging the animosity between them. "I wonder which of us would regret that the more? I, married to a man with no civility? Or you, married to a woman with a less-than-spotless reputation?" She was vexed to see how quickly his face darkened into anger. How dare he think so ill of her? Rumors or not, how dare he look at her with such contempt? She'd been worthy of Paul's love, hadn't she? No matter how false the circumstances.

"How very unbending you are," she said, her lips drawing together in a tight line. "I can understand that you want to protect Paul's future. I can even appreciate that the rumors you may have heard about me—though false, I can assure you—might cause you to be unkind...to treat me with less courtesy than you ought. But to behave as though it were impossible for Paul and me to have any affection for each other, that there might even be a spark of love..." She frowned in disgust. "What gives you your moral superiority?"

He laughed—a cynic's laugh, sharp and humorless. "Love? There's no such thing as love. There's passion, rooted in self-interest."

"Can you admit of no emotions beyond our control?"

He stared at her, his burning eyes focused on her mouth. "Yes," he growled at last. "Desire."

She gulped. She was aware that her pulse had begun to race, that she was finding it difficult to breathe. That his eyes were frightening and wonderful. That they were alone and isolated in this carriage, racing along to God knew where. She had never felt more helpless in her life, dreading—yet oddly craving—the moment when he would reach out and pull her into his arms.

Then his eyes shifted, and his hungry expression changed, as though a curtain had dropped in front of him. "But unless we're no better than savages," he said, "we resist our desires. Now, if you'll forgive me..." He took off his hat, leaned into a corner of the coach and closed his eyes. "I've been up since dawn." He waved his hand in the vague direction of the carriage door. "Should you wish to read, there are books in the pocket there."

Seeing that he meant to sleep, Céleste turned her attention to the books he'd offered. A curious collection, she thought. Intelligent, discerning, oddly quixotic: two recent novels by Balzac and George Sand, a book of poetry, a new translation of *Hamlet*—all of France was still buzzing over the "discovery" of Shakespeare's works. A scientific monograph on the cultivation of grapes, and, most peculiar of all, a picture book of medieval armor and two Gothic tales of troubadors, dragons and damsels in peril.

She chose the Balzac, rereading a chapter she'd enjoyed before, but she found it difficult to concentrate. As she had feared, her hastily downed breakfast was now sitting heavily; her discomfort was intensified by the pressure of her tight corset. She closed her eyes and slept, but when she awoke, her distress was even greater, with rumblings and sharp twinges beneath the whalebones of her bodice. Beaufort still slept; his face in repose was soft and strangely young.

They passed through a small village—a cluster of thatch-roofed cottages and barns, and a sprawling inn. The carriage lumbered onto a rickety bridge, then stopped. From the sounds of the shouting outside, Céleste guessed that another coach or wagon had come onto the bridge from the other direction; the two drivers were now arguing as to which one should be forced to back up.

I wonder, she thought, eyeing the still-sleeping Beaufort. With the hullabaloo outside, it would be a simple matter to slip away from the carriage, race back to the village and beg for sanctuary. She put out her hand and grasped the handle of the carriage door.

"Don't try it." Beaufort's voice was dark and menacing.

Startled, she jerked her head toward him. He was now sitting upright, alert, clearly poised to lay his hands on her if it should become necessary. "I wasn't planning an escape," she said with cool sarcasm. "But we've been riding for some time now. I thought, as long as we were stopped... Certain necessities... The inn, there..." She intended to loosen her corset at the first opportunity.

He smiled. "A quick answer for everything. Does nothing shake your poise?" He pulled down the window and peered out. "We seem to be starting again. If you can wait a few minutes, you can avail yourself of the privacy of the woods."

She smiled in her turn. "I'm agreeable to that," she said calmly. She wasn't about to let him enjoy his small victory!

They rode for another ten minutes, and then Beaufort rapped on the roof of the coach with his walking stick. When they stepped from the carriage, he gestured toward a small wood not far from the road. "You won't be disturbed there. However—" he held up a warning finger "—if you are thinking to escape, I should tell you that there are wild boars in this region." He raised a sardonic eyebrow. "Though I'm not sure you couldn't charm them with those eyes of yours."

She sniffed in disdain. A grudging compliment. "I'll return in a few minutes. If I intended to escape, I'd plan it with more care than this." She made her way into the midst of a thicket, where the trees and heavy underbrush shielded her from the carriage. She lifted her skirts and relieved herself, then moved farther into the wood. She unhooked the front of her redingote from the bosom to just below her waist, reached in and began to work at the lacings of her corset. It was awkward, with her petticoats in the way and her fingers stiff with the cold of the January day. She struggled for a few minutes, then gasped in dismay when the tape snapped. "Oh, bother!" she muttered, feeling the corset give way completely. There was no way to repair the tape; she'd have to refasten her redingote as well as she could. She certainly wasn't about to call for her trunk and change her clothes from her chemise outward!

She tugged and pulled at her gown, trying with all her might to force the front edges together; but with the release of her confined body and the bulk of the now-useless corset in the way, the snug redingote refused to close. She grunted and strained, managing to fasten one or two hooks, but that was all. Despite the chilly day, she was beginning to feel the perspiration roll down her back with the effort.

"Are you contemplating escape after all?"

She whirled to face Edmond de Beaufort, clutching her arms in front of her to shield her gaping dress. "A slight...a minor inconvenience ..." she stammered, feeling a flush of embarrassment on her checks. "Go back to the carriage. I'll join you presently."

He grinned. "Is that a blush? Are there some things that disturb even the perfect Madame Valvert?" He examined her carefully, attempting to peer under her protective arms. "Come," he said, "I'm not unfamiliar with a woman's garments. What seems to be amiss?"

She hesitated, then gave in. Unless she intended to keep her hands wrapped around her for the rest of the journey, he'd know soon enough. "The tape of my corset broke," she said. "And now my gown won't close."

The grin deepened. "A very real concern. You might seduce my footman or coachman with your charms revealed. And then we'd never reach my château. Here." He untied his dark silk cravat, unwound it from his neck and held it out to her.

"Thank you." She took the cravat and turned away from him, then stared down in dismay at her bodice. "If...if I could just fasten one hook at my waist..."

"Here. Allow me." Despite her feeble protests, he turned her around and grasped the two sides of her gown. "Hold your breath." He bent down, tugged at the fabric, swore softly, then grunted in satisfaction. "There. Now, if you don't eat too much at lunch, it should hold for the rest of the day." He looked at Céleste and grinned again. His teeth were white and even, and his smile was unexpectedly warm, lit by the intense blue of his eyes. "I may keep you a prisoner, but I don't intend to starve you."

She turned away quickly to escape his gaze. She tied the cravat around her neck, allowing the ends to hang loose and cover the open front of her gown. When she faced him again, she returned his smile. The loan of the cravat had been thoughtful, and he'd seen to the fastening of her gown without humiliating her or stressing the intimacy of the gesture. "Now, at least, I'll be able to eat," she said.

He chuckled. "I begin to understand what Paul saw in you. You have a natural ease about you. A self-assurance that's very pleasant. And rare. Not many women would have managed a personal catastrophe with such aplomb."

She shrugged. "If I've learned nothing else through the years, I've learned to be comfortable with myself."

"And where have you learned? Who taught you?"

She shook her head and smiled at his maneuver. "Ah, no, *monsieur*. You'll not pry my secrets from me quite so easily."

He threw back his head and laughed aloud. "By all the devils, you're a challenge, Madame Valvert. Perhaps your enforced captivity in the next few weeks won't be such a trial after all." He offered her his arm. "Come," he said. "Lunch."

Lunch turned out to be a lavish meal, produced from a large hamper by Beaufort's footman. Though they ate in quiet civility, side by side in the carriage with the food laid out before them on the seat opposite, Céleste found herself more and more troubled. "Keep you a prisoner," he'd said. "Enforced captivity." As though he had every right to do with her as he wished.

The more she thought of it, as the carriage resumed its journey, the angrier she became. She lapsed into a distant silence as the afternoon wore on, staring out the window at the passing countryside. They must be deep in the heart of Burgundy by now, she guessed, and she had no idea where they were going, nor how long he intended to keep her. It wasn't so much the thwarted trip to Rome that she resented. Nor even his stubbornness in refusing to believe that she'd give up Paul. It was his high-handedness, his arrogant subversion of her plans, that rankled.

By the time night fell and she saw the dark shape of a château looming in the distance, her anger was at the boil. How dare he presume to control her life? Even if she had

actually intended to go to Paul, he had no right to stop her!
Well, she'd outwit him. Lull him into thinking he'd won,
and then . . .

She was careful to hide her feelings, to moderate her behavior toward him—friendly, but not too warm. He'd never
believe she was softening *that* much! She declined his kind
offer of supper with him after she was settled in her rooms,
preferring, she said, a light snack on a tray. She smiled en-
ticingly at the groom who helped her from the coach. The
man who kept the horses was decidedly the man to culti-
vate! She graciously acknowledged the housekeeper's welcome, she admired the handsome vestibule and grand
staircase of the count's home, and she bade him a civil good-
night.

But all the while she thought: Tomorrow. I'll make my
escape tomorrow.

Chapter Nine

"You're up early, *madame*." The maid knelt before he fireplace in Céleste's bedchamber, stacked a fresh supply of logs and kindling and struck a match to them.

Céleste shivered and wrapped herself more snugly in her coverlet, waiting for the warmth of the fire to fill the room. "Yes," she said. "I seem to sleep better in the quiet of the countryside." She watched the maid bustle about the handsome room, opening the curtains, fetching her paisley dressing gown from a mirrored armoire. Edmond de Beaufort was rich, that was clear enough. But someone had furnished this suite with a refined taste that had nothing to do with a lavish expenditure of money, and someone had trained the servants to a degree of care that was thoughtful yet unobtrusive, and entirely out of the ordinary. Her trunks and boxes had been unpacked in no time last night, and her simple snack had been served on a tray with fresh flowers from the winter garden.

She stretched and yawned, admiring the embroidered tulle hangings that curtained the bed, the soft blue velvet swags that draped the walls and windows and doors. After a few minutes, she ventured out of bed, hurriedly slipping into the dressing gown that the maid held for her.

"I have tea waiting in your boudoir," said the girl. "After that, what do you wish, *madame?*"

Céleste frowned in thought. The wise general took the time to reconnoiter the territory, to gauge the strengths and weaknesses of his enemy. "I think I'll stay in my rooms this morning, *en déshabillé*.... In front of the fire. With a good, filling breakfast, if the cook doesn't mind. Once I'm settled for the morning, you needn't trouble yourself about me any longer. You can go about your business as though I weren't here. I can always ring if I need anything."

The maid bobbed politely. "Very good, *madame*."

The morning went as she had hoped. She was bathed, dressed in a demicorset and a loose, comfortable *robe de chambre*, tended, fed, and finally left alone with her thoughts. By the time the bronze clock on her mantel had struck the hour of one, she had made her plans.

Her rooms in Rochemont, Beaufort's château, were located in a corner of the pavilion. One set of windows looked out upon distant hills, while the other gave her a view of the lawn and gardens at the front of the building. Recalling their arrival last night, she was able to figure out in which direction lay the stables and the road that led to freedom. And when she caught a glimpse through her window of Edmond de Beaufort riding out in the opposite direction, she was set on her course. They'd passed a village last night—some five leagues distant, she guessed. If she could reach it, explain to the local gendarmes that the comte de Beaufort was holding her against her will, she might be able to arrange an escort back to Paris.

She shed her *robe de chambre* and quickly pulled on her riding habit. The sun was shining, but it might be cold on a long ride, so she put two petticoats over her stirruped riding trousers before finishing with a heavy velvet riding skirt and jacket. Her tall beaver hat had a long crêpe veil that she wrapped snugly around her head and neck. At the last moment, she remembered her cameo. Once he found her gone, Edmond de Beaufort might be reluctant to release her belongings right away, and she didn't want to leave Alex's gift behind. She pinned it to the wide collar of her jacket, picked up her gloves and walked softly to the door of her boudoir.

She opened it a crack and peered out. No one seemed to be in the passageway. She moved to the staircase, treading softly, but without seeming to appear furtive, as though she had no business there. She breathed a sigh of relief when she found an outer door and went into the sunshine. No one had stopped her.

She found the stables and her groom of the previous night, using all her charm to persuade him to saddle a horse for her. When he expressed a momentary doubt, she assured him that *monsieur le comte* was waiting for her just beyond the avenue of trees that led to Rochemont. She handed him a sou to encourage his cooperation, mounted the horse he gave her and took off at a gallop. She rode down the graveled avenue, passed winter-bare fields with row upon row of staked grapevines, and soon reached a wooded road that hid her from view of the château. An hour or so of hard riding, she imagined, would bring her to the village. She rode at a steady pace, her horse's breath clouding the cold air.

She wasn't sure at what moment she first noticed a distant, faint sound on the road behind her. But when she turned in the saddle, she gasped in horror. Edmond de Beaufort was racing toward her, flying down the road like some mad jockey at Longchamps. Or a dark bat out of hell. His shoulders were hunched, and he leaned far forward in the saddle, wielding his whip with ferocious intensity. She couldn't see his face at this distance, but she could imagine the savage grimace. His horse—mane and tail streaming— was as black, as wild and frightening, as Beaufort himself.

"Dear God," she whispered, feeling her heart constrict. She didn't know what the count intended if he caught her. And she wasn't sure she ever wanted to know! But if she could elude him long enough, she might yet reach the village. She jerked on the reins and cantered her horse toward the trees, swiftly guiding the animal among the dark trunks and bushes with all the skill at her command. In, out. A frantic, evasive dance. Increasing her pace when she could, slowing only to keep the horse from colliding with the looming trees. And still Beaufort gained on her.

The worst of it was, she had no idea where she was going. This way could be leading her right back to his château, or so deep into the woods that she would need his help just to find her way out! The trees seemed to be thinning up ahead. If she was lucky, that might indicate the outskirts of a town. She came to a large meadow covered with tufts of dead grass and small clumps of bushes. Beyond it was a canal—a long, straight, man-made channel. It sparkled in the afternoon sun. Thin wisps of steam rose into the frosty air from its glassy surface. Thank God! she thought. This might prove to be her salvation. For where there was a canal, there were surely barges and people and busy little market towns.

Abruptly she wheeled her horse about to parallel the direction of the canal, prodding the animal with a sharp smack to its flank. At that moment, a bird, hidden among the grasses and startled by her sudden approach, rose up in front of her with a noisy, frightening flurry of wings. Her horse whinnied and reared up in alarm. She felt herself flying through the air, arms waving wildly. And then... nothing.

She awakened to the sound of her name, an urgent "Céleste!" from Edmond de Beaufort. She opened her eyes and groaned.

"Are you hurt?"

"I don't think so," she said in a tentative voice. "It merely...took my breath away." She wriggled gently to feel the movement of her limbs. "Nothing seems to be broken, as far as I can tell."

He moved with quick assurance, his hands at her clothing. He unwound the veil from her neck and hat, pulled the hat from her head and tossed it aside, and loosened her collar. Then he put his arm around her shoulders, supporting her so that she was able to sit up. "What the devil did you think you were doing?'' he growled. ''You don't know these woods. You might have been killed.'' Strangely, though his words were angry, his blue eyes were soft with concern. ''Here,'' he said. ''This will help.'' He reached into the pocket of his riding coat and pulled out a small flask. ''Cognac. Drink it.''

She was beginning to recover her wits, as well as her equilibrium. Alert now, she glanced around the open meadow, scanned the nearby trees. Her horse was gone. No doubt it had bolted after it had thrown her. Only Beaufort's horse remained, panting and snorting from its wild gallop. Céleste felt an unexpected surge of anger at her situation; if not for Edmond de Beaufort, she wouldn't be lying here in the first place, feeling dazed and winded. Still... She suppressed a look of cunning. She might still best him, the scoundrel! Kidnap her, would he? Keep her a prisoner against her will?

She allowed him to guide the flask to her lips. She took a small sip and pretended to choke. ''Oh,'' she gasped. ''I can't... It's so strong. Perhaps a bit of water?'' She contrived to look helpless, her eyes pleading with him to excuse her feminine weakness.

''Of course.'' He looked abashed at having offered her the cognac. He stood up and strode to the canal, emptying the flask of its alcoholic contents as he went. At the water's edge, he knelt on one knee, bent over and dipped the flask.

In that moment, Céleste was on her feet. She raced to him, put her hands at his back, and pushed with all her might.

With a roar, he toppled headlong into the canal.

She turned around and dashed for his horse, grabbing frantically at the reins. Oh, bother! she thought. She might have guessed that he'd ride a high-spirited animal, skittish with strangers. Despite her eagerness to escape before Beaufort could recover himself, she made a conscious effort to slow her movements, to speak gently and soothingly to the horse. It would be difficult enough to get her skirts out of the way so that she could mount and ride astride; she didn't need a temperamental animal besides! She hitched up her skirts, held them to one side, raised her leg. She was near to swearing aloud in frustration. The horse was so *big*, and the cursed stirrup so high! She slipped her boot into the stirrup for a second, lost her footing, tried again. Perhaps if she gave a little leap as she put her foot into the stirrup, she'd have enough momentum to swing her other leg over the saddle.

She shrieked when she felt a strong arm around her waist. It was cold. It was dripping wet. "Get down from there, damn it!" Beaufort's voice quivered with rage. She turned and twisted, tore wildly at his arm and struggled against his superior strength. It was useless. She was dragged from the horse and held, suspended, above the ground.

"Let me go, you—you monster!" she cried. She kicked and wriggled, vainly trying to reach the ground, and pounded at his wet coatfront and shoulders with flailing fists. To no avail. He marched purposefully toward the trees, stopping only long enough to scoop up her veil from the ground. Roughly he set her on her feet in front of a tree, pushed her back against the trunk and began to wrap her veil around her waist, looping it in with the tree trunk. While she hooked her thumbs in the veil and squealed in protest, he brought the ends behind the tree, tightened them with a savage jerk and tied them securely, out of reach of her clutching fingers.

She writhed and twisted, pulling at the veil and swiveling her body within the confines of her bonds in a vain attempt to free herself. She felt like a butterfly impaled through its middle—able to flutter its wings, but helpless nonetheless. In a fury that was quite unlike her, she pulled off her gloves and threw them to the ground. If the villain came close enough, she intended to scratch his eyes out!

He moved around to stand in front of her, just beyond her reach. He was panting from his exertions, and canal water was still dripping from his dark curls. "By God," he muttered, "I must have been an imbecile not to warn my servants what a tricky, lying devil you are!" He shook his head, looking like a shaggy mastiff, and droplets went flying. "I should leave you here to freeze to death," he growled, beginning to shiver in the cold air.

Her lip curled with contempt. "That would solve the difficulty with Paul, wouldn't it? On the other hand, surely your château has a dungeon somewhere."

"Brazen and unrepentant to the end, I see. You're more trouble than you're worth." He unbuttoned his wet riding coat and stripped it from him. Then he worked on the buttons of his brocaded waistcoat, pulled if off and eyed it with disgust. "Twenty gold louis. And the damned thing is ruined." He untied his cravat, unbuttoned his stiff collar.

Céleste was growing uneasier by the minute. If he began to work on his riding breeches, she was prepared to fight for her virtue with the last ounce of strength in her body. "Don't you think you've gone far enough?" she asked. Her voice betrayed her by quavering.

He smiled sardonically. "Has it finally occurred to you that this isn't a game?" He unbuttoned his shirt and pulled it free from his breeches, then slipped it from his shoulders. His torso was hard and firm, his muscular chest covered with a thick patch of straight black hair that made him seem all the more ominous.

"See here—" she began, but he cut her short with a wave of his hand.

His eyes held hers. They had darkened to the blue of night, filled with anger and...something else? Something frightening and unnameable? She trembled in terrified fascination. His voice, when he spoke, was low and menacing.

"Take off your skirt," he said.

"Wh-what?"

"You heard me," he snarled. "Your skirt. Take it off."

She faced him with cold defiance, though her heart was pounding. "I will not."

"If I take it from you, you might not like my technique. I'm not feeling particularly chivalrous at the moment. Take the damned thing off!"

It was madness to argue. Especially when the man seemed capable of any manner of violence. Despite the tightness of her bonds, she wedged her hands between her skirt and the tree trunk, managing with some difficulty to find and open the hooks at her back that held the garment closed. She eased it over her petticoats and pushed it down to her ankles. "Now what?" she said with sarcasm. "I can't bend over to pick it up."

"Step out of it and kick it toward me."

She did as she was told, but with ill grace.

He scooped up the skirt and held out his hand. "Now give me your brooch."

"It's an heirloom. And precious to me. No."

"Damn it, I don't intend to swallow it! Just borrow it. Give it here."

She sighed in defeat and unpinned Alex's cameo. At least, whatever Beaufort intended, there seemed to be no further danger to her person.

His teeth had begun to chatter. He blotted his wet hair with a corner of her velvet skirt, then wrapped it around his naked shoulders like a cape and fastened it close with the cameo. "Not exactly Paris fashion," he said with a smirk, "but I don't plan to freeze on your account. Now..." He crossed his arms against his chest; he seemed to be making a deliberate effort to curb his anger. "We're going back to Rochemont on my horse," he said evenly. "Together. You'll either behave—no tricks, no attempts to escape—or it will be a long and uncomfortable ride for you. You have my word on that."

"Your word?" she said with a sneer. "A rascal who stoops to kidnapping women?"

He laughed sharply. "The word of a 'rascal' who is rapidly learning the strengths of his adversary. Now, I want your oath to behave before I release you."

"Or?" she prompted, curious to learn just how uncivilized the man could be.

"You behave—and you share the saddle with me. If not, you ride facedown, trussed across the rump of my horse."

She gave him a tight smile. "An amusing choice." She held up her hands. "You may untie me. My fingers are growing cold. I need my gloves."

"Your oath?"

She shrugged. "The rascal has the oath of a— What did you call me? A lying, tricky devil?"

"Fair enough." He untied the veil, mounted his horse and pulled her up to sit in front of him. "An unexpected bounty," he said, circling her body with his arms to reach for the reins. "You're warm."

Why had he said that? It only made her aware of his bare flesh pressing against her back, of the strong, hairy arms that enveloped her. He held her close to feel her warmth; she wondered if he could feel the mad pounding of her foolish heart.

Weak-willed idiot! she thought. Why was she so susceptible to him? To his nearness, his scent, the power of his strong body? She'd felt a certain triumph in besting him, if only for the moment; now, wrapped within the warm tent of his seductive arms, she felt sadly defeated.

They rode in wary silence, marshaling their forces, no doubt, for the next engagement. They were met at the château by a swarm of somber-faced servants. To each anxious question, Beaufort simply replied that he had had an unfortunate accident while riding. Both he and Madame Valvert were well, thanks be to God, though cold and wet. He sent a groom back to the canal to look for *madame's* horse and fetch whatever clothing he might find lying about. He bowed politely to Céleste as he saw her up the steps, then hurried to his own suite to get out of his sodden boots and riding breeches.

The early night of winter was falling by the time Céleste had changed into a flannel dressing gown and warm slippers and pulled up a chair before a blazing fire in her boudoir. The maid had lit several lamps; their soft alabaster glow touched the room with warm gold. She took up a book, propped her feet on a little footstool and sighed in contentment.

It was absurd to feel so content, she thought, after the bizarre farce of the past two days. The madness of her captivity, her wild escape and recapture. But she couldn't help herself. Rochemont seemed to have been designed for domestic comfort and ease. No doubt the late Madame de Beaufort had set her imprint on every detail of the house. She wondered how Edmond could still live here, surrounded by reminders that were surely painful.

"May I come in?"

She closed her book and turned in her chair. Edmond de Beaufort had entered the room and was now moving across the carpet toward her. "Would it avail me anything to refuse?" she asked. The chill in her voice matched the cold night beyond the windows.

He held out her riding skirt and cameo. "I came to return your belongings."

She made no move to take them from him; indeed, she had neither risen in welcome nor offered him a chair. "You could have sent them by way of a servant."

He shrugged and threw the skirt across a divan, then ambled to the fireplace and leaned against the mantel. Céleste noted that he was dressed in well-cut evening clothes. He turned the cameo in his hand, inspecting it from every angle. "A handsome piece. An heirloom, you said?"

"It was given me by someone very dear to my heart."

"Oh?" One dark eyebrow raised in curiosity.

She smiled. There was no harm in tossing him a useless crumb. "Yes," she said. "My late husband."

"Ah. There *was* a husband, then."

"Did you doubt that?"

He examined her with care, a slow smile playing around his lips. "*Madame*, I have doubted everything about you from the moment I first saw you. I've tried to be on my guard—and not without cause. This afternoon proved to me the folly of trusting you even for a second.''

She waved her arm around the room. Her prison. ''You seem to have the advantage at the moment, not I. This scarcely looks like Rome to me. Nor even Aix-les-Bains, since you seem to think that was my destination. Perhaps *I* was the one who wasn't sufficiently cautious.''

''Enough,'' he said in annoyance, slapping the cameo down on the mantel. It made a click that sounded like a door closing. ''This begins to feel like a chess match.'' He strode to the door of her boudoir, and then turned. ''We dine at seven in the country.''

''I intend to eat in my rooms.''

''And I should prefer that you change into a suitable gown and join me in the dining room.''

''Prefer what you wish,'' she said with a shrug. She opened her book and resumed her reading.

He swore under his breath, marched to her and snatched the book from her hands. ''Damn it, let us come to an accommodation, once and for all!''

She felt strangely threatened as he hovered above her, glaring down with those intense blue eyes. She rose from her chair with great dignity, trying to still her unease, and moved away from him, placing several pieces of furniture between them. ''An accommodation?''

''A truce, if you will. I have no quarrel with you beyond your relationship to Paul. But I intend to keep you here until his wedding, by whatever means. The manner of your captivity is up to you. For myself, I should prefer civility, not unending warfare.''

She snorted. ''Surely you don't expect my friendship.''

''I said a truce. Nothing more. If you choose to be stubborn and view this as a battle, I can keep you locked in this room, if need be. With guards at the doors and windows. A dreary prospect for six weeks, it seems to me. But if you agree to the truce, you'll have the freedom of the château.

I'll permit you to ride—not alone, of course. But otherwise, you'll be treated as a guest, not an enemy. What do you say?"

She wavered. He held the advantage, and they both knew it. And it *was* a tempting offer. Her wild behavior of this afternoon—recklessly pushing him into the canal, fighting him like a savage beast—was very far from her usual demeanor. It frightened her. She seemed to lose control whenever he challenged her, seemed to give in to strong emotions that she normally kept in check. She didn't like what was happening to her.

"Let me explain it again," he said when she still hesitated. "I assure you, you have no choice in the matter of your going or staying. Your only choice is between a *pleasant* stay and a decidedly *unpleasant* one. I regret to be so harsh, but—" he shrugged "—there it is."

She sighed. There was no point in fighting any longer. She couldn't win. And it wasn't as though she were still planning to disrupt Paul's wedding, so there was no reason to return to Paris. What did it matter? She would have her "vacation" in Burgundy instead of Rome. "A truce," she said, and held out her hand.

He took her proffered hand and shook it, his face breaking into a pleased smile. "Dinner at seven?"

"Yes." He didn't have to be quite so smug!

"Good." He still held her hand. His grasp was warm, pulsing with life. "I'll tell them to set a place for you." He bent and kissed her fingers, then strode to the door.

"Wait," she said. She looked at him, looked away, worked at a design on the patterned carpet with the toe of her slipper. Her face felt hot with embarrassment. "I...regret my behavior this afternoon," she said. "You might have taken a chill or...or drowned, or..." She lifted her chin and stared boldly at him to see if he was gloating at her humble apology.

Instead, his eyes were filled with warmth. "I enjoyed the ride home," he murmured, his voice low and thrilling. And then, as she blushed again, he added, "Wear the perfume that you had on this afternoon." He grinned unexpectedly, a glinting, wicked smile. "I might be tempted to take off my clothes again." He laughed, and left her to her confusion.

Truce or no truce, she thought, sinking weakly into a chair, she wasn't sure how she'd get through the next few weeks.

Chapter Ten

Someone was breathing.

Céleste lay motionless in her bed, her eyes closed, and strained to listen. Yes. There was the soft whisper of someone's breath, very close to her head. It was what had wakened her, crept in to disturb her dreams—the eerie sense that she was no longer alone in her bedchamber. It wasn't a servant, surely. The maid, Nicole, would have knocked, or waited for her to ring.

Beaufort? she thought with a sudden thrill of alarm. Had he come to overpower her while she slept? No, it wasn't likely. He wasn't the type to behave like a sneak. Not at all! She had the uneasy feeling that if he wanted her he'd be quite direct. As he had been that night in the conservatory.

Besides, there had been nothing in his manner at dinner last night to show that he either disliked or desired her enough to want to invade her rooms. She wondered why he had insisted on her company. They had dined in near silence—civil, correct, distant—taken coffee in the sitting room, then wished each other a polite good-night.

The breathing was growing louder. Or perhaps...could there be two people bending over the bed? Yes, that was it. And one of the creatures had made a funny little squeak. Bursting with curiosity, Céleste opened her eyes an imperceptible crack and strained to see through the veil of her thick lashes.

Two children hovered over her. A boy and a girl. It was difficult to see clearly, with her eyes almost closed, but she had the impression of bright red hair, wide blue eyes, solemn faces. They seemed to be about the same age. Céleste waited for a moment, wondering what they were planning. When they continued to do nothing but stare, she blinked open her eyes.

"You see?" cried the boy, breaking into a grin. "I *told* you she wasn't dead or enchanted!"

The little girl looked disappointed. She frowned down at a gnarled and weather-beaten branch in her hand. "We didn't even get to try the magic of the sacred unicorn's horn."

Céleste suppressed a chuckle. "I'm glad not to be dead," she said.

"And not enchanted, either," said the boy in a tone of finality. He looked at the girl. "I told you."

"Well," said Céleste, "if I *were* enchanted—" the girl brightened "—and I'm not saying it's so—" the boy smiled smugly "—I feel sure that the magic of the horn restored me."

"But we didn't even wave it and say the words."

"No matter. Its power was so great that it filled the room and touched me where I lay." She was delighted to see them both smile in satisfaction. Both were missing the same two front teeth. "Now—" she sat up in bed and reached for several pillows to place behind her back "—if you will present yourselves, I should like to know to whom I am beholden for my rescue."

The boy smoothed back his curly red hair and bowed solemnly. Céleste noticed a sprinkling of freckles across his upturned nose. "The Chevalier Albert de Beaufort," he announced.

Edmond's children? thought Céleste in surprise. Surely not. Hadn't Thérèse told her that Edmond's son had died with his wife years ago? Perhaps these were distant Beaufort relations—Edmond seemed autocratic enough to take responsibility for his entire family. And they certainly didn't look like his children, with their copper hair and open countenances.

The girl curtsied, holding out her skirts in a graceful gesture. She tried to look as serious as the boy, but she giggled as she gave her name. "Mademoiselle Albertine de Beaufort."

"Albert and Albertine. Twins?" asked Céleste, though it seemed an unnecessary question, given the matched faces before her. She received two vigorous nods for answer. "And how old are you?"

"Eight, last November," said Albert. "What's your name?"

"Madame Céleste Valvert."

"You're pretty," said Albertine.

Céleste reached out and fingered a long bright lock of hair that rested on the girl's shoulder. "So are you."

"Can you play trictrac?" demanded Albert.

Céleste grinned. "I'm a master of the game. And jackstraws."

Albertine clapped her hands. "Can you come to our schoolroom this afternoon and play? We should so like—"

"Allie! Bertine! What are you doing here? You know this isn't your part of the house!" A heavyset woman with gray hair stood in the doorway of Céleste's bedchamber. She wore the usual somber garb of a governess—a simple black dress trimmed with white embroidered linen, and a ruffled white muslin cap. Despite her scolding words, her eyes were kind behind thick spectacles, and her mouth seemed more inclined to smile than to frown.

"I've been up and down, in and out, this past hour, looking for you children," she said with a shake of her head. "Now, off with you. Your lessons are waiting. If we're to take a carriage ride before lunch, I want your sums finished this morning." She waited until the twins had scampered from the room, then approached Céleste's bed. "Forgive the children's intrusion, *madame*. I don't know what possessed them. Perhaps when they heard the chambermaids whis-

pering about a guest... We get so few, here at Rochemont."

"No, no. They're charming. Whose children are they?"

"Why, Monsieur Edmond's, of course."

"Oh!" she said, surprised anew. "I'd heard..." She
smiled in pleasure, though she didn't know why it should
matter to her that Edmond de Beaufort hadn't lost his entire family in that tragic accident. "How fortunate for him
to have them."

The older woman snorted. "Humph! Fortunate? As if he
cared! He doesn't see them. Gallivanting around the world
the way he does. And when he's home, he doesn't want them
near."

"Oh, but he must! They're sweet and beautiful.
They're—" She stopped, too upset to continue. What kind
of father could he be, not to see the treasure under his own
roof?

The other woman looked uncomfortable. "If you'll forgive me, *madame*. I spoke out of turn against Monsieur
Edmond. It was not my place." She sighed. "Ah, well...
Please excuse me, now. I want to be sure the children get to
their lessons."

"Of course. Mademoiselle—?"

"Mademoiselle Camille Daumard." She smiled. "I hope
you'll visit the children in their wing while you're here, *madame*. I'm sure they'd enjoy the company."

Edmond's children. She thought about them all morning, as she breakfasted and dressed, filled with dismay and
an odd disappointment. Edmond had been cold and distant to her, to be sure. But, given his defense of his family,
his imagined need to protect Paul, she could understand his
behavior, if not enjoy it. But what kind of man ignored his
own children?

She read in her boudoir for the rest of the morning, until
a maid came to tell her that *monsieur le comte* wished her to
join him for luncheon. She met him coming down the stair-

case. They exchanged cursory greetings and crossed the vestibule together toward the dining room.

Just then the door burst open and Albert and Albertine came barreling into the hallway, dancing around in little circles and laughing uproariously. They were followed by a breathless Mademoiselle Daumard. The children's cheeks were red from the cold, and their blue eyes sparkled with joy—a joy that was veiled when they saw their father. They stood still, made their little bows, and smiled shyly.

"Good afternoon, Papa," said Albert. "We've had a carriage ride."

"Good afternoon, Papa," said Albertine. "*Mademoiselle* thinks we may skate if the ice freezes on the pond."

Edmond matched their formality with his own. "Good afternoon," he said. He indicated Céleste. "Let me introduce my guest."

"We met this morning," said Céleste. "Good afternoon, children," she added, and was rewarded with two wide and toothless grins.

Edmond cleared his throat. "Mademoiselle Daumard tells me you're enjoying the books I brought."

The grins melted away. "Oh, yes, Papa. Thank you so much."

"You're doing well in your lessons? Albert, your penmanship has improved? And Albertine—geography is coming easier for you now?"

The children nodded, but they seemed as eager to leave their father's presence as he seemed to have them go. They looked relieved when he dismissed them with a wave of his hand. They went racing up the stairs, breaking into giggles as they reached the landing. Beaufort turned around and glared up at them. The smiles faded from their shiny faces. Chastened, they hurried up the rest of the steps and vanished through a door.

Céleste frowned. "Monsieur de Beaufort . . ." she began.

He turned back to transfix her with his penetrating gaze. "Do you have anything to say that is of concern to you, *madame?*" he demanded.

No, of course not, she thought. It wasn't her place to intrude. She followed him meekly into the dining room, but her thoughts weren't on the meal, or on his desultory conversation. She was thinking of his children.

He had used *vous* with his own children! *Vous,* not *tu.* The impersonal *you* of the salons, of casual friends and meaningless acquaintances, not the warm, loving *thou* of a father to his children. She wondered if Albert and Albertine were aware of the slight. But surely they were—even the humblest peasant father used *thou* to show his love and concern.

"I have work this afternoon," he said as they finished their coffee. "Estate matters."

"Of course. You and your steward must have business to discuss. After your trip to Paris."

"I have no steward. I manage Rochemont myself."

"But surely... such a burden..."

His expression made it clear that he wished to end the discussion. "I have a secretary in Paris who is most helpful when I need him," he said impatiently, as though the entire matter were beyond her understanding. "Now...I trust you won't mind being left alone this afternoon."

"I can amuse myself. I should very much like to explore Rochemont."

"On foot, you understand. No one will give you a horse. Not anymore." He seemed pleased with himself for having thought to prevent another escape.

"I meant the rooms," she snapped. "But if I go out-of-doors, it will only be to stroll in your gardens. I won't try to get away. I gave you my word, didn't I? Even the word of a woman—that poor, inferior, weak-willed creature—can be as steadfast as a man's, whatever you may think."

He raised a quizzical eyebrow. "Is that what I think? That women are less worthy than men?"

"Isn't it?" she asked dryly, and rose from the table.

She spent the next hour or so grudgingly admiring the glories of Beaufort's château. She had already enjoyed the warmth and intimacy of the *petit salon,* the sitting room, with its thick upholstery, rich velvet hangings, lush carpet. But there was also a billiard room, and a well-stocked library, paneled in dark woods and curtained with purple velvet draperies. There was a magnificent drawing room, and a vast ballroom done in gilded wood and silk brocade, and a charming, elegant music room in the style of Louis XV, with delicate tapestry on all the chairs. And all enclosed within a well-proportioned building of pale cream granite. Céleste felt again what she'd sensed in her own rooms: For all its splendors, Rochemont was a *home,* not a showplace. A place to live, love, raise children, grow old in sublime contentment.

They why did Edmond de Beaufort treat the very centerpiece, the heart of such a place—his children—with such indifference?

She remembered the twins' plea, and was suddenly eager to see them. She found her way to the separate wing of the château that housed the children and the chief servants, and knocked softly on the schoolroom door.

"Oh, Mademoiselle Daumard, look!" cried Albertine, opening for her. "It's our enchanted lady!" She grinned at Céleste. "Have you..." she began.

"Come to visit with us?" finished Albert.

"No," said Céleste with a wicked grin. "If Mademoiselle Daumard will permit, I've come to be your *foe.* Didn't you challenge me to trictrac?"

The children begged to be excused from their afternoon lessons, and Mademoiselle Daumard relented at last. Céleste found them delightful: clever, well-read, imaginative and filled with high spirits that were contagious. The hours of play flew by, until Mademoiselle Daumard called a halt and closed up the board, insisting that it was nearly suppertime and there was still reading to be done. She thanked Céleste for her visit and walked her to the door.

"I'm sure you want to dress for dinner, *madame*," she said. "But do come again to see us."

Céleste frowned. "The children sup with you?"

"Of course. Sometimes we go down to the kitchen to join the servants, but most of the time we sup in these rooms."

"Never with their father? Not even to come in for dessert?"

Mademoiselle Daumard looked uneasily toward the twins, then guided Céleste out into the corridor. "It's as Monsieur Edmond wishes," she said. She clearly disapproved.

"He had another son, didn't he?"

"The one who was killed. Yes."

"What was he like?"

"I don't know, *madame*. I wasn't hired until after the accident. He was ten at the time, I've heard. He would have been fifteen this year."

"Does Monsieur Edmond never talk of him? Never share his memories?"

"No, *madame*. Not a word. And who should he talk to, even if he wanted to? The twins were too young to remember their brother. And every servant at Rochemont was replaced after *madame la comtesse* and the boy died."

"It must have been a frightful blow to lose them both that way."

"I'm sure it was. Now, mind you," added the governess in a low voice, leaning close to Céleste, "I'm not one for idle gossip, but they say in the village that it was a terrible scene in the churchyard that day. Monsieur Edmond was a wild man, they say. Raging and crying. He leapt into his son's grave and forbade them to lower the coffin. The priest had to beg him to remember he was on holy ground." She shivered. "I should not have wanted to be there that day."

"Nor I," whispered Céleste, her heart aching for Beaufort. She had wept for days—wept uncharacteristic tears—

after her stillbirth. How much worse for Edmond, to lose a son he had loved for ten years? Perhaps that was why he was so distant with the twins. Why he kept himself apart. He had lost one beloved child; if he allowed himself to love the others, who knew what cruel fate might take *them* from him?

She went to dress for dinner, wishing she knew the man well enough to tell him she understood his suffering and pain.

She looked at him with more sympathy as they sat across from each other at dinner. His coldness toward his children was understandable, if unwarranted. It seemed a pity for a father and his children to be almost strangers because of a tragedy that had left them mutually bereft.

All during dinner she tried to maintain a friendly conversation, regretting the stiff silences and polite small talk that had filled their previous mealtimes. She complimented him on Rochemont and was pleased to see that his pride of family—so clear in his protection of Paul's future—extended to a modest and seemly pride of home, as well. She smiled when he passed a witty remark, praised the skill of his cook, promised to ride with him on the morrow when he asked. And when they moved into the sitting room for coffee and he reached for his usual Havana, she lit a taper at a candle, crossed to his chair and held out the light for him.

"Thank you," he said, looking up at her through a cloud of smoke. His eyes searched her face, in an odd examination that left her wondering what he saw there. "Don't go up after you've finished your coffee," he said as she regained her seat near the fireplace. "Do you play billiards?"

"In point of fact, I do."

"Would you care to chance a game or two?"

She nodded. "I must warn you, however, that I'm skilled at the game."

He appraised her with the same searching look. "I have no doubt you're skilled at many games."

She bristled. "Is that meant to be an insult?"

His expression was bland. "Not at all. I looked for you late this afternoon. My valet told me you'd spent hours playing trictrac with the children."

"Do you object?"

"Not if it helps to pass your time here."

As though his own children were mere diversions! "I enjoyed it very much," she said with some heat. "Your children are delightful. It's a pleasure to be in their company. They have a rare bond between them. When Bertine starts a sentence, so often Allie will finish it. It's charming."

He scowled. "Allie? Bertine? Don't you mean Albert and Albertine?"

She glared in exasperation. "You might call them by their nicknames once in a while," she said. "If it wouldn't hurt your pride."

For a moment, she thought he'd take it as a challenge. Then he softened, and even managed a sheepish smile. "I didn't even know that was what they were called."

Seeing his unexpected humility, she pressed her advantage. "Well, I don't wonder," she scolded. "Keeping them hidden away in their rooms like that!" She gestured around the comfortable sitting room, with its soft chairs and its large round table in the center. "I don't know why they're forbidden this room. It's so much larger and more pleasant than their schoolroom. And it isn't as though they were ill-behaved. Merciful heaven, they're more like prisoners than I am, confined to their wing as they are."

He had the decency to blush at her sharp words, in a warm tide that darkened his naturally swarthy complexion. "Don't be absurd," he muttered. "They're not 'confined.' It's only that—" He cleared his throat—a rumble of embarrassment. "I like my solitude. But you must think me a monster, if you think I forbid my children their own home."

"Of course not," she said soothingly. She suppressed a smile of triumph. Tomorrow afternoon she would invite the children into the sitting room for trictrac. Let him forbid *that,* if he dared. "Now," she said, standing up and smoothing her skirts, "I'm ready for billiards."

They played for several hours by the bright light of an Argand lamp that hung over the elaborately carved table. As skilled as Céleste was, she was no match for Beaufort. He won every game handily, his strokes sure and deft. He seemed to relax as the evening wore on; she found herself responding to his friendly encouragement with warm smiles of her own.

At last she sighed and laid her cue across the table. "Enough. You're far too skillful for me."

"You're very good yourself," he said. "Are you sure you didn't lose deliberately?"

"Why should I do that?"

"One of your many skills, perhaps. To flatter my masculine pride."

He was beginning to vex her again. "What nonsense. I played to win."

"Still…your behavior tonight… You seem to have been trained to please a man."

"Have I been a specimen under a microscope tonight?" she asked bitterly, feeling an odd disappointment that their pleasant evening should end this way. "I was only trained to be civil," she went on. "Who taught *you* to be so suspicious of people?"

"Not 'people,'" he said sardonically.

"Ah, yes, of course. Only women. How gratifying it must be for your daughter. To know with what little esteem you view the members of her sex."

He gripped his cue so tightly that his knuckles turned white. "You will please refrain from interfering in my affairs," he said.

"Interfering?" Her lip curled with contempt. "The way you've interfered in Paul's affairs?"

"I'm only trying to save him from women's treachery," he growled.

It was all she could do to keep from hurling a billiard ball at him. "Yet you magnanimously allow him to marry Élise de Malecot."

"There is a world of difference between *her* kind and yours."

She gasped in outrage. Would he forever look at her and see Whore written across her forehead? "And which kind was your wife?" she asked maliciously.

"Damnation!" he roared, and smashed his billiard cue against the table. It splintered into little pieces. With a growl of disgust, he threw away the end he still held. He glared at Céleste, his chest heaving in anger, and then turned his back on her.

But not before she caught the look in his eye, the pain behind his fury. Merciful heaven, what had she done? What foolish cruelty had prompted her words? Surely, if he mourned his son so deeply, his grief for his wife must be boundless. "Monsieur...Edmond..." she murmured. "I'm sorry. That was cruel of me. I beg you to forgive my hasty words."

"Get out of here," he said in a strangled voice. "What do you have to be sorry about?" He turned back to her. His handsome face was a study in pure misery. He reached out and gripped her by the shoulders. "For being young and beautiful and seductive? And having nothing more in your head than the desire to collect as many trophies as you can?" His wild eyes burned into hers. For a moment she thought he would kiss her. Then he pushed her from him and turned away.

"Get out," he said hoarsely. "For God's sake, get out."

Chapter Eleven

He stayed in his rooms for most of the next day. There was no invitation to lunch with him, no offer to ride. When it became clear to Céleste that she had been abandoned, she took a bold tack. Just because he chose to sulk, that didn't mean she had to sit in her rooms all day like a penitent. She sent a note to Mademoiselle Daumard requesting that the children be sent to her for play when their afternoon lessons were done. Since Monsieur Edmond had given her the freedom of the château, she said, she thought it would be pleasant for them to meet in the *petit salon*.

The children were delighted to be in the sitting room. While Albert set out the trictrac board on the round center table, Albertine wandered about the room, examining the various decorations, admiring a figurine, touching a plush pillow, a polished table, with awe and wonder. It was clear that to enter this forbidden sanctuary had long been their desire, a chance to explore their father's world. They took turns sitting in Edmond's armchair, perched like royalty in a splendor of red velvet, laughing in delight.

They had been playing trictrac for nearly an hour—each child taking a turn against Céleste—when they heard Edmond de Beaufort's voice outside the door. The twins looked startled and guilty. Céleste smiled reassuringly at them—Albertine at the table, bent over the board, Albert comfortably cushioned in his father's chair. "Have no fear," she whispered.

Beaufort came through the curtains at the doorway, frowning. "What the devil—" he began.

"Ah! Monsieur de Beaufort," Céleste said quickly, to forestall an explosion, "the children and I are enjoying these pleasant surroundings together, as you hoped we would. Won't you join us?"

Beaufort looked toward his chair. Albert blushed to the roots of his red hair. "Excuse me, P-Papa," he stammered, starting to rise. "I didn't mean to..."

Edmond glanced at Céleste and smiled gently. She didn't know if the smile was an acknowledgment of their conversation about the children, or an apology for his behavior of the night before. She only knew that it warmed her heart, filled as it was with goodwill and understanding. "No, Albert," he said, "stay where you are. I'll watch your sister play awhile with Madame Valvert." He perched on the edge of the table and watched with some interest as Albertine and Céleste cast their dice and moved their stones around the board; he nodded his approval and murmured an occasional "Good move!" when Albertine took her turn, making the girl beam with pleasure.

"You'll gammon me this time for sure, Bertine," said Céleste, groaning in mock dismay when Albertine rolled a double.

"She will if she takes your blot there," said Edmond, pointing toward the board.

Albertine looked up at him, her blue eyes wide with surprise and joy. "Oh, Papa, thank you! I never saw that move."

"I protest!" cried Céleste. "Will you conspire against me? The two of you?"

"No, of course not. It isn't fair," he answered solemnly. "However..." He shook his head when Albertine put her finger on a stone, then nodded in agreement when she chose another to make her move, a hit that put Céleste's stone on the bar. When Céleste complained loudly about their plotting, Beaufort stared in wide-eyed innocence. "I never said a word."

By the time the game was over and Céleste had been soundly drubbed, Albert had left his chair to join the laughing group at the table. They were about to begin a new game—Albert begging his father's help against Céleste—when the warm domestic scene was interrupted. Mademoiselle Daumard appeared and announced that she'd come to fetch the children for supper. Albert started to protest, but then he looked at his father and held his tongue.

As for Edmond, he suddenly seemed uncomfortable with his informal manner, as though he'd just recalled his position as head of the household. He inclined his head solemnly to the children and shook their hands. "It has been an agreeable visit," he said. "I'm pleased to see that your mathematical skills are being sharpened even while you play." He turned to Céleste and allowed his face to relax into a smile. "Dinner at seven, Madame Valvert?"

She returned his warmth. "Of course."

Dinner was a lively affair. He had spent most of the day reading his translation of *Hamlet,* and was eager to discuss it with her. Since Céleste had read the play, in English, they debated the relative merits of each scene with some heat. Beaufort was keen and intelligent; Céleste didn't know when she'd had a more stimulating conversation. "All in all, a fine play," he said in conclusion as they rose from the table. "I think it would make a superb opera."

She nodded in agreement. "Ophelia's mad scene. It should have an aria like Amina's in *La Sonnambula.* All soft and clear and sweet, like the sighing of a zephyr."

"Ah, yes. Amina," he said, smiling in remembered pleasure. "I heard la Malibran sing that role. In '31." He turned to the footman in attendance. "We'll take coffee in the music room. I should like to hear you sing tonight, *madame,* if you wouldn't mind."

She smiled wickedly. "Are you sure? You didn't like my choice of song the last time." She wasn't sure he'd enjoy the reminder of that night at Madame de Cloquet's musicale, but she thought she'd chance it.

His mouth twisted in a droll smile. "Since that time, I've put on my suit of armor. I shall be as dispassionate as a music critic."

"I trust you won't be quite so critical. I don't practice the way I should anymore."

"I'll chance it. Come." He offered her his arm and led her into the music room. The piano was old and exquisite, painted in soft hues, with a scene on the opened top of shepherds and shepherdesses in a pastoral setting. Although cabinetmakers were beginning to make copies of pre-Revolutionary furniture for an increasingly affluent society, the piano was clearly an original. "I found it in Saint Petersburg," he said, when she voiced her admiration. "It was in a state of disrepair, but I had the workings replaced with a modern pianoforte action." He tossed back the tails of his evening coat and sat down at the bench. "Now, what will you sing?"

She was still in a teasing mood. "There's a ballad I've been hearing of late. 'Prends garde à ton coeur.' 'Guard your heart.'"

He refused to yield the advantage. "Though I've taken the words as my anthem," he said with a sly smile that acknowledged her gibe, "I fear my fingers can't play the notes. You'll have to be content with my choice. Do you know this song?" He began to play an aria from a Mozart opera, a slow, lilting song that showed off his considerable skill at the pianoforte.

Would the man never cease to surprise her? Céleste was so entranced by his wonderful playing that she refrained from singing; she merely listened and watched. His hands were strong and supple, the long fingers managing the difficult passages with an ease that was marvelous to see.

He dropped his hands to his lap. "You don't know it? I thought surely you would," he teased. "It's a very seductive aria, in which she invites her lover to put his hand on her heart." He looked her straight in the eye, allowed his glance to drop to her bosom, then returned to her face. It was a challenging look, but as good-humored as her teasing had been. He, too, seemed prepared to forget the past and simply enjoy their lighthearted banter.

She waved away the challenge with an imperious flick of her hand. "Will you have the aria in Italian or German, *monsieur le comte?*" she asked smugly.

He stifled a laugh. "A neat riposte, *madame*. In German, I think. Italian is too seductive. A man could lose his heart." Shifting to a more serious mood, he began the introduction to the aria once more, nodding at her to sing at the appropriate moment.

She nodded in answer, her mouth twitching in a smile; then she deliberately sang the song in Italian. When she was finished, he complimented her voice and chided her wickedness, insisting that she was surely the most perverse woman he had ever known. At his urging, she sang a half-dozen more songs. One was a duet for which he accompanied her in a rich, if not particularly distinguished, baritone.

"Do you know Rossini's 'For Him Whom I Love'?" she asked at length. "From *The Italian Girl in Algeria?*"

His blue eyes twinkled. "Is your repertoire nothing but captivating love songs?"

She shrugged. "We adventuresses know how to use our charms."

"Adventuress?" He seemed surprised by her choice of word.

"You did call me that. Have you forgotten? The first time we met. Do you still think I am?"

He eyed her thoughtfully. "In all fairness, I don't know. But you're charming and quite beautiful. And I can see how other women might envy you enough to spread rumors."

It was, she supposed, the closest he would ever come to an apology. "Thank you," she said. "Now, do you know the Rossini?"

"Not well enough. How does it begin?"

"Here," she said, indicating the piano bench. "Make room for me." When he slid over to one side, she tucked in her skirts and sat next to him.

"You play, as well as sing?" he asked.

"Not very well, I'm afraid. But I was expected to learn."

He laughed. "My father used to say that a woman takes up the piano to show off graceful arms and a trim waist, and nothing more."

She rolled her eyes. "What a cynical thing to say. And if some poor creature has neither attribute, what is she to do? Banish music from her life?"

"Not at all. My father felt that if the lady wasn't as slender as she might be, she should take up the harp. That instrument, at least, would call attention to a swelling bosom. And hide the rest."

She giggled. "Merciful heaven, was your father as wicked as he sounds?"

"He was a wonderful man. I never had a moment of regret in my childhood." He sighed; it was a gentle sound, filled with fond remembrance. It made him seem quite young and vulnerable. "The Rossini?" he prompted at last.

"Yes, of course." She began to play, haltingly at first, as she tried to recall the notes, then with more confidence.

He listened for a few minutes, then tentatively repeated the chords that she'd played, embellishing them with trills and little runs.

She stared at him, astonished and delighted at his skill. "How much more easily you reach the chords than I," she said in wonder. "I can scarcely make the octave."

"Don't disparage yourself," he said kindly. "My hand is larger, that's all. Look." He held up his hand, inviting her to put her palm against his.

She touched his hand, flesh to flesh. His fingers were warm, and when he moved his hand slightly to align their palms, she could feel the whorls and ridges of his skin under her fingertips. Her own skin tingled at the sensual touch of his hand. A wild thrill raced through her. She looked into his eyes, blue pools of mystery and danger. They had joked tonight about her seductive singing in Madame de Cloquet's salon. Now she remembered how the evening had ended, the burning kisses that had devastated her. Was he remembering, too? Was that what she read in those eyes?

Or was it only her own desire that spoke to her? She trembled, and was saved by the clock chiming on the mantel.

"Good heavens!" she cried. "Is it that late? If you intend to ride tomorrow, *monsieur le comte,* I should be pleased to have an invitation to join you. In the meantime, I'd best get my rest. Good night." She rose from the piano bench and fled his disturbing presence.

Chapter Twelve

The weather turned mild. February had begun, and it seemed as though spring could scarcely wait to appear. The sun seemed to shine more brightly; the earth smelled raw and new. Céleste's days at Rochemont settled into a comfortable routine. She would ride with Edmond in the mornings, watching with a mixed sense of admiration and pride as he toured his estates, dealt with his tenants, consulted with his vintners on the maturing wine from the previous grape harvest. Though *why* she should feel pride was more than she could understand. Except for this brief, enforced coexistence, what did his life have to do with hers?

They would lunch together, then go their separate ways—he to his rooms, for work or reading, she to her afternoon's play with the twins. After that first day, she had taken to meeting them in the *petit salon,* and the cozy room rang with their laughter as they played children's games, or read together, or drew pictures.

Once in a while, Edmond joined them to watch their play. He was still distant and formal with his children, but it seemed to Céleste as though he were making an effort to reach out to them. She wondered how he could fail to see that every crumb of goodwill he offered, no matter how small, was welcomed by the twins as though they were receiving a treasured prize.

In the evenings, Céleste and Edmond would dine together, discussing a book they had both read, or sharing their opinions of an opera, a composer, a ballet. Afterward, they would play billiards or make music. More and more she found herself looking forward to their hours together, aware for the first time how lonely she had been since leaving Rome. How much she had missed the company of someone who loved music as much as she. In the La-Granges' château in Normandy—that gloomy old manor—she had always felt that her music was an unwelcome intrusion, like a bright beam of sunlight in a sickroom. Disturbing the living and unsettling the ghosts.

There came a rainy afternoon when the twins grew restless and bored. They had had their fill of trictrac, of cards and dominoes. Charades had ended in a quarrel over one of Albert's pantomimes, and drawing was too sedentary for children who were used to an outdoor romp almost every day. Grumbling their discontent, they were ready to retire to their schoolroom.

"Wait a moment," said Céleste. "I just recalled an old game. Run to the housekeeper and ask her if she can spare any buttons. Round and flat. Three of them at least this big—" she made a measurement in the air with her fingers "—and perhaps a dozen or so smaller. All of the same size, if possible."

"But why?" asked Albertine.

"What kind of a game can you play with buttons?" complained Albert.

"It's a game I used to play with my landlord's children in Germany. *Knopfspiele.* Now, no more questions. Just see if Madame Léopold has what we need."

When the children returned, carrying a sack filled with buttons, Céleste explained how they would use the edge of the large button to pop the smaller ones into the shallow bowl she'd set on the floor. In no time at all, they were on their hands and knees, scrambling in every direction on the floor in their pursuit of errant buttons. Céleste's pale silk skirt was covered with dark lint from the carpet, and one of her braids had come unpinned and hung loose over her breast. But the children were laughing and declaring that they had never had a better time. She was content.

"Are you all mad?" Céleste looked up from the floor. Edmond stood in the doorway, scowling. "By all the devils, Madame Valvert, what is this? My *petit salon* may be a comfortable place for games, but it is scarcely a gymnasium!"

"Oh, but, Papa! We're having such a jolly time!" cried Albert.

"Come and play! It's such fun," said Albertine.

"You want me to *play* with you? A child's game?" There was tolerance in his voice, though he was still frowning.

Céleste smiled beguilingly at him. He was particularly handsome today, in a well-fitted blue frock coat and snug gray trousers that accented the breadth of his shoulders, the fineness of his limbs. She wasn't sure, dressed as he was, that he'd want to risk the knees of his trousers, but she was willing to chance it. "Do join us. It's an amusing game. And one that—I think you'll be surprised—will challenge your skills. My landlord in Germany had a half-dozen children. We used to play on many a rainy afternoon."

For a moment, she had thought he was weakening, but then his expression turned cool. "In Germany? With Monsieur Desrosiers?"

She was surprised that he'd heard the name. Although, given his thoroughness, she should have guessed that he'd try to delve into her past. There was no danger to the LaGranges or their plot, she realized; however much Beaufort might learn of her years of travel, there was no way he could connect her to Alex. "Yes," she replied. "It was in Nauheim, where he took the waters almost every year. Come," she added, her eyes warm and entreating, "won't you join us? Allie and Bertine can't be allowed to think that only children are good at games."

The cool expression had become a frozen mask. He looked with disapproval at her rumpled gown, her disheveled hair. "I think the game is a bit too undignified for my taste, *madame*. I trust you yourself will join me at dinner tonight looking less like a hoyden than you do at this moment." Without waiting for a reply, he turned on his heel and stalked from the room.

The children looked at Céleste in dismay. Even in the short time that Céleste had been at Rochemont, the twins had come to expect more warmth from their father. She smiled to hearten them. "I feel sure your papa is as downcast with this rain as we are. So close and uncomfortable. Even a saint could be allowed a little testiness. Your father isn't angry at *you*."

Their eyes shone with hope. "Do you think not?"

"Of course not. And to prove it for yourselves, why don't you come downstairs tonight before you go to bed? See if *Mademoiselle* will permit it. I'm sure your papa will wish you a fond good-night." And he would, even if she had to shame him into it! she thought with determination.

Sitting across the dinner table from him later, however, she wasn't as confident. Something had angered him. Something had created a wall between them so that he looked at her with the same contempt she'd seen on his face that first night at the opera.

She put down her soupspoon. She wasn't about to spend the whole meal in this cold silence. "Would you prefer to dine alone tonight?"

"Why should I?" He shrugged, a careless gesture that made it clear he didn't care if she stayed or went.

She tried another approach. "Did you do any reading this afternoon?"

"Some of Alfred de Musset's poems. I didn't enjoy them."

"Oh, but the ones he wrote last year..."

"Damn it!" He interrupted with such venom that Céleste flinched. "Tell me about Desrosiers!"

"Grandpapa?" she said in astonishment. "Is that what this is about? My grandfather?"

He sat back in his chair as violently as though he'd been shot. "Your *grandfather?*" he asked with a snort.

She eyed him curiously. What had prompted this sudden, strange behavior? "How did you know about him?" she asked.

"The baron de Lansac."

"Of course. Maurice. A dear old man, but growing senile, I'm afraid."

"Not too senile that he couldn't remember Achille Desrosiers and his inamorata."

She chuckled. "Which one? He had many in his wild youth."

Edmond's eyes were as frosty as a winter day, as the blue ice on a frozen pond. "The one in his old age. The one in Rome."

She gasped in stunned surprise and horror. "Lansac... I... He said *that?*"

A sardonic laugh. "It seems to have been the rumor. The widely held belief."

"Oh, my God, my God," she moaned, fighting to hold back tears. "People thought that of us? Grandpapa and I? I never knew. I never guessed.... Oh, how ugly! What a young fool I must have been."

"He *was* your grandfather?"

"But of course!"

He shook his head. His expression was dark with doubt. "You're very skilled at stories. But Desrosiers never married."

She looked at him with accusation in her amber eyes. "You believe it, too. You think I was his..." She covered her mouth with her hand, as though to hold back the hateful word. She was finding it painful to recall the past, and suddenly wondered how many people, in how many cities, had thought as Lansac had. She waved away the servant who had hurried forward with the next course, and started to rise from the table. It was too difficult to control her churning emotions with Beaufort staring at her so intently. "If you don't mind. I'm not very hungry."

"No, stay," he said quickly. "Please." It was a sincere plea, and when she looked at him, she saw warmth in his eyes. Perhaps even remorse. It gave her heart. "Tell me about him," he went on. "I've heard of his career in Paris, of course. They say he was a fine diplomat."

She nodded, her thoughts suddenly flooding with sweet memories of Grandpapa. "He was a man of steadfast loyalty and conviction," she said. "No one who met him failed to love him. He had a dear friend, an aristocrat, who was arrested during the Reign of Terror. Grandpapa could do nothing to get him released. Every day he lived in dread that his friend would go to the guillotine. He loved the man's wife with as much tenderness. When it was feared that she might follow her husband to prison, Grandpapa took her to his heart—and to his bed—hoping that the revolutionists would not be so bloodthirsty as to arrest a woman carrying a child. But it was not to be. Evil times beget evil deeds. She was allowed to give birth to the baby—my father—before her arrest. Then she and her husband were beheaded on the same day."

He swore softly. "My family escaped the worst of the Terror, thanks be to God. The peasants in the parish protected us. And when Napoleon came to power, my father and uncle were among the first of the old aristocrats to be welcomed into the new court." He shook his head. "But sometimes I hear cruel stories like yours, and wonder how France survived at all. What happened to your father after that?"

"Grandpapa sent him to Champagne to be safe. A foster home. He took the name Valvert from the family there. He was raised in ignorance of his circumstances; he knew only that he had a patron who paid for his keep. In time, he met a young woman and married..." She smiled sheepishly.

"You see, I *am* legitimate. When I was a year old, the Allies invaded France."

"Through Champagne."

"Yes. My parents, it would seem, died of one of the plagues the Russian army brought into that unfortunate province." She sighed. "And Grandpapa, conscience-stricken after the years of neglect of his natural son, took me under his care."

"You traveled, I've heard."

"Almost constantly. He was a man who wanted to taste all of life. To see, to feel, to learn."

His eyes were soft with concern. "But it must have been so lonely for you, as a child."

"I didn't think so. There was a nursemaid when I was very young. After that, I took care of Grandpapa. We didn't need anyone else."

"But no friends?"

She smiled. "I played with the children wherever we were."

"The games you play with Albert and Albertine."

"Yes. And Grandpapa had many friends throughout Europe. Older men, of course, but . . ."

He almost looked ashamed of his past thoughts. "And so you learned to be charming to men."

"It wasn't very difficult. Grandpapa treated me like a princess. It's very easy to learn to be gracious when others are gracious to you. He was my teacher and my friend. What more did I need? You said once, I think, that your childhood was happy. Well, so was mine. I didn't feel deprived, or envious of the children I saw around me. On the contrary, I felt blessed. We traveled to all the great cities. Grandpapa was treated with great respect wherever we went. We were sometimes the guests of princes and emperors, of great writers and musicians." Her eyes shone. "It was wonderful to be a little girl in those circumstances."

"Did you come to Paris?"

"Once or twice, a long time ago."

"Do you like it?"

"The city? Yes. It's very beautiful. I like it better than Saint Petersburg or Florence."

He nodded. "I agree."

"You've traveled, too, Mademoiselle Daumard tells me. We might have met."

"I would have remembered you," he said softly.

She trembled at the look in his eyes—more open, more tender than it had ever been. But if he had believed the stories of that fool Lansac, he must have thought her wicked indeed. It seemed a good time to correct the rest of his misconceptions. "I don't like the *people* of Paris very much, however," she said. "It's a society of overweening ambition and greed...without standards of conduct, conscience, or pity. It seems to be dominated by concerns about money, petty jealousies, and little else. Except, of course, the spreading of gossip," she added bitterly. "I, for example, have been linked with a deputy of the Chamber, a baron and a journalist." It was better to tell it all, she thought, since she didn't know what he'd heard.

He laughed ruefully, and scratched his chin. "And a retired general from the Auvergne."

"Merciful heaven!" If Thérèse had been near, she wasn't sure she wouldn't have boxed the girl's ears! "It's a wonder I ever sleep, with all the lovers I'm presumed to have had."

"But your grandfather—?"

"When his rich friends began to die off—the ones whose hospitality we had relied on for years—we moved to Rome. He was happy to settle down after all the wandering. He taught singing to earn a little money."

"I think you were his finest pupil."

She blushed at that, caught by surprise. "He'd be pleased to hear you say that," she murmured. "He was always scolding me for not practicing enough." She sighed at the memories. "So you see, I had a perfect life."

"Did you?" He frowned. "What about...young men? Suitors? Surely you know you're exquisitely beautiful. I can't imagine the men in Rome were blind. Did you never think of marriage? A home? Men of your own age?''

She shrugged. "They bored me. Besides..." She hesitated. Without knowing it, he had touched the raw pain, the wound that still throbbed from her loss. "I thought..." She looked across the table at him, her eyes brimming with tears, "I thought somehow he'd live forever," she whispered. "I never saw my life without him. Next to Grandpapa, other men seemed... of no consequence." She gulped and covered her eyes with her hand.

In a second he had left his seat and was kneeling beside her. She felt the warmth of his hand on her shoulder. "Here," he said.

She opened her eyes. He was holding a glass of water to her lips. She took a sip or two and nodded her thanks. "I'm quite myself again," she said. She even managed a small smile.

He shook his head. "My God, I never cease to be astounded at your poise and self-control. Any other woman would be sobbing like a child at this point in the story."

"I'm not sure I know how. Grandpapa expected a miniature adult from the moment I learned to walk and talk."

"And what happened when he died?" He shook his head in consternation. "No. Forgive me. That was too painful a question to ask."

She took a deep breath. "I'm quite recovered now. I can speak of it. When he died, I was very lonely. Devastated by the loss."

"And there was a husband, I believe you once said?"

Something in the way he said that, leaning slightly forward, eyes burning with intensity, alerted her. She had said too much already. Revealed too much. Perhaps it was just sympathetic interest on his part. But it could also be the curiosity of a man who had gone to extraordinary lengths to protect his cousin's future. She must remember her pledge to the LaGranges; she mustn't say anything that Beaufort could trace to Alex or his parents. "Yes," she answered guardedly. "I had a husband. He's dead now."

As if he'd seen the door close, he stood up and resumed his seat, motioning for a hovering servant to bring the next course. "Did you love him?" he asked, in exactly the tone of voice that he might have used to inquire about the weather.

She remembered her desolation after her grandfather's death, and the sunshine that Alex had brought to those black days. "I'll always love him for what he did for me," she said softly.

"I don't suppose you'll tell me his name?"

She smiled and picked up her knife and fork. They had returned to their chess game. "Lord! I've suddenly recovered my appetite." She smiled again. A superior smile, to let him know that his tender sympathy, whether real or shammed, wouldn't drag her secrets from her. "I don't suppose I shall."

Chapter Thirteen

They took coffee in the music room. It seemed to Céleste as though a subtle change had come over Edmond since dinner. As though all his certainties about the wickedness of her character had been thrown into confusion. He sat at the piano, idly playing a Chopin étude, as if his thoughts were far from the keyboard.

While he played, Céleste leaned against the marble mantel of the fireplace and stared at her face in the mirror above. Her features were the same. The almond-shaped amber eyes were as veiled and mysterious as ever, and the full-lipped mouth was as enticing. She hadn't suddenly been transformed, her face becoming as bland and innocent as a milkmaid's. Yet something was different. The air was newly charged with an electricity, an undercurrent of warmth between her and Edmond, that was totally unlike the skeptical, not-quite-trusting cordiality that had marked their encounters before.

It was as though the rumors, the stories he had heard in the past, had put a stain on her, the vile mark of Jezebel and Messalina. And now it was gone.

To be replaced by... what? Surreptitiously she watched his reflection in the glass. What was he thinking as his hands glided over the keys? She knew what was in *her* thoughts, God help her. The memory of his kisses. The warmth of his arms. She ached with a yearning to turn back time. To go to

Paris again with no tainted suspicions about her past, no false tales and gossip to reach his ears. To meet him, unburdened by duty and family and ugly schemes—both of them as pure and fresh as two innocent lovers in the Garden of Eden. How sweet, how magical, it might have been.

He looked up and caught her eye in the mirror. "Céleste..." he said softly. Was it an invitation? Was he, too, remembering the thrill of their embraces? She trembled with longing and hope.

"Pardon, Monsieur Edmond." Mademoiselle Daumard stood in the doorway, the twins in tow. They were dressed in nightclothes. "The children would like to say good-night. I know it's not your usual custom, but I was sure you wouldn't mind. Just this one time."

Céleste suppressed a smile. She should have guessed that the governess would be her ally. She beckoned to the twins before Edmond could say a word. "Come in," she said.

The children advanced shyly. "This is a pretty place," said Albertine, looking about the elegant music room, her clear blue eyes wide with curiosity.

"I like when you play that song on the piano, Papa," said Albert. "It sounds like waterfalls."

Edmond finished the étude in silence, then looked at his son. "But when have you heard me play?"

"Sometimes the children sit outside the door in the afternoons when you play, *monsieur.* Just to listen," said Mademoiselle Daumard. Céleste wondered whether Edmond had heard the reproach in her voice.

He had heard. He cleared his throat and stood up, his color darkening. "Yes. Well...you must come inside the next time I'm playing. No point in..." He cleared his throat again and fiddled with the ruffled cuffs of his evening shirt. "You came to say good-night, I think?"

Céleste had a sudden vexing recollection of his formal greetings and adieux, and the impersonal handshake that accompanied his use of the distant *you,* not *thou.* Perhaps this time . . . She moved quickly. She knèlt and held out her arms. "I, for one, want a good-night kiss."

The twins beamed and ran to throw their arms around her neck, their eyes shining for joy. They kissed her exuberantly, all the while babbling about a jaunt Mademoiselle Daumard had planned for the morrow.

"If the rain stops . . ." began Albertine.

"We'll take a pony cart," finished Albert.

"That will be delightful, I'm sure," said Céleste, laughing and hugging them. She disengaged their clinging arms and stood up. "Now say good-night to your Papa."

The twins hesitated. Albert started to put his hand out for a handshake, and Albertine shuffled her slippers on the carpet.

Edmond frowned. It was an awkward moment. Céleste was beginning to regret her interference. What right had she to intrude upon the relationship between a father and his children, no matter how distant it was?

Then Edmond glanced at Céleste—a look that was part embarrassment and part reproach, as though she'd shamed him into something that he wasn't sure he wanted. He bent down toward the children and thrust out his face in invitation. "Well?"

They came to him slowly. First Albert, then Albertine. They leaned forward, kissed him formally on each cheek. Albert drew away at once, blushing, but Albertine allowed herself to stroke her father's chin for a moment before she turned away.

In the silence that followed, the steady patter of rain outside was deafening. "Papa, would you . . . play one more piece before we go?" Albert ventured at last.

"Of course." Edmond's voice had a peculiar, rasping quality to it, as though he were choking on some deep emotion. "Do you . . ." He seemed to recover himself. "Do you have a favorite?"

"Something fast," begged Albert.

Edmond chose a spirited mazurka. While he played, Albert stood transfixed beside the piano and watched his father's flying hands. His sweet face, topped with its crown of bright red hair, shone with wonder in the light of the candles set on either side of the keyboard. Albertine, forever curious, wandered around the room as her father played, touching everything, as though the mere contact would bring her closer to the distant stranger who grudgingly shared his house with them.

When the mazurka was finished, Albert clapped his hands with as much enthusiasm as if he were part of a paid claque at the opera. Albertine was more restrained, but she seemed to have been distracted by something she had found. She pointed to an inlaid rosewood box on a corner table. "What's this, Papa?" she asked.

Edmond peered in her direction. "A music box. Wait. There was a key..." He stood up and crossed to a painted commode, rummaging in a drawer until he produced a large brass key. "Yes. Here. Wind it up."

Albertine did as she was told. The room was immediately filled with the metallic tinkle of notes plucked from a cylinder.

It was an old folk song. Albertine began to sing softly. "'Ah, vous dirai-je, maman'..." She stopped and smiled sheepishly. "I don't know the rest of the words. Do you, Madame Valvert?"

Edmond chuckled. "A song about love? I'm sure Madame Valvert does. She knows *all* the love songs." He said it good-naturedly, with a twinkle in Céleste's direction.

She shook her head, returning his laughter with an innocent smile. "There's another version, which I've heard children sing. It has nothing to do with love and broken hearts. I think the twins would like it better." She rewound the music box and began to sing in her clear, sweet voice:

Mama, shall I tell you now
What has brought me grief, I vow?

Papa wishes me to reason
Like a grown-up, every season.
Me, I think that one sweetmeat
Betters thought. Oh, what a treat!

For a moment, the children looked uncomfortable at this indirect gibe at their father. Then Edmond threw back his head and roared with laughter, and their little faces relaxed into smiles.

"You must ask Madame Valvert to teach you the words one day," said Edmond, when he finally stopped laughing. He reached out to the music box and pressed a little button. "There are more songs, I think." After a moment, another melody began to play, a sprightly tune that made the children clap their hands in time.

"I remember that," said Céleste. "It's a Bohemian song. I don't know if it has words, but I remember the peasants used to dance to it in Warsaw. A gay step—like a waltz, but with a little hop to it."

"If it's the same dance, it was all the rage among the nobility in Vienna last year," said Edmond. "You couldn't go to a ball without expecting to dance it. They call it a 'polka,' I think."

"Can you dance it, Papa?" asked Albertine.

"Not without a partner." He raised a questioning eyebrow at Céleste. "Madame Valvert?"

She nodded. "As luck would have it, my Polish landlady had an extremely plain-faced son. He thought that if he learned to dance well, he might attract a young woman of his class at a country fair." She smiled apologetically. "I can only dance it the way the peasants did then. If it changed when it reached Vienna and the aristocrats, you'll have to guide me."

"Fair enough." As Mademoiselle Daumard wound up the box again, Edmond pulled Céleste to him, wrapped one strong arm around her waist and clasped her fingers with his other hand. His grasp was firm and his steps were sure as he swirled her around the polished floor of the music room. They danced until they were breathless, spinning giddily, hopping on the beat with a liveliness and enthusiasm that made them both laugh aloud. Though Céleste hadn't danced the polka for almost five years, it was so easy to follow Edmond that she found herself doing variations that she wouldn't have believed herself capable of. She was floating on a cloud of happiness, lost in the joy of the dance and the thrill of being in his embrace.

The music box wound down, and still they danced, slowing their pace as the music slowed, but unwilling to stop, to be parted from one another's arms. Edmond's eyes searched her face, focused on her lips, then returned to stare deeply into her eyes. "We were meant to dance together," he murmured in a throaty voice. He stopped dancing entirely and put his other arm around her, pulling her close to his breast. Time—as well as the music—had stopped. The air vibrated with unspoken longings.

"Monsieur," Mademoiselle Daumard said softly, as though she were reluctant to shatter the mood. "I think it's time I took the children to bed."

"Yes, of course," he said absently. He was still holding tight to Céleste and his gaze never left hers. Whatever was in his thoughts, it was clear he wanted to be alone with her. He turned his head briefly to his children, and nodded. "Good night, then." It was a kindly adieu, but a dismissal nevertheless.

Oblivious of the charged atmosphere, the children said their good-nights and allowed Mademoiselle Daumard to bustle them toward the door.

Albertine turned. "Papa," she asked innocently, "did you ever dance the polka with Mama?"

The spell was broken. Céleste—pressed close to Edmond's body—felt him stiffen. He looked down at her and frowned, as though he were surprised to find himself still holding her. He released her and stepped back, bowing formally as he did so. "Thank you for the dance, Madame

Valvert. It was a pleasure. We shall have to do it again." His
words were the mechanical recitation of a well-bred man
remembering his etiquette. He smiled distantly at his
daughter. "No, Albertine," he said, in answer to her question. "Your mother died before the dance became popular."

Mademoiselle Daumard hurried the children out the door.
After the warmth of the dance, the intimacy of Edmond's
embrace and his searching glance, his sudden frosty distance was bewildering. Céleste covered her dismay by
crossing the room and pouring herself another cup of coffee. Beaufort rang impatiently for a servant.

"I've not enjoyed the coffee tonight," he said to the
footman who answered his summons. "Bring me some cognac instead." He looked at Céleste. His eyes were guarded,
hiding thoughts she could only guess at. "I hope you don't
mind, *madame,* if I drink cognac."

She wanted to die. What had happened to ruin their magic
moment? She fought to keep control of her chaotic emotions, to ignore the awful feeling in the pit of her stomach—the sense that someone had dropped her from a great
height. "I don't mind at all," she said. "In point of fact,
that madcap dance has given me a headache. If you'll forgive me, I'll go to my rooms." She scarcely waited for his
approval but fled before she could shame herself with un-
wonted tears.

It wasn't until Nicole, her maid, was readying her for bed,
brushing her long brown hair at her dressing table, that she
allowed herself to review the strange and disturbing evening. He had warmed to her after her story about Grandpapa, and that warmth had grown and blossomed like a
hothouse flower when they'd danced together. And then?

And then Albertine had asked her question.

She glanced at Nicole in the mirror. "Did you know *madame la comtesse?*"

The girl tied back her hair with a pink satin ribbon that
matched her dressing gown, and shook her head. "No, *ma-*

dame. I didn't come to Rochemont until after she was gone. None of us did.''

"Yes, I know that," she said, remembering what Mademoiselle Daumard had told her. "But surely you—or some of the others—had met her before. Seen her in church, perhaps. In the village."

"Oh, no. This isn't my parish. Not where I grew up. Monsieur de Beaufort hired us all from Dijon."

She stared in surprise. "How very peculiar. To dismiss the old servants and bring in new from so far away. Was he dissatisfied with them?"

"He couldn't have been, and that's a fact. They say he paid them so handsomely that most of them went off to Paris or Lyons to make their fortunes."

"Then you know nothing about *madame?*"

The girl scratched her chin. "Well, I remember an old woman from the village, when I first came to Rochemont. She said *madame la comtesse* was beautiful, quite fragile and delicate, with flaming hair and bright eyes."

"Are there no miniatures of her, no paintings hidden away in the attics?"

"They say Monsieur de Beaufort took them down himself, before he brought in the workmen to redecorate the château."

"*He* did?" She gestured to indicate her charming boudoir. "Do you mean this wasn't *her* doing?" She was astonished. She had admired Rochemont, its warmth and elegance; she had never suspected it represented Edmond's taste and sensitivity. "What did he do with his wife's paintings?"

Nicole clicked her tongue. "He burned them, *madame*. Every one."

"Dear God," she whispered. "To be unable to live with his memories . . . How he must have mourned her."

"I think it must have been so. He cut himself off from all their old friends."

"How do you know?"

"Oh, *madame,* that first year... before he started traveling so much... He warned Madame Léopold, the housekeeper—oh, in such a fearsome voice!—that she was to tell everyone he was gone. No one was to be admitted or received at Rochemont. Especially not people who claimed to have known him in the old days."

It was too much to bear. She closed her eyes against the pain. "You may go now," she said. "I want to sit up for a while. I'll turn down the bed myself, when I'm ready."

She sat in a chair before the fire, listening to the rain outside, and stared at the flames. She wished she were capable of weeping easily; she envied women who could burst into tears at every minor catastrophe. For here she was, her heart breaking, and she could do no more than sigh.

I love him, she thought, wondering how it had happened so quickly. It was more than just physical desire, as strong as that was. More than the longing to be held and kissed, to be made love to. She ached to cradle him in her arms, to reach and soothe the pain that must lie behind so much of what he did. That was why he had drawn back at the last minute tonight. That was what she had seen in his eyes. If only she had been wise enough to read them with her heart.

He was afraid. Even more than he had loved his son, he had loved his wife. And he had lost her tragically. Perhaps, in some irrational way, he even blamed himself for her death. It wasn't so odd, when she came to think of it. Hadn't Grandpapa blamed himself when her parents died of the plague? Hadn't he convinced himself through the years that they would still be alive if he had acknowledged his son?

She knew Edmond was attracted to her. She'd felt it often enough, even in their most innocent moments together. Perhaps he felt guilty, because of his wife. Or perhaps he was afraid to love—and lose—again.

She leaned back in her chair, overwhelmed by hopelessness. How could she compete with a ghost? How could she teach him to open his heart again?

"Oh, Edmond," she whispered. "Why can't you love me as I love you?"

Chapter Fourteen

She had fallen asleep in her chair.

A scratching noise awakened her, the sound of someone fumbling with the latch at her boudoir door. The clock on the mantel showed the hour of two. She jumped up in alarm, her heart pounding wildly. At this hour, whoever it was could only be up to no good. She glanced about the room. If she moved quickly, she might be able to draw the portiere over the closed door; the heavy velvet curtain wouldn't afford much protection, but it might slow the intruder and give her a few extra seconds to flee to her bedchamber, which had a key.

It was too late. The door swung open. Edmond stood there, holding a lit candle in a silver candlestick. "I saw the light under your door," he said. The words were slurred, and he seemed to be having trouble standing without his body swaying. His coat and waistcoat were off; his cravat hung—untied—around his neck.

She frowned, not knowing whether she was relieved it was Edmond, not a strange intruder, or concerned because of his condition. "Have you been drinking all evening?" she asked.

He beamed—a wide, proud, silly grin—and nodded his head. "Not a drop of cognac left in the bottle."

"Well, I don't have another bottle in hiding," she said indignantly. "So why have you come creeping around my door?'' He looked suddenly downcast. She recalled that tonight he had been painfully reminded of his dead wife. Perhaps, under those circumstances, his intoxication was understandable. She softened her tone. ''Why don't you go to bed?'' she said, more gently.

''Don't want to,'' he said with a pout. ''Want to sing. No fun to sing alone. I saw your light. Come...'' He held out his hand. ''The music room... Sing with me.'' He looked like an unhappy little boy, his dark curls drooping over his forehead.

''*Monsieur*... Edmond...'' she said. ''Do you know how late it is?''

He put down his candle and staggered toward her. '' 'Course I do. My fool of a valet kept reminding me, until I sent him away. Must be asleep on the floor of my bedchamber by now. Curled up like a puppy dog.'' He nodded vigorously. ''A good man. Loyal man.''

She felt like a mother with a wayward child. She tucked her hand under his elbow, steering him gently but firmly toward the door. ''Then go to him. Have him put you to bed.''

''No.'' He turned unexpectedly and wrapped his arms around her, holding her close. She suddenly wondered if he was as drunk as he seemed. He smiled—it was a wicked smirk—his eyebrows arching. ''*You* put me to bed.''

She tried to free herself without antagonizing him; she kept her tone mild and reasonable. ''Edmond, please... you're not yourself.''

He continued to grin, ignoring her plea. ''Or I can put *you* to bed...'' In one deft movement, he lifted her from the floor and cradled her in his arms, turning toward her bedchamber at the same time.

Her alarm was growing. She felt small and helpless in his firm grasp. And vulnerable. She was wearing only a thin muslin nightdress and her silk dressing gown, and she could feel clearly the pressure of his arms under her back and knees, the intimate warmth of his body against hers. Whatever his mental state, he was strong, capable of overpowering her once they reached her bed. She had no idea how dangerous he could be when he was drunk, nor how many of his normal constraints had been drowned in the cognac tonight.

The bedchamber was to be avoided, that was certain. But the passageway outside her door was dark, as well, and there was probably not a servant still awake at this hour. The music room might be the safest place. At least it would give her the chance to weigh the situation. "Do you still want to sing?" she said quickly. "If so, put me down. At once!" she added, as he hesitated. "Or I'll sing off-pitch deliberately."

"Perverse woman," he said with a chuckle, and set her on her feet. He reached for her wrist and curled his fingers around it, then picked up his candlestick. "Come, then." He pulled her into the passageway and down the stairs, stopping at the landing to light a large candelabra on the newel post. It made an oasis of golden light in the darkness of the great staircase and hall. He wobbled for a moment, and his hand shook, causing the candle to drip on the polished mahogany floor.

"Oh, here," said Céleste, reaching for the candlestick, "let me take that before you fall on your face."

He relinquished the candle, but kept his hold on her wrist. "It's a handsome face," he mumbled. "Don't you think so?" He waggled his finger at her and smiled slyly. "Yes, you do. I see the way you look at me."

She snorted. "Is your head this swelled when you're sober?"

Unexpectedly he raised her hand to his lips and pressed a burning kiss into the flesh. "When I'm sober," he said in a husky voice, "I can only see how beautiful *you* are." His eyes were smoky blue and seductive. The drink and the hour had softened his features; he looked like a god, all dark perfection.

Her heart melted. "Edmond," she whispered.

His mood shifted abruptly, in that disjointed manner peculiar to drunkards. He tugged at her wrist, pulling her down the rest of the stairs. "Come. Singing."

The music room was still brightly lit when they reached it, though the candles had begun to burn low, and a few had already sputtered out. Edmond's evening coat and waistcoat lay in the middle of the floor. He pulled off his cravat and threw it on top of his other garments. The cognac bottle—quite empty—rested on its side on a serving table, and a broken glass lay in a corner of the room.

Céleste shook her head. "What a night you've had. Are you sure you can still play the piano?"

"Always play the piano," he muttered. "Only good thing left in life. Music." He sat down at the instrument and ran his fingers over the keys. His hands were surprisingly sure and agile, as though the cognac had had no effect on them. He closed his eyes and began to play. He seemed to have forgotten about the singing. It was a Beethoven sonata, and he played it with concentrated intensity, as though nothing else existed for him but the liquid passages. Except for the occasional missed note or uneven tempo—due, no doubt, to his condition—his exquisite playing might have been the performance of a sober pianist in concert.

Watching him with eyes that drank in every feature, Céleste wondered how often he had escaped the pain of his losses in just this way—seated at the piano, his music both a solace and a shield against the world. Did the abstract beauty of the music help him to forget the reality of a dead wife? A child killed in the sweetness of his youth?

The third movement of the sonata was coming to a close in a crescendo of sonorous chords. Edmond's hands attacked the keys with great raging blows that seemed like the crashing of angry waves against the shore. His eyes were now open and staring, and his face was contorted in fury, as though his playing were a kind of vengeance.

Dear heaven, thought Céleste in a paroxysm of pain. She wished she could turn and run; she had no right to be here.

His emotions were too raw, too personal. He was a proud man, a man of reserve and self-control. Surely, if he was sober, he wouldn't grant her this glimpse into his tortured soul.

He uttered a cry of bitter triumph as he pounded out the last chord. Then he shuddered and dropped his arms on the keys, burying his head against his forearms. He groaned. "My head hurts."

Céleste ached with pity. She hurriedly moved behind him and began to massage his tense neck and shoulders. The thick curls at his nape clung damply to his skin; she stroked them with her fingertips, noting the way they caught and held the golden candlelight in each dark coil. On an impulse, she leaned down and kissed him where the curve of his ear met the line of his jaw.

He stiffened, sat upright and shook off her hands. "We never sang," he said. His eyes were clearer now, and far more focused than they'd been all night. He pulled her down to sit beside him on the bench.

"Perhaps we should wait until morning," she said, beginning to feel uneasy again. Was the cognac wearing off? She wondered if she should stand up and leave while she could. "Your head..."

He shrugged. "Will hurt as much in the morning, no matter what I do." He began to play and sing—the song from the music box that the children had enjoyed. This time, however, he sang the words that were meant for grown-ups—words of love and desire. When he came to the last line of the verse—"Can one live without a lover?"—he looked straight at Céleste, his eyes searching her face.

Did she read desire there? The hunger he had denied since that night in Madame de Cloquet's conservatory? She wasn't sure. But she suddenly knew she didn't want to see desire in his eyes—she wanted to see love. To be desired, with no stronger emotion than that, was to be less than a woman. And little more than the adventuress he'd called her.

She laughed lightly to turn aside his mood and stood up, moving away to the other side of the piano. "I prefer the words I sang to the children," she said.

His mouth twisted in a cynical smile. "Subversive words. Undermining my authority."

She felt a twinge of guilt. "I...hope you didn't mind..."

"Mind? That you've interfered where you had no right?"

The words were said with such unexpected ill humor that it made her feel defensive. "At least I give them some attention," she said hotly. "Which is more than you can say. They're lovely children. They deserve an amiable parent, not a cold stranger."

He laughed. It was a sharp, unpleasant sound. "Do you want them? I'll give them to you. With my blessing. Then you can meddle all you wish."

She gasped in horror. Drunk or sober, what kind of man would offer to give away his children? "How can you say that? They're your own flesh and blood!"

His expression became a sardonic grimace. "Are they? They're Joséphine's, sure enough. They have her coloring. But mine? I never saw a jot of resemblance."

"J-Joséphine?" she stammered.

"My late wife. She had red hair, my Joséphine. And the face of an angel."

"You must have loved her," she said with sympathy.

His eyes glowed with an odd light. "Yes, I must have. To link the Beaufort name with hers. Her father was only an upstart, you understand. A parvenu of the Revolution who wormed his way into the Emperor Napoléon's favor. In appreciation, the old man—oh, how prophetic!—he named his daughter after Bonaparte's fornicating whore."

Céleste dropped into a chair, her jaw falling open. The ugly words hung in the silence. She stared at him. Surely it was the cognac that had caused him to speak so coarsely. "But of course the times in which the empress lived... It was so different. To judge her with such harshness..."

"I didn't mean the empress," he muttered. "I meant my wife."

She gasped. "But...but you *loved* her." Hadn't that love colored all his behavior? She shook her head in bewilderment, all her certainties fading away.

He looked tired and drawn. "I loved her madly, when I was twenty. So much so that when my ailing father begged me to marry her and produce an heir before he died, I willingly gave up my music to take Joséphine to my bed and bosom. She was sixteen then. Delicate and frail. And I was her champion, her protector." He laughed bitterly. "You can't imagine the smug pride I felt in those early years. I had become the count. She was my countess, my jewel, my sweet responsibility and burden. And when Jean-Claude was born..." He gulped several times and covered his eyes with his hand.

After a few moments—during which Céleste wondered what comfort she could give him—he stood up from the piano and began to pace the room in an agitation of emotion. "I kept my illusions for nearly ten years. Even though she didn't like to accompany me to Paris, and she complained that my music disturbed her. I still found her lovable, blaming myself for the restlessness that made me leave her side." He stopped pacing and looked at Céleste, his mouth curving in a cynical smile. "I was the perfect husband, allowing her to entertain our friends in the country because she was too fragile to enjoy travel. I understood, I made allowances for her delicacy, even when she began to deny me...her bed...." He sighed and turned away.

"Edmond," she murmured, "you've had too much to drink. You shouldn't tell me these things. In the morning..."

"In the morning, I'll regret it. And you're so well-bred, you'll pretend I never spoke at all. But tonight..." He shook his head. "Every day you look at me with questions in your beautiful eyes. God knows why, but I want to give you answers." He glanced impatiently around the room. "Damn,

I wish there was more cognac." He rubbed his hand across his mouth and continued his narrative. "You were surprised, I remember, when I told you Rochemont had no steward. It did, once. A competent man—I relied on him while I was away in Paris. He was capable, efficient and intelligent. He was also my wife's lover."

"Oh, no..." she breathed.

"One of many, you understand. Once I learned the truth, she was only too happy to cite me chapter and verse. To rub my nose in it. The great catalog of her indiscretions." He groaned. "Everyone at Rochemont, it seems, had known for years. *Everyone*... except the poor cuckolded husband."

She wondered how such a proud man could have endured the humiliation of being surrounded by people who, no doubt, thought him a blind fool. And then she remembered that he had dismissed all the old servants and paid them handsomely to leave the region. "What did you do when you learned of it?" she asked gently.

"I was nothing if not... morally unbending, I think you called me once. I gave her a choice. She was to renounce her past and her lovers and return to the chastity of a wife, or I would seek a divorce."

"What did she say?"

"She laughed in my face, said I was foolish. Out of step with the times. She had the advantage, I suppose, knowing how little I wanted a divorce, how much I dreaded a scandal attached to my family's name. She proposed that we should go on just as before. She had been discreet, she said, had conducted her affairs far from the gossip of Paris. There was no reason for anything to change. I would have the satisfaction of knowing that society would continue to see a picture of domestic bliss, she said. And she would have the freedom of her love affairs."

Céleste's heart was breaking. "She cannot have been so cruel."

"Cruel? I don't think she saw it as cruelty. Nor even hypocrisy. She was young and selfish and self-indulgent. And

I had encouraged it through the years. She felt no obligation to me, no sense of duty. She had been my child wife, pampered and petted. And perhaps that was my defect of character. To take such overweening pride in my stewardship of another person's life.''

Yes, she thought, remembering his behavior toward Paul. Viewing it now with more tolerance and understanding. She had seen it as interference; but it was second nature to him to take command. "How did you answer her proposal?" she asked. "What did you do?"

"Not what I should have done, I suppose," he said, his voice filled with self-loathing. "She had behaved like a child, I reasoned. Ergo, I treated her like a child. I threatened to take her across my knee and punish her like a child, lock her in her room like a child, unless she changed her ways." He sighed. "And so, of course, she repaid me by taking a child's spiteful revenge." He whirled and slapped his hand against the side of the piano. "Damn it, there must be some cognac in the drawing room. Wait."

He strode from the music room and returned in a few minutes, bearing a half-filled bottle of liquor. He took a swallow directly from the bottle and looked at Céleste, his eyes dark with misery. "Do you want to know what she did? She and the steward decided to elope. At the last minute—knowing how dear Jean-Claude was to me—she took the boy with her. It was winter. The roads were icy." He took a hasty gulp of cognac, choked on it, and turned away.

She stood up, wondering if to go to him would be an intrusion on his grief. "Oh, my dear..." she murmured.

His voice was muffled when he continued at last. "They were all crushed in a ravine, including the coachman. I had the steward's body removed and buried in secret, so that he would never be associated with Joséphine's death."

"And you cut yourself off from the past," she said with sympathy, wishing he'd turn around so that she could see his eyes. "That much I know."

"Wouldn't you? The new servants, the fresh decorations. Everything. I thought it the only way to keep my sanity. To shut out the past."

"But your friends?" It seemed a needless sort of punishment, to isolate himself further. "Even your friends?"

He laughed bitterly, his rigid back shaking. "Most especially the friends. I found myself wondering how many of them she'd slept with. Now I travel as much as I can. But, sooner or later, business calls me back to Rochemont. Where the twins are a daily reminder of her perfidy."

"Those lovely children? But surely you can't blame them for her sins."

He spun around to glare at her. "Don't you understand yet? There's almost no way they can be mine!" He closed his eyes and groaned. "Jean-Claude was mine. His hair was dark, and he..."

"Edmond, don't," she said. She reached his side, put her hand on his arm, gently removed the bottle from his grasp. "It's late. You're tired, and you've had too much to drink. You can't let the past twist your whole life. In time, you'll forget."

"*Forget?* Forget my shame? Forget that my wife was a whore?" he snarled.

She felt as though she were fighting for her own happiness. "But not all women..." she began.

"After Joséphine, my eyes were opened," he said. "I've not found a woman yet who can be trusted."

"That's not so!"

"Isn't it?" he said with a sneer. "A week after Joséphine was in her grave, the wife of one of my friends came to me, offering solace. The comfort of her bed. I suppose her husband bored her and she wanted amusement." He sighed tiredly. "What does it matter? We're all self-interested. There's nothing more in life."

"There's love," she whispered, all her yearning in her eyes.

"Love killed my son," he growled. "If the witch hadn't known how dear he was to me, she would never have taken him away." He shook his head. "No. Love is for fools—like young Edmond de Beaufort, the devoted husband." He reached for the cognac and took another swallow, then slapped at his breast. "*This* Edmond has learned a new creed. Desire. It approximates the same emotions as love, but it's safer."

His cynicism, his bitterness, cut her like a sharp knife. "Edmond, my dear..."

He seemed not to hear her. "Desire," he said again, as though he were musing over the word. He put down the bottle, reached for Céleste's chin and cradled it in his hand. "I want you," he said in a husky voice. "God knows I do. I don't know what magic spell you weave. I don't know if it's planned...if it's as calculating as it seems—that spell you cast. But I look at you and want to devour you. To cover you with kisses, to feel your heart beating against mine..." His eyes were burning sapphires, glowing with desire; his breath rasped in his chest.

She jerked her chin from his grasp and backed away, holding her hands before her in an involuntary gesture of protection. "No, Edmond. It's late. You're not yourself. I beg you...no."

"Yes," he growled. "Show me how you loved that phantom husband of yours."

He reached for her, his shoulders hunched and menacing. She eluded his grasp and turned and fled, racing toward the stairs. He caught her at the foot of the staircase and clutched at her hair. She wrenched away, tugging her curls from his grasp.

"Wait," he said. "Don't go. Just a kiss."

"No!" She took the steps two at a time, her heart pounding in fear. She had almost reached the landing, then she tripped on the top step and went sprawling. She felt his strong hands on her shoulders, turning her. And then he was on top of her, his mouth grinding down on hers, his body hard against her soft length. Her hair was in her face, and her lips burned from his passionate kiss.

Not like this! she thought, anguished. Not with hatred in his heart. Not with anger and jealousy and pain to poison the sweetness. She went limp, overwhelmed by despair. He lifted his mouth from hers and sought her bosom, kissing the soft flesh where her dressing gown had fallen open. "Don't," she said with a moan.

He raised his head and looked at her. His eyes were bewildered, lost and weary, glazed with drink. "All whores," he mumbled. "All lying cheats. Every one of you." He sighed once and collapsed against her breast. In a moment, he was snoring softly.

She eased herself from under him, fighting her tears. She crept up the stairs, clinging to the banister to keep herself from trembling in grief and horror. In the passageway, she turned toward her rooms. She stopped, seeing the light from Edmond's suite at the end of the corridor. She hesitated, wondering whether she should awaken his valet and send him for his master.

No. It would be too humiliating to try to explain what she was doing wandering around the château at this hour. Besides... She felt a surge of unexpected anger. Let the wretch stay where he was for the night. Perhaps a cold, hard bed would make him regret his behavior. If he even remembered any of it in the morning!

She extinguished her candles and crawled into bed. Perhaps she should lock the door to her bedchamber, she thought. She decided against it. She was safe from him for now, and her maid might wonder.

It was hours before she fell asleep. Again and again she reviewed Edmond's story in her mind. And each time her despair grew. It had been painful enough to think that she was competing with the love of his dead wife. But to learn of his dark hatred... to know that her true opposition was his deep and bitter mistrust of all women...

She moaned and curled herself into a tight ball of pain. How could she win his trust, when almost everything he knew about her was a lie?

Chapter Fifteen

"There, Madame Valvert. Do you like it that way?" Nicole gave a last pat to her coiffure and handed her a silver mirror.

Céleste peered into the mirror and turned about, surveying the sleek chignon on the top of her head, the soft clusters of curls at her ears. "Yes," she said, "it's very charming." Though why—after last night—she should care about how she looked was more than she could imagine. To please Edmond? She wasn't even sure she wanted to see him at all. More than that, after his savage behavior, his revealing confession, he might be unwilling to face *her*.

Nicole had already told her that Monsieur de Beaufort had been found lying on the stairs this morning. Not hurt, but clearly the worse for too much cognac. He had been roused and bundled off to his bed, where—it was supposed—he would spend the day nursing his aching head and regretting his unwise indulgence. "It's not like him, *madame*," said Nicole, "and that's a fact. He's always been moderate in his behavior."

Céleste eyed her with curiosity. "Do you like your master?"

The girl shrugged. "It's hard to tell. He's fair to us here, that's sure. And he works hard, and takes good care of Rochemont. There aren't many that way. But for the rest…" She frowned. "It's like he's wearing a mask. Some of the servants think it's strange and fearsome, the way he's so distant. Madame Léopold says she's never been house-keeper to such a cool one in all her life. Me, I say a person can't know what fish lie at the bottom of the pond.'' She smoothed a final dark brown curl into place and peered at Céleste's reflection in the dressing table mirror. ''Do you want a ribbon bow, *madame?* Or a bit of lace to finish the look?''

Céleste turned and glanced out the window at the gray day. The heavy rain had ended, but the sky was still overcast. ''Yes, it might cheer me.''

Nicole fetched a large covered basket that contained Céleste's ribbons, rummaging through them until she found one that complemented Céleste's plum-colored gown. ''This would be pretty, I think.''

Céleste scarcely acknowledged the girl; she stared into the basket, her eyes wide with surprise. Her pink satin ribbon was neatly rolled and tucked in among the other ribbons. But she'd wakened this morning without it, her hair un-bound and wild on the pillows. And she remembered Beau-fort reaching for her with frantic hands.

Nicole followed Céleste's glance to the pink satin. ''It was at the foot of the staircase this morning,'' she said quietly. ''Near *monsieur le comte.* I took the liberty of removing it.'' Her smile was bland and innocent. ''I can't imagine how it would have gotten there, you understand. But there was no point in giving busybodies anything to talk about.''

Céleste returned her artless smile. ''Of course not. Thank you.'' Did *anything* happen in a household that the ser-vants were unaware of? She remembered Edmond's humil-iation because of his wife's affairs. She was grateful that Nicole was discreet and sympathetic.

She spent the rest of the morning in her rooms and had her lunch brought in on a tray. Perhaps it was cowardly of her, but she wanted to hide away forever. As though her boudoir were a snug refuge that would somehow, magi-cally, ease her pain. It was no use. She was too discouraged, too confused by everything that had happened, to shake her melancholy. And when the children sent to ask why she hadn't come to play with them, she begged them to forgive her absence, pleading a headache.

What was she to do about Edmond? It was clear, after his heartbreaking story of last night, that he was damaged beyond measure by his wife's infidelity. How could he forgive what Joséphine had done? And even if he could, how could he ever forget the loss of his child, the pain that a woman's betrayal had brought to him? He was wounded, suspicious and afraid to trust his heart. He would never see beyond his anger and bitterness to accept the love that Céleste felt for him. He might desire her, and his passion might be hot and strong and hungry. But that was all. His heart would remain closed. Only a fool would hope for more.

And in the meantime she was losing her self-control. Each day, each moment, that she spent with him shredded her emotions a little more, leaving her raw and vulnerable, her feelings exposed to every shift in his mood. How could she go on this way, wanting him, yet dreading a repetition of last night's madness? What to do? She paced her room for hours, torn by indecision. To go? To stay?

She stared out at the gloomy day. It wasn't raining, at least. Perhaps she'd just go for a walk to clear her head. She put on a heavy velvet pelisse and wrapped a shawl around her head and shoulders, then slipped outside. The weather had turned sharply colder; she was glad she'd thought to dress warmly. She stayed to the road, walking between the rows of large, overarching trees that bordered the woods.

She didn't know at what point her mind was made up, at what moment she knew that she couldn't bear to see him again. She only knew that her steps had become more purposeful and sure, that she found herself calculating the distance to Saint-Rémy, the nearest village. Five leagues or less if the servants could be believed. She could reach it in little more than two hours of steady walking. Long before nightfall, even under this dark February sky.

It began to drizzle—a light, misty rain that inconvenienced her more than soaked her. She pulled her shawl far forward to shield her face, and continued on. What was a little rain measured beside her confusion and unhappiness? She'd have a warm drink when she reached Saint-Rémy. Surely there would be an inn or two in the village.

She laughed softly. How we deceive ourselves, she thought. In the pocket of her pelisse, she had a few coins wrapped in a handkerchief. Not much, but enough for a drink, a meal, an overnight stay. But there had been no reason for her to take money at all—not for just a simple walk. Surely she'd known, somewhere in the back of her mind, that she meant to run away today. To escape the painful burden of love that her heart could no longer bear.

The rain was beginning to turn to snow, a light sprinkling that became slush almost as soon as it hit the ground. Céleste was glad she'd worn warm, ankle-high boots. If the snow persisted, her feet would be thoroughly soaked long before she reached the village. Still, she'd come this far; it seemed foolish to turn back now.

The snow began to fall more heavily, the flakes becoming large white puffs that drifted down and clung damply to the bare branches of the trees. And still she wasn't alarmed. The temperature seemed to be hovering around the freezing point; at any moment she expected the snow to turn to rain again. She pushed on, her eyes on the distance.

It was really quite beautiful—the snowflakes as big as a child's fist, soft white against the ebony branches of the trees and the wet brown earth of the road. Here and there, the snow had begun to stick, softening the harsh, dark colors. It lay like downy clouds on the tops of bushes, across the lengths of tree branches, plastered to gnarled trunks. To wander in this magical world gave her a sense of peace and isolation that was soothing to her troubled heart. She found herself forgetting Edmond's drunken conduct of last night, and remembering instead the sweet times: the music around the piano, the rides through the woods, the thrill of dancing in his arms. She smiled dreamily and brushed the snow from her pelisse.

The storm increased in intensity. She plodded on, sure that at any moment it would end or turn to rain. But the longer she walked, the more frightening her situation became. She was in a world of white, far from help or comfort. The snow was now thick on the ground, wet and icy. It caught at her skirts, slipped into the tops of her boots. The trees bent under the weight of their snowy burden. She could hear the cracking of heavy-laden branches all around her, a counterpoint to the soft whisper of the flakes as they fell.

She looked about, peering into the swirling gusts that obscured the road. This was madness! She must be halfway to Saint-Rémy by now, trapped at the midpoint between the château and the village. Why in God's name hadn't she turned back as soon as the snow began to fall? She stopped to gauge her chances. It made more sense to turn around and go back to Rochemont. If it was noticed that she was missing, they would surely come out to search for her.

The snow now filled the air so thickly that she could barely guide herself by the rows of trees; once she stumbled off the road and had to plow through tangled underbrush and drifts before she could regain the path. It seemed to be growing darker. She didn't know if night was falling or if the clouds were thickening. Neither prospect was of much comfort.

She heard a loud snap and looked up in alarm. A huge tree branch, weighted down with more wet snow than it could support, had cracked and was bending toward her. She tried to move, tried to dodge it, but her foot slipped on the icy ground and she went flying, sprawling on her back. She felt the thick snow beneath her, cushioning her fall, and then—a mere second later—the weight of the branch landing on her body. She gasped with shock and cried out, fearing herself grievously injured.

She lay still for a moment, waiting for the expected pain. Strangely, she felt nothing except the weight of the branch pressing her to the ground. It lay aslant across her hips and torso, but her thick coat and skirts had kept it from doing real harm. She was grateful it didn't quite reach to her breast; it might have crushed her ribs or pressed the air from her lungs. She breathed a sigh of relief and tried to sit up.

"Dear God," she whispered. Though no bones seemed to be broken, she could scarcely move; the heavy branch, made heavier by the damp snow, kept her pinned. She grunted and struggled frantically, aware that the snow was continuing to fall unabated; each moment she remained on the ground only increased the weight on her trapped body. She fought the waves of panic that threatened to rob her of her common sense. Surely there was a way out.

But her attempts to free herself only seemed to make things worse. The more she twisted and turned, tried to slide herself out from under the branch, the deeper she sank into the wet snow. She was enveloped by it, surrounded, overwhelmed. And if it continued to fall this heavily, she thought, brushing it from her face, she would soon be suffocated.

With a great deal of effort, she managed to pull her shawl loose, resting it on her upraised arm to shield her face from the blizzard and create a pocket of air. At least she could breathe while she tried to figure out a way to free herself. Perhaps if she struggled out of her pelisse, unhooked her skirts and petticoats, she might wriggle free of her clothing and the branch at the same time.

But the branch was so heavy, and her clothes were now thoroughly soaked and impossible to manage. And she was so cold, and so very, very tired...

The voice was low and urgent. "She's breathing, thank God. Take the reins from my horse, Gaston. We'll hook them around the branch."

Céleste felt her shawl being pulled back from her face. She opened her eyes, blinked, and stared into Edmond's scowling face. "I thought I'd...die here." she murmured weakly.

"Little fool," he muttered, clearing the snow from her head and shoulders. "What happened to your promise not to run away?" He glared at her and motioned to the servant, who waited with the horses. "Here, Gaston. The reins."

Her anger grew as her awareness returned. He didn't have to take that tone with her! she thought. *She* was the one who'd been driven off by his drunken attack. *She* was the one who was lying here, trapped and miserable. And it was his fault. "*My* promise?" she said. "You promised me civility! A welcome guest, you said. I scarcely think that last night's self-indulgence—"

"I was prepared to offer an apology," he growled. "You might have demanded it. You might even have asked for a lock for your boudoir door, if you felt so threatened! But to run away in the middle of a storm . . . !" He swore softly.

"I might even have asked for a pistol to keep you at bay!" she snapped back. "And it wasn't storming when I left! Now, do you intend to spend the rest of the day quarreling, or do you think it's possible to dig me out?"

He scowled even more fiercely at her words, then stood up. With the help of his servant, and the strength of their two horses, he managed to loop the reins around the tree branch and drag it from Céleste's body. She winced as it rubbed over her legs and tore her stockings. Edmond knelt beside her. "Can you stand? Is anything broken?"

"I don't think so." She felt strangely light with the weight removed from her body, and her limbs were numb. She suddenly remembered that it hadn't been snowing when she opened her eyes to Edmond, though the air had been thick with flakes when she fell. She guessed she must have been lying there, asleep or unconscious, for a very long time before he found her. The realization of her brush with death set her to trembling, as though she could allow herself to feel fear only now that the danger was past. "I'm c-cold," she said, her voice shaking.

He cradled her in his arms and lifted her from the ground. "Your garments are soaked. We'll get you back to Rochemont as soon as possible." He set her on her feet for a moment, to be sure she was strong enough and unhurt, and then he put her on his saddle and swung up behind her. He held her tightly on the ride back; although she was wet and uncomfortable, the cold seeming to settle in her vitals, she felt secure and safe in his embrace.

Night had fallen, dark and clear and frosty, by the time they reached the château. The waxing moon shone brightly on the expanse of white snow. The serenity of the scene almost made Céleste forget the frightful storm that had nearly killed her. Despite her protests, Edmond refused to let her walk, but carried her to her room, setting her down only when she was in front of the warm fire in her boudoir.

Nicole threw up her hands in horror. "*Madame,* what a sight you are! You frightened us all half to death, and that's a fact, when we found you'd gone."

She shivered. "It was very foolish of me," she said, peeling off her wet pelisse and pushing the sopping curls from her forehead. "I had a headache and thought to go for a walk. The storm came up so suddenly it caught me unawares. I was on my way back to Rochemont..." She stared pointedly at Edmond. His superiority, his smug conviction that she'd been attempting to run away, was not to be endured. She hoped he'd recall that she'd been facing toward the château when he found her. Let him have at least a few uncertainties! "On my way *back,*" she repeated.

He raised a skeptical eyebrow. "I tend to doubt it, but perhaps you were wiser than I gave you credit for, *madame.*"

She smiled thinly. The wretch couldn't even concede her a single point. "You've always underestimated me, *monsieur.* It's astonishing how often you misjudge my strengths. Now, if you don't mind—" she indicated her gown "—I'm wet and cold."

He bowed. "Of course. I'll return in a little while to be sure you've recovered from your ordeal."

"It isn't necessary." She didn't know why she felt such irrational anger. He'd saved her life, after all. And here she was snapping at him, trading barbs with him like some quarrelsome fishwife in the marketplace.

"I think you should have some wine," he said, "to stave off a chill. I'll bring it when I return." He bowed again and started for the door.

His overbearing manner set her teeth on edge. She wasn't in the habit of being dictated to. She threw him a parting shot. "Bring cognac, instead. I'm told it has great restorative powers." The success of her thrust, measured by his heightened color, oddly brought her no satisfaction. She sagged with weariness, suddenly tired of their fencing. "Better still, don't come back."

When he'd gone, Nicole stripped her of her wet clothes, toweled her dry, bundled her into warm nightclothes. She combed out her long hair and left it loose to the drying heat of the fire. A bowl of soup was fetched from the kitchen; Céleste downed it gratefully, enjoying its warmth, as well as its nourishment. She sat in a large armchair before the fireplace, her slippered feet on a little footstool. She still felt chilled clear through to the bone. "I think I'll never be warm again, Nicole," she said.

"I've brought you cognac. Here." Edmond stood in the doorway, holding out a glass. He was dressed in a heavy brown silk dressing gown with a velvet collar, and his snug pantaloons were of buff leather that accented the strength of his long legs. The firelight glinted in his blue eyes.

Céleste glared at him. How dare he look so handsome, when she was feeling weak and vulnerable? "I told you not to come back," she said sharply. "I don't want your cognac."

He marched across the room, his eyes narrowing in anger. He waved Nicole toward the door. "You may go."

For a moment, Céleste thought to countermand his high-handed order; then she decided against it. If they were going to have a battle royal, let it be in private. "I'll ring if I need you again tonight, Nicole," she said.

Edmond thrust the cognac toward her. "Now drink it," he commanded. "Get a bit of color in your cheeks again."

"I will not," she said through clenched teeth. "Leave me alone."

"Shall I pour it down your throat?" he growled. "You're still shivering."

She couldn't deny it. Hating herself for yielding to him, she took the cognac and downed it in a gulp. It seemed to help; the quivering deep within her stopped.

"That was a stupid thing to do," he muttered. "To run away. You could have died."

"I wasn't thinking of dying," she said defensively. "I was thinking of being quit of you!"

He laughed—it was a cynical bark. "It would seem our truce hasn't held."

"Our truce died last night," she said, still filled with resentment. "On the staircase." She shifted impatiently in her chair, wishing he'd go away and leave her alone. The heel of her slipper caught on the edge of the footstool and fell to the carpet.

He stooped and picked it up. "Give me your foot." He knelt in front of her, waiting for her to hold out her leg. When she stubbornly refused, he swore under his breath and wrapped his long fingers around her ankle, pulling her foot toward him. But instead of replacing the slipper, he frowned and pushed up the hem of her dressing gown. "Your leg is scratched."

"The branches..." she began, then stopped, her heart catching in her throat. He had bent his head and was now kissing her leg, his lips gentle and feathery on her bare skin. It was too much. She had had the strength to quarrel with him, but this unexpected tenderness—after all she'd been through—left her defenseless. She ached with the desire to reach out and stroke the dark curls on his bent head. To kiss him. To fall into his embrace. She began to weep—silent tears at first, then great, wrenching sobs that shook her body to the core.

He looked up at her in surprise. "Céleste. Don't," he said. He reached up and pulled her down to the floor beside him, wrapping his arms around her. He held her tightly and rocked back and forth, murmuring her name.

She wept for a long time—all her grief, all her frustration, pouring forth with her tears. Her head was buried against his chest. He smelled of cologne and spicy tobacco. A man's scents. They only fueled her need and her despair the more. At last she quieted, pulled away from him and dabbed at her eyes. She felt ashamed of her unfamiliar weakness. "That was foolish of me."

His voice was gentle and warm with understanding. "Nonsense. It's very human." He smiled wryly, clearly remembering his own drunken lapse. "Sometimes we're not as self-sufficient as we think." He pulled a handkerchief from the pocket of his dressing gown and blotted her eyes and nose. His arms were still around her, firm and strong, and his eyes had deepened to the blue of a troubled sea, a whirlpool drawing her in with its power. He seemed unwilling to speak, to break the spell that shimmered in the air between them. The fire crackled behind them—warm on her body, and as warm as the heat that raced through her blood. He bent her back across his arm until her head nearly touched the floor. His beautiful face was a heartbeat away from hers.

"Say it," he growled at last. "Say you desire me as much as I desire you."

She closed her eyes in an agony of longing. She wanted his love. And he had no love to give.

He took her silence for consent. "I knew you did," he said, and pressed his burning mouth to hers.

Chapter Sixteen

They clung to each other in a frenzy of passion, lips and tongues tasting, exploring, savoring the sweet delights so long denied. Céleste matched his hot kisses and caresses with her own. She was at a banquet, and her ravenous senses couldn't get enough of him: the moist warmth of his mouth, the glide of his tongue on hers, his musky scent. Even the rough scratch of his chin stubble excited her. She tangled her fingers in his hair. His curls were as silken as she'd always known they would be. Thick and soft. It was like stroking fur, and her hands tingled with the sensuous pleasure of it. And when she dropped her hands to his nape, she could feel the thrilling strength of muscle and sinew beneath her fingertips.

She hated his clothing, the dressing gown and shirt that came between them. She moaned and clawed at him, pulling his dressing gown from his torso; then she worked frantically at the buttons of his shirt. Why didn't he take it off? Why couldn't she touch his skin? She was hot and impatient, starving to know and taste every bit of him, to gratify her hungry senses.

He seemed as impatient as she. He pushed her roughly to the floor, parted her dressing gown and unhooked the neckline of her nightdress to reach her straining, eager breasts. He bent his head to the soft flesh; his teeth were like darts of fire, nibbling at her tender nipples until they hardened into burning peaks. She groaned in pleasure and dug her nails into his back, feeling his muscles tense beneath his shirt.

His hands had ranged over her body, stroking her flanks through her nightdress. Now, with the urgency of his own need, he abruptly pushed the garment above her waist and spread her legs, exposing the trembling, pulsing core of her desire.

No, she thought suddenly, remembering Alex and the ultimate disappointment of their lovemaking. It was too soon. She wanted more kisses, more caresses. She wanted— "Oh!" she cried aloud, her eyes widening in surprise and joyous pleasure. What was he doing? This was always the moment when Alex would cover her body with his own and seek his satisfaction. But Edmond still lay beside her, and had plunged his fingers deep within her; his teasing hand moved with a tantalizing skill that left her gasping and writhing. Again and again he thrust his fingers, touching sensitive places that she hadn't known her body possessed. She closed her eyes and surrendered to the wild dominion of his hands, his mouth. She was on fire, aching for the final sweet release, yet wanting this delirium never to end.

His body stilled, his fingers withdrew. Céleste opened her eyes. Edmond was poised above her, his face tense with passion, his eyes filled with a strange triumph. "I knew you'd be like this," he murmured. "I dreamed of it." He fumbled with the fastenings of his pantaloons, uncovering his potency, and placed himself between her legs. "Well?"

She was in agony. "Yes," she groaned. "You know I'm yours."

He plunged. He was hard and thick, filling her completely, his mere possession of her a heart-stopping joy. And when he began to move, his hips rocking in a sensual rhythm, she wanted to die for sheer pleasure, wondering how she could endure much more of this exquisite torment. The firm rhythm grew to wild, frantic strokes that made her head spin and took her breath away. She gasped and cried out—soft whimpers torn from her heaving bosom. "Yes, yes," she panted. "Yes!" Her body exploded in release, and she trembled violently, shaking as though she were tumbling down a steep incline.

Edmond clenched his teeth, threw back his head and let out a roar. At the same moment, he gave a final, savage thrust and fell forward across her body.

She felt too weak to move. His soft curls were against her face, and his head rested on her breast. She wanted to put her arms around him, but she was too sated, too lazily content, even for that small movement. She had never known such pleasure before. Perhaps it was because she loved him that she felt such satisfaction. But she'd loved Alex, hadn't she? And their lovemaking—exciting while they kissed and caressed—had always ended in his disappointment at her ultimate lack of passion, her inability to move beyond preliminary excitement to the wild abandon that he seemed to expect and demand.

She sighed, feeling regret for the past. Perhaps tonight had been different only because it was new—the thrill of making love with Edmond after the long weeks of yearning. Or perhaps the exhausting day had left her emotions shaky and vulnerable.

At last Edmond stirred, sat up and began to adjust his clothing. "My God, you're a wonder." He stood up and pulled her to her feet, wrapping his arms around her and taking her mouth in a hard kiss that filled her with renewed desire. She felt an odd tickle in the back of her throat, and a stirring of her vitals. It was foolish and greedy of her, but she wished their sweet night of love was just beginning, not ending.

He made no move to leave her. Instead—and before she could stop him—he slipped her dressing gown from her shoulders, gathered up her nightdress and pulled it over her head.

"What are you doing?" she said in protest, shielding her naked breasts with her arms. She had felt no shame while they'd been locked in the intimacy of a lovers' embrace. But the moment had passed, and now, to stand before him like this...

His blue eyes glittered as he scanned her body. Swiftly he shed his own dressing gown and shirt. His dark-thatched chest still rose and fell in the heavy rhythm of passion. He ran his tongue across his lower lip. Then, unexpectedly, he grinned. "I'm not inclined to end this evening yet. Are you?"

She felt giddy with happiness, and deliciously wicked. She giggled, her eyes straying to the buff pantaloons stretched taut across his groin. "In point of fact, *monsieur,*" she said, "I don't really know your 'inclination' at this moment." She was suddenly aware of the unladylike boldness of her double entendre, and she blushed and looked away.

He roared with laughter. He lifted her chin with strong fingers and smiled into her eyes, and her embarrassment melted away. "A charming blush," he said. "How I enjoy it when you lose your composure."

She snorted. "I think you like it because it makes you feel superior, you arrogant dog."

The smile faded from his face. "Arrogant? No. I'm humble before your beauty, God knows. The power you have over me." He reached out and stroked her bare shoulder, his fingers gentle and tantalizing on her flesh. When she shivered in delight, he smiled again and swept her up in his arms. He carried her into her bedchamber and laid her across the bed.

Nicole had left an alabaster night-light burning on the bedside table. By its glow, Céleste admired the perfection of Edmond's torso as he loomed above her. The power of contained muscles, of potent vigor waiting to explode. It made her heart pound just to look at him. She stretched like a cat and purred. "Will you... take off the rest of your clothing and join me, *monsieur le comte?*" She held out her arms in invitation.

"Seductress." He leaned over the bed and grinned down at her. "Not yet, you impatient creature. I want to look at you first." His smoldering eyes ranged her body, filled with a warm approval and admiration that made her feel like a princess. "If you knew how often I watched you," he said, "cursing the corsets and petticoats that hid your charms..."

She smiled her most engaging smile. "It's all part of a woman's allure. I don't think you'd watch me as much if I went around in my chemise."

He laughed—a low, wicked sound deep in his throat. "I'd watch you if you went around without a stitch. And never tire of the sight." He frowned as though a sudden stray thought had come into his mind. "Last night..." he began, then stopped and turned away.

She sat up and stared at his rigid back. The muscles were tense, a hard wall that seemed to keep her at a distance. She wondered if he was remembering that he'd bared his soul last night, told her things he'd kept hidden from the world for years. "Last night is forgotten," she said gently.

He turned and glared at her. "And my drunken behavior? Do you think I can forgive myself so easily for that?"

She shrugged. "I've seen men in their cups before. Grandpapa didn't mind a revel now and then."

"Did you feel the need to run away from *him* when he drank too much? Preferring the safety of a storm to..." He stared at the lamplight that flickered on the ceiling.

"Edmond." His remorse was touching. "Do you think I ran away because I was afraid of you?"

He ran his hand through his hair. "You had every right to be. I behaved like a barbarian."

How could she ease his sense of guilt? She couldn't very well tell him that it had been not fear, but the pain of her hopeless love, that drove her away. She couldn't risk revealing her heart that much. "But, you see, I didn't run away," she lied, repeating the story she'd told to Nicole. "Your behavior was abysmal. I'll grant you that. I was very angry. But I merely went for a walk to clear my head. I suppose I was simply too lost in thought to notice the storm. Until it was too late.''

He looked relieved at her words, but then he shook his head. ''Still, when I think of what might have happened to you out there...''

''But it didn't.'' She smiled teasingly. ''Did you miss me? Is that why you came after me?''

''Miss you? Not I.'' He groaned. ''I was too busy nursing an aching head.''

''Well deserved,'' she told him. ''All that cognac...''

He laughed shortly. ''I have no doubt it was fitting retribution. But Mademoiselle Daumard came to trespass on my misery. She had gone looking for you. She found it strange, not at all like you, when you declined to play with the children. She came marching in to me as though she thought your disappearance was my fault.''

''How ridiculous.'' Céleste clicked her tongue. Perhaps Nicole hadn't been quite as discreet as she thought. ''But, you see, it wasn't your fault at all. Now...'' She lay down again and motioned to him. ''Do you intend to talk for the rest of the night?''

He laughed and came to her, sitting on the edge of the bed to lean down and kiss her with fervor. He lifted her dark hair and inhaled its perfume, then spread the tresses across the pillow. His eyes were heavy-lidded with renewed passion. ''How do you do it?'' he murmured. ''Make a man desire you so much?''

''By wanting him in return,'' she whispered, and reached up to pull him down to her. She ached to feel his chest against her naked breasts.

He stared at her, then frowned and pulled away. ''Is it as simple as that? Is that how you women play your games?''

She sat up in alarm, disturbed by his sudden shift of mood. ''Edmond?''

''By all the devils! How blind could I have been? Is that how you bewitched Paul?'' he growled. ''By letting him know you wanted him?''

"Oh, dear God," she groaned. It had all seemed so far away. Paul and Paris, the LaGranges and their mindless, vindictive feud. "I—I never made love with Paul," she stammered. "You know that."

"But he loves you. And you love him. You told me so, often enough, in Paris. And I've seen the love letters you wrote. Aunt Charlotte spirited them away from Paul's desk to show me. You love him."

"No, I—" She choked on the words.

His eyes had darkened, and his mouth was twisted into the cynical sneer that had been his aspect in Paris. "You *don't* love him, then?"

"Edmond!" she cried. "Please..."

"Was I right to distrust you from the first? Do you have a reason to destroy Paul?"

"Of course not! I don't want to hurt him."

"Then you do love him," he said quietly.

"No." The look in his eyes was a torment.

"You can't have it both ways," he said with a sneer. "Either you love him or you don't."

Short of blurting out the truth, how was she to make him understand? "I...I cared for Paul," she said. "But I didn't love him."

He paced the room for a few angry seconds, then stopped to glare at her. "I'd forgotten how skillful you are. You didn't love him, you say. And the inn? How do you explain that? Are you in the habit of eloping with men you don't love? My God, even my trollop of a wife persuaded herself that she was in love with my steward before she ran away with him."

She was drowning in her own lies, in her past. "I...I thought I loved him. I was so lonely. But the moment I met you, Edmond, I knew Paul wasn't the man for me."

He laughed mockingly. "It gets better and better. Now I'm to understand that *I* turned you away from my cousin?"

She wondered if he could read the love that shone in her eyes. "Yes," she whispered.

"And yet you wrote him a tender letter the very morning after our love-crossed meeting at the opera." He smiled, an ugly grimace. "Forgive my cynicism. I intercepted the letter, of course. I remember it begged him for another rendezvous. The opportunity to prove your love." His voice grew sharp. "But perhaps I was mistaken. Perhaps I was unaware of my own power to attract you. Perhaps that letter was meant for *me* that morning."

"The letter meant nothing. I was finished with Paul, I tell you!" she cried in desperation.

"Then why were you going to Aix-les-Bains?" He was relentless, attacking her from every direction.

She pulled the coverlet around her trembling body and sat curled up on the bed, her arms tight around her knees, as though she could contain her pain with the gesture. "I was going to Rome," she said tiredly. "To Rome. Not to Paul. I planned to give him up. Before he left, I told him . . ."

"What? That it was over between you?"

She couldn't lie, not with his scornful glance challenging her. "No. Not exactly. But I gave him to understand . . ."

"What a damnable liar you are," he growled. "His valet told mine that he planned to rent a large house in Aix. With two bedchambers, I believe. And a music room. Paul neither plays nor sings, as I'm sure you know. It would seem to me that he expected you to join him."

She sighed. She was fighting a useless battle. "I don't know what he expected. I told him I wouldn't come." She buried her face in her hands. What was she to do? Tell him the truth? Betray Alex's memory, her final promise to him? Once more betray the LaGranges—who had asked only for her silence after she had disappointed them?

And even if she were to tell him the truth, what in the name of heaven could she say? That she was a LaGrange by marriage? That she was part of a vicious plot to destroy the Malecots? And that—most callous of all—she had been willing to break Paul's heart to do it? And how could she explain to him what she herself still didn't understand? She had allowed the LaGranges to use her for their own ends; her grief and guilt at Alex's death had persuaded her to compromise her own sense of decency.

Edmond's wife had betrayed him cruelly. But his pain had been as much for his blindness as for anything else. The humiliation of knowing that a woman could so easily dupe him. Could she tell him the truth now—after all her lies—and confirm for him that she was no better than Joséphine? A "lying cheat," as he'd called her?

No. That was too hurtful a truth. If she had to tell him something let it be something good, at least. Something of which she could be glad and proud. She lifted her face to him. "Edmond," she said softly, "Paul has nothing to do with you and me. I love you, and no one else. With all my heart, I love you."

He strode to the bed and grabbed her by the shoulders, his eyes glowing with fury. "You *love* me? You shameless bitch! Is there no trick too low for you? No lie you won't tell?"

She stared at him in horror, her heart constricting at the way he'd turned on her, the depth of his mistrust. "Do you think it was a lie, what happened between us tonight? Do you think I'm capable of such deception?"

"No." His voice had dropped to an ominous growl. "It was real. You felt what I felt tonight. This!" He tore the coverlet from her in one savage wrench and pinned her to the bed, covering her naked body with his own.

"Let me go," she gasped.

He ignored that. "I don't know what is between you and Paul," he said. "But *this* is what's between you and me. Desire." He crushed her lips with his mouth. The kiss held such anger and pain that she moaned aloud, hot tears springing to her eyes. She tasted blood from her own bruised lip.

She wrested her mouth from his and turned her head aside, fighting to keep the sob from her voice. "You have no cognac for an excuse tonight," she said bitterly. "Will you justify your cruelty by cursing Joséphine in my name?"

He stared at her for a long moment, his face twisted with an unfathomable emotion. Then his expression went blank. He released her and moved off the bed. He bowed stiffly. "Your pardon. I am at fault, not you. You were just doing what comes naturally to a beautiful woman. You'd think being at Rochemont would remind me of how little women can be trusted." He bowed again. "Good night," he said, and left her alone.

"Damn you, Edmond de Beaufort," she whispered to the empty room. "Go and bury your wife, once and for all. I'll not be her proxy. Not anymore." Then she threw herself facedown on the pillow and gave way to wrenching tears.

Chapter Seventeen

By midmorning, the snow had melted away. Céleste sat at her boudoir window—in morning *déshabillé*—and watched the water drip from the eaves. It seemed strange to remember that the frightful blizzard and her brush with death had happened only yesterday; stranger still to recall that she had made love with Edmond on the floor of this very room. And quarreled bitterly over Paul. Only half a day ago, though it seemed an eternity.

And now she would have to face him over the luncheon table today. She sighed. She found herself envying those fragile creatures who could conjure up a sick headache at a moment's notice. Who could languish, pale and frail, and beg the world to forgive their absences. She laughed wryly. She was certainly not of their ilk! Hadn't Mademoiselle Daumard come looking for her yesterday because she doubted her excuse?

She turned from the window as Nicole came into the room to help her dress. Perhaps Edmond would spare them both the embarrassment of a meeting by declining to lunch with her. If not, perhaps she could refuse him. Of course, there was always the risk that he would consider that an insult and come storming into her rooms to demand an explanation.

And what could she tell him? That she couldn't face him after all that had happened between them? The angry words, the burning passion, the secret intimacies and revelations... She sighed again. There was one thing to be grateful for, at least. He hadn't believed her confession of love. And it was just as well, she decided upon reflection. She didn't want him to think she was a lovelorn female, helpless and susceptible to his domination. She was at enough of a disadvantage, having granted him the last favors. Let him think that her behavior of last night had simply been prompted by desire, as he'd been driven by his own hungers.

"What shall I wear today, Nicole?" she asked. "Not the blue *gros de Naples*." Edmond had particularly admired her in that gown. It would be a tactical error to go out of her way to please him. "Perhaps the puce silk?"

"Oh, there's no point in your dressing so grandly today, *madame*. Not with Monsieur de Beaufort away."

She stared. "Away? Where is he?"

"He told Madame Léopold he was going to Dijon on business. And not to expect him back for a few days."

This was what she'd wanted, wasn't it? To avoid his company for a little while? Then why did she feel oddly disappointed? She bit her lip in consternation. "Does he... often go to Dijon on business?" she asked. Or was he afraid to face her? she wondered.

"I'm sure I don't know, *madame*," said Nicole, looking away uncomfortably. "But I'm sure Monsieur de Beaufort has his reasons."

"Yes, I'm sure he does," said Céleste stiffly, wondering—not for the first time—how much Nicole knew or suspected. "I'll just wear my green cashmere, then. And you might ask Mademoiselle Daumard if she and the children would like to join me in the dining room for lunch. I'm sure *monsieur le comte* wouldn't mind."

Nicole smiled archly. "And if he's not here, who will know?"

Céleste laughed. "You're a shrewd one. I wonder if there's anything that happens here that you don't know."

The girl shrugged. "Well, I keep my wits about me, and that's a fact."

Céleste dressed quickly. In some strange way, with Edmond gone she felt free. She could quiet her wayward desires for a while, forget that nothing had been resolved in the matter of Paul, swallow her guilt at the betrayal of the LaGranges and Alex's memory. Pretend that her heart wasn't in turmoil. She was free to enjoy the innocence of the children, to make believe that her life was no more complicated than theirs.

It was a day for exploration. They lunched together in the dining room, they played cards in the sitting room, moving from there to the music room, the billiard room, the elegant drawing room. They even tiptoed through the cavernous ballroom, noting how their voices echoed off the vaulted ceiling. With Céleste's encouragement, the children reveled in the pleasures of Edmond's part of the château, which had been denied to them in the past. And when Madame Léopold, the housekeeper, complained that night before dinner, Céleste demanded to know whether or not *monsieur le comte* had granted her the freedom of the manor house.

"Of course, Madame Valvert," said the woman. "You are an honored guest."

"Then I wish to have the company of the children, wherever I am."

Madame Léopold frowned. "But they're only children, Madame Valvert. So much added work for the servants..."

"*Wherever* I am," she repeated. "And that includes dinner tonight."

"As you wish." The housekeeper nodded politely, if coldly, and turned to go.

"One moment..." said Céleste, as a sudden notion struck her. "Has Monsieur de Beaufort actually *forbidden* his children to enter any of the rooms of the château?"

Madame Léopold looked defensive, and that only confirmed Céleste's suspicions. "No, *madame*," she said, her mouth pinched and tight. "But he has never found fault with the way I manage his household. Not in all my years of service here. Monsieur Edmond likes his solitude, you understand. He has impressed that upon me, many a time. It seemed sensible to discourage rowdy children from intruding upon him."

"Rowdy? To the contrary," snapped Céleste. "They're very well behaved. Perhaps you should have asked Monsieur Edmond himself, before you took it upon yourself to shut out his children." She whirled on her heel and stormed away, feeling as angry toward Edmond as toward the housekeeper. If he hadn't spent so much time traveling, he might have been aware of the cruel prohibition that Madame Léopold had enforced in his name!

The next few days were filled with a happiness that flooded Céleste's soul. Madame Léopold had retreated without a battle; the children now freely followed Céleste about the château, grinning in wonder and delight at the change in their routine. The weather had turned cold again, but the sky remained clear and blue. The ornamental pools and canals in the vast park of Rochemont froze, shining like hard, glittering jewels under the February sun. Mademoiselle Daumard found skates for the three of them, and they spent hours gliding and spinning and turning in gleeful enthusiasm. And when the twins' cold-touched cheeks turned as bright a red as their hair, they would troop inside and settle themselves before the fire in the cozy sitting room, downing steamy cups of chocolate and finding laughter in everything.

More and more, the children were drawn to the music room. Albert would sit at the piano, frowning "like Papa," and try to pick out tunes; Albertine would pretend she was a great opera singer. Her eyes shone as Céleste told of the renowned singers and performances she'd seen in her travels. And then they would ask Céleste to play, and she would teach them gay little songs and folk airs.

It seemed natural to Céleste to begin to use the personal *tu*, the intimate *thou*, when she spoke to them. She had used it with Alex and Grandpapa, of course. But Edmond's heart had seemed too distant—even in the throes of passion—for anything but the more proper *vous*. *Thou* was for love, tender and trusting. And surely she was growing to love these children, with their bright, open faces, their sweet charm. *Thou,* she said to them. Not *you.* And they heard, and they understood. And they bloomed like twinkling crocuses in the snow.

"Don't ever go away, Madame Valvert," they would beg. And at night she would lie awake in bed, her heart breaking for those two lonely children who needed a father.

No matter how he thought about it, he hated his cousin.

Edmond de Beaufort stared out at the lines of bare trees that flew past his carriage window. They were almost at Rochemont, and he still hadn't put his churning thoughts in order. Still hadn't decided what to do about the woman.

He could have stayed away longer, but it wouldn't have made any difference. He'd done everything he could in Dijon to drive her out of his mind. He'd sought out old companions—the ones he'd gotten drunk with in those terrible, pain-crazed months after the accident. He'd gone to the theater, looked for actresses, whores, loose creatures who would help to remind him that there was nothing good or honest or true about womankind. All to no avail.

She wasn't that way. She wasn't like those women, for all the mystery of her past, the unanswered questions. He had begun to doubt the vile rumors he'd heard in Paris, the stories of her liaisons. But even if every one of them was true, she wasn't . . . what the gossips would have her.

She was everything Paul had said she was. And more. Beautiful, elegant, charming, with a warmth in her smile that made a man feel invincible. And an indomitable spirit that never ceased to amaze him. She'd nearly died in the snow, yet she'd still had the pluck to talk back to him, even as she lay trapped. And she had a wonderful serenity about her; it came, he supposed, from being so loved as a child. He wished he'd known her grandfather, Desrosiers. The husband, whoever he'd been, had left her with money, that was clear. But her grandfather had given her the priceless treasure of self-confidence.

Small wonder that Paul was prepared to ruin his life for her. To jilt his fiancée, to run away, to risk everything to win her. It only surprised him that his cousin had known her for all those weeks and hadn't carried her off to his bed after their first kiss! She fired a man's blood. Made him long to possess her. She... He gnashed his teeth. Damn Paul, for knowing her first! That night in her bed, after they'd quarreled and he'd attacked her, it had been Paul he was thinking of. He had burned with the need to overwhelm her, to force Paul from her mind. The need to see only *his* image in her eyes, her desire for him alone. He groaned aloud. And even now, when he should be feeling disgust for his vile, cowardly behavior that night, all he could feel was jealousy.

He still had the letter she'd written to Paul that morning after the opera. He didn't know why in the name of God he'd saved it—with its avowals of love and devotion, its tender pleas, its sweet words. He had thought it cunningly skillful, at the time. The artfulness of a scheming woman. He had suspected a plot, had delved into her past as much as he was able, hoping to prove to himself that she was two-faced and treacherous. He had been so sure that she had darker motives, that she hoped to destroy Paul's reputation with the rendezvous at the inn.

But... what if the letter was genuine? And he, merely a bitter cynic who saw the worst in every woman? What if she truly loved Paul, and he loved her in return? What right had he, Edmond, to stand in their way? Because of family pride? His fear of scandal? He'd buried Joséphine's secrets when he buried her. Everyone in Paris still looked at him with pity: the grieving husband who had lost a pure and virtuous wife. But did it ease his pain and anger that no scandal had touched him? It was an absurd reason to deny Paul his happiness.

And if Céleste loved Paul... Oh, God! he thought, torn with new doubts. Then who was the hot-blooded creature who had melted in his arms? He thought of her body responding to his, writhing in ecstasy beneath his caresses. Who had given her that passionate nature? Had there been other men besides the husband? He thought again of all the rumors. All the men she had been linked to. So many stories, so many lovers. Surely not even the gossips could make up stories out of thin air!

He leaned back in the carriage and closed his eyes, filled with bitter torment. The fickle creature wanted every man she could get, that was clear enough. She'd spent a lifetime being pampered and petted by men. She enjoyed it. She expected to be treated like a princess. Wasn't that what she'd said? And never mind the Élise de Malecots of this world who might get hurt along the way. The jade might truly *love* Paul, though he doubted it. But she wanted him for a sexual conquest, as well. And in the meantime... What was the old proverb? *Far from eyes, far from heart.* Paul was in Aix-les-Bains. Edmond was at hand. And she didn't mind taking advantage of that to satisfy her desires.

Well, the devil take the minx, he was prepared to enjoy the game, too. To satisfy his own hungers with her voluptuous body until this madness ran its course. It had been a long time since he felt this way. Why should he deny himself, if she was willing? The sooner his hungers were sated, the sooner he could return to the world of calm reason, the world of passionless distance that had sustained and protected him all these years.

The carriage crunched over the gravel of the drive, then slowed and stopped. Edmond nodded to the footman who opened the door and gave instructions for the baggage to be unpacked. He strode into the vestibule and looked around. It felt good to be home—an unfamiliar sensation. As comfortable as he'd made Rochemont, as much as he'd tried to eliminate all traces of Joséphine in the decorations, his first steps through the doorway had always reminded him of her. He had always felt the painful urge to turn and leave again. To escape to a safe and unfamiliar place. But this time...

This time he had a mental picture of Céleste, radiant in blue, floating down the staircase. And Rochemont glowed with a freshness for him. He turned to Madame Léopold, who had hurried to greet him. "Our guest was well cared for while I was away?"

"Of course, *monsieur.* She has enjoyed the run of the house, as you instructed."

Did he only imagine that her lips puckered with disapproval? "And Madame Valvert is in her suite this afternoon?"

"No, *monsieur.* She and the children are in the park. At the large reflecting pool."

"Well, then..." He thought for a minute, then turned nonchalantly toward the door. "Perhaps I'll go and say good-day to them." He went out into the sunshine and turned toward the rear of the château. It was probably cowardly of him, but he welcomed the idea of greeting her in the company of the children. The words of their last encounter hung like an embarrassment between them: his thoughtless and cruel insults, accusing her of all manner of vile designs, and her absurd, defensive excuse—claiming to love him, like a child willing to say anything to put off a scolding. The twins' presence would be an effective silencer. Neither of them would have to apologize, or even refer to that night ever again.

As a matter of fact, he thought perhaps he'd ask Mademoiselle Daumard to bring the children to dinner tonight. He saw so little of them, it might be a pleasant diversion. And keep him from saying anything to Céleste that he'd regret.

He followed a garden alley bordered by neatly clipped hedges, and emerged where two wide canals—frozen solid—

converged and led to the reflecting pool. He stopped in surprise and stared. Unaware of his presence, Céleste and the children skated happily, flying across the ice like brightly colored birds. Albert's cheeks and nose were as pink as a puppy's tongue. Albertine's bonnet had slipped from her head, and her vivid red curls swirled around her face each time she turned.

But it was Céleste who caught and held his eye. She was dazzling, her sweet curves enveloped in a pelisse of ruby velvet that accented the pale clarity of her complexion and called attention to the graceful span of her waist. She was fresh and captivating and alive, glowing with health and pleasure.

She turned her head and saw him. At once her eyes lit up with a joyous delight that gave him an odd sensation in the pit of his stomach. "Look, children," she cried, skidding to a stop, "it's your papa!"

Why should she be so glad to see him? he thought. Was it because there were no other men at Rochemont to pay her court? Or was she simply displaying that coquettish charm she had perfected? He watched, vague irritability scratching at him, as she and the children skated to the edge of the pool and gingerly made their way across the frozen lawn toward him. He scowled. "Where do you find such joy?" he muttered darkly.

The smile faded from her face, to be replaced by a look of such disappointment that he cursed his own cynical mistrust. Fool! he thought. Perhaps she *was* glad to see him.

But it was too late to know. Her amber eyes had become as cold as the pond behind her. "I assume your business went badly in Dijon," she said. "Otherwise, I can't imagine why you should want to be so disagreeable." She turned to the children. "Come, Bertine, Allie. Let's go inside to the schoolroom. I'm sure Mademoiselle Daumard has chocolate waiting for us." She knelt and unbuckled her skates and helped the children with theirs.

The twins straightened and smiled uneasily at their father. He stared back, wondering if he should offer his hand or his cheek. They were clearly torn between their desire to greet him and their wish to follow Madame Valvert, who was already marching angrily toward the château. When he made no move, they settled for a hasty bow and curtsy and went racing after Céleste.

Edmond watched them go, then cursed softly. He'd managed that like a complete imbecile. They'd held open the door to him; he'd wrapped himself in his pride, his doubts and his suspicions, and slammed it in their faces. He sighed heavily. Well, perhaps he could make amends at dinner tonight.

"Will you have another pickled walnut, Allie?" Céleste smiled at the boy across the dining room table and held out a crystal dish piled high with the savory treats.

Mademoiselle Daumard adjusted her spectacles on her nose and shook her head. "I'm sure both children have had more than enough to eat tonight, *madame*. Perhaps it's time for us to say good-night."

From his place at the head of the table, Edmond held up his hand. "No, no. Not yet. I brought back a magic lantern from Dijon. I've had it set up in the sitting room. The children can't go to bed until they've seen the pictures." He turned and smiled at Céleste. "Don't you agree, Madame Valvert?"

Céleste nodded. "Oh, indeed. If you brought it especially for the children..." He was really behaving splendidly this evening, she thought. Perhaps he meant to atone for his sour arrival this afternoon. He'd sent her a very civil note, delivered to her rooms by his valet, inviting her to join him at dinner. And when she came into the dining room, she had been astonished to discover that Mademoiselle Daumard and the children had been invited, as well. He had chatted pleasantly throughout the meal, raising friendly, impersonal topics when the conversation seemed to flag. He was still somewhat stiff with the children, but he seemed to be trying, pulling them into the discussions from time to time.

He'd seemed not to notice the first time Céleste used *thou* with the twins, but when she caught his eye, he'd turned red and looked away. An acknowledgment of his failings as a parent, perhaps—even if he wasn't ready for that kind of intimacy with the children. And the gift of the magic lantern had been thoughtful. Céleste suddenly remembered that he'd brought books for them on his last visit. Perhaps it was his way of compensating for his cool reserve.

"They can sleep a bit later in the morning, can't they, Mademoiselle Daumard?" she asked.

The governess nodded. "Let me take them to their rooms first, and get them into nightclothes. We'll join you in the sitting room in a few minutes."

"An excellent idea, to get comfortable," said Edmond. He snapped his fingers at a hovering servant. "Have my valet bring me a dressing gown and slippers to the *petit salon.*" He looked at Céleste. "We shall have a domestic evening, *madame.* Lest you think I don't know how," he added with a smirk.

She couldn't resist the gibe. "On the contrary," she said, "I know a great deal about your domestic capabilities."

Mademoiselle Daumard cleared her throat and rose quickly from her chair. "Children?" She ushered them from the room like a mother hen guarding her brood from wickedness.

They moved to the sitting room for coffee. The magic lantern had been set on the table in the middle of the room, and a large white sheet was pinned to one wall. The valet appeared, and Edmond's evening coat and waistcoat were exchanged for a handsome flowered silk dressing gown, his patent leather pumps for slippers. In a few minutes, the children, dressed for bed, came in laughing excitedly. They threw themselves onto a mound of pillows on the floor, facing the sheet.

When they'd settled down, Edmond lit the oil lamp in the magic lantern and inserted a glass slide. Immediately a brightly colored image appeared on the sheet—a ferocious-looking tiger in shades of deep gold and brown against a dark green jungle. Albertine exclaimed in alarm at the size of the creature's teeth, but Albert declared that it wasn't such a frightful sight for a *boy* to see. The tiger was followed by a dozen more exotic animals, and then a set of colored drawings showing the mysterious cities of North Africa, still a novelty, since France had only recently conquered Algiers.

"Now," said Edmond, producing a large book and a new box of slides, "we shall need Madame Valvert's assistance for this set."

Céleste moved toward him. "Of course."

The slides turned out to be a children's fairy story; the book was the accompanying text. While Edmond showed the pictures, Céleste read aloud in her clear voice. It was a story of noble adventures and exciting rescues, of a beautiful heroine and a brave hero. The pictures were so wonderfully drawn, and Céleste's reading was so vivid and dramatic, that the children were enthralled. They clapped with delight at the successful conclusion of each episode, and sighed when the last slide had been shown and Céleste closed the book.

Edmond turned off the lamp in the lantern, picked up his cherrywood pipe and sat down in his large velvet armchair before the fire. He stretched out his long legs, crossing them lazily at the ankles, tucked up the skirts of his dressing gown and smiled at the children. "To bed, now. We'll leave the magic lantern here. Perhaps Mademoiselle Daumard will show the pictures again in the morning. Good night." He hesitated, then offered his cheek for the children's kisses. They came to him with an easy manner that warmed Céleste's heart—though they still kissed him formally on both cheeks. Then they skipped to Céleste to receive their usual hugs and scampered from the room.

When they had gone—their happy laughter fading up the staircase—Céleste leaned against the mantel and played nervously with a little silver matchbox. She wasn't sure whether she should leave or stay; she and Edmond hadn't been alone once since his return. She dreaded the moment he'd ask about Paul again, and yet she ached to tell him everything.

"An amusing book," she murmured at last, for want of something better to say. "And the pictures were charming."

"Yes."

"The children seemed to enjoy themselves."

"Yes." He frowned at his unlit pipe. "Would you care to play cards tonight?"

"No, thank you."

"Music? Billiards?" He seemed as uneasy as she, as though he wanted to apologize but didn't know how.

"No. I think I'll go to bed soon. Skating always tires me."

"Of course."

The fire gave a pop, and a live coal leapt onto the carpet in front of Edmond's chair. Céleste quickly extinguished it with the toe of her slipper. She smiled, filled with an old memory. "A *bourguignon,* my grandfather used to call them. A Burgundian, full of noise and fire."

"Careful," he said, scowling. "You're in Burgundy now."

She looked down, regretting more than her words. "I always seem to say the wrong things, don't I?"

"No more than I," he growled. He lifted his chin and stared fixedly at her. His eyes were deep blue, dark with remembrance and remorse for his last cruel kiss.

She couldn't bear the intimacy of his look. She turned away and picked up the matchbox. "Permit me." She moved to him, struck a match and held it to the bowl of his pipe.

He puffed for a few minutes, his eyes never leaving her face. Then, when his pipe was lit, he put it aside, took the matchbox from her and set it on the table next to his pipe. "Thank you," he said. Before she could turn away, he clasped her hand in his and brought it to his lips for a gentle kiss. She trembled, moved and touched by the sweetness of the unexpected gesture. What did he want from her? There was no passion in the kiss, only a heartbreaking tenderness. It left her confused, her thoughts spinning, her fragile emotions tossed about like a ship on a far sea.

While she foundered, still trying to recover herself, he wrapped one arm around her waist and gently pulled her down to sit on his lap. There was nothing threatening in the way he'd done it. It felt as natural as sitting on Grandpapa's knee when he'd let her stay up late as a little child. She felt neither embarrassed nor self-conscious. She belonged here, safe in the harbor of Edmond's embrace. She sighed and leaned against his chest.

He said nothing. He held her more tightly and reached for his pipe again. They sat that way for a very long time, while the aromatic smoke curled above their heads and the fire burned down. There seemed no need for words; the magic of the blue-tipped flames and the glowing embers cast a spell that filled the silent room with the beating of their hearts, the serene contentment of the moment.

At last Edmond stirred and put down his pipe. "It grows late," he said," and the fire is dying. I fear we'll need another log."

"No." She stood up. It was too dangerously comfortable to be on his lap, to feel the warmth of his arms around her, the quickening of her senses. "It's very late. Nicole will be waiting for me." She moved to the door. She was suddenly afraid to look at him. Dreading to see . . . What? Indifference? But surely not. Not after they had so intimately shared the night and the fire and the companionable silence of the room. Desire? Raw, naked hunger? She couldn't bear that tonight, either. "Good night," she murmured without turning around and reached for the door.

"Céleste." His voice was low and thrilling, vibrating with a tenderness that sent shivers down her spine. She turned, hope and fear shining in her eyes.

He rose from his chair and came toward her, his steps unsure and hesitant. "Thou art beautiful," he whispered. There was pain on his face, uncertainty in his eyes, as though he waited for her rejection and dreaded the sentence that would plunge him into despair.

She ached with longing. What to do? "Thou," he had said. Did he mean it? Or was it just the easy, careless seduction of a lover, hungry for his mistress? He was clearly waiting for a sign in return. She could hold fast to her pride and leave, unwilling to gamble that his feelings ran deeper than mere desire. Or she could stay, take a chance, hold out her hand...

Foolish Céleste, she thought. As though her heart had any choice! She smiled and returned his impassioned gaze. "My door will be open."

There was no unseemly triumph on his face, only warmth and gratitude. "In half an hour?"

"Yes."

He returned her smile, his clear blue eyes praising her with a glance that swept her trembling body. "Beautiful Céleste. We shall have a night of passion that neither of us will forget." He kissed her on the lips and put his hands on either side of her braided coiffure. "Wear your hair unbound for me," he said, "and let me drown in its scented glory."

Oh, Edmond, she thought. Thou art my beloved. How can I teach thee to see it?

Chapter Eighteen

"**Y**ou left your hair up." Edmond stood in the doorway of her boudoir and frowned at the dark curls piled high on her head.

She smiled at him through half-closed eyes. How handsome he was by the light from the hearth. She had extinguished all the lamps; only fireplaces lit this room and her bedchamber. She laughed softly at the look on his face. "Perhaps I like to be perverse," she said teasingly.

He closed the door behind him and strode to her, pulling her roughly into his arms. "Do you take such joy in tormenting me?" he muttered, and pressed his mouth to hers.

His kiss was hot and impassioned, inflaming her senses. But it wasn't what she wanted. She stiffened, deliberately refusing to respond to his lips. And when he released her and stepped back, scowling, she thrust out her lower lip in annoyance. "Do you think you can bully me by behaving like a big, angry bear?" she asked. "Suspecting my reasons, whatever I do?"

He looked disconcerted. "Céleste...I..." He made a growling sound in his throat.

"I didn't leave my hair up to torment you," she said, "but to please you. I thought you might prefer to take it down yourself. It's only held with a few pins."

He swore softly. "What a fool I am. Why do I treat you with such distrust?"

Because I'm no different for you than any other woman, she thought sadly. There was still a war going on in his heart, and she—womankind—was the enemy. She shook off her melancholy. She wanted tonight to be different, to be wonderful and magical. To continue the sweet tenderness that had begun downstairs, in the sitting room. She sighed and moved into his arms. "Oh, Edmond, can't we pretend tonight that we have no past, and no future?"

He kissed her gently. "We shall begin afresh." He returned to the doorway, and this time, when he looked at her, he smiled. "You look charming that way, *madame,* but will you let me unpin your hair?"

She returned his smile with an innocent giggle and held out her hands. "Only after a forfeit. At least half a hundred kisses, I should think."

He groaned. "Sweet forfeit. I can scarcely wait." He took her hands and kissed them, finger by finger, until she trembled for joy. Then he released them and began to work on the ties of her dressing gown.

"So soon?" she said, dismayed at his seeming haste.

He laughed and stripped the dressing gown from her.

"Edmond..." Couldn't he understand that she wasn't ready? "But my kisses..."

"I haven't forgotten." He lifted her nightdress over her head and tossed it down. His hands returned to caress her naked body, and he laughed again. "But I claim the right to choose *where* the kisses go. For example..." He bent his head to her breast.

His kisses were soft, arousing her flesh in a gentle crescendo of pleasure. His tongue circled the pink tips of her breasts, his lips teased and stroked the firm white curves. She gasped in delight and threw back her head, thrusting her straining bosom closer to his hot mouth.

His kisses drifted lower. He dropped to his knees and put his strong hands around her hips. His hands cradled her buttocks, and his mouth sought her flat belly—and below.

"No more," she panted, breathless with ecstasy, "I can barely stand."

"But I must earn the privilege of being your coiffeur," he said mockingly, and teased her with his tongue and his lips until her whole body throbbed.

"Merciful heaven." She sank to the carpet, quivering. It was too sweet, too exquisite, to be endured.

He stood up and shrugged out of his dressing gown. He was naked beneath it, and his beautiful masculine body was hard and poised for her. He picked her up and carried her into the bedchamber, laying her gently across the sheets. She burned with a wild heat, wanting him, waiting for him. She let her knees fall wide.

He shook his head. "Not yet. Turn over." He loomed over her, the outline of his shoulders massive in the dimness. She smiled uneasily. "Do as you're told. Turn over," he repeated.

"Edmond?" She couldn't be sure, but she suspected that he was more annoyed about her hair than he chose to admit.

"Don't you trust me?" he asked. "I thought that was what we needed between us. Trust."

Reluctantly she did as he had ordered, burying her face in the pillow. After all, she did trust him, didn't she? Ah, but did he trust *her?* Were thoughts of Paul hovering in his brain? She gulped and waited.

The first kiss was delivered to the nape of her neck, the second a scant inch lower. While she writhed in delicious agony, he kissed every inch of her back—her spine, her rounded bottom, the backs of her legs. Even the soles of her feet. By the time he was finished, she was moaning, her body taut with an aching need. "For the love of God, Edmond," she gasped, "you've earned your privileges. And more. Don't torment me any longer."

He lay down on the bed and lifted her so that she was straddling his body, her throbbing core poised above his manhood. His eyes glittered with passion, but he didn't move.

Now! she thought. Why was he waiting? The agony was more than she could endure. She tried to force her body down onto his hard shaft, but he prevented it.

"It's time for *your* forfeit," he growled. "Loose your hair for me."

She was a captive of her own desires. If this was a war, in some subtle way he'd won it. She reached up with shaking hands and pulled the pins from her curls. At once the heavy tresses cascaded down to cover her shoulders and hover above his heaving chest.

As if to reward her obedience, he pulled her hips down to his loins and thrust into her. She cried aloud at the exquisite sensation, her blood pounding in her temples. They rode out the tempest together, twisting and tossing on the bed in an excess of frenzied passion that was even more thrilling than their first coupling had been. As before, Edmond signaled his climax with a great, savage roar that quickened Céleste's own release.

At length Edmond stirred, untangled himself from Céleste's long tresses, sat up and smiled down at her. "I'm not sure I should tell you this," he said, his mouth twitching, "but it is a very great pleasure to make love to you. You're a woman of fire and passion."

She was glad the room was dim, to hide her blush. "It must be all those lovers I've had," she said with a giggle.

His brow darkened. "Is it?"

"Oh, Edmond!" She sat up in her turn. "Surely you don't still believe those rumors... Dear God, you *can't*."

He looked uncomfortable. "No, I..."

"I had a husband. You know that. But he was the only man who ever shared my bed, until now. I swear it."

He lay back down against the pillow and covered his eyes with his hand. "Forgive me. I don't know why I do that."

"Not every wife is unfaithful," she said gently.

"Nor every husband so rigid and unforgiving? Is that what you mean?"

Did it trouble his conscience? "Who knows?" she said. "Perhaps you could have forgiven your Joséphine in time, if chance hadn't taken her from you. Perhaps you can find it in your heart to forgive her even now. And lay the ghosts to rest," she added fervently.

"Never," he groaned. "Not after Jean-Claude."

She remembered the dreadful story that Mademoiselle Daumard had told, of Edmond weeping, not wanting them to bury his child. She nestled closer to him, to give him the warmth and comfort of her body. "Tell me about Jean-Claude," she said softly.

He gulped and rubbed his hand across his mouth. "Why should I tell it?" he growled. "Let the past be gone."

She stroked the curls at his forehead. "But it isn't. It torments you every minute of every day. I see it in your eyes."

He looked fixedly at her. It was a look almost of fear, as though it dismayed him to have his soul revealed. He closed his eyes on her searching gaze and turned his head aside. "He was my shadow," he said at last. "My mirror image." His voice was a hoarse croak. "He would follow me around Rochemont, aping my gestures. From the time he was very little. And sometimes I'd find him in my wardrobe, marching about in my shoes and waistcoats. I taught him to play chess when he was five. He had a fine mind, and a depth of understanding... Sometimes I'd forget he was only a child. We rode together. Went fishing together. And sometimes we—" His voice cracked. "Oh, God," he cried, "what's the point of this?" He stared up at the canopy of Céleste's bed. Even in the dimness she could see the sparkle of tears in his eyes.

"Did he have a talent for music?"

He brushed at his eyes and laughed softly. "Not a bit. He couldn't hold a tune, and his fingers were short. But he liked to listen. And criticize my playing. We sometimes joked that he would become a sharp-penned music critic when he grew up, and make and break careers. When he grew up," he repeated bitterly. *"Nom de Dieu!"* he burst out, sitting up and running his hands through his hair. "This is absurd. I can't bring him back by dwelling on the past."

She hesitated, wondering if it was her place to interfere, then plunged ahead. "How fortunate that you still have two children."

His eyes glowed with dark anger. "Damn it, you can say that to me? Knowing what you know of their lineage?"

She shook her head in exasperation. The man was completely blind! "Tell me," she demanded, "do you intend to repudiate them? To reveal Joséphine's adulteries and deny to the world that you're the twins' father?"

He looked surprised at such a scandalous suggestion. "Of course not."

"Then why can't you embrace them as your own? Mademoiselle Daumard, as kind as she is, is a poor substitute for a loving father."

"Whoever he may be," he said bitterly.

"*You* are the only father they know. What else matters? And didn't you tell me that there is some possibility that they could be yours?"

"Yes, but..."

"Then why deny them the devoted father that Jean-Claude had? The twins are blameless. And they worship you. Albertine goes around touching everything that belongs to you. With such love in the gesture..."

"This isn't your affair," he growled.

She ignored that. "They're very musical, by the way. Albert has a good ear. You might consider hiring a piano teacher. Eight isn't too young to begin."

"I don't need your interference."

She clasped his bare shoulder and shook it. "Edmond, you have a *family*. Do you know how blessed you are? I'm all alone, and I envy you. Children, aunts, cousins..." She bit her lip. The only Beaufort cousin she knew about was named Paul. What a stupid thing to say! She wondered if her words had reminded Edmond of Paul, as well.

They had. His mouth twisted in an unpleasant smile. "But you collected admirers, instead...to make up for your lack of family."

"I told you," she snapped, "I was faithful and chaste, even after my husband died."

"Until you met me, of course." He peered at her, one eyebrow arched sharply in curiosity. "Why did you choose me?"

She wasn't fool enough to confess her love again. Certainly not while he was looking at her with such skepticism. She shrugged. "I had my reasons."

He smiled seductively and stroked her forearm with one long finger. "I think I can guess," he said. "But, of course, you wanted Paul before me. I haven't forgotten the inn. Save for my interference, you might now be sharing Paul's bed, and not mine."

Her heart was filled with pain. Would they quarrel about Paul again? Tonight of all nights, when she had hoped to shut out reality from their sweet paradise of love? She struggled against her tears. "Please," she begged, "I don't want to talk about Paul tonight. We said we wouldn't."

"No," he said, gathering her into his arms. "The devil with Paul. And anything else that makes us sad or angry tonight." He bent and kissed her. And when his caressing mouth teased her and sent her emotions spinning out of control, she knew that Paul had ceased to exist.

His lovemaking was leisurely, with a sweet gentleness that took delight in every unhurried kiss, every soft caress. Céleste found herself responding in kind, touching and kissing him in ways that she wouldn't have dreamed of with Alex. There had never been enough time with Alex. He had always been too impatient for his own release, impatient for her passion to take fire.

But Edmond seemed to enjoy every moment, to savor the lingering embraces, the tender glances, the exquisite tension that quickened to the final heart-stopping, thrusting climax. When it was over, they sighed in the same breath and collapsed in exhaustion.

Edmond stroked back the tangled curls from her brow and smiled tenderly. "You enchanting creature. Why is it I'm so helpless to resist your allure?"

"You say that as though it were a weakness to care for someone else—to need them."

"Isn't it? Aren't we better off in our own separate worlds?" His voice was so joyless that it broke her heart. He sighed again and kissed her. "But you wouldn't know that, would you? You have a heart that's big enough to embrace the world." He pulled the coverlet over their two bodies, and tucked Céleste into the curve of his arm. "I'll stay till morning, if you're agreeable. I'm sure my servants won't be surprised."

Céleste laughed softly and scratched at the thatch on his chest. It gave a sensuous thrill to her fingers. "I'm not sure if Nicole knows, but she almost smirked tonight as she was helping me get ready for bed. I think she's hopelessly romantic."

"Or very practical. I'll see that she gets a generous tip, to ensure her discretion." He grunted in contentment, kissed Céleste once more, and closed his eyes. In a few minutes, he was asleep.

But sleep eluded Céleste. Her body was sated and comfortable, still filled with remembered pleasure. She thought at first that was why she couldn't sleep. Her senses were still too aroused, her nerves too excited to allow her to relax. But after a while she knew that it was her churning brain, not her overwrought body, that was keeping her awake. She eased herself from Edmond's arms and crawled out of bed. The fire had died down; a few glowing embers and smoldering logs remained. She sat curled up before its warmth and thought of Alex.

She had never pleased him in bed. And, until tonight, she had always thought it was her fault. One more reason to feel guilty toward his memory. But now, with her lips still tingling from Edmond's kisses, she found it difficult to escape the thought that perhaps Alex had really tried to please her. He had always forced himself upon her with such violence and haste that her body—aroused though it was by his kisses—was still unprepared to receive him. While she would struggle to hide her discomfort, he would quickly satisfy himself. It had always been an angry moment for him, because she was unable to match his fire.

And always afterward... That was the most disturbing to recall. They would lie together, still joined. Céleste would feel him within her, feel the reawakening of his desire, feel the stirrings in herself of a passion that hadn't had time to blossom the first time.

In a little while, Alex would withdraw from her, and she would wait. Hoping, anticipating. But he would arise from the bed—his face a study in strained patience and noble forbearance—and dress and leave her alone.

Remembering, Céleste felt her back stiffen in sudden anger. To go to a whore! That was where he had gone, night after night. She'd denied it to herself all this time. But Edmond's lovemaking had made her understand at last. Alex had been ready and eager to make love again, and she had been too naive to realize it. Too innocent to understand how utterly selfish he was. Not only had he been repeatedly unfaithful to her with other women, but he had also withheld the pleasure he might have given *her,* had he stayed. Pleasure that Edmond had shown her she was capable of experiencing.

And Alex had sworn he loved her—at least while they were still in Rome. And she'd believed him, and mourned the death of her lover, and suffered remorse because of her imagined failings. But for Edmond, she would have gone on feeling guilty forever.

She hugged her knees and began to weep. She didn't know if she was mourning the loss of her illusions about Alex, or weeping in gratitude for Edmond. He might be incapable of losing his heart to love, but in the few weeks she'd known him, he'd shown more thoughtful concern than Alex had in more than two and a half years of marriage. She wept for a very long time—hot, bitter tears—hunched over the fire and quivering.

At last she stilled. It was late, and she feared to disturb Edmond. She dried her eyes and returned to his side. In his sleep, he reached out and pulled her close; she smiled in contentment and snuggled into his embrace. She didn't know what would happen between them. She thought that, in spite of the LaGranges, she might tell Edmond everything in the morning. If not, she could tell him after Paul was safely married to Élise de Malecot. When he saw how happy she was, how could he doubt her love for him?

But in the meantime, she was home. Tonight she was where she belonged.

"Good morning, *madame.*" Nicole set the tea tray on the bedside table and went to build up the fire.

Céleste stretched and sat up. Strange. She was wearing her nightdress, and her dressing gown lay at the foot of her bed. Edmond? she thought. She remembered it as if it were a dream, his strong hands lifting her shoulders, slipping the nightdress over her head. She looked at the place beside her in the bed. It was empty. And the pillows had been plumped to look as though no one had slept on them. Had he decided on discretion, after all? Or was he regretting something he hoped would never happen again?

She frowned and punched at her pillows, then leaned over and helped herself to the tea. "What time is it?"

"Well after nine, *madame.*"

"Did...Monsieur de Beaufort indicate that he wants to go riding this morning?"

"He didn't say, *madame.* But he went out early in his coupé. And he had a traveling bag with him, so perhaps he intends to be gone a good part of the day."

"How strange. He didn't tell me he was going anywhere." She was growing more and more uneasy. The last time he'd left like this, they'd quarreled. Had she done something last night to drive him away? "I'm sure it's just a short errand," she said, trying to reassure herself.

"I have no doubt of it, *madame*. I'm sure he'll return in time to see you off on your journey."

She nearly choked on the tea. "My journey?"

"Yes. It was the last thing he said to Madame Léopold. That she was to have the large carriage prepared to take you back to Paris this afternoon."

She set down the cup with shaking hands. "He can't have said that."

"I heard it myself, and that's a fact," said Nicole, with an emphatic nod of her head. "And then he gave me a letter to give to you."

"Dear God! A letter? What are you waiting for? Give it here."

"No, *madame*. Monsieur de Beaufort wanted me to wait until you were bathed and dressed and settled comfortably."

To cushion the blow of the letter? she thought, dreading the worst. "Give it to me now. I'll be no more calm than I am at this moment. She took the letter and tore it open, reading the words with a mixture of pain and disbelief.

Sweet Céleste, I leave this morning with a heavy heart, but with the belief that it is the only decent thing to do. I hope you will understand that I do this out of my deepest respect for you.

I have not always thought as well of you as I should. I know what has existed between us from the first—a passionate attraction that could only conclude as it did. But, while I could forgive that weakness in myself, I held you to a higher, more rigorous standard.

I remember once your anger that a man could have affairs and flaunt them proudly, while a woman was expected to be a saint. It shames me now to think of my narrow-mindedness, however much I justified my reasons because of my own history.

And then I saw you weeping before the fire last night. Yes, I confess it. I was awake. I cannot begin to tell you how your tears moved and touched me. You, who are always so calm and self-contained.

I realize now that you wept because of your confusion. Your heart is with Paul, as it always was. And I was cruel to seduce you away. To beguile your senses and make you think—even for a moment—that desire could ever be the same as love.

I curse myself now for what I did. I seduced you and betrayed my cousin. Not to protect my family's name, but because I wanted you. I shall continue to want you, my sweet angel of the night. But you love Paul and he loves you. And I am a poor substitute, I assure you.

I want you to be happy, my sweet Céleste. I've left my carriage to take you back to Paris. When Paul returns to you from Aix, I pray your happiness will be complete. I give Paul to you with my blessing. Edmond.

The letter dropped from Céleste's hands. "The fool," she groaned.

"What is it, *madame?*"

"He's gone away. He wants me to go back to Paris and wait for his cousin."

Nicole gaped. "His cousin? *You,* Madame Valvert? Were you the one who—? We heard the stories about a woman in Paris, when Monsieur Paul's mother was here, but— You were the woman?"

She buried her face in her hands. "Oh, it's all so stupid."

"Shall I pack, *madame?*"

"Yes. Pack. Why not?" she said with bitterness. She had been dismissed by her lover. The blind fool, he had misun-

derstood everything! "I'll leave for Paris this afternoon."
She frowned. All she really wanted to do was run away. Why
should she return to Paris and throw herself back into that
cauldron? "No. Tell the coachman I'll go to wherever I can
catch the *diligence.*"

"But the coachman can take you where you want to go,
madame."

She smiled crookedly. "Even to Rome?"

"Rome? But why do you want to go there? If Monsieur
Paul is in Paris—"

"For the love of God," she exclaimed, "I don't *want*
Paul."

"I knew it!" Nicole beamed with satisfaction. "You're in
love with Monsieur Edmond."

"Is it so obvious?"

"Well, maybe not to some. But it is to me."

Céleste sighed. "What does it matter? His interest in
me... Well, you're clever. I think you can guess what he
wants from me."

"Twaddle! All men start off that way. It takes them time
to know what they want. Besides, Monsieur Edmond has
feelings he doesn't even know of. I see it in his eyes when he
looks at you, and that's a fact. You give him time, and he'll
come around." She snorted. "But it won't do you any good
if you're in Rome!"

Céleste wondered if the girl was right. If she pursued him,
could she make him love her? Did he love her already, as
Nicole seemed to suggest? Perhaps he was sending her to
Paul because he was afraid of his own feelings. Afraid that
he was growing too fond of her for his own heart's safety.
But... "I don't even know where he's gone," she said. "Nor
do you. For all we know, he's off to foreign lands."

Nicole shook her head. "He has to be in Paris before
Lent. On business. I remember hearing him tell Madame
Léopold. That's only—" she counted on her fingers
"—twelve days. If you leave today, you won't get to Paris
until Tuesday. And then its just a week." Her eyes lit up.

"And you'll be there for Carnival, which should make the time pass. Oh, how I envy you!'

Yes, thought Céleste, it made sense. She'd go back to Paris and wait for Edmond. It would give her time to close the book on the past. She would write a letter to Paul at Aix-les-Bains, telling him once and for all that it was over. She would make her peace with the LaGranges. She would wait for Edmond to come to Paris. And then she would begin her campaign for his heart.

Saying goodbye to the children was the most difficult. They wept bitterly. She held them tightly in her arms and kissed them and promised to write. Though it was a sad parting, her heart was filled with a secret, joyous, wild hope. If she could get Edmond to admit the strength of his feelings for her, there might come a time when these lovely children could call her "Mama."

"May it be so," she whispered, climbing into her carriage. She turned and gave a final wave to the twins, then settled herself for the long ride to find her heart.

Chapter Nineteen

"**Y**ou're already dressed for the masked ball?" Madame de LaGrange scanned Céleste's gold satin gown and turban, her multicolored mantle, brocaded in exotic designs, and the lace-edged black domino mask she held in her hand.

"The baron de Lansac is giving a small dinner party before we go on to the opera house," replied Céleste. She had been back in Paris for nearly a week; in that time, she'd sent Joseph to Edmond's *hôtel* in the rue Saint-Dominique twice a day, to inquire discreetly if Monsieur de Beaufort had yet returned. Even though she'd been disappointed, she had kept herself busy.

She had rehired her servants and arranged a secret meeting in the Bois with the LaGranges. She had turned aside their prying questions, managing to suggest—without actually lying about it—that she had returned from a brief holiday in Rome. After their initial surprise at seeing her again so soon, they had left her in peace for most of the time—until today.

She had next gone to see Monsieur de Lansac, her grandfather's old friend. She had chided him for unkindly suspecting that she had been Desrosiers's mistress, then had enlisted his aid. If she was to have any chance to win Edmond, she guessed that a good name and a restored reputation would go far toward persuading him. After the shame he'd felt because of his wife, he would be sensitive to gossip about Céleste. With Lansac's influence, she had had herself invited to the most proper gatherings this week, and she had dressed sedately and behaved with a restraint that seemed to cast doubt on all the previous rumors that had swirled around her name.

"Are the streets as crowded as I expected?" asked Monsieur de LaGrange in his usual mournful tone.

"Oh, yes. Everyone is anticipating tomorrow's carnival parade. I think half of Paris has begun to celebrate early. No one paid any attention to my carriage. It was perfectly safe to come here this evening. As you surmised." She looked around the disordered room. They were in the viscount's study. LaGrange was in the habit of taking down books from the shelves and leaving them scattered about—a habit that infuriated Madame de LaGrange. Céleste removed a pile of books from a chair and perched on the edge of it. "Why did you want to see me?"

She could tell from the looks they exchanged that something was troubling them, but she couldn't guess what it could be. They hadn't asked her to do anything against the Malecots, though she feared they were simply waiting for Paul's return in order to urge her to continue her seduction.

Madame de LaGrange lifted her little dog and set the creature on her shoulder, turning to nuzzle it softly. "Did you hear that, Pépin?" she asked. "Our son's widow wants to know why she's here."

Oh, Lord, thought Céleste. It was always something dreadful, when Madame de LaGrange talked to her through her dog. She sighed. "What have I done?"

"Nothing important," said LaGrange sarcastically. "You merely broke your pledge to us."

She shook her head, bewildered. "No. Not as far as I know."

Madame de LaGrange clicked her tongue. "How we suffer, Pépin..." She raised her head and glared at Céleste.

"Did you, or did you not, write to Paul de Beaufort at Aix-les-Bains this morning?" she demanded in her sharp voice.

How could they know that? "Yes, I did. But..."

"And rejected him out of hand?"

"Yes, but..." Now she really was going to box Thérèse's ears! When the girl's loyalty to the LaGranges extended to snooping! She distinctly remembered she'd left her writing table for a moment to fetch an envelope for Paul's letter. And Thérèse had been in the room. "I told you I was going to do it," she said defensively.

"But you swore that it wouldn't be until Paul returned from Aix. Didn't it occur to you that that might change all our plans?"

"If your plans involve Paul, I said I wouldn't go through with that scheme. That I was finished with it. Under the circumstances, I saw nothing wrong in writing to Paul now." She took a deep breath. "Besides," she said, "I... I think I'm in love with Edmond de Beaufort. I don't want him to fear his cousin as a rival. In point of fact, if it should become necessary to convince him of my feelings, I intend to tell him the truth."

"Oh, my God, my God! You *have* been seeing him! That scene in your box— Faithless, lying schemer!" Madame de LaGrange shook so violently that Pépin was dislodged from her shoulder and went scrambling to the floor, where he hid under her chair.

LaGrange began to pace rapidly around the room, grimacing and rubbing at his shoulder. "Is there anything more you can do to make your betrayal complete?" he asked. His voice was agitated, and high-pitched with outrage.

"Please," she said, taken aback by the extremeness of their reaction. She stood up and put her hand on his arm, trying to placate him. "I... didn't mean it to happen. And I swear I won't tell Edmond unless I must. And once Paul gets my letter, I'm sure that he'll retire from the field like a gentleman. There will be no need to say anything, I'm sure."

LaGrange shook off her hand. "You killed our grandson in the womb with your carelessness. And now you even forget your vow to Alex." His blue-green eyes—so like his son's—bored into her, dark and accusing, playing the old familiar chords of guilt.

But this time she remembered how Alex's eyes had looked at her, so open, so loving—even as he was betraying his own vow of marriage. "I'll never forget Alex," she said. "But what I do is between my conscience and me."

"And the Malecots?" LaGrange had begun to quiver.

For the first time, Céleste felt pity for him, this maimed, embittered old man who had already depleted half his fortune on this mad feud. "Dear God," she pleaded, "why can't you let it rest, once and for all? It's destroying you. Lent begins on Wednesday. The Easter season. The time of redemption. Can't you make your peace with the Malecots, after all these years?"

LaGrange nervously pulled down a book from the shelves, riffled through it, then tossed it on a large pile of books on his desk. "It will all be resolved when I have a new plan," he said.

She sighed. They would never let go of their hatred. "What plan? Short of dueling with the man, what can you do?"

"I'll think of something. But in the meantime, for God's sake, say nothing to Edmond de Beaufort."

He seemed so distraught that she dared not quarrel with him. "Of course not." She picked up her gloves and reticule. "What time will you be at the Opera Ball?"

Madame de LaGrange, a little more calm, had coaxed Pépin back onto her lap and was now scratching the animal's ears. "Not until eleven. I shall wear my blue gauze ball gown. Monsieur will be costumed as a bat."

"I'll look for you. I think I can safely nod a greeting, don't you? We've seen each other often enough in public. To snub you entirely would cause more gossip."

"Do as you wish," muttered LaGrange bitterly as Céleste moved toward the door. "I shall die knowing my enemy still lives content in the bosom of his family."

The opera house was blazing with lights. The great foyer, where the patrons usually milled about with the opera singers and ballet dancers in hopes of arranging a rendezvous, had been turned into a dancing floor for the masked ball. The balcony surrounding the *foyer* had been set up with small tables and a buffet that served refreshments and champagne. Some of the guests, anticipating Mardi Gras, the highlight of carnival week, had arrived in full costume, and the room was a swirl of brilliant colors and fabrics and spangles.

Céleste removed her own colorful mantle of "Ali Baba" cloth and handed it to the maid in the cloakroom, receiving a numbered slip in return. Her gold gown had a low, wide collar that rested on fashionably large leg-of-mutton sleeves—the width of the neckline accented her trim waist, her white, sloping shoulders. She felt quite beautiful tonight as she peered at the crowd through her mask. Wouldn't it be wonderful if Edmond should appear unexpectedly?

The evening passed pleasantly enough, though it seemed somehow empty without him, despite the crowds. She danced with a great many partners. The anonymity of a mask removed all constraints, including the need for proper introductions. Of course, the masks scarcely deceived anyone. Indeed, Céleste heard her name whispered more than once as she passed a cluster of gossiping women.

She drifted in and out of the theater, where a ballet was being presented on the large stage. No one seemed to be paying much attention to it, except for a handful of aging roués and young dandies, who had come merely to see, and comment on, the dancers' scanty costumes.

Céleste saw the LaGranges several times, and nodded politely when they passed on the stairs or in the *foyer*. Madame de LaGrange was overdressed, as usual, with far too many silk flowers and glittering bows for her ample bulk. Monsieur de LaGrange was indeed costumed as a bat, with a headpiece that covered most of his face, and a pair of bat wings that cleverly concealed his missing arm. At midnight, almost everyone removed their masks and pretended to be surprised at the faces beneath.

After a while, Céleste began to regret that she'd come at all. The baron de Lansac had gotten quite tipsy and gone home early, and the rest of his dinner guests had drifted off into the crowd. She was tired of dancing with strangers, and sated from food and drink. It was still quite early, perhaps only one or two in the morning, but she decided to call for her carriage and go home. She reclaimed her mantle and started down the broad staircase, ignoring the LaGranges' look of surprise as they watched her from the balcony.

"Madame Valvert. If you please."

She stopped on the landing and turned. A young woman, still masked, was coming down the stairs toward her. Céleste frowned. There was something familiar about her—the soft blond curls, the frail delicacy of the woman's limbs.... Dear God, she thought, it's Élise de Malecot! She swallowed her surprise and managed to smile graciously. "You wished to speak to me, *mademoiselle?*"

"Forgive my mask," the girl whispered, "but..."

"But it would be lowering your station to be seen talking to me?" she finished, not without an edge of bitterness to her voice. If society considered her a less-than-perfect woman, she had no one but herself to blame. She had willingly agreed to the LaGranges' mad plans in the first place.

"Please, *madame,* this is so difficult." The girl opened her fan and cooled her flaming cheeks. "I have no right..." She stared at Céleste through her mask; her eyes were a silvery gray, and as innocent as the dawn. "You *do* know who I am?"

Céleste nodded. "Yes, of course. How old are you?" she asked on impulse.

"Almost nineteen, *madame*."

Just the perfect age for Paul, she thought. Edmond was right. "What did you wish to say to me?" she said gently.

The delicate mouth trembled, and tears glittered in the eyes behind the mask. Élise's words rushed forth in a breathless torrent. "We were supposed to be married on the seventh of March, but he wrote to me from Aix. He wants to... postpone it, and... Oh, *madame!* I know I have no right to ask it, but I beg you—" Her voice caught on a sob. "I shall go to church and pray every day for your future happiness and peace, if you'll only give him up. Release him to me, *madame*. You, who are so lovely, with so many admirers... Why do you need one more? And I love him..."

Deeply moved, Céleste held up her hand to silence the girl. "Please, my dear. Don't shame yourself. Say no more. It is I who have wronged *you*. Foolishly trampling on true love, for my own selfish reasons. Oh, I admit it. It was a simple flirtation on my part. Thoughtless and cruel. While I amused myself, your heart was breaking. But it's ended. It's over. I've already written to Paul at Aix, telling him so." She might as well repair as much of the damage as she could. "He never really cared that much for me, my dear. It was just a mad infatuation, which I selfishly encouraged. He may sulk for a bit—as men do—but in the end you'll discover that it was only his pride, and not his heart, that was damaged. Be patient, and forgive him." She clasped Élise's small hand in hers. "And forgive me, if you can," she said fervently.

The girl began to weep. "Oh, *madame,* how good you are. How noble. I shall never forget—"

"Élise! By all the saints, are you mad, to talk to that creature? Have you no pride or dignity?"

At the sound of the harsh voice, half the people in the *foyer* turned to stare at the figures on the landing. The man who came bounding toward Céleste was short and powerfully built. His features were coarse, and his brown hair was beginning to gray at the temples. His face was red, as though he'd had a great deal to drink. He glared at Élise and tore her hand from Céleste's grasp. "Explain yourself!" he demanded.

Élise trembled in terror. "Papa . . ." she whispered.

So this was Julien de Malecot, thought Céleste. The man who had killed Alex. He looked wild and savage; she could imagine him shooting Alex without a moment's hesitation. If all the other Malecots had been like this, small wonder the feud had never died. She felt a surge of unexpected anger. She hadn't thought she could still feel resentment toward Alex's killer. But she wasn't prepared to create an embarrassing scene to indulge her wrath. She controlled her emotions and bent her head in a nod of civility. "My discourse with Mademoiselle de Malecot is concluded, *monsieur*. And to her satisfaction, as you will learn. Please excuse me." She turned to go down the stairs.

He lurched forward to stand in front of her and block the way, his arms across his barrel chest. "What do you mean, satisfaction?"

"I mean, *monsieur,*" she said quietly, conscious of the gossips who had crowded closer, "that Paul is Élise's fiancé. I have no designs on him. Pray let me pass."

His lip curled in a sneer. "Why? So you can run and find another victim to toy with? Oh, I know your sort, *madame*. And so does everyone here." He made a sweeping gesture with his arm. "While you have your looks and youth, you parade your beauty at the opera or on the promenades of the Bois. You collect your men like charms on a watch fob, and with as little care. Your generals, your barons . . . You ride in your carriage and scorn the *filles publiques* who take their nightly walks along the boulevard des Italiens. But how many times can you turn a man's head? How many stories must make the rounds of the salons before you are no longer welcome, *madame?* Before the streets become your domain?"

Céleste felt the blood drain from her face, felt her heart contract with shock and horror. She stared, breathless, and when she finally managed to speak, it was through clenched teeth and punctuated with controlled gasps. "I have restored your daughter's happiness, *monsieur*. Would that you were as merciful in your dealings with others. Now let me pass."

"You won't escape the truth, *madame*. All of Paris shall know what you are!"

Her shock had turned to outrage. The drunken boor! Everyone was gawking in curiosity and fascination. Was there no man to defend her honor against such a vile attack? If only Edmond were here, she thought, feeling wretched and alone, Malecot wouldn't dare to say such dreadful things to her! Even now, she could imagine his fury when he learned of it. "I warn you, *monsieur*," she said, her voice rising in anger, "that I will not permit you to sully my name. Do you hear? You will regret any vile rumors you spread. I give you my word on that! Now, get out of my way!" She pushed him aside and stormed down the rest of the stairs.

She caught sight of the LaGranges on her way. Their smug smiles seemed to say, "What did you expect from a Malecot?"

She was still trembling when she reached her *hôtel,* and she felt sick at the memory when she awoke in the morning. She sat up tiredly in her bed, wishing she could sleep all day, and watched Thérèse prepare her tea.

"That dreadful man last night," said the girl, handing her a cup. "How could he say such things to you, *madame?*"

She frowned. "How do you know about him?"

"Oh, you slept for a long time, *madame*. I had time to visit the LaGranges and hear all about it. What awful things he said!" Thérèse's face was a study in sanctimonious disapproval.

She smiled sourly. God knows she'd brought it on herself, but still . . . "He might not have had as much to say, if you and the LaGranges hadn't spread so many rumors about me.''

The maid shrugged. "Well, what's done is done. And today is Shrove Tuesday, so you can have a gay time and forget all the horrible things he said. Now, let me see... You're dining with the baroness de Cloquet, then on to the Cirque-Olympique to see the bareback riders, then the ball at the École Militaire, then the ball at...''

She shook her head. "No. I don't want to go out at all today. Not after last night.''

Thérèse's face fell. "But, *madame,* you *have* to go out,'' she said anxiously. "How will it look? That Monsieur de Malecot's words have driven you from society? And then... what about me?''

Céleste nodded in understanding. It was Mardi Gras, after all. Except for her coachman, she'd already dismissed her servants for the next two days, and she'd told Thérèse that she might take the night off. With all the invitations she'd received, she had assumed that she wouldn't arrive home until dawn. And Thérèse was right: If she didn't put in an appearance *somewhere* tonight, the gossips would be convinced that every word Malecot had spoken was the truth, and that the wicked Madame Valvert was too ashamed to show her face.

"Well, perhaps I'll go to dinner at Madame de Cloquet's *hôtel,* at least. A small affair. My absence would be noted. And then I'll come home and go to bed. Around ten, I should guess.'' She caught sight of Thérèse's expression. "Now, don't fret,'' she added. "You can still take the whole night off, as we agreed. And come back late in the morning. I can let myself in after my dinner party.''

Thérèse brightened at once. "Oh, *madame,* how kind of you. And I have an idea. I'll leave a little cold snack in your boudoir. A fruit compote, and biscuits and wine. I know you like that sometimes before you go to bed.''

"Thank you. I think a sweet would be very agreeable. After an evening with the sour faces at the baroness's.''

She spent a quiet day in her studio, sketching and trying to ignore the sounds of revelry in the street outside. The music of a passing parade, the loud pops of firecrackers, the laughter and the singing. What did all that merriment matter to her when Edmond still hadn't returned?

She couldn't concentrate; her sketching went badly. She had reread *Hamlet* while at Rochemont; Edmond's copy of the book contained several handsome lithographs by Delacroix. She'd been struck by the ironies of Shakespeare's plot, and by the parallel with her own situation—a man forced against his will to avenge a wrongful death. It had stayed with her. And when, upon returning to Paris, she'd seen an ancient skull in an apothecary's shop window, she had determined to create a *Hamlet* still life. She'd found a beautifully carved old dagger in a shop filled with antique curiosities, a Renaissance goblet, and a length of ruby velvet. She'd even persuaded a florist to give her a handful of faded flowers and herbs to put beside the skull. She'd set everything on a pedestal, arranging and rearranging the various items until the composition satisfied her eye.

But her sketches today were abysmal. She worked for several hours, then gave it up. She tried to read, but that was no use, either. She felt edgy, but tired at the same time. At last she retired to her boudoir, lay down on a chaise longue and slept until Thérèse woke her to dress for dinner. The girl was already in a pretty little costume—a shepherdess's gown with a laced bodice and large panniers on her skirts. She bubbled with excitement as she helped Céleste dress, describing the balls in Montmartre, which were—she assured Céleste—far more lively than the balls of fashionable society.

Clad magnificently in silver gauze, Céleste put on her mask and the same colorful mantle she'd worn the night before, then hurried downstairs to her carriage. She insisted that Thérèse join her. "Let me take you to your ball before I go to Madame de Cloquet," she said over the girl's protests. "You'll never get a fiacre for hire tonight, and it's madness to try and walk."

Happy chaos reigned on the street. Costumed revelers crowded every inch of pavement and road, tooting horns and waving at everyone and everything. Party guests leaned out of windows, toasting the occasion with bottles of wine and tossing confetti down to the mobs below. The streets glittered with lights: torches carried aloft, lanterns hanging from trees and gateposts. Every house was ablaze. Thérèse clapped her hands in delight at everything. Her eyes were unnaturally bright, as though her anticipation of the night's events had already intoxicated her.

For Céleste, the evening wasn't nearly so exciting. Everyone at Madame de Cloquet's soirée was excessively polite and tried not to look directly at her, which only convinced her the more that every soul there had heard the scandalous gossip concerning Malecot and the masked ball at the opera house.

She excused herself as soon as she could without appearing to retreat, and sought the refuge of her carriage. She had her coachman drive past Edmond's house once more. She nearly burst into tears when she saw that the windows were still dark, and there was no sign of life. Oh, Edmond, she thought, anguished, where are you? Nicole had said he planned to return before Lent; tomorrow was Ash Wednesday, and he still hadn't come back to Paris.

When they reached her *hôtel*, she dismissed her coachman, brushing aside his fervent gratitude that he was now free to enjoy carnival like the rest of the Parisians. The clock in her large drawing room was just sounding the hour of ten when she crossed the threshold of her *hôtel*. She felt tired and defeated. When she'd first agreed to help the La-Granges, she'd thought only of her duty to them, her debt to Alex's memory. She hadn't thought that what they were doing might poison her chances for happiness in the future. Now she wondered with a sinking heart what Edmond would say when he learned of her latest social embarrassment with Malecot. Would the shame be too much for him to overlook, even if he loved her?

She sighed, dropped her cloak and mask in the vestibule and picked up the single lamp that had been left on a small table. She dragged herself upstairs, filled with a weariness that came as much from her soul as from her body. The comfort of her rooms cheered her a little. There was still a small fire burning in the grate of her boudoir, and her snack awaited her on a large silver tray. She readied herself for bed, had her fruit and crackers and wine, then took out a book to read before the fire.

She'd read scarcely one chapter, however, when she found herself yawning. "Merciful heaven," she murmured aloud as she stepped into her bedchamber and crawled between the sheets of the soft bed. "I should never have lasted through the circus, let alone the balls!" She yawned again, closed her eyes, and slept.

Chapter Twenty

The bell echoed throughout the silent house like the clamor of doom. Céleste struggled up from the depths of a sound sleep, her head pounding, her ears ringing almost as loudly as the bell.

She sat up in bed and groaned, cursing the LaGranges for bothering her with one of their nocturnal visits. She blinked her eyes and looked around the room. But that was *sunlight* filtering through the crack in the heavy draperies. She looked toward the clock on the mantel. After eight. Still half-asleep, she listened to the ringing at the gate for another full minute before she realized that it was too early for Thérèse to have returned.

She sighed and dragged herself out of bed. Who in the name of God could it be, so early in the morning after the Mardi Gras revels? Surely not the LaGranges, who had planned a full night of parties and balls.

She threw on a dressing gown and slippers, retied her hair with its ribbon, and hurried down the stairs. She glanced at herself in a mirror beside the door and pinched a little color into her cheeks, then went outside into the glaring sunshine of the courtyard. "Yes, yes!" she cried, as she neared the gate. "I'm coming."

The ringing stopped.

She breathed a sigh of relief. Now if only her head would stop pounding. "Who is it?" she called, taking the key down from its hook and unlocking the gate.

"Police. Open up."

Dear God, she thought, and threw wide the door. Several gendarmes stood in the street, the gold buttons of their blue-and-yellow tunics glittering brightly. Beside them were two gentlemen in long, dark greatcoats. All of them looked so solemn that Céleste felt a thrill of fear. "What is it?" she asked in alarm. "Has something happened to one of my servants?"

One of the gentlemen—a man as tall and thin as a cadaver—stepped forward. "May we come in?"

"Yes, of course." Céleste led the men through the cobbled courtyard to her door, then stepped aside and watched them file into her vestibule. One of the gendarmes went to the door of her drawing room and peered inside. "Will you tell me what this is about?" she demanded, scarcely hiding the irritation in her voice.

The thin man who had first spoken bowed politely. "Are you Madame Céleste Valvert?" At Céleste's nod of affirmation, he swept his hat from his head and bowed again. "Permit me. I am Inspector Raphael of the Paris police. This gentleman—" he indicated the other man, who had also removed his top hat "—is Monsieur Claudel, the confidential man of her grace, la duchesse de Tallon."

The duchesse de Tallon? But that was Élise de Malecot's maternal grandmother! Céleste puffed in exasperation and pressed her hands to her aching temples. "I have been importuned by the daughter and insulted by the father. Am I now to be plagued by a third generation of that family? And at this ungodly hour of the morning?"

Monsieur Claudel smiled thinly. "I can assure you, *madame,* that her grace's concern in this matter is not frivolous. Her grace is a woman of the highest integrity, a woman who—"

Céleste interrupted him by turning to Raphael. "Inspector," she said, "you have wakened me from a deep sleep, and I've not had my morning tea. My servant hasn't returned yet, but if you'll follow me to the kitchen, I shall brew a pot for all of us."

"Of course," he said. He turned to one of the gendarmes. "Bernard," he said, "go back and watch the courtyard. A necessary precaution," he added to Céleste.

She smiled sourly and led the way through the vestibule and into the large kitchen. They sat around the kitchen table and drank their tea; Céleste didn't bother to apologize for the informality of it; nor did she offer to serve them in the drawing room. Anyone who was so graceless as to disturb a person the morning after Mardi Gras scarcely deserved civility! "Now," she said, pouring herself a second cup, grateful that the warming drink had moderated her headache, "what is this about?"

Raphael cleared his throat. "Baron Julien de Malecot left his wife's side at the École Militaire Ball last night. He told her he had another engagement and would see her later. He has not returned."

Céleste stared at him in indignation. "Good God! What has that to do with me? More than one man, I'm sure, spent Shrove Tuesday in wild revelry and never came home this morning."

"But he had promised his wife and daughter that he would take them to early Mass."

"A holy promise that was drowned in too much champagne, no doubt," she said with a mocking snort. "I was not overly taken with Monsieur de Malecot's piety when I met him."

Raphael frowned. "Madame Valvert, I don't think you appreciate the gravity of this matter. You quarreled with Monsieur de Malecot the other night, at the Opera Ball, I am told."

"A passing misunderstanding. I endured his insults, yes."

"And threatened him?"

She shrugged. "If you mean vague warnings spoken in a moment of heat . . . yes, I suppose I did."

"Where were you last night, *madame?*"

"I? I came home at ten from a dinner party and went to bed. And until your ringing woke me, that's where I've been." She looked at Monsieur Raphael with a sarcastic smile. "My dear Inspector, did you think I'd carried away Monsieur de Malecot on my broomstick? But it was Shrove Tuesday, not Allhallows Eve." She put down her cup and stood up abruptly. "I'm afraid I can't help you further. The good Lord knows I don't have any idea where the man went. Now, if you'll excuse me, I should like to dress."

"A moment, *madame.*" Raphael's slow, deliberate manner made Céleste think of a spider, drawing its prey into the web. "When Monsieur de Malecot didn't return this morning, his wife sent a note to her mother, the duchesse de Tallon, who dispatched Monsieur Claudel at once to her daughter's house. Monsieur Claudel searched Monsieur de Malecot's study, and then sent for me." He reached into the breast of his coat and pulled out a folded piece of paper. Céleste gasped in surprise. Raphael smiled craftily. "Ah, I see that you do recognize the paper."

"It . . . certainly looks like my notepaper," she said.

He unfolded the sheet and thrust it under her nose. "And is this your handwriting, *madame?*"

Céleste had time to read a few phrases before Raphael snatched the letter away. "*I must see you. . . . Come to my* hôtel. . . ." But it had been enough. "It . . . it looks like my handwriting," she stammered, "but I never . . ." She didn't remember writing those words. She had always lived too privately to receive many callers, let alone invite them.

Raphael pocketed the letter, smiled in satisfaction and leaned back in his chair, tapping his long fingers together. His hands looked like two giant spiders stretching their legs. "As far as we can determine," he said, "this is what happened. Somewhere before three o'clock, Monsieur de Malecot received this note at the École Militaire. He excused himself to his wife, took his carriage home, then sent the coachman back to wait on Madame de Malecot, when she should wish to leave the ball. *Monsieur le baron* left his evening cape in his study—along with this note—had a groom hitch up his cabriolet, and left his *hôtel*. He drove himself. One presumes he came here."

"That's ridiculous. If he came, he would have found a darkened house. And if he rang, I certainly didn't hear it! More than that, Inspector, I didn't send that note to Monsieur de Malecot. I don't know how it could have come into his possession. In point of fact, though it's my handwriting, I don't remember writing it. It seems to me it could be a clever forgery. Scores of people overheard our quarrel at the Opera Ball. Any one of them could have wished Monsieur de Malecot harm."

"Ah, so it *was* a quarrel?" crowed Raphael.

The web kept growing tighter. "Not really a quarrel," she said, conscious of how lame her words sounded. "There was no reason for me to harbor any ill will toward him, despite his intemperate behavior. I ascribed it to too much champagne."

"Come now, Madame Valvert." A sly smile lit Raphael's face. "It's common knowledge that you have been attempting for some months now to come between Monsieur de Malecot's daughter and her fiancé. To insinuate yourself so much into the affections of Monsieur Paul de Beaufort that he would spurn his intended and leave her desolate."

She clenched her fists and bit her tongue. It was all she could do to keep from showing her impatience with the man's self-important manner. It was as though he were prepared to find her guilty of a crime if she merely told him the time of day! "Really, Inspector," she said, "an affair of the heart is not exactly a crime against the state, though you seem to equate the two. But my brief liaison with Paul de Beaufort was ended before the night I quarreled with Monsieur de Malecot. I told the baron so. There was no need for him to insult me. As far as I'm concerned, the matter is closed. Monsieur de Malecot..."

"Inspector." Bernard, the gendarme who had waited outside in the courtyard, came hurrying into the kitchen. He carried a pair of gloves in his hand.

"Yes, what is it?"

Bernard held up his find. "A gentleman's gloves, *monsieur*. I discovered them in the carriage house, on the seat of a carriage that is still hitched to its horse."

"What kind of carriage?"

"A cabriolet, Monsieur."

Raphael's spider body tensed, as if he sensed the kill. "Do you own a cabriolet, Madame Valvert?"

She frowned. She was becoming more uneasy by the minute. "No," she replied.

The inspector got to his feet. "Then I fear you must allow me and my men to search your *hôtel*."

She rose in her turn. "This is absurd. No one has been in my house except myself since yesterday evening."

"Your servants?"

"I gave them two days off to enjoy the holidays. My personal maid is expected back sometime before noon."

Raphael gestured toward the door. "Will you show us the way, *madame?* I should prefer that we conduct an orderly search, under your supervision."

She sighed in agreement. Did she really have a choice? She led them back to the vestibule and watched as they pulled aside draperies, looked behind chairs and peered under divans; then she ushered them into the drawing room, where the procedure was repeated. One of the gendarmes even removed the music scores from the top of the grand piano and raised the lid to peek inside.

"I scarcely think Monsieur de Malecot would be hiding there," said Céleste dryly.

Raphael moved toward a closed door. "What is this, *madame?*"

"The door to my studio. I sketch and paint to amuse myself."

Raphael opened the door. He turned back to Céleste; his eyes had become glittering buttons of malevolence. "Do you also commit murder to amuse yourself, *madame?*"

"What? Are you mad?" Céleste hurried to the door of her studio and looked inside. She gasped in horror, one hand going to her mouth. Her stomach lurched, and she swallowed repeatedly to keep herself from vomiting. She closed her eyes to drive away the image, leaned against the doorway for support, then opened her eyes again. The horror remained.

Julien de Malecot lay, facedown, on the floor of her studio. He was still in evening clothes. His head was turned to one side, so Céleste could see the greenish pallor of his cheek, and the blood that fouled his mouth and chin. His hands were stiffened claws, tangled in the folds of her Mardi Gras mantle. But it was his back that made Céleste shudder. A dozen gaping wounds, from shoulder to rib to the small of his back, glistened red and dark crimson with his drying blood; in the very center, between his shoulder blades, there rose the hilt of an elaborately carved dagger.

Monsieur Claudel pushed past Céleste into the studio and uttered a cry. "My God! Malecot! What will I tell the family?"

Raphael knelt beside the body. He felt for a pulse, touched the cold flesh with practiced hands, leaned close to listen for a breath. "Dead, alas," he said. "For some time now, I should guess." He glanced at Claudel. "You positively identify this unfortunate wretch as Monsieur le Baron Julien de Malecot?"

Claudel clutched at his throat and nodded. "Yes," he said in a strangled voice.

Raphael turned to one of the gendarmes. "Bernard, write this down. You are a witness to Monsieur Claudel's identification." Gingerly the inspector pulled the cape from

Malecot's rigid fingers. It was stained with blood. He held it up to Céleste. "Yours, *madame?*"

She was too overwhelmed to speak. She could merely stare at her mantle, at the bright colors dimmed by gore.

"Come, come, *madame.* I see that it is a festive garment. If you wore it to any of the balls this week, half of Paris will be able to recognize it."

"Yes, it's mine," she whispered. "I left it in the vestibule when I came in last night."

"And the knife? No, don't touch it," he said to the gendarme, Bernard, who had leaned down to pull the blade from Malecot's back. "The doctors can determine, from how long the wound bleeds, at what time the man was killed." He looked at Céleste again, his eyes bright with triumph. "It is your knife, *madame,* is it not?"

"Yes." She pointed to the pedestal that held her *Hamlet* grouping. "I was sketching yesterday...." Even her drawings condemned her, filled as they were with sketches of the unusual knife.

Raphael stood up and squared his shoulders as though he were donning his cloak of office. "I must now warn you, Madame Valvert, that everything you say may be used against you."

She gasped. "Dear God, what are you saying? You surely can't believe that..." She indicated Malecot's bulky form. "*Monsieur le baron* is—was—far stronger than I. It would take more strength than I possess to—" She shuddered.

"It takes no great strength to stab a man in the back. Certainly not if he has been taken by surprise. Even a woman can do it."

Her head had begun to pound again. She shook it to clear her thoughts. "Someone must have come in, while I was asleep..."

"*Madame,* you yourself unlocked the gate for us."

She was trembling in every limb—the prey caught in the spider's net. "I swear to you..." she began.

Raphael held up his hand for silence. "Madame Céleste Valvert," he announced majestically, "in the name of Louis-Philippe, king of the French, I arrest you for murder. You will please come with me now."

Céleste sank into a chair, fighting against her panic. No! she thought. She was Achille Desrosiers's granddaughter; she had been raised with pride. Whatever might come next, she would face it. She took a deep, steadying breath. "I trust you will allow me to dress, Inspector Raphael. If you wish, a gendarme can accompany me and wait outside my rooms." At his nod, she arose proudly and climbed the stairs to her boudoir.

But as she dressed in her simple green cashmere, her head was spinning. Malecot dead. Murdered, with a savagery that could point to only one person: Vicomte Philippe de La-Grange. He had seen the quarrel at the Opera Ball. And if the note to Malecot was a forgery, the LaGranges would have dozens of examples of her handwriting from which to arrange forgeries.

Still, it made no sense. Could they hate her so much that they were willing to see her sent to the scaffold? No. She couldn't accept that. Save for their mad obsession, their unswerving hatred of the Malecots, they were not evil people. And God knew their history justified the hatred. Besides, there was the matter of the locked gate. How could they have found their way into her *hôtel* in the middle of the night?

She smoothed her hair into a tight knot and picked out a simple redingote and bonnet. For the time being, she would say nothing to the authorities. Certainly nothing that might implicate the LaGranges. Surely some clue would emerge in Inspector Raphael's investigations that would indicate who could have done such a vile deed.

Followed by the gendarme, she went downstairs and into the courtyard, where Raphael and Claudel were waiting. "I trust it won't be necessary to manacle you, *madame*," said the inspector.

"Of course not," she said. With Bernard recording it in his book, she surrendered the key of her *hôtel* to the inspector, receiving in return his assurances that he would be responsible for her possessions while his men searched her property. She moved aside while a gendarme opened the gate, then stepped forth into the street.

"Oh, my God," she gasped. "Edmond!" She stood still, numb with shock, and willed her quivering limbs to continue to support her.

Edmond de Beaufort had leapt from his carriage and was striding toward her. He smiled at the sight of her, his beautiful eyes lighting up with joy. Then, as if he had recalled himself and the circumstances of his visit, he erased the smile from his face. He gestured toward his coach. "I've brought Paul back from Aix for you," he said softly. "He's waiting in the carriage, afraid to credit his good fortune. Go to him. Go to your love, and with my blessing." He frowned when he saw Raphael and the gendarmes follow Céleste out of her gate. "What's the meaning of this?" he muttered.

At that moment, Paul bounded from Edmond's carriage, his expression filled with hope and fear. "Well?" he said. "What does she say?"

She was dying of shame. "Go away, Edmond," she whispered. "And take Paul with you."

Edmond looked beyond her to Raphael. *"Monsieur,"* he said, "I insist on knowing what is your business with Madame Valvert at this hour of the morning."

Raphael put his hat firmly on his head and looked down his thin nose at Edmond. "I don't know you, *monsieur,* but I am Inspector Raphael of the Paris police. And I am under no obligation to answer your questions."

Monsieur Claudel swore softly. "But it is Monsieur Paul de Beaufort there," he said, pointing to Paul. "We met when her grace was discussing the terms of the marriage contract."

Raphael's eyes lit up. "Ah! We have heard *that* name in connection with this matter. Judging by his appearance here, and yours—'' he nodded at Edmond ''—one would say that Madame Valvert is in the habit of receiving gentlemen at strange hours, for a respectable woman.''

Edmond growled at the disrespect in Raphael's tone. ''By all the devils, *monsieur,* I will not have you speak of Madame Valvert in such a disdainful and insulting fashion. She is a woman of honor and virtue. A gentlewoman. *Nom de Dieu,* can we expect no civility from our police? Are there no standards left in this city?''

Raphael colored at that, clearly humiliated to be rebuked by a man with a noble crest on his carriage. He pinched his lips together in anger, and defended himself with an attack. ''Since the newspapers will soon be broadcasting the news, I can inform you now that this *gentlewoman,* as you call her, lured Monsieur Julien de Malecot to her house last night. We have the note in her handwriting to prove it.''

''Céleste?'' Edmond's blue eyes were suddenly dark with the old suspicion. Hadn't he himself read her note to Paul, enticing him to her opera box that long-ago night? ''Why?'' he demanded of her. ''Couldn't you wait for Paul to return? Or did you need another trophy in the meantime?'' The accusation in his voice tore at her heart.

''Madame Valvert had a darker purpose than merely satisfying her vanity this time, *monsieur,* '' said Raphael.

''And what was that?'' asked Edmond, scarcely dragging his angry glance from Céleste's face.

The inspector smiled coldly, tucked his hand under Céleste's arm and steered her toward his carriage. ''The murder of Julien de Malecot,'' he said with satisfaction.

Chapter Twenty-one

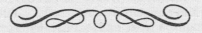

"I saw a few snowdrops in the garden this morning, Madame Valvert. Spring is surely here." Thérèse stacked Céleste's empty dinner plates on the tray and covered them with a napkin. "Shall I leave the rest of the wine?"

"Yes, please. And thank Monsieur Jacques for me. It's been a long time since I've enjoyed his bill of fare at the Maison d'Or. And he still remembered what I liked to order." Céleste allowed her eyes to stray up the whitewashed walls of her cell to the single barred window near the ceiling. "There must be a tree up there," she said wistfully. "I heard a robin this morning, quite close." She smiled at the maid. "You and Joseph are managing the *hôtel* well enough?"

Thérèse clicked her tongue. "It's taken us all these weeks to set things to rights after that inspector and his men were through tearing apart the rooms. My God, I thought they were going to dig up the garden, hoping to find another body!" She twisted the edge of her apron. "But Joseph wanted me to ask you... He knows it's expensive, what with the cost of Monsieur Dupin, your lawyer, and all. But could he rehire Pierre to help him safeguard the house?"

Céleste frowned. "Can't the two of you manage?"

"Well, *madame,* with me coming back and forth to the Conciergerie with your meals and clothes, and all my secret visits with the LaGranges, Joseph is alone much of the time.

And ever since *Le Temps* began printing those nasty articles, it's all he can do to keep the gawkers away. And now, with the trial beginning tomorrow..."

"*Le Temps*," Céleste said with contempt. "That vile Monsieur Soulanges and his scurrilous articles! Never quite open enough to be libel, under the law. Only explicit enough to feed the gossips. And his malice, I'm sure, is prompted by the fact that the wicked Widow Valvert has refused to see him or grant him an interview. Ah, well... Tell Joseph we can't afford to hire Pierre, unless it's really necessary." She sighed. "How is Monsieur de LaGrange?"

"Not well at all. I would have thought he'd be glad, with Monsieur de Malecot dead. But it's like he has no reason to live now. He spends hours in his study, pulling down books and talking to himself. He never reads more than a line or two, but he won't let Madame de LaGrange or any of the servants touch a single book! He doesn't eat, and he scarcely sleeps. I think it was too much of a strain for him—that dreadful day he spent with Inspector Raphael. Madame said the questions went on and on and on."

"How could it be otherwise? The inspector has nothing to connect *me* to Malecot, except through Paul. But the LaGrange-Malecot feud is known to every washerwoman in Paris. Raphael had to question him that way."

Not that it had come to anything. Monsieur de La-Grange was clearly innocent of Malecot's death. There hadn't been a single moment, the whole night of carnival, when LaGrange hadn't been with friends; the inspector had taken depositions from a dozen witnesses. It didn't help Céleste's situation, and Raphael had been lax about searching out any other enemies of Malecot's as possible suspects. But at least Alex's father was no longer under suspicion.

Not that the inspector had a very good case against her, Lord knows, despite her knife and mantle. Whoever had entered her *hôtel* that night would have found the items without any trouble. She'd told Raphael and the examining magistrate almost nothing beyond the facts of that night. Let her remain Céleste Valvert, the woman of mystery. If there was nothing to connect her to Alex or to the La-Granges, her motive for killing Malecot seemed too weak to build a case on. Certainly not with the defense she and Monsieur Dupin had worked out.

"Is there any other news before you go?" she asked.

Thérèse thought for a moment. "Madame de Malecot is still in her sickbed, mourning her husband. And the wedding has been postponed again."

"Oh, God," she moaned, cursing herself and the mischief she'd caused. She wished she could write to Paul and urge him to marry Élise and get on with his life. But that would be madness. Every letter, every visitor, was inspected, scrutinized, probed by Raphael. In view of Paul's connection to the Malecots, to write to him now or ask him to call on her could only jeopardize her case.

Her reasons for denying Edmond, however, were more complicated. He would have learned by now of her final rejection of Paul. Her letter had gone to Aix—which Paul had already left—then followed him back to Paris. But Paul had eventually received it and, no doubt, shared its contents with his cousin. Still, she wondered if Edmond would ever understand her feelings. He seemed so determined to believe she loved Paul. Hadn't his mad trip to Aix-les-Bains to fetch his cousin shown how little he saw into her heart? Or, perhaps, how little he wanted to see.

And then there was the scandal. She didn't want his name connected with hers. Not while this cloud hung over her head. Not after his wife. She loved him too much for that. And perhaps she was too ashamed to face him in her cell. It was her own stupidity, her naiveté, that had brought her to this place. She knew that Edmond had come to the Conciergerie more than once to see her, but had been turned away at her request, along with the rest of her visitors—friends and gossips and ghouls. And she had refused to accept any letters. It was easier to be alone these past weeks. To have her music and her drawing and her solitude.

Besides, what could she tell him if she saw him? That she was carrying his child? Oh, she could scarcely deny it to herself. She'd pretended at first that it was the shock of her arrest, the dampness of her prison cell, that had affected her monthly courses. But she was three weeks late already, and the queasiness in the morning had nothing to do with the food she ate. She couldn't deceive herself for very long; after all, she'd been pregnant before.

There was no point in telling Edmond now. If she was found guilty, she'd go to the guillotine long before the child was born. She doubted the law would be as merciful to her as it had been to her grandmother. She felt a pang, thinking about the child. Perhaps she could beg the court's mercy until the baby was born... She shivered. That thought was too frightening to contemplate. She would wait for the verdict, and pray for the best. If she was acquitted, there would be time to decide what to do.

Thérèse picked up the tray. "I'm going now, *madame*. I'll be here in the morning to help you dress." She walked to the front of the cell and peered through the bars at the gendarme in his antechamber. "Well, Gervais, you can let me out now."

The gendarme unlocked the door and ushered Thérèse into the little cell. "Did the prisoner give you any letters this evening, *mademoiselle*?"

"No."

"I'll have to search you anyway."

Thérèse giggled. "I know." She put down the tray and held out her arms, submitting to the by-now-familiar ritual, which had more to do with seductive play than a search.

Céleste turned away and sought the curtained alcove at the back of her cell, where her bed was set. The sounds of kisses and laughter only made her feel more wretched. Her prison was certainly as comfortable as she could afford to make it, and far better than the communal cells inhabited by those poor wretches who couldn't pay for private accommodations. Joseph had brought furniture from her *hôtel:* a small bed, a table and chairs, a comfortable divan, a stove to ward off the March chill. Even a prie-dieu for when she said her prayers, and a music stand. She'd spent the month since her arrest sketching, reading, and practicing her singing, which entertained her jailers. Thérèse brought in her meals, cooked by her own hand; upon occasion a restaurant or café would send over a meal gratis. As appreciative as she was for the favor, Céleste admitted to a little cynicism. She had no doubt that the proprietor would spend the next week boasting that he personally had fed Madame Valvert, the notorious murderess awaiting the judgment of God and the court.

And yet, despite her comparative comfort, she was so miserable that she wanted to die.

She was grateful when she heard the outer door close on Thérèse at last. She fetched a book from the table and sat down in a chair, ignoring Gervais, who had thrown himself onto his little cot in the antechamber and was now beaming up at the ceiling in smug contentment. How simple life was for him.

There was a knock on the outer door. Gervais opened it a crack and held a whispered conversation with the jailer on the other side. Céleste saw a gloved hand with a fistful of banknotes. Gervais grinned, took the money, and opened wide the door. A dark-caped figure, with a drooping black felt hat that hid his features, strode into the antechamber.

Céleste leapt to her feet in alarm. Was some unknown enemy sending an assassin against her?

The figure pointed to the barred door that separated the two cells. "Open this door," he barked, "then leave us alone for an hour."

Oh, my God, she thought, sinking back into her chair. "Edmond," she whispered.

Gervais shook his head. "I have to stay here and watch the prisoner at all times," he said, "when the crime is a capital offense."

Edmond swore and reached into his pocket, producing another handful of bills. "I'm sure you can find a hole that will swallow you for an hour," he growled.

Gervais nodded, unlocked the door of Céleste's cell, and vanished. Edmond moved across the room to Céleste, throwing down his hat and cloak and gloves as he came. He pulled her from her chair, wrapped his arms around her and crushed her mouth with his.

Céleste responded with all the aching need in her, twining her arms around his neck and pressing her breast close to his. They moved in an urgent dance toward the curtained alcove—kissing, touching, holding, with a hungry desperation that fired their passion all the more. Céleste fell back on the bed and tugged at the buttons of her bodice. Edmond tore off his coat, fumbled with his own buttons and threw himself on top of her. One impatient hand plunged into her bodice to violently caress her heaving bosom, while the other pushed aside her skirts and petticoats.

"Oh, yes," she gasped. "I want you."

He took her with a passionate savagery that wrung a cry of ecstasy from her lips. They rocked together, mouths and arms and bodies joined, in a pounding rhythm that spoke of desire and desperate need, of love and tenderness and aching despair. It was over quickly—the ending announced by Edmond's throaty roar, Céleste's sigh of release. They lay together, eyes closed, arms around each other, and kissed softly.

At last, Edmond rolled away and straightened his clothes. "Why the devil did you refuse to see me or receive my letters?"

"How could I?" she said bitterly. "How could I stain you with my shame? Give *Le Temps* something more to write about?"

"That damned Soulanges," he muttered. "I intend to call him out when this is finished." He turned to her, his eyes suddenly dark with uncertainty. "Did you mean it? What you wrote to Paul at Aix? That you no longer love him?"

"Yes."

He laughed—a short, ironical bark. "I was a fool, rushing off to fetch Paul that way. All I did was raise his hopes. I thought he'd go mad at Aix. It snowed for two days in the mountains, and we couldn't leave. He talked about you all the time. And then, when he finally received your letter, forwarded from Aix... What a disappointment for him."

She reached over to stroke his lips with loving fingers. "I wasn't waiting in Paris for Paul. I was waiting for you. That's why I sent the letter."

He shuddered at her touch, and kissed her fingertips. "We arrived the night of carnival. We drove past your *hôtel*, but it was dark. Paul went home. But I couldn't sleep. I took a small carriage, drove around, came back at midnight—" He glared at her suddenly. "Damn it, where *were* you?"

"Asleep in my bed."

He stood up and pulled her to her feet, holding her close to his heart. "Oh, God..." he groaned. "If I'd wakened you and taken you away with me that night, perhaps none of this would have happened. I've heard the stories... what Malecot said to you at the Opera Ball. I think I would have killed him myself, had I been there." He sighed and moved out of the alcove, slipping into the coat he'd discarded with such haste. "I wish you'd let me help you. Pay for another lawyer. Something!"

"I have confidence in Monsieur Dupin. I don't need anything."

"But it looks so bad, from what I hear. They say your *hôtel* was locked that night...."

"Monsieur Dupin intends to argue that there was time for someone to come into the courtyard after I returned home that night. My coachman had gone. It wasn't until I was ready for bed that I remembered to go out and lock the gate.

The murderer could have stayed inside all night, after he'd let in Malecot and killed him. In the morning, when the police came, the gate was left unlocked again. He could have departed then.''

"That's not a very strong defense.''

"No. But Monsieur Dupin means to raise the question of my motive. The insult at the Opera Ball was something that might drive a man to a duel. But it's usually assumed that a woman wouldn't react so violently. Certainly not to commit murder. My only other motive would have been to keep Julien de Malecot from coming between Paul and me. *If* I loved Paul.''

"Ah! That was why Monsieur Dupin asked Paul for the Aix letter.''

"Yes. He intends to produce it in court, to show that I had already jilted Paul before that scene with Malecot. If I must, I'll have Élise de Malecot testify that I told her I was through with Paul. Not five minutes before her father appeared. I don't want to do it—the poor thing has suffered enough, with her father dead and all. But...''

"But what about your love letter to Malecot, luring him to your *hôtel* that night?''

She frowned. "I wish I'd been allowed to read it thoroughly. It looked like my handwriting, when the inspector showed it to me. But I didn't recognize the text.''

"Could it have been one of the letters you wrote to Paul?''

"No. Dupin asked him. Paul's store of letters seems untouched. It *must* be a forgery.'' She sighed. "Well, everything will be resolved, starting tomorrow.''

"You know I'll do anything I can,'' he said fervently, clasping her hands in his. His eyes were soft and filled with tenderness.

It was too frightening to think that she would lose him if the trial should go against her. "I don't want to talk about it anymore,'' she said. "Tell me something happy.''

He poured two glasses of the wine that Thérèse had left and handed one to her. "Meyerbeer presented a new opera on Leap Year Day. *Les Huguenots*. Very stirring. We shall go together when this is over. And there's a pianist from Austria, a young man named Sigismund Thalberg, who has been challenging Monsieur Liszt as the pet of the salons and the musical soirées. They've been playing at concerts in turn. All of Paris is divided into two camps." He smiled and kissed her gently. "You shall hear Thalberg play, soon enough." His eyes twinkled. "And then we shall quarrel about it."

"I have no doubt." She smiled back. How she had missed the sight of him. The sound of his voice. The clear blue eyes, the smile that warmed her. And now he spoke of their being together as though it was the most natural thing in the world to him.

"Do you love me?" she asked softly.

"What?" The clear blue eyes clouded with doubt. The smile faded. "I . . . care for you deeply, Céleste. I wouldn't have gone to fetch Paul if I hadn't thought that would make you happy."

"And you're glad I don't love him?"

"More than I can tell you," he said, his voice hoarse with emotion. "I couldn't have lived if I hadn't been able to see you tonight."

"But that was desire. You said it in your letter. Remember? That you believe the two are different. And so I ask you . . . do you *love* me?"

He scowled and scooped up his hat and cape from the floor. "Don't ask for more than I can give, Céleste. My heart is still in chains. You know that."

She held him with her glance, all her devotion shining in his eyes. "Cannot my love break the chains? For you know I love you, Edmond. With all my soul."

He hesitated, his face twisted with agony and doubt. Then he turned away and threw his cape over his shoulders. "I'll stand next to you during your trial," he muttered. "I'm sure I can bribe someone to arrange it."

She shook her head. "No. It might affect my case adversely, to have you there. Besides..." All evening she had read doubt in his eyes. Not only about his feelings toward her. But doubts about her honesty, the true disposition of her heart, even her complete innocence in Malecot's death. "Unless you can believe with all your heart, Edmond, that I wasn't Paul's lover, that I wasn't Malecot's lover, that I wasn't all those things the gossips said, then we have nothing. Nothing but the passion you spoke of. And how can you believe in my love if your memories of Joséphine keep you from opening your own heart?"

"Céleste..." She could see that he was battling his ghosts.

"Go away, Edmond," she whispered. "Wish me well. But stand in the courtroom with all those others who think there is something wicked about the mysterious Widow Valvert. I'll not make it easy for you by telling you my secrets. Love me as I am ... or go away."

The ghosts had won. "Good night," he said softly, and left her.

Chapter Twenty-two

"God's mercy be with you today, *madame.*" Gervais's plain peasant face radiated goodwill as he unlocked the door of Céleste's cell. "They tell me people have been petitioning all week for tickets of admission. It will be a circus at the assizes." He led her through the doors, then handed her over to the gendarmes who would escort her to the trial.

She blinked in the bright noon sunlight as she emerged from the Conciergerie. The day was so sweet and mild that she almost didn't need the cape that covered her simple, demure dress. The gendarmes hustled her toward a waiting carriage for the short ride to the Gothic royal palace that was now the Palais de Justice. There seemed to be hundreds of people crowded together on the narrow street, pushing and jostling each other to get a closer look at her. She tried not to hear the catcalls, the ugly epithets, the accusations of crimes that would have made Attila himself blush. A line of gendarmes struggled to keep the crowd under control, with limited success. They shoved and screamed and pressed near; within their ranks, someone even held up a child to watch the frantic scene.

A short, balding man, well dressed, broke from the mob, eluded a gendarme and thrust himself in front of Céleste. She frowned, recognizing him. Monsieur Soulanges, of *Le Temps.* He was breathless from his efforts, and his eyes glittered like black stones. "Madame Valvert, will you grant me an interview tonight in your cell?" he shouted above the noise and tumult.

"Not if I were on the way to the guillotine," she said with a sneer. How dare he ask such a thing, after the lies he'd written!

"I think you'll regret that!" he cried as a gendarme pushed him back toward the crowd. "I have the power to destroy you!" His mouth twisted in an evil smile.

"The truth will set me free," she said, and hurried into the carriage. She heard his final shout as the coach moved off.

"Be warned!" he cried.

She shuddered at his tone. That vile man. Tomorrow's story in the paper would no doubt be dripping with acid.

She was heartened by the sight of her lawyer, Monsieur Dupin, in the antechamber of the courtroom. He had the young, innocent face of a schoolboy, but a lively and clever mind. He murmured a greeting, helped her off with her cape and indicated a small door. "Come," he said. "Shall we go in?"

She nodded, waited for the gendarmes to take their places on either side of her, and then entered the courtroom. It was a large and handsomely appointed room. On a raised platform at one end was the judge's bench, graced with the tricolor of France and a bust of King Louis-Philippe. On either side of the judge's bench, facing each other, were two rows of benches. One set for the defendant and her lawyer and guards, the other for the *procureur du roi,* the king's prosecutor and, behind him, the jury. In the middle of the room was a semicircular dock where the witnesses would stand to testify. At the side of the room opposite the judge was a guardrail that held back the spectators. They crowded the banked rows of seats, leaning forward and murmuring excitedly when Céleste came in and took her seat on the defendant's bench beside Dupin. Half a score of gendarmes were in the courtroom: two standing behind Céleste, the rest at attention in front of the spectators.

The prosecutor and his assistants were already in their places, stiff and proper in their magisterial robes. Franz, the chief prosecutor, nodded curtly in acknowledgment of Céleste's entry. She all but ignored him. She glanced briefly at the jury, taking in their neutral expressions, then turned her attention to the rows of seats at the back of the room.

She saw Edmond first, in the second row, frowning his concern and looking as though he wanted to leap over the guardrail and carry her away from this dreadful place. Beside him, to her surprise, was Paul. The expression on his face made it clear that, while he had reluctantly accepted Céleste's having fallen out of love with him, his feelings for her hadn't changed. Young fool, she thought tenderly. If only she could think of a way to send him back to Élise. It was clear that Edmond hadn't told his cousin of their affair. She wasn't sure that she herself was prepared to further break Paul's heart by telling him.

She saw a number of reporters, all looking like vultures, their notebooks and pencils at the ready. As she watched, Soulanges pushed his way through the crowd and took his seat in the front row. Several rows above him, and dressed entirely in mourning, was Monsieur Claudel, representing the interests of the Malecot-Tallon families in this place.

But the most shocking sight for Céleste was the viscount de LaGrange, seated in the top-most row with his wife. He seemed to have aged a dozen years in the month since she'd seen him last. His graying hair had gone completely white, and his cheeks were drawn and thin. His mouth drooped on one side, and his one arm twitched as though he were palsied. Thérèse had wondered if, after all those years of hatred, he'd lost his reason for living when Malecot died. But Céleste saw the decline of the man and suspected a mild stroke. Though she had never liked him very much, her heart went out to him—a fading old man with no heirs to carry on the family name. A man with nothing but lost moments.

A loud pounding, repeated three times, echoed throughout the courtroom. "The court, gentlemen!" called out the doorkeeper, and everyone rose to his feet. The judge entered and mounted his bench. He was dressed in an ermine cape, and the Legion of Honor hung on a red ribbon around his neck. He rang his bell for order and nodded to the prosecutor. "You may deliver the deed of accusation," he said.

"Thank you, *Monsieur le président.*" The prosecutor cleared his throat and took out a large sheaf of papers. He began to read the charges against Céleste in a deep and emphatic voice. It was a long, dismaying catalogue of accusations, suggesting that he intended to bring in stories about the questionable character of the accused, the facts of the night of the murder that would surely convince the jury that she was guilty and the quarrel she had had with the deceased, which would establish a motive. He ended by saying that he intended to show that this was more than just a simple murder. He would produce a doctor to describe the many knife blows Malecot had suffered.

"This is a heinous crime, gentlemen," he concluded to the jury. "This woman, so innocent in her youth and beauty, was not content merely to kill. No. She struck the poor man again and again and again. Look at her now," he said, pointing to Céleste. "So calm, so self-contained. I tell you, I will prove to you that that reserved exterior hides the soul of a bloodthirsty monster!" He bowed to the judge and sat down.

The effect of such an impassioned denunciation was to bring half the spectators to their feet. The judge rang his bell furiously and demanded that the gendarmes keep order. Dupin whispered words of reassurance to Céleste, but they weren't necessary; Achille Desrosiers's granddaughter had her pride. She even forbade her cheeks to color with shame.

When order had been restored, the judge leaned over and addressed Céleste. "What is your name?"

She answered in a clear voice. "Céleste Valvert."

"Your age?"

"Twenty-three."

"And where were you born?"

"In Champagne, *Monsieur le président.*"

"Are you guilty of the crime before this court?"

"No, I am not." Her answer was delivered in such a ringing tone that it caused the spectators to stir.

The judge made a note on a paper before him, then turned to the prosecutor and instructed him to begin his case against the accused.

Franz, the prosecutor, was nothing if not thorough. He and Inspector Raphael had done their jobs well. It seemed as though they had interviewed every rumormonger in Paris. Franz attempted to have several people testify, but Dupin—warned by Céleste to expect such ugly testimony—protested, shrewdly arguing that unsubstantiated gossip didn't belong in a court that searched for truth alone. To Franz's evident annoyance, the gossip was suppressed. Céleste breathed a sigh of relief.

"But the liaison of the accused with this man," said Franz, pointing to Paul de Beaufort, "is far more than gossip." While everyone looked at Paul, whose face turned red, Franz brought witnesses to detail the number of times Céleste and Paul had been seen together. The testimony was damning. Franz beamed in triumph.

Céleste, cursing herself for every meeting, every indiscreet tête-à-tête, rose to her feet in dismay. "I do protest, *monsieur le président.*"

The judge scowled down at her. "Do you deny the testimony of these witnesses?"

"No, *monsieur,*" she said, with the cool self-control of one who knows herself to be the injured party. "But what they describe is merely a flirtation. As common as breathing in this city. If everyone who flirted were to be accused of murder, the Conciergerie would have to be as large as the whole Île de la Cité!'' She smiled innocently at the jury and sat down to the laughter of the spectators. Edmond nodded and winked in her direction.

But Franz wasn't finished with the subject. He produced the innkeeper of the Three Feathers who testified about the rendezvous the accused had arranged. Dupin demolished his testimony at once by forcing him to admit that the couple had never come to the inn that night; indeed, he didn't even have proof that the woman who had arranged the meeting was the accused, whom he had never seen until this very moment.

Confounded, Franz shifted tactics, choosing to move at this point to the night of the murder and the quarrel leading up to it. There were witnesses who spoke of overhearing the argument with Malecot, there was a doctor to testify about the condition of the body when it was found. Céleste's knife and bloodstained mantle were produced. Dupin allowed them without protest.

Thérèse, nervous and frightened, was called to the witness box. In a quavering voice, she told about seeing her mistress for the last time that evening, before she'd gone on to her own Mardi Gras ball. Céleste's coachman told the same story.

Inspector Raphael took the witness box, and had just begun to describe the events of the morning of Ash Wednesday when a juror raised his hand.

"If you please, *monsieur le président,*" he said, addressing the judge, "we are wondering why the victim was at the *hôtel* of the accused."

"Yes, so was I," said the judge, and proceeded to take over the questioning himself. Raphael immediately produced the letter that had been found in Malecot's study. He was, he said, prepared to bring in experts to give testimony, based on samples he had obtained from her *hôtel,* that the

handwriting was indeed that of the accused. He insisted that
Céleste again verify her own handwriting. When the clerk
brought the letter to her, she nodded reluctantly, then
frowned as she scanned the entire page.

"But this isn't my signature," she said. "I'll swear to that.
It looks like it, but . . . not quite. Merciful heaven, I think it
must be forged!" she added boldly, before Franz could silence her. The spectators murmured among themselves, and
several members of the jury had the courage to look her in
the eye for the first time. A good sign, she thought.

"Will you read the letter to the court, Inspector?"
snapped Franz, clearly trying to recover the direction of his
case.

Raphael nodded. "I must see you at once," he read.
"Come to my *hôtel* directly you receive this letter. I know it
is imprudent for you to call on me, but I desire peace and
harmony between us. If you are of the same mind, do not
fail to come."

Céleste leaned back on her bench and closed her eyes. For
the life of her, she couldn't remember writing those words,
though they sounded vaguely familiar. Could someone have
copied them from one of her letters to Paul?

Beside her, Dupin patted her hand. "At least now we
know *what* the letter says," he whispered. "Even if we can't
disprove it, it shows goodwill on your part. The hand of
friendship. Surely not the words of a murderess."

At last Franz concluded his case, and Dupin rose in re-
buttal. He was a forthright young man, and his sincerity was
clearly conveyed to the jury. Céleste was glad that she hadn't
confided to him anything more than she'd told the police;
she suspected that he was too straightforward and honest to
lie knowingly for Alex de LaGrange's widow. Skillfully he
questioned Céleste, drawing out her account of the night of
the murder, and emphasizing the long period of time when
anyone could have slipped into her unlocked *hôtel*. He had
her repeat her charge that the letter must be a forgery, and

brought out the point that the note bore no salutation. How could Monsieur Franz prove that the letter had been meant for Malecot?

Dupin then moved on to the key to Céleste's defense: the lack of motive. He dismissed her momentary pique at Malecot's insults as unimportant. The man clearly had been drunk; a woman of Madame Valvert's breeding would find it in her heart to forgive him. As to Malecot's supposed interference between Paul and Céleste...Dupin produced her letter rejecting him, which had a strong impact on the jury. They seemed torn between sympathy for Céleste and for the clearly suffering Paul de Beaufort, the spurned lover.

Dupin ended his case by declaring that the murder of Monsieur de Malecot, though a dreadful crime, could have been done by anyone who had seen or heard the quarrel and wished to implicate his client while destroying the baron. Some wicked person had crept into her home, let in Malecot and killed him, leaving the incriminating evidence of the mantle and knife behind. And all this while his client slept in pure innocence in her room above. He begged the jury to take note that such a charming and poised young woman could scarcely be capable of the crime of which she was accused.

The long day was over at last. Céleste was tired but heartened as she was taken back to her cell. The jury seemed to look on her with favor, the spectators had murmured words of encouragement as she was led from the court, and Edmond had smiled at her from across the room with a warmth that gave her hope for the future. And when she arrived at her cell and found waiting there an anonymous gift of flowers and a folio of several of Schubert's love songs, she wanted to cry for joy. Perhaps he couldn't say the words, but his heart was learning to speak to her. She went to bed and slept more soundly than she had in weeks.

"I think it will be finished before the day is done," said Dupin as he led her into the courtroom the following noon. "Franz and I will present our summaries, and the jury can begin to decide. I think you have a very good chance of being acquitted."

She nodded. "They looked me in the eye. Every man of the jury, when I got up to leave yesterday afternoon. That's a good sign, you said."

"Yes. It's been my experience that jurors are reluctant to look at someone they plan to send to the scaffold."

She took her place on her bench, looked for Edmond and mouthed her thanks for the flowers. God willing, she'd be in his arms by this evening. The mood of the crowd in the courtroom had changed; the hostile air was gone, replaced by sympathy and optimism. Even Thérèse, who had been afraid to stay in court yesterday, had come today to await the expected happy conclusion. She waved to Céleste from her place in the stands.

The judge entered. Franz stood up to speak. "*Monsieur le président,* I should like to ask several questions of the accused." Upon receiving the judge's consent, he turned to Céleste. "Madame Valvert, you are a widow, I believe."

"Yes," she said, glancing with some alarm toward Dupin.

"And the name of your late husband?"

Dupin had understood the message in her eyes. He jumped to his feet. "I must protest," he said. "What has that to do with the case of the *procureur du roi?* A husband who has been dead for years." That was all that Céleste had told him; he hadn't even thought it important enough to ask for a name.

"Indeed, *monsieur le président,*" said Franz, "this information is central to the case. I received an anonymous message last evening, which has kept me up for half the night. I ask the right to pursue this."

The judge scratched at his chin, then nodded. "Granted."

Franz smiled, looking like a crafty fox. "Now, *madame*, the name of your husband, if you please."

"I decline to answer," she said coolly, though her pulse had begun to race in dread.

"Then let me ask you another question." He strode to the guardrail and pointed up at the spectators. "Do you know that elderly gentleman and lady there?"

Her heart sank. "Yes," she said in a low voice. "That is Monsieur and Madame de LaGrange."

"The sworn enemies of the Malecots, as all Paris knows. Is it not so, *madame?*"

"I have heard the rumors. Yes."

"Isn't it true you were once married to their son?"

The courtroom was as hushed as the tomb. Céleste looked at Edmond and saw fresh doubt in his eyes. Beside him, Paul was leaning forward and frowning. The LaGranges looked stricken, their faces drained of color. Every spectator sat on the edge of the bench, straining to hear Céleste's reply.

Only Soulanges of *Le Temps* looked serene. Dear God, she thought. He was the one. She didn't know how, but he'd discovered the truth and was taking his revenge on her. She glared at him with hatred in her eyes and said nothing.

"Come, come, *madame,*" said Franz in a self-satisfied drawl. "We have already sent to Rome and Normandy seeking the necessary documents."

Madame de LaGrange let out a shriek and toppled forward. It was the signal for the stands to erupt in chaos. While Monsieur de LaGrange, quivering violently, called for a smelling-bottle of vinegar for his wife, everyone began to shout at once. It took the gendarmes several minutes to restore order, during which time Dupin growled his disgust with Céleste for not having trusted him with all her secrets. Only when the judge began to threaten the mob with contempt of court did the spectators settle back on their seats.

"Well, *madame?*" demanded Franz. "I have a man who is prepared to testify that he had often caroused with your late husband in Rome, and remembered him speaking of his wife, Céleste. Will it be necessary for me to produce this witness? Or ask for a postponement of this trial until your marriage papers arrive from Rome?"

She sighed. What was the use of protesting? "No, *monsieur le procureur.* I was indeed married to the chevalier Alexis de LaGrange. In Rome, four years ago." She had stopped looking at Edmond. She couldn't bear the accusation in his eyes.

Madame de LaGrange, moaning softly, had to be helped from the courtroom into a small antechamber. Her husband remained, trembling, his bloodshot eyes imploring Céleste's silence.

"How did your husband die?" Franz went on.

"In a duel, *monsieur,*" she murmured.

"Let us talk again of the Malecot-LaGrange feud," he said, with a smile that indicated that he knew everything. "If you were married to Alexis de LaGrange, *madame,* you do indeed have a motive for this crime we prosecute today. Am I mistaken, or was it not Julien de Malecot himself who killed your husband?"

"Yes, but..." She shook her head. "I forgave him long since. I had no wish to kill him."

"Only to destroy him?"

"What do you mean?"

"The gossips are very helpful, Madame de LaGrange. They tell us many things. One of them was the fact that the duchesse de Tallon was prepared to disown her son-in-law, Malecot, should there be any family scandal. Have you heard that rumor, *madame?*"

"Yes," she whispered.

"I submit to you that you carried on an extremely public love affair with that man..." he pointed to Paul in the gallery "—in order to humiliate and disgrace the Malecots, and bring them down. That you have plotted from the first to revenge yourself on your husband's killer—whatever means you might have to employ." Paul's face went white, and he buried his head in his hands.

Céleste tried not to notice, tried not to see Edmond's face, which was set in an expression of bitter anger and betrayal. She was fighting for her life. There was no way she could ease their pain at this moment. She assumed that Franz was only guessing about the plot, putting the facts of her true identity together with all that had happened. She drew herself up proudly. It wouldn't pay to appear weak. "Do you have any proof of this, *monsieur?*" she asked in a challenging tone. "This wild scheme you say I've concocted?"

Franz shrugged. "You make this very difficult, *madame.*" He turned to the judge. "I should like to call monsieur le Vicomte de LaGrange to testify."

"No!" cried Céleste. What was the point in dragging in that pitiful old man? She herself was doomed in any event, unless she could make the jury believe her. "Leave the LaGranges out of this. They had nothing to do with the scheme," she said.

"Are we to believe that? You were in Paris with people to whom you had been related through marriage, and you didn't acknowledge one another?"

"It was my idea alone. I insisted upon secrecy. They didn't know what I had in mind. I didn't wish to involve them." She calculated quickly, ignoring Dupin's signaled pleas for restraint. If she was open on this point, the jury might more readily accept her honest denial of Malecot's murder. "You made a very clever and accurate guess, Monsieur Franz," she went on. "My scheme was as you divined. To disgrace the Malecots through Paul de Beaufort."

"Damn you!" Paul let out a bellow of pain and outrage and leapt to his feet. Before Edmond could stop him, he shoved through the row of spectators and ran from the courtroom.

Céleste closed her eyes for a moment, fighting her tears, her self-loathing. She took a deep breath and continued. "I freely confess all this to you, Monsieur Franz. I had hoped that Paul and I would be discovered together at the Three Feathers. But you've heard the innkeeper's testimony. You've read my letter of renunciation to Paul. None of this came to pass, as you have seen. It seemed too cruel to take my revenge on Malecot by hurting Paul de Beaufort."

"An attack of conscience, *madame?*" sneered Franz.

"Perhaps. I decided to go away. I no longer wished to pursue my vengeance."

He smiled slyly. "At least not through Beaufort. You struck on a better plan. To lure Malecot to your *hôtel* and kill him."

"No! I told you, I found forgiveness in my heart. Even for a Malecot."

At the name Malecot, LaGrange began to mutter softly and rock back and forth. Immediately Thérèse rose from her seat and pushed her way to him. She motioned to a gendarme to help him from the room. Then, seeing that the courtroom had fallen silent—all eyes on her—she blushed furiously and resumed her seat.

"How very curious," said Franz in a low voice. "*Monsieur le président,* I should like to recall that witness."

Thérèse's red face turned white, and she began to shake almost as much as LaGrange. It took several gendarmes to drag the terrified girl from her seat and bring her to the witness box. "I told you everything before, *messieurs,*" she whimpered.

"Don't be afraid," said Franz. "You have only to answer my questions truthfully." He held up a warning finger. "But remember, you are still under oath. Now, I noted your attention to Monsieur de LaGrange just now. What is your connection to him?"

She twisted her fingers together. "I . . . was born on his estate in Normandy. I've served the family all my life."

"You became the personal maid to Madame Valvert? That is, Madame de LaGrange?"

"Yes. After her marriage to the chevalier."

"Then you knew, of course, that your mistress was deliberately hiding her true identity here in Paris."

"N-No, I . . ."

The judge scowled, raised himself up on the bench and pointed to the quivering girl. "Come, come, *mademoiselle.* Don't take us for fools. You must tell the truth. Do you know what the court does to liars?"

She clasped her hands in supplication. "Have mercy on me, *monsieur le président.* Yes, I knew of *madame's,* plot. How could I not? But I swore not to tell."

"Don't be afraid," repeated Franz soothingly. "No one means to harm you. Did Madame Valvert force you to help her?"

His tone seemed to reassure the girl. She relaxed and even managed a small smile. "Oh, no, *monsieur.* Of course . . ." She hesitated, her eyes darting to Céleste.

"Yes? You can speak freely to me."

"She was very interested in all the gossip about her. She knew that it would make it look worse for her and Monsieur Paul."

"And of course that's what she wanted. The scandal."

"Oh, yes! She encouraged it. Sometimes I think she enjoyed it—to be talked about. No matter what she said."

Céleste chewed at her thumb in dismay. It was bad enough that Franz was trying to turn Thérèse against her. But she had the sudden uneasy feeling that the girl was actually enjoying her damaging testimony. It made no sense, of course, but . . .

"Now, *mademoiselle,*" said Franz, "Madame Valvert has told us that she abandoned her plan to elope with Monsieur de Beaufort. Is that true?"

"Well, that's what she *said*."

Céleste stirred uneasily at the girl's tone.

"You don't believe it?" asked Franz.

"Well, *I* never saw her give him up. All I know is that she was doing everything she could to seduce him." Now she made no effort to disguise her dislike.

Céleste leaned toward Dupin and whispered a suspicion that was beginning to form in her brain. Had that hostility always been there, and Céleste too blind to see it? Thérèse's answers had cast doubt on her own testimony, making it appear as though she were far more scheming and calculating than she seemed. Since the girl knew that the plot had been the LaGranges' doing in the first place, her testimony could only be meant to blacken Céleste further. She fretted with impatience until Franz was finished with his questions and Dupin could rise to her defense.

"*Mademoiselle,*" he began, "do you like Madame Valvert?"

Thérèse sniffed. "I serve her, don't I?"

"But do you serve her because you like her, or because she was one of the LaGranges, whom you have served all your life?"

"I don't know what you mean." The girl tossed her head in contempt. She was clearly enjoying herself now. The attention of the spectators. The power she held over Céleste's fate.

Dupin smiled. "No, perhaps you don't understand the distinction. Tell me about the chevalier de LaGrange."

That caught her by surprise. She looked stricken. "He's dead. What more is there to tell?"

"Was he handsome?"

"Oh, yes."

"And strong and brave?"

Thérèse sighed. "Oh, wonderfully so. Ever since he was a boy."

"Indeed? You knew him even then? How fortunate for you." He stepped closer to the witness box. "Tell me, *mademoiselle,* did you love him?"

Thérèse turned pink. "What do you mean, *monsieur?*"

"I mean," he said, his voice growing harder and sharper with every word, "were you his lover? Did you sneak out of the château to meet him in a barn, to kiss in a dark passageway and couple under a haystack?" He thrust his face closer still. "*Did* you, *mademoiselle?*" he growled.

"Yes!" she cried, as though he had physically torn the unwilling confession from her lips.

Céleste clutched the oaken railing of her bench to keep her balance. Oh, Alex, she thought, anguished. Under my very nose? And Thérèse, burning with resentment and jealousy. No wonder she'd sometimes felt uneasy about the girl's loyalty. She'd thought it was merely her devotion to the LaGranges. But perhaps it had been more: her hatred of Céleste, who had taken her lover from her. And how she must have despised Malecot, who had killed him! If Thérèse had had the wit to do it, Céleste might have begun to think that *she* had murdered Malecot. But the girl wasn't clever enough.

Dupin was now pacing the floor, allowing the jury to absorb Thérèse's damning admission before he went on. "Let me submit to you, *mademoiselle,*" he said at last, "that everything you have told us here is a tissue of lies. That you hated your mistress for marrying the man you loved, and you would say anything to see her convicted." He turned to the judge. "*Monsieur le président,* I should like to see this creature charged with perjury."

Thérèse's face turned a brighter shade of red, and the veins in her neck stood out. "You want the truth?" she demanded. "Very well! Madame Valvert *did* decide not to seduce Monsieur Paul. But only because she thought he didn't deserve to be hurt by something that had nothing to do with him. That doesn't mean she didn't still hate Monsieur de

Malecot." She smiled at Céleste, her mouth set in an ugly twist of malice. "Do you want to know what she said? I'll tell you. It's not right to hurt Monsieur Paul, she said. I'd rather take a knife and stick it into Malecot's heart if I want to be revenged! *That's* what she said, her very words! And you can ask her!" she finished defiantly.

If chaos had reigned before, now it was pure madness. The spectators poured down from the stands and pushed against the guardrail and the beleaguered gendarmes, shaking their fists at Céleste. Even the judge looked at her as though he had already decided she was guilty. "To the guillotine with the widow!" shouted a man in a butcher's smock who was immediately ushered out. The doorkeeper pounded for order, the judge rang his bell furiously. Soulanges held up his notebook and waved it mockingly at Céleste.

She sank down on the bench, all her strength gone. The hatred of the mob was like a hot wave pressing against her. She looked at Dupin and sighed wearily. "You did your best. And I didn't make it any easier for you."

"Don't be so pessimistic."

"But I did say those words, I remember, though I didn't mean them. How can I deny it?"

He looked thoughtful. "Perhaps we can still..."

"Monsieur le président!" Edmond's deep baritone boomed out above the uproar. "I wish to give testimony," he went on, as the room quieted and all eyes turned to him.

"Monsieur le comte de Beaufort," said the judge. "I recognize you, Your Excellency. What do you mean by coming forward at the eleventh hour?"

"I wish to testify. I have information that pertains to this case."

The judge looked irritated. "And you've kept silent until now? Well, come and be sworn, if you have something to say. I'll question him myself, *messieurs,*" he said to Franz and Dupin.

Edmond strode the length of the room to murmurs of speculation among the crowd, and stood before the witness box as Thérèse scurried away. He took his oath with an impatience that was scarcely hidden.

Céleste stared at him. What could he possibly say that would be helpful? Or did he despise her so much now, after what he'd heard, that he wished her further harm?

"Now, Your Excellency," said the judge, "does your testimony have anything to do with the sordid matter that involves your cousin, Paul de Beaufort?"

"No, *monsieur le président*. It is the matter of Madame Valvert's alibi. She has said nothing because she wished to protect me. But I can no longer keep silent. Madame Valvert couldn't have killed Monsieur de Malecot, because she wasn't in her *hôtel* that night."

"Then where was she, *monsieur?*"

Edmond's voice was cool and controlled, with a richness of tone that sent a thrill racing through Céleste's body. "She was with me," he said quietly.

"Edmond," she whispered, her hand going to her throat, "don't." How could he perjure himself, dishonor his proud name on her behalf?

He smiled; his eyes were warm and tender. "I will tell it, Céleste." He nodded to the judge. "Despite the false rumors linking her with others, Madame Valvert has been my faithful mistress for some time." He turned toward the gallery with a look that bordered on contempt. "There are those gossips among you who could, I'm sure, describe for this court every single moment we were together in public, beginning at the opera. For nearly a month, *madame* stayed with me at my château in Burgundy. If it please the court, I can send for my servants to testify that she was more than a guest. Servants always seem to know about these matters, you understand." He laughed softly, ironically. Céleste knew he was thinking of Joséphine.

"But the night of the murder," said the judge impatiently. "That is what concerns us now. Not the woman's wanton behavior, of which we've heard much."

Edmond glared at him, but continued. "I returned to Paris, with my cousin Paul, on Shrove Tuesday. We drove past Madame Valvert's *hôtel*. It was before ten. The house was dark. I took my cousin home and returned to my own *hôtel*. But I was eager to see *madame*. She had written me a love letter. You may read it," he said, fishing in the pocket of his waistcoat and holding it out to Franz with a disdainful air. "If you wish to authenticate it, you'll find it is indeed the woman's handwriting. Including the signature."

The prosecutor took the letter and read it aloud. It was an impassioned note, filled with love and devotion, telling him all the reasons she adored him. It begged him to arrange a rendezvous as soon as possible, to soothe the fires of her desire.

Céleste pressed her hands together. It was all she could do to keep her composure. This time she recognized the letter. It was the one she'd written to Paul the morning after the opera. She remembered that Edmond had told her he'd intercepted it. And kept it next to his heart all this time? she thought. Oh, Edmond! Beloved...

"What did you do when you received the letter?" asked the judge, as soon as Franz had finished his reading.

"I returned to Madame Valvert's *hôtel*."

"Your coachman can attest to this?"

"No. I drove myself. I took my tilbury. I went to Madame Valvert's *hôtel*—it was around midnight—and fetched her back with me. Monsieur de Malecot, I understand, was falsely summoned at three in the morning. I had been truly summoned, and I did not return my mistress to her *hôtel* until somewhere between five and six."

The judge looked skeptical. "Have you any witnesses?"

Edmond shook his head. "Among my servants, no. They had all gone out. A few drunken revelers, and a street cleaner on the boulevard, perhaps. But otherwise, you must take me at my word.''

''Is it not possible, *monsieur,* that you would lie to save this woman?''

Edmond drew himself up proudly, every inch the aristocrat. ''I am a man of honor, *monsieur le président.* With a name that goes back for centuries in the annals of France. I have sworn an oath here. And I tell you again—every word I have spoken is truth!'' He glared at the judge, who glared back, but seemed afraid to rebut such nobility and pride.

The courtroom shimmered with tension for a moment. Then the prosecutor raised his hand to the judge. ''This is important testimony, *monsieur le président.* And it does great harm to my case—*if* it's true. I should like to ask the witness one question, with the court's permission.'' The judge nodded. ''Now, Monsieur de Beaufort,'' said Franz, ''this is my question. Do you love the accused?''

Edmond looked at Céleste. His blue eyes seeming to drink in every detail of her face, he smiled tenderly. ''With all my heart,'' he said, ''I love this woman. Yes. Till the end of time. I love her.''

There was a burst of applause from the spectators, who seemed won over by Edmond's noble bearing, his air of scrupulous honesty. Only one man disagreed. Soulanges rose from his seat and waved his arms at the crowd. ''The man is lying! Can't you see? He only testifies to save the whore from the guillotine!''

Edmond whirled to him, his face dark with fury. ''I demand satisfaction from you, *monsieur!* Tomorrow morning. On the Champ de Mars!''

The judge rang his bell and pounded at his desk with his other hand. ''I will have order in my court!'' He pointed to Soulanges. ''Take that man out!'' He scowled at Edmond. ''And you, Your Excellency—if you have no more testimony, you may return to your seat. *Messieurs,* we will hear your summations.''

Céleste sat in a trance as first Dupin and then Franz gave their closing arguments. What did it matter what they said? Edmond had said he loved her, for all the world to hear. He loved her, in spite of the lies she'd told, the dishonesty and deception, the cruel game she'd played with Paul's heart. He loved her, and she could only gaze at him across the vast distance of the room—all her love, all her devotion, shining in her eyes.

The summations were finished. Céleste was taken out of the courtroom and returned to the Conciergerie to await the jury's decision. Within an hour, she was summoned back. The jury had decided quickly. The courtroom was hushed. The judge asked the jury's verdict. Céleste held her breath.

"Not guilty, *monsieur le président.*"

Céleste, standing to hear the verdict, sagged back into her seat. She trembled from head to foot, as though her body were only now acknowledging the frightful tension she'd endured all these weeks, the effort at rigid self-control that now failed her. Tears poured down her cheeks, and she wept softly.

The spectators had begun to babble noisily almost as soon as the verdict was announced. Now, the judge silenced them. "Madame Céleste Valvert," he began, then corrected himself. "Madame Céleste de LaGrange." His tone was one of extreme dislike and scorn. "This jury has found you innocent of the charge of murder. So be it. The court has no choice but to accept this verdict, though we may perceive it as a grave miscarriage of justice. I *will* speak. I have the right," he said, as Dupin started to protest.

The judge allowed his cold eyes to sweep over Céleste with a look of contempt, and then he continued. "I have no doubt that it was the testimony of the comte de Beaufort that was this woman's salvation."

The spectators murmured, and several members of the jury nodded their heads.

"It has been my experience," the judge went on, "that beautiful women have the power to influence men to do their bidding. I have listened to the testimony in this case. I have heard of schemes and deceptions and scandalous behavior. Of lies and shameless seductions. Of a woman who would stop at nothing to avenge her husband's death. But none of this saddens me more than the sight of an honorable man lowering himself to commit perjury—if indeed you did, Your Excellency. But you must live with your conscience." He nodded to Edmond, who had risen angrily from his seat and was attempting to break through the line of gendarmes to enter the court. The judge rang his bell. "The sitting is adjourned, gentlemen," he said, and left the room.

But his words of condemnation remained. The fickle spectators, previously swayed by Edmond's testimony, now turned on Céleste. They rose in a body and began to curse her, hurling insults that made her tremble. The mob surged forward, trampled the gendarmes and broke down the guardrail. While Edmond frantically sought to reach Céleste's side, the crowd rushed toward her, hands clawing in her direction, mouths filled with vile insults.

"Harlot!"

"Temptress!"

"Delilah, who leads men astray!"

With the help of her guards and Dupin, she was rushed out of the courtroom and into the antechamber. She sagged against a wall as the gendarmes barred the door to the mob, her body trembling in horror at the savagery directed against her.

One of the gendarmes touched his hat politely. "Come, *madame.* The carriage is waiting to take you where you want to go."

Dupin took her arm. "Will you return to the Conciergerie for your belongings?"

"No," she said. "I'll send Joseph for them in the morning. If he still wishes to serve a harlot," she added bitterly. She began to weep again, still hearing the curses of the mob. Oh, Edmond, she thought in anguish. What had she done to him, to his good name? She couldn't bear to face him. She turned to Dupin and welcomed the comforting arms he put around her.

"Take me to my *hôtel,* Monsieur Dupin," she whispered.

Chapter Twenty-three

"Careful, *madame*. The glass will cut your shoes." Avoiding the shards and debris that glittered in the late-afternoon sun, Joseph guided Céleste through the bottle-strewn courtyard of her *hôtel* and opened the door for her and Monsieur Dupin. The vestibule was as dark as night, for the shutters were closed at every window. "I'll light some lamps and candles as soon as I finish sweeping up." Joseph smiled, his eyes warm with sincerity. "I didn't expect you so soon. And with such welcome news."

"Thank you for your good wishes all these weeks, Joseph," she said, and sighed. "Leave the courtyard for now, and stay inside. I'm sure there will be more bottles and rocks thrown before the day is finished. We might as well wait until morning to clean. Were any windows broken before you could close the shutters?"

"No, *madame*. I've had them closed since last week. The worst we suffered was the night someone threw a dead cat over the wall and we couldn't find it. The courtyard stank for days. Thérèse and I—"

"You are not to speak of Thérèse," she said tightly. "I want you to go to her room and pack her things. If she comes here, hand them out to her. But I don't want to see her. I don't want her to cross my threshold." She didn't know which distressed her more—the girl's betrayal in the witness box today, or her furtive affair with Alex.

There was a furious ringing at the outer gate. Dupin clicked his tongue. "It begins already."

"Whoever it is," said Céleste, "tell them I'm indisposed, Joseph. I'll light the lamps myself." She smiled tiredly. "Come, Monsieur Dupin. Let me see if I can still remember how to be hospitable." She led him into the drawing room, lit several lamps and found sherry and glasses for them both. The comfort of being home again warmed her, and she relaxed in her chair.

Joseph appeared at the drawing room door. "It's a reporter from the *Gazette de France,* Madame Valvert."

"I told you, I'll see no one. If need be, we'll ignore the bell. Sooner or later the vultures will grow weary and go away."

"But, *madame...*"

"Not a living soul, Joseph. *No one.*"

He nodded and left the room. Dupin laughed softly. "Not even the man who saved your life? The man who tells the world he loves you?"

She leaned back in her chair and thought of Edmond. He had said he loved her. But only to save her life? A noble gesture inspired by the overwrought intensity of the courtroom, and nothing more? And even if it were true...

The judge, in his condemnation, had only said what all of Paris must be thinking of her. A scarlet woman. A deceiving, lying harlot. Possibly a murderess. How soon before Edmond would begin to regret linking himself with her in so open a fashion? How soon would he begin to compare her to his dead wife, who had lied and cheated and shamed him?

He had shown how much he cared for her when he surrendered her to Paul and brought his cousin back to her, despite his own desires. And she had made a fool of him, debased his good intentions. Left his family open to the malice of the gossips. She had told the court that the Beaufort name was to be mocked, that his cousin Paul was nothing more than a poor dupe in a larger, uglier scheme.

And now he intended to fight a duel with Soulanges to defend her honor. How many more duels would there be? How much more disgrace would she bring down upon him? No more, by heaven! She shook her head. "Most particularly not that man," she said to Dupin. "I don't want to see him again. Ever."

He looked at her thoughtfully. "I wish you had confided in me, *madame*. Perhaps I could have spared you some of the painful drama in the courtroom." He finished the last of his sherry and helped himself to another glass. "For what it's worth," he said, "I don't believe you killed Malecot. But I don't believe Monsieur de Beaufort's story, either."

She smiled, keeping her expression inscrutable. "The trial is over, *monsieur*. My secrets will remain my secrets." She frowned. The ringing at the gate had begun again. "I can't stay here," she said. "They'll drive me mad. I should like to leave the city. Tonight, if I can. When it's dark, perhaps they'll all be gone, and I can slip away." She looked around the drawing room, her brow wrinkling in dismay. "But how can I leave? There's so much to do. It will take days. Sublet my *hôtel*, pack..."

"Where do you intend to go?"

"Rome, I think. I had friends there, once."

"Then go this evening. Your servant and I can arrange everything. We'll sell the furniture, get a tenant. I can have my own housekeeper come and pack your belongings and send them on to you when we have an address."

"Why should you do all this for me? Your fee was modest. I can pay no more."

He blushed, two bright spots of color appearing on his smooth-shaven cheeks. "Madame Valvert...Céleste... We have worked together these past weeks, you and I, planning your defense. To be perfectly frank, I found myself envying those imaginary lovers of yours, and wishing I had been one of the men fortunate enough to be gossiped about." He smiled sheepishly. "And I'm soon to be happily married!"

"Keep your love pure," she said fervently. "You see what scandal has done to me."

They supped together with Joseph as twilight fell, quietly discussing the details of closing up the house, shutting the door on Céleste's life in Paris. Afterward, while Céleste packed a small valise for her trip, Joseph took Dupin through the *hôtel,* pointing out which pieces of furniture were rented and which had been bought outright. The piano would be sent to Rome, but the handsome drawing room furniture would be sold.

While Dupin made himself comfortable in the upstairs sitting room, poring over Céleste's lease and bank papers and arranging for the transfer of her funds, Céleste retired to her boudoir. She had one last painful chore.

She wrote to Paul first. That was the easier of her two letters. She begged him to forgive her. She urged him to forget, to find comfort with Élise, who loved him truly. She assured him that, though she'd used him badly, he was more than worthy of a woman's love. She had found him good and kind, she said; she had sometimes wished that their love affair could be genuine. She closed with a prayer for his happiness.

The letter to Edmond was an agony to write. More than once she had to dab at her cheeks to keep her tears from staining the paper. This was the last lie she would ever allow herself to tell, and the most dreadful. But it had to be done. She would *not* ruin his life any further. She had to drive him away, make their break so irrevocable that he would forget her and find a good woman to mother his children.

His children. She choked back a sob. How she would miss them. And she hadn't even allowed herself to think about the child she might be carrying. She almost prayed that her suspicions were baseless, that she wasn't pregnant at all.

The letter to Edmond was as cold and as unfeeling as she could make it. She tried not to think of his burning kisses, the warmth of his arms, the tender light that had shone in his eyes when he announced to the court that he loved her.

She began by thanking him for saving her life. But, she said, she was scarcely worthy of such a noble gesture. He had been right about her all along. As her testimony in court had shown, she had been prepared to use Paul to avenge her late husband. Society would be horrified, she knew, if the Malecots continued to link Élise with Paul—a man who had allowed himself to be openly seduced by an adventuress.

But when Edmond had come along, intruding in her opera box that night, it had given her a better idea, she said. If she seemed to be toying with *both* men, it would create even more of a scandal. If the Malecots chose to marry Élise into a family that saw nothing incestuous in the cousins sharing the same woman, it would send the duchesse de Tallon into a fury. The very purpose of her scheme, after all, she told him.

She hoped Edmond would understand. But of course nothing she had ever said to him was the truth. Certainly not her vow of love. A woman with her sort of reputation was scarcely capable of love. She hoped he would accept her letter as final, and not try to pursue her. A meeting would only embarrass them both.

She sanded the letter and shook it off, then buried her face in her arms, fighting her tears. Courage! she thought, and tried not to imagine his face as he read the awful words. She was aware of pounding footsteps on the stairs, and she raised her head. What new disaster now? The bell had rung repeatedly while she was writing her letters. Now it was silent.

The door of her boudoir burst open. Edmond stormed into the room, followed closely by a red-faced Joseph. "I— I tried to stop him, *madame*," stammered the servant.

She stood up and waved him away. "I understand. Please go."

Edmond glared at her. "Was there a reason I was denied your door?" he growled. "Didn't you think I'd want to see you? To hold you?"

She hesitated. She was going away, and she'd never see him again. Why should she care what he thought of her? But she did. "To forgive me for the lies I told?" she asked.

He snorted impatiently. "Of course. Should I blame you for your loyalty to your dead husband? You did what you thought was necessary." He started to gather her into his arms.

"Wait," she said, holding him off. "But can you forgive me for what I did to Paul?"

His steady glance wavered for a moment. "It's for Paul to forgive you," he said at last. "For myself... God save me," he muttered, "I was glad to know you'd never loved him."

She turned away before he could see the tears in her eyes. He understood. He loved her. He forgave her. If only the gossips could be so forgiving. But it would never be. Better to break his heart now than to ruin his life. "I'm going away," she said firmly, as though she were trying to strengthen her own resolve. "Tonight. I shall return to Rome."

He spun her around, his hands strong on her shoulders. "Are you out of your mind? Run away? No, by all the devils! We shall go to the opera tonight, and show everyone we have nothing of which to be ashamed!"

"No, *you* don't," she said bitterly. "You're simply a man with a mistress. All very natural and acceptable. But I? I have no standing. I shall forever be 'that Valvert creature.'"

He scowled. "Not when you're my wife. Not when—"

She held up her hand. "Please. Don't say another word. Don't say things you'll regret in a moment. I had just finished a letter to you when you came in. Perhaps you should read it now." She took the letter from her desk and handed it to him. She couldn't have felt more doomed if she'd handed him a knife and asked him to pierce her heart with it.

The color drained from his face as he read. He reached the bottom of the page and returned to the top, as though he hoped the words would magically change in the rereading. At last he finished, and looked at her. "Is this true?" he asked hoarsely.

"Yes."

"I was simply a part of your scheme?"

"Yes."

"And the passion? The desire? Was that as false? Are you that good an actress?"

She couldn't lie about that. Not while her body quivered with the needing of him, not when she wished she could throw herself into his arms and pretend it had all been a bad dream. "No," she said. "The desire was real. But you always knew that."

He clenched his jaw so tightly that she could hear the grinding of his teeth. "Do me the honor to be frank. If you're capable of it," he added with a sneer. "Did you ever love me?"

She swallowed hard and reminded herself that she was doing this for his happiness, his family honor, his pride. "No," she said. "I only told you so as part of my schemes. To keep you in my power."

The words seemed to hit him in the pit of his stomach. He drew in a deep, sighing breath and turned away from her. "Well, then, damn you," he said softly. "Go to Rome. And good riddance. Joséphine was only going as far as Marseilles."

She almost broke down at his words. She was grateful his back was toward her and he wouldn't see the anguish on her face. He had been an angry, bitter man after his wife died, mistrusting women, guarding the currency of his heart like a poor man protecting his last few coins. And she had taught him to love again, to trust again, to stand up and trumpet it to the world: I love this woman. And then she had robbed him of everything.

Let it be ended, she thought, drowning in misery. It was too painful to prolong this encounter. "Please go," she said, controlling her voice only with the greatest effort. "I have much to do this evening."

He whirled to her suddenly, his eyes burning. "Then let me leave you with a memory." He pulled her into his arms and kissed her fiercely, his mouth hot and possessive, his lips claiming the sweetness of hers until she trembled and moaned and ached with desire.

Abruptly he pushed her away and laughed—an ugly, humorless bark. "When you're in Rome, and gloating over the success of your Paris adventure, think of that!" He turned on his heel and left her. She could hear the thunderous sound of his footsteps on the stairs. It was as hollow as the sound of her heart pounding against her ribs.

Hands shaking, she finished what she had to do, took up her redingote and left her rooms for the last time. Joseph and Dupin were both waiting downstairs, tense and concerned about Edmond's visit. She ignored the questions in their eyes and made her final arrangements. She felt a last duty to say goodbye to the LaGranges. She would hire a fiacre. Joseph would take her luggage and meet her in an hour at the coaching inn. She would take the *diligence* to Rome from there. She turned to Dupin and thanked him again for all he'd done for her.

"I've almost finished with your papers tonight," he said. "I'll come back in the morning, and Joseph and I can begin our work."

"There's a letter on my desk. Please see that it gets to Paul de Beaufort. And one more thing..." She held out Alex's cameo. Confronted with all his infidelities, she could no longer bear to keep it. But it had brought her joy in those early days, when she had needed the love he had seemed to give her. "For your fiancée, Monsieur Dupin," she said. "May it bring her as much joy as it brought to me when first I received it."

Thoughts of Alex had reminded her of something. She returned to her rooms and opened a small chest. It was still there—the bottle of Julien de Malecot's wine, laced with the sleeping potion that had been intended to put her and Paul into a deep sleep at the Three Feathers Inn. She couldn't leave it for someone to drink by accident. She supposed she could pour it out. But perhaps the LaGranges would want it, as a memento. She put it into a basket, descended the stairs once more and left her *hôtel*.

She was shocked at the condition of the LaGranges. The study in their *hôtel* looked like a scene out of the madhouse at Charenton. It was as though the trial had unhinged them completely. Madame de LaGrange sat huddled in a large upholstered chair in the corner, her clothing in disarray. Pépin lay curled in her lap; she stroked him and whispered to him as though he were the only reality for her. She looked up when Céleste entered the room. "Oh, Pépin," she said with a moan, "how could that woman let them know she was a LaGrange? We shall die of shame!"

Monsieur de LaGrange was even worse. He had pulled down half the books from his shelves. He pored over them, squinting as though he could scarcely read them, though the light of a half dozen Argand lamps blazed in the disordered room. "Well," he said impatiently, looking up at Céleste, "why have you come? I have no time. Can't you see that?" He turned the pages of the book before him. "There must be a way," he muttered. "A plan..."

"I came to say goodbye," she said. "I'm leaving." When they didn't respond, she sighed. She reached into her basket and pulled out the bottle of wine, which she placed on the cluttered desk. "I thought you might want this back."

LaGrange scowled at the bottle and rubbed his stump. "The wine... I wonder... Élise... Is there a way?"

"My God," said Céleste in disgust. "Are you still bent on revenge, after all that's happened? Malecot is dead, for the love of heaven. What more do you want?"

LaGrange paced the room feverishly, his eyes bright and staring. "She can still carry a Malecot in her womb, can't she? That's why I must find a way. Somewhere among these books...here or here or here..." He swung his arm in a wild arc and jabbed the air with a finger, pointing at the volumes that surrounded him. His wayward hand struck the bottle of wine and sent it crashing to the polished floor. Pépin yelped and leapt from Madame de LaGrange's lap.

The wine flowed in all directions, forming dark red puddles on the floor. Seeing that the LaGranges seemed too distracted to do anything, Céleste rang for a servant to clear away the mess. At once, Thérèse appeared. Céleste frowned. "What is that girl doing here?"

"Why not? She's more loyal than you've ever been," said LaGrange with contempt. "Are you leaving us?" He jerked his chin toward the door. "Go, then!"

She wondered why she'd even bothered to come. She turned to the door. "Goodbye."

A high-pitched shriek stopped her. Madame de La-Grange rose from her chair and threw herself to the floor beside Pépin. The dog whimpered and thrashed convulsively, rolling in the spilled wine until his pale gray fur looked bloody. "My God, my God!" cried Madame de LaGrange. "He drank it!" She cradled the dog in her lap and began to weep hysterically.

"But he'll only sleep," said Céleste. "It's only—" She gasped in horror. "Dear God! It's *poison,* isn't it? You put poison in the wine! And Paul and I were meant to be found dead that morning . . . not asleep.''

LaGrange smiled craftily, ignoring his sobbing wife. ''With Malecot's bottle of wine. He would have gone to the guillotine for murder.''

She trembled and sank into a chair, overwhelmed with the enormity of their hatred. For the Malecots. And for her. ''Did you despise me so much?'' she whispered.

LaGrange's blue green eyes were as cold as the sea in winter. ''You killed the last hope of the LaGrange line.''

Thérèse planted herself before Céleste's chair and thrust out her chin in resentment. ''I would have borne him healthy children,'' she said. ''He'd even talked about marrying me. And then he went to Rome. And met you.'' She spat out the word.

Céleste stared at her and shook her head in disbelief. There had been a serpent in her midst all this time. A serpent who did the bidding of two revenge-crazed monsters. And they all had conspired against her. She felt their hatred like waves of venom, choking her. Everything the three of them had done had been as much to destroy her as to destroy the Malecots.

Even the murder! Now she remembered why the letter that had lured Malecot to her *hôtel* had seemed familiar. It was part of a letter that she'd written to Paul and never sent. A letter that she'd left on her desk. She pointed a trembling finger at Thérèse. ''You sent my letter to Malecot . . . You killed him.'' Her voice was flat, drained of all emotion by the horror of it.

The girl was suddenly panic-stricken, as she had been in the courtroom when Franz had called her to testify. ''It wasn't my idea to kill him! I just did what I was told.''

LaGrange laughed, his face twisted in an ugly smile. ''It was one of my best plans,'' he boasted. He pointed to Madame de LaGrange, who was still bent and weeping over Pépin. ''She didn't even know.'' He sneered. ''She didn't

ind poisoning, but she would have been too squeamish for
utright murder. But Thérèse..." He looked at the girl and
aughed sharply. "My dear, you're stupid, but very loyal. I
knew I could rely on you."

"But—but how did you do it?" stammered Céleste.

"I had meant to kill him at your empty *hôtel* while you
were at the ball. Then Thérèse came and told me that afternoon that you planned to stay at home. We had to be sure
you'd sleep soundly through the murder."

"Dear God," she gasped, remembering her headache the
next morning. "My snack...such a kind gesture..."

He grinned in evil satisfaction. "Yes. I had made a copy
of the key to your gate. Thérèse dressed in your cape and
mask and let in Malecot, who had been summoned by your
letter. I was watching. She led him into the studio and held
out her arms. 'Come, embrace me,' she said, 'and let us be
friends.'" He cackled softly. "And he—the fool, the
dupe!—took her in his arms. His back was toward me. I
struck again and again. For my son. For my manhood. For
my arm. For all the LaGranges who had suffered and died
on the guillotine, thanks to the Malecots!" His eyes glittered with righteous fury.

She felt sick, and swallowed frantically to keep her gorge
from rising. "But how could you?" she said. "All those
witnesses who saw you at the Mardi Gras balls..."

He tapped his nose and winked, as though he were merely
describing a clever chess move. "Don't you remember my
costume? I was a bat. With wings. Who was to say that the
man inside the costume had one arm? Or two? I hired a
drunken reveler to take my place for a few hours. He dozed
for much of the time. Not even my wife guessed it wasn't
me. She even scolded me the next morning for being such
poor company."

Céleste stood up to leave. "If I were as vindictive as you,"
she said in disgust, "I would go to the police. But I leave you
instead to live with your conscience. If you ever had one."

She scowled at him, her eyes narrowing. "But now I warn you. Leave Élise in peace, or I'll go to the authorities with the whole ugly story. It ended as you hoped. With Malecot's death. Be content with that."

"As I hoped?" he said bitterly. "Not quite. *You* were supposed to be convicted. *You* were supposed to pay for what you'd done to the LaGranges." His eyes glittered with a crazed light. "But it's not too late for you to pay!" He leapt at her, his hand going to her throat.

She gurgled and slapped at him, fighting against the strength of his grasping fingers. They struggled fiercely, careening from one side of the room to the other. Locked in their deadly battle, they stumbled over a pile of books on the floor and fell against a table. A lamp crashed to the floor, spilling its oil in all directions. Instantly the flames shot up, lapping at books, consuming scattered papers, racing through the oil to reach a chair, the combustible draperies at the windows.

Thérèse screamed and tried to reach the door. Céleste gasped and choked. Despite the smoke that filled the room, LaGrange still clung to her neck, so mad with hatred that he seemed willing to die in the fire, as long as she was destroyed, as well.

She thought—wildly and irrationally, as the smoke thickened—that at least the murderer of Malecot would die.

He was an imbecile. He had felt her trembling in his arms, had seen the look in her eyes—and still he'd believed her words. But it was absurd, her letter! She loved him, no matter how much she denied it. She'd sworn it to him in prison, long after Malecot was dead, long after there was any need for her to pursue her cunning scheme. She loved him. He reached out of his coach window, rapped on the outside and ordered his coachman back to Céleste's *hôtel*.

He frowned. Yet now she denied her love. Why? Did she carry more secrets within her that she feared to have revealed? Did she think he hated her for what she'd done to Paul? But there was a kind of nobility in what she'd done. She might have been misguided, but she had shone with a fierce and admirable loyalty, putting her sense of duty to her dead husband above the dictates of her heart. She had gone through the fires of hell to avenge LaGrange's death. And if the facts had proven the man unworthy of such devotion, it brought her no less glory. Until now, he had thought of women as the weaker sex, incapable of the same sort of nobility as a man. But her proud bearing in the face of all that scorn, all that false and ugly gossip, put everyone else in the shade.

Perhaps she had denied her love because she was simply ashamed of the way she'd used and hurt him and Paul. Or perhaps it was his fault that she wanted to go away. How often had he judged her, held her to his rigid moral standards? And for what? He knew the answer in the darkest recesses of his soul. To quiet his own guilt, to bury the dreadful thought that still lurked in his heart, eating away at it.

Had *he* killed Jean-Claude? Had his unwillingness to bend to Joséphine's all-too-human weaknesses driven her away? She had wanted lovers. Half the married women he knew kept lovers, and no one seemed to care. Were his standards too cruel, too impossibly high for any creature except a saint? He groaned and urged on his coachman, praying he wasn't too late.

Her *hôtel* was dark and shuttered when he arrived and threw himself out of his carriage. Only that lawyer of hers, Dupin, was at the gate, turning the key in the lock. It took only a few frantic questions to learn that she had gone to the LaGranges to make her final farewells. "Do you know where they live?" he said to Dupin. At the lawyer's nod, he took him by the coat sleeve. "Come, then. Show me the way." He scowled during the entire ride, conscious that

Dupin was grinning at him like some smug guardian angel, as if to say, I wondered when you'd come to your senses!

There seemed to be a great deal of commotion on the street as they turned into the rue de Varennes. The sky was lit with an unnatural glow, turning the night to day. A fire wagon careened around the corner, its bell clanging loudly. The air was thick with acrid smoke, and people were running up and down the pavement, shouting.

"Nom de Dieu!" said Dupin. "I think that's the La-Grange *hôtel!*"

Edmond barreled from his carriage even before it had stopped and raced to the courtyard of the burning *hôtel.* By the light of the flames, he saw Thérèse, smoke-blackened, gasping and sobbing by turns. "Where is your mistress?" he cried.

"Inside . . ." she panted. "The study . . ."

He didn't wait to hear the rest. Holding his hand over his mouth and nose, he dashed into the burning building. One side seemed entirely consumed, but the vestibule he was in was still intact. The smoke billowed around him, and the room glowed blood-red from the approaching fire. "Céleste!" he called, above the crackle and roar of the flames. Then again, more desperately, "Céleste!"

He heard a choked cry from near the staircase. "Here. Edmond?"

He found her on her knees in front of a quivering mass that—as he blinked against the smoke—revealed itself to be Madame de LaGrange, curled up and rocking softly.

"Oh, Edmond, thank God," said Céleste, giving way to sobs.

"Come!" he said urgently, tugging at her sleeve. "Before this part of the house catches fire."

"I can't. I won't. Madame de LaGrange . . ." Céleste coughed violently, then went on. "She won't leave without her dog. But the dog is dead. And in the burning study."

"Pépin," whimpered the old woman. "Where are you?"

"Where's Monsieur de LaGrange?" he asked.

Céleste shook her head. "A bookcase fell on him."

"Come," he said again, taking Madame de LaGrange by the arm. "Help me get her out of here." With a fierce effort, they managed to drag Madame de LaGrange through the vestibule and out of the door, into the waiting arms of Dupin and the servants.

Edmond gulped great draughts of fresh, sweet air into his lungs and looked at Céleste. She was as pale as snow, and had begun to cough again. His heart contracted with fear, the belated realization that he might have lost her. "Beloved," he whispered. "My dearest one." He reached out to enfold her in his arms.

She gasped in pain and clutched at her belly, staring in horror at the spreading red stain on the cobblestones beneath her feet. "Oh, Edmond!" she cried, collapsing into his arms. "Our child! Forgive me! Forgive me!"

Chapter Twenty-four

She was a princess, borne on a scented litter. Cradled in flowers, and surrounded by warmth and love and beautiful music that filled her senses and soothed her. And she was so happy. So very happy...

Céleste opened her eyes and squinted at the face that hovered above her. "Nicole?" she whispered in a hoarse croak.

The maid grinned. "You recognize me today?" At Céleste's mystified frown, she smiled more broadly. "Well, it's the first time you've known who I am, and that's a fact."

"How long have you been here?" Her throat felt parched; she drank gratefully from the glass of water the maid offered.

"A week. I came at once when Monsieur Edmond summoned me."

She was trying to make sense of it. All the way from Rochemont? But that was a long journey. "My God," she said, struggling to sit upright in the bed, "how long have *I* been here?"

"More than two weeks, and Easter come and gone."

"I must have been very ill. Was I conscious at all?"

"Oh, yes, these last few days. On and off. But you didn't seem to know anybody. You still had the fever." Nicole touched Céleste's forehead. "I think it's finally gone."

Céleste looked around at the handsomely appointed bed-chamber. "Is this Monsieur Edmond's *hôtel?*"

"Yes."

"Is he here?"

"Not now. He drove to the outskirts of Paris. He's waiting for an important delivery at the Vincennes gate. Are you hungry?"

She ran her tongue along her lips. "And still thirsty." She rubbed her face; her skin felt dry and old. "I must look frightful. I wish I could have a bath. What will Edmond say when he sees me?"

"He'll be pleased, no matter what."

She was remembering everything, now. The horrible fire, the miscarriage... "Will he be pleased that I lost his baby?" she asked bitterly. Alex had never forgiven her.

Nicole looked astonished. "Oh, *madame!* He was just glad you were safe. The doctors said he was a madman those first few days, when they didn't know if you'd live. You had a dreadful fever. You'd toss and turn and thrash about on your bed. It was heartbreaking to see." She pointed to the adjoining boudoir. "There's a piano. He'd play it for hours, with the door open. Hoping, wherever you were, that you could hear."

She blinked away the tears that had sprung to her eyes. "I think I did," she whispered. "I remember the music." She brushed at her cheeks and managed a smile. Where was Grandpapa's self-controlled little girl now? Edmond had crept into her heart, stirred her deepest emotions—and now she wept at everything. "I should so much like to look pretty for him," she said.

Nicole smiled. "We'll see what we can do, *madame.*" While the maid fed her and gave her a sponge bath and brushed her hair, she told Céleste all that had happened since the day of the fire. Madame de LaGrange, still mourning Pépin's death, had somehow decided that her husband was completely to blame. In her grief and anger, she had told the authorities everything.

"Everything?" asked Céleste.

"Oh, yes! How the whole scheme with Monsieur Paul was Monsieur de LaGrange's idea, not yours. And how they forced you to help them. How they tried to poison you and Monsieur Paul. And how he and Thérèse killed Monsieur de Malecot. *Nom d'un chat,* I couldn't believe it when that nice Monsieur Dupin told me all that happened here."

Céleste sighed. "I think Monsieur de LaGrange was totally mad at the end. His hatred of the Malecots finally consumed his soul, just as the fire..." She sighed again. "What did the authorities do when they learned the truth?"

"They let Madame de LaGrange go back to Normandy. She's a broken old woman, and she didn't know about Malecot's murder. But Thérèse will be brought up before the next assizes."

Céleste frowned. "Perhaps I'll hire Monsieur Dupin to defend her. She didn't do the actual killing. And the La-Granges played on her simple mind, and her love for their son."

"Trials, murder..." Nicole shook her head. "It's much quieter in the country, and that's a fact!"

She had a sudden, frightening thought. "What about Monsieur Edmond's duel?"

"There was no duel. Monsieur Dupin said that that nasty Soulanges was too cowardly to show his face at the Champ de Mars. And the next day, *Le Temps* printed an apology to you and Monsieur Edmond."

"Thank God he didn't fight," she breathed. She had enough on her conscience. "And what about—" she hesitated "—Monsieur Paul?"

"Oh, you mustn't worry about him. He's young. I think he's begun to call on Mademoiselle Élise again, even though she's in mourning. Very discreet, you understand. But I think we'll have a wedding one day."

"But the duchesse de Tallon..."

"Well, she wasn't happy at first. But it was Malecot she didn't like. Not Mademoiselle Élise or Monsieur Paul. And when Monsieur Edmond, as head of the Beaufort family, called upon her and pleaded on Monsieur Paul's behalf, the old woman relented. Now, enough talking—let me finish your toilette. You don't want to be so tired that you can't greet Monsieur Edmond when he comes in." She dressed Céleste in a charming dressing gown and helped her into a comfortable chair to doze and wait for Edmond.

He came bounding into the room at last, his handsome face wreathed in smiles. Clearly Nicole had told him of her recovery. He knelt before her chair, wrapped his arms around her waist and kissed her as though he never wanted to stop. At last he sat back on his heels and looked at her, his blue eyes sparkling with joy as they took in every feature. "How can you still be so bewitching, after all you've been through?" He clasped her hand tightly and pressed it to his lips. "Now, my love," he said, "do you want a large wedding or a small one?"

"No." She shook her head, all the happiness draining from her. "We can't marry, Edmond. I won't do that to you."

He raised a questioning eyebrow. "Can't marry? But I love you, and you love me."

"Let me be your mistress, then. But I won't shame your good name."

He swore softly. "What nonsense is this?"

"Don't you see? There's been too much gossip. They'll accept me, even welcome me, as your mistress. But that's all. You'd be excluded from the best aristocratic circles with a scandal-ridden wife."

"Then they're not the best circles, if they won't accept you. And if we tire of their stupidities, we'll go to Rochemont." He kissed her tenderly. "And be happy and have lots of children."

"Children? How can I?" she asked bitterly. "I lost Alex's child. And now yours. What kind of a woman am I?"

"You're the only woman I want," he said, gazing fervently into her eyes. "Do you think I could love you less simply because you can't bear children? Besides, the doctor thinks there's no reason why you can't conceive again, *and* carry safely to term." He smiled, his blue eyes twinkling. "And, if need be, I'll keep you a prisoner in bed for the whole nine months! Now, my foolish, sweet, dear Céleste, does that convince you to marry me?"

She wavered. His words helped to ease the pain and guilt she'd been suffering because of her miscarriage. But they didn't resolve everything. "No," she said, beginning to weep again. "There's still the gossip. I won't disgrace you, Edmond. Don't press me. I won't marry you. I've made up my mind." She reached out with tender fingers to stroke the frown lines between his brows. "Please try to understand. Please forgive me."

He stood up. She couldn't read his expression. "There's nothing to forgive," he said. "I haven't given up yet. Let me see if I can still persuade you." He turned about and left the room.

Céleste sighed and leaned back in her chair, closing her eyes against the pain. There was nothing he could say that would persuade her to change her mind. To bring scandal upon his head. She loved him too much.

She heard the sound of the piano in the next room. "Ah, vous dirai-je, maman." The song from the music box. Was that meant to remind her of their days together in Rochemont? To blot out the shame and disgrace that had followed?

And then, incredibly, she heard the soft, sweet, piping voices of children. She opened her eyes, laughing and crying at the same time. The twins. She stood up and walked unsteadily to the boudoir door.

Still in their traveling clothes, Albert and Albertine stood beside the piano as Edmond played, singing the verse that Céleste had taught them. Mademoiselle Daumard and Nicole watched from a corner. They smiled benevolently, like two fairy godmothers in the old tales.

"Allie! Bertine!" cried Céleste, and held out her arms to them. The children stopped singing and threw themselves at her, hugging and kissing her with all the fervor in their hearts. Their adoring faces shone up at her. She saw their bright sparkle through a mist of tears. She swayed and would have fallen, but Edmond sprang from the piano and lifted her in his arms.

"No more," he said tenderly. "Back to bed." Trailed by the children, he carried her into her bedchamber and laid her down, wrapping her in the coverlet like the gentlest nurse. Then he turned and smiled at the twins. It was a tentative smile, as though he were seeing them for the first time, and enjoying what he saw. "Is this the enchanted lady thou hast told me about, Allie?"

The little boy glanced at his sister, then dropped his eyes. He seemed uncomfortable with the form of address his father had used, as though he thought perhaps it was a mistake. *Thou,* not *you.* "Yes, Papa," he said at length. "We found her sleeping in the blue bedchamber at Rochemont."

Edmond turned to his daughter and stroked the bright red curls at her cheeks. "How shall we keep the enchantment, Bertine, and make her stay with us? For she is as precious to me as she is to thee."

Albertine looked at her brother and smiled. It hadn't been a mistake. "I can search for a magic unicorn's horn, Papa," she said. She blushed and giggled and turned away, suddenly shy in the face of such unfamiliar intimacy.

"No," said Edmond, taking Céleste's hand in his and gazing down at her with tender devotion, "there's only one magic spell. *Je t'aime.* I love thee."

"Please, Edmond," she said in desperation. "Be reasonable. It will be a terrible scandal."

He shrugged. "A week or two of malicious whispering before the next scandal captures the attention of those Parisians who have nothing better to do than chatter. I want you, Céleste, and the children want you. I won't hear another foolish reason against it."

"But..."

"And I have at least one reason of my own why you should marry me. Rochemont is too big to manage alone."

Her jaw dropped. "That's all? That's your reason?"

His eyes were beginning to twinkle wickedly. "Well, I need a proper hostess and countess."

"Please, Edmond, be serious."

His face was a mask of innocence wronged. "I am serious. But if you insist... The children need a mother, I suppose. Though Mademoiselle Daumard does very well for them."

She rolled her eyes, beginning to enter into his game. "And?"

"You need more reasons? Because I'm tired of the gossip about which man has captured Madame Valvert's heart this week."

"Oh, very good," she said dryly. "And I suppose it's also because you need someone to share your music with."

"I hadn't thought of that reason," he said, grinning. "You have agreed, of course, haven't you? You'll marry me?"

"Of course," she said, suddenly misty-eyed. "Because I have the best reason of all. I love *thee.*"

He laughed like a young boy, and hugged her and kissed his children. Then he perched on the side of the bed and held her hands in his. "As for the gossips," he said, "after a while they'll have only one thing to say. 'My dear,' they'll whisper, 'have you heard? Monsieur le comte de Beaufort adores his very own wife, and doesn't care who knows it!'"

Céleste returned his laughter, her heart overflowing with love. "What a scandal!"

Some weeks later, the count and countess Edmond de Beaufort entered their carriage on the way to the opera. It was a beautiful spring night, with the chestnut trees beginning to blossom along the Champs-Élysées. Madame de Beaufort looked radiant, fully recovered from the fire and the illness that had nearly killed her.

In the darkness of the carriage, Monsieur de Beaufort put his arm around his wife and held her close. "I don't see why we have to go," he said. "I hate *Guillaume Tell.*"

"Oh, nonsense," she said. "It's your favorite opera, and you know it. Besides, Madame de Marsan expects us for a little supper beforehand."

He grumbled and kissed her on the neck. "I'd just as soon spend the evening at home with you and the children."

"There'll be time for quiet evenings when we go to the country next week. I want to find a good piano teacher near Rochemont for Allie."

"Will you start Bertine on her singing yourself?"

"I think so. I haven't forgotten *everything* my grandfather taught me."

He sighed. "I'm only afraid we'll have visitors at Rochemont. Now that you've been all but canonized by the gossips."

Céleste chuckled softly. It was laughable the way everything had turned out. As soon as the whole story had made the rounds of the salons, all of Paris had decided that Céleste was the noblest, most self-sacrificing woman who had been seen in a long time. The gossips admired her devotion to the LaGranges, though it meant her own ruin; her willingness to keep from implicating them at the trial, though it nearly cost her her life; her heroic desire to save Madame de LaGrange from the fire, despite the wrongs that had been done to her by the family. After their quiet wedding—attended by the grinning children—Céleste and Edmond had been buried in invitations to all the most fashionable parties.

Of course, the one invitation that had truly pleased them had been for the small supper that Edmond's aunt Charlotte was giving next week. She proposed to honor the formal announcement of Paul and Élise's wedding in the fall. Paul, recovering from his heartbreak with Élise's loving help, had called upon them only the other day. He had forgiven them both with a wry smile.

"We can't help whom we fall in love with," he said, laughing ruefully, "even though I shall always think you chose the wrong Beaufort. But it would have been nice, dear Cousin Céleste," he had added, "if *some* of that charm had been genuine."

"Paul," she'd said, taking his hand in hers, "the friendship I gave you was always genuine. And always will be, God willing."

Edmond stirred in the carriage and kissed Céleste more passionately, his lips burning on the soft flesh of her bosom. "I wish it were a very short opera tonight. I can think of so many delicious ways to spend the evening."

She shivered in delight and anticipation, and returned his hungry kiss with her own. Then she pushed him away and grinned wickedly. "We could always create a fresh scandal by leaving early."

*   *   *   *   *

Harlequin® Historical

HARLEQUIN HISTORICALS
ARE GETTING BIGGER!

This fall, Harlequin Historicals will bring you bigger books. Along with our traditional high-quality historicals, we will be including selected reissues of favorite titles, as well as longer originals.

Reissues from popular authors like Elizabeth Lowell, Veronica Sattler and Marianne Willman.

Originals like ACROSS TIME—an historical time-travel by Nina Beaumont, UNICORN BRIDE—a medieval tale by Claire Delacroix, and SUSPICION—a title by Judith McWilliams set during Regency times.

Leave it to Harlequin Historicals to deliver enduring love stories, larger-than-life characters, and history as you've never before experienced it.

And now, leave it to Harlequin Historicals, to deliver even more!

Look for *The Bargain* by Veronica Sattler in October, *Pieces of Sky* by Marianne Willman in November, and *Reckless Love* by Elizabeth Lowell in December.

Take 4 bestselling love stories FREE

Plus get a FREE surprise gift!

Special Limited-time Offer

Mail to Harlequin Reader Service®

3010 Walden Avenue
P.O. Box 1867
Buffalo, N.Y. 14269-1867

YES! Please send me 4 free Harlequin Historical™ novels and my free surprise gift. Then send me 4 brand-new novels every month, which I will receive before they appear in bookstores. Bill me at the low price of $2.94 each plus 25¢ delivery and applicable sales tax, if any.* That's the complete price and—compared to the cover prices of $3.99 each—quite a bargain! I understand that accepting the books and gift places me under no obligation ever to buy any books. I can always return a shipment and cancel at any time. Even if I never buy another book from Harlequin, the 4 free books and the surprise gift are mine to keep forever.

247 BPA AJHV

Name	(PLEASE PRINT)

Address	Apt. No.

City	State	Zip

This offer is limited to one order per household and not valid to present Harlequin Historical™ subscribers. *Terms and prices are subject to change without notice. Sales tax applicable in N.Y.

UHIS-93R   ©1990 Harlequin Enterprises Limited

Coming in October!

From

Harlequin® Historical

It was a misunderstanding that could cost a young woman her virtue, and a notorious rake his heart.

Award-winning author of JESSIE'S LADY and SABELLE

Available wherever Harlequin books are sold.

Harlequin® Historical

Nora O'Shea had fled to Arizona seeking freedom, but could she ever find love as a mail-order bride?

MARIANNE WILLMAN

From the author of THE CYGNET and ROSE RED, ROSE WHITE comes a haunting love story full of passion and power, set against the backdrop of the new frontier.

Coming in November 1993 from Harlequin

Don't miss it! Wherever Harlequin books are sold.

Harlequin® Historical

From *New York Times* bestselling author

Elizabeth Lowell

Reckless Love

The powerful story of two people as brave and free as the elusive wild mustang which both had sworn to capture.

A Harlequin Historicals Release
December 1993

HHRLOVE

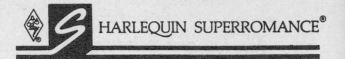

HARLEQUIN SUPERROMANCE®

VERONICA SATTLER

Joins Harlequin Superromance with her first contemporary novel.

You've enjoyed her in the past; now enjoy her in the present!

Don't miss *Wild Cherries* by Veronica Sattler.
Coming to Superromance in 1994.

Praise for *The Bargain:*

"Veronica Sattler . . . transports readers into a Cinderella story filled with Regency charm and sizzling sensuality . . . the best gothic ending since *Ashes in the Wind.*"

Kathe Robin, *Romantic Times*

Praise for *Sabelle:*

"This book will move you as it moved me. Five stars."

Affaire de Coeur

VS-SR1

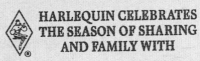

HARLEQUIN CELEBRATES
THE SEASON OF SHARING
AND FAMILY WITH

Friends, Families, Lovers

Harlequin introduces the latest member in its family of
seasonal collections. Following in the footsteps of the popular
My Valentine, Just Married and *Harlequin Historical Christmas
Stories,* we are proud to present FRIENDS, FAMILIES,
LOVERS. A collection of three new contemporary romance
stories about America at its best, about welcoming others into
the circle of love.... Stories to warm your heart ...

By three leading romance authors:

KATHLEEN EAGLE
SANDRA KITT
RUTH JEAN DALE

Available in October, wherever
Harlequin books are sold.

1993 Keepsake

Stories

Capture the spirit and romance of Christmas with KEEPSAKE CHRISTMAS STORIES, a collection of three stories by favorite historical authors. The perfect Christmas gift!

Don't miss these heartwarming stories, available in November wherever Harlequin books are sold:

ONCE UPON A CHRISTMAS by Curtiss Ann Matlock
A FAIRYTALE SEASON by Marianne Willman
TIDINGS OF JOY by Victoria Pade

ADD A TOUCH OF ROMANCE TO YOUR HOLIDAY SEASON WITH KEEPSAKE CHRISTMAS STORIES!

HX93